BIOSTORM

Vector, Book One

ANTHONY J. MELCHIORRI

Biostorm (Vector, Book One)

Copyright © 2021 by Anthony J. Melchiorri. All rights reserved.

First Edition: July 2021

http://AnthonyJMelchiorri.com

Cover Design: © Damonza, Damonza.com

ISBN: 9798735206880

This is a work of fiction. Names, characters, places, and incidents either are the product of the author's imagination or are used fictitiously, and any resemblance to locales, events, business establishments, or actual persons—living or dead—is entirely coincidental.

10 9 8 7 6 5 4 3 2 1

-Dedication-

For my good friend, Luis, and all those who dedicate their lives in pursuit of scientific advancement to make the world a better place.

ISTANBUL, Turkey

ALEX WOLFE SEARCHED through a crowd of hundreds for his target. He needed to find just one man hurrying through a busy Turkish marketplace in possession of an engineered pathogen.

Millions of innocent lives might be at stake.

And so was Alex's job.

The hot June sun soaked into his trim sports coat and matching black slacks. Not the most comfortable clothing for a jaunt through Istanbul in the summer. His blond hair and decidedly Scandinavian appearance weren't much help, either, if he wanted to blend in with the locals. But that wasn't the point. Instead, he slipped into the stream of people clad in business attire that had descended on the city for the Biodefense World Summit.

The timetable his analyst had provided told Alex that the Summit's scheduled afternoon break had just begun. An ideal time for his target to escape using the cover of the crowd.

He navigated through the crush of conference-goers with name tags swinging from their necks and tourists leisurely passing over a cobblestone street. Knockoff designer bags spilled from shops where hawkers touted, "The real thing, my friend! Good deal just for you!"

Merchants accosted people in front of stores with shelves of stone animal statuettes and double-stacked Turkish tea kettles. Children ran through the street and neighboring square. A few kicked a soccer ball between the streams of tourists. Behind the souvenir stands and chaos, the iconic minarets of the historic Blue Mosque speared the sky.

Alex passed a stand with a man roasting chestnuts and paused near an open-air restaurant where a cook grilled sizzling kebabs over an open fire. Somewhere in the hordes of wily salesmen and hapless tourists was his target.

Where are you?

Istanbul marked Alex's first mission as an operative on the newly formed Vector Team. This was their trial run. Their chance to prove the black-box organization was more than just a discretionary line item on a federal budget. That they could be instrumental in fighting the shadowy war against biological and chemical weapons.

But only if they found this damned scientist.

"See our friend yet?" Alex asked through his throat mic.

"Not yet," Skylar Cruz called through the receiver pressed into his ear. She was the only other Vector Team member on the ground.

Cruz was stationed somewhere at the south end of the street, a black-and-pink modesty scarf around her dark brown hair. Loose-fitting khakis and a light sweatshirt completed the ensemble, all to help her masquerade as a sightseeing traveler.

He wasn't sure that would be enough.

Before Vector, she had been a helicopter pilot in the Marines.

It showed.

She had a habit of walking with her shoulders back, chin up like the world belonged to her. Not the best way to meld into your surroundings when trying to tail a suspect. But this was Alex's first time working with her in the field outside of simulations and training exercises. He wanted to give her the benefit of the doubt.

Problem was, their target wouldn't.

"We miss him, that's it for us," he said.

"No pressure." Cruz paused. "Wait. Think I got him. He lost the beard from the pictures in his file. Should have kept it. Guy's got a face like a blind carpenter's thumb. Headed your way."

Alex looked over the bobbing heads of other pedestrians.

"You should see him right about now," Cruz said.

There. He spotted their guy walking in front of an art gallery. An older man in his sixties. Black cap. Olive polo tucked into cargo shorts.

Felix Breners.

The scientist had come to the conference from Latvia. He was the scientific advisor for EnviroProct. The company had developed a prototype device to detect dangerous contaminants and bioweapons. Intercepted emails from Breners to an encrypted address claimed the company's prototypes had identified a brand-new—and potentially deadly—microorganism in China.

Vector Command believed Breners planned to deliver a sample of that unidentified microorganism to someone in Istanbul. While Alex had every reason to believe this was a dangerous bioweapon, he had no idea who Breners was meeting, what exactly this pathogen was, or why he was meeting someone in secret instead of going to the authorities.

The most obvious answer was the most frightening: Breners was about to sell it to the highest bidder.

The scientist cut straight across the street. He stuffed his left hand into his pocket. Alex expected him to pull out a phone. Instead, Breners kept his hand there like he was hanging onto something.

"The sample must be in Breners's left pocket," Alex said.

"You're telling me he's not just happy to see me?" Cruz called back.

The joke didn't deserve a reply.

The target took out his cell from the right pocket and pressed it to his ear. He seemed to be talking to his handler, or maybe the people he planned to meet. Didn't look happy, in any case.

Breners was headed straight to a place packed with tourists and vigilant police cradling submachine guns. A place full of winding corridors and tiny shops.

The Grand Bazaar.

The scientist reached a security checkpoint with a metal detector and three guards holding automatic rifles.

Alex could not lose him in that labyrinth.

But the SIG Sauer pressed against the bottom of his spine meant Alex couldn't just waltz through the metal detector. Every entrance to the bazaar was secured to prevent a catastrophic terrorist attack like those that had hit Istanbul in 2016. The Turkish police would find his gun, and he would land himself a long-term stay in a musty, hot jail cell with twenty other men.

As part of Vector's operational protocols, he and Cruz were not officially employed by the United States government. No intelligence agency would claim them. That gave the US government plausible deniability in case their mission devolved into an explosive scandal.

Which meant no one would be coming to bail Alex out of that jail cell.

The security guards waved Breners through the metal detector.

Alex needed to follow him. But there was no way to get past those guards without going through the detector.

Screw it. The gun had to go.

All he needed to do was track Breners. Take a picture or two of the people the man was meeting then steal the sample.

He didn't need a firearm for that.

He turned into a nearby alley. Smashed crates and soggy cardboard boxes lay around overflowing trash cans. Trash bags clawed by stray animals bled puddles of brown, watery goop. The lingering smell of rot was enough to make him gag.

Good. Not a place people would want to hang out.

He looked up and down the alley to make sure no one was watching.

"Cruz, I'm following Breners into the Bazaar." He slid his pistol out from its holster and pushed it under a pile of particularly rank bags.

"I'll go with," she said.

"No way to get in carrying hardware."

"Then I'll leave mine too."

Alex thought of the kids he'd seen kicking a soccer ball down the street. He could hear more children laughing as they ran between the nearby shops. The last thing he wanted was for one of them to stumble on the weapon. The thought of it repulsed him to his core, reawakening memories he had no time to deal with now.

"No, you've got to pick mine up," he said. "I'll follow Breners."

"Wolfe—"

"Cruz, I don't want anyone stealing it. Or worse, hurting themselves. I got to move."

"Damn, you're stubborn."

"You don't know the half of it," Alex muttered.

He left the alley and walked to the security gate. He handed his phone over to the guard then walked through the detector. Ahead, Breners curved around a corner near a store selling colorful glass lamps. Alex snatched his phone from the guard and took off.

Voices echoed off the walls from shopkeepers in front of souvenir T-shirts or shelves of faux antiques down the next corridor. The cloying smell of caramelizing sugar drifted from a candy shop next to another store with open wooden boxes filled with colorful spices. People swarmed every one of those shops and the passages between them.

Alex spotted Breners turning left into a narrower corridor and followed him. Sunlight glowed in from another checkpoint up ahead. Breners marched straight out of the bazaar and stuck his hand in the air, looking down the street.

Alex's gut tightened. "Cruz, I think we're going to need a ride."

"I'll find one."

Twenty seconds went by before a cab pulled up. Breners got in.

"You far?" Alex asked over the comms, wading through mobs of people.

"ETA five minutes."

Breners's taxi peeled off.

"Not going to cut it," he said.

Alex waved down his own taxi and slipped inside.

"Where to?" a man with a graying beard said with a strong accent.

"Follow that cab," Alex said, pointing at Breners's car. "But don't make it obvious."

"Are you serious, my friend?" the cabbie asked, his voice hitching up in excitement.

"Deadly," Alex said.

"I thought this was only in the movies."

"Not today."

They followed Breners over the Golden Horn River. When the scientist's car stopped to drop him off, Alex directed his cabbie to halt about half a block away. He handed the driver a wad of lira that would more than cover the fare and, he hoped, buy some discretion then got out.

Breners joined the crowds walking down a brick-paved pedestrian street. In contrast to the more ancient and lived-in ambience around the Grand Bazaar, this part of the city had a distinctly Western European feel. Ornate couture shops, bakeries, and restaurants lined the street, all of which might appear at home in Paris or Rome. Breners turned left onto a single-lane road next to a coffee shop. As Alex followed him, a multitude of languages collided in an alcohol-induced cacophony.

The scientist entered one of the many neon-sign-laden bars.

"He's at the Squealing Hog Irish Pub," Alex said. "I'm going in."

"Okay, okay." Cruz sounded distracted, wind blowing over her mic. "I'm about five, maybe ten minutes away. Got your weapon and found a ride. Don't do anything crazy without me."

Alex slipped into the bustling pub. His feet stuck to the floor. The cloying smell of stale beer filled the air, mixing with the sweaty body odor of the happy-hour patrons. A long carved wooden bar stretched to his left. To his right, Breners was climbing a winding iron staircase leading to a second-floor seating area that wrapped above an empty stage.

Alex needed to buy a little time and cover. He jostled for a space at the bar and signaled the bartender. "A Guinness, please."

Once he got the drink, he went up the stairs and acted as if he was looking for a good seat. The second floor was organized in a U-shape, wide enough for a single line of booths and tables around the perimeter overlooking the stage below. Only a few tables were unoccupied. At one end of the U, Alex spotted the back of Breners's head.

Two Asian men in suits were at the table with the scientist, one facing Breners, the other sitting beside him.

He was too late to stop the handoff.

Alex walked past a couple cuddling in a booth. He chose a seat at the closest table where he could watch Breners from the corner of his eye.

Conversations and laughter rose around him. He was just near enough to Breners to hear the scientist and the other two men whispering but couldn't quite make out their words.

With his cell phone, he snagged a discreet picture of the man sitting across from Breners. He looked to be in his mid-fifties. Maybe Chinese, judging by the snippets of his accent Alex could hear.

A few curses, the sound of dropped glasses breaking, and angry yells from the first floor dashed any chance he had of eavesdropping. He turned to see three large men barging up the stairs. All wore black T-shirts. Intricate tattoos coiled around their arms. Each of them had a Cyrillic A emblazoned amid the ink patterns. They talked between themselves in Russian.

Their demeanor set off every alarm trained by Alex's decade of service in the CIA.

"Possible hostile contacts on the scene," he whispered. "Might need backup."

"On it," Cruz said. The whine of what sounded like a motorcycle engine screamed over the comms. "Just a couple minutes."

The first man cresting the stairs reached behind his back and drew a pistol.

Two minutes might be too long.

A second passed before the nearest bystanders realized what was about to happen. The first shriek from a woman in a booth set off a chain reaction of screams from the other patrons.

Time seemed to slow. Adrenaline plunged through Alex's vessels, his grip tightening around the glass of Guinness.

Were the Russians after Breners too? Where had they even come from?

This was not how the mission was supposed to go. Vector had no knowledge of a third party being involved in the handoff.

The holster where his pistol should be suddenly felt a lot lighter.

People began rushing down the stairs, the cacophony of panic growing louder.

The Chinese man across from Breners started to stand, his face going pale. He held up his hands and waved in that universal gesture of surrender. The second Chinese man with Breners turned, jumping to his feet and beginning to reach under his suit coat.

Must be a bodyguard, Alex thought.

"Please, do not shoot!" the older Chinese man said in stilted English.

"Come with us," the lead Russian said in a thick, unmistakable accent. He aimed his pistol at the older man.

Breners was shaking. He cowered in the booth as if he was trying to sink straight through his seat.

The Russian surged toward the booth.

"Come with us," he repeated.

The Chinese bodyguard suddenly reached toward his back. Before he pulled out whatever weapon he had, the Russian opened fire. Bullets lanced through the man's chest. He collapsed, and a pistol clattered from his grip, just five feet from Alex.

More screams and cries rang through the bar. Over the railing, Alex saw people on the first floor stampede toward the exits. Somewhere outside this madness was Cruz. She had Alex's pistol—but he couldn't wait for her.

One of the Russians was looking at him.

Alex was the only person up here that hadn't made a run for it.

The Russian said something to his buddy, and the pair began to close in.

With nowhere else to go, nowhere to run, Alex had to act. Now. He threw his pint glass at the Russian with the pistol. The glass slammed into his face, beer splashing over him, and the gunman recoiled, his aim breaking.

Alex kicked over a table and dove for the handgun that the Chinese man had dropped. He scooped up the weapon and began firing. Rounds plunged into the gunman, stitching up his leg and into his stomach.

The man shot back three times, but he was already going down. His bullets punched into the ceiling and wall.

"Taking fire," Alex called over the comms. "Two men left. Russian. Second floor."

Drawing their own handguns, the other two Russians took cover behind the booths near the stairs.

"Copy," Cruz replied. "I'm coming!"

Frantic voices downstairs clamored for help in a storm of languages. Alex hoped those weren't the cries of people who had been shot in the fray, but he couldn't help them now.

The toppled table obscured his position. But it wasn't bulletproof. Rounds slammed through it. Woodchips flew. He needed better cover.

Only one place to go. He launched himself toward the booth where Breners was.

The older Chinese man was still there, hands raised in pointless surrender. He twisted toward Alex, mouth open.

Before the man could so much as speak, the Russians filled him with bullets.

Alex shoved his way past the now-dead man and into the booth beside Breners. He popped up and fired at the two Russians' positions, forcing them down for a moment. His rounds cut through the plush booths. Stuffing flew from the seat cushions, and splinters of wood burst in small geysers.

The Russians fired back blindly. Most of the shots punched into the nearby wall, shattering glass picture frames. A few pounded into the thick wood of the booth. It provided just enough protection to keep the incoming 9mm rounds from tearing into Alex and Breners.

"What is happening?" Breners asked, voice shaking.

Ignoring him, Alex fired back, desperate to hold off the Russians.

Four shots.

The slide on his stolen pistol locked back.

Empty.

He didn't have any more ammunition.

The bodyguard probably had a spare magazine, but he was lying in the middle of the open aisle.

As soon as Alex stepped out of the booth, he was a dead man. In a couple seconds, the Russians would realize he didn't have anything left.

"Cruz, I could use that backup now!"

2

SKYLAR PUSHED through the people surging past her. A few crouched under tables or hid behind the bar. Sobs came from a woman crouched in a booth.

"Get out of here!" she yelled. "Go!"

She took the stairs toward the second floor two at a time, urged on by another burst of gunfire. They hadn't planned on anyone else showing up to Breners's party and causing a shootout. But if her time in the Marines had taught her anything, it had hammered home that no good plan survived contact with the enemy.

After the gunfire settled, she heard a pair of voices shouting in Russian. Sounded like they were on her right. She made it to the top of the stairs and swung her handgun toward where she thought they were.

One was leaning over a booth. She plugged two shots straight into the man's chest. The second gunman twisted and fired back.

She ducked behind the closest booth. Bullets slammed into the wood. A few rounds broke through, slicing past her. Frustrated, she ripped off the damn pink scarf that was impeding her peripheral vision.

Crouching, she swung around the other side of the booth to fire at the Russian.

But he had advanced while she was hiding. He stood close enough to slam his boot down hard on her wrist. A shock of pain spread up her bones, forcing the fingers open, and her pistol fell from her grip.

The Russian swung his handgun toward her. No way he could miss.

"Cruz!" Wolfe dove out from where he'd been hiding. Instead of doing anything remotely useful, the former spook started going through the pockets of a dead man on the floor. The Russian turned on Alex before he could grab whatever he was looking for then let loose a few shots forcing Alex back into cover.

At least Wolfe had bought her a few seconds' distraction.

She kicked her leg up straight into the Russian's groin. His face flushed, and he let out a yowl. He staggered but didn't drop his weapon like she'd hoped. When she tried for a second kick, he caught her ankle, twisting her leg until a violent pop sounded.

Suddenly, her foot was dangling from her ankle at an unnatural angle.

The Russian leveled his weapon at her, clearly expecting her to be frozen by this debilitating injury.

Instead, Skylar put all her power into a gut punch that sent the Russian reeling. She lunged at him, pushing herself up with her good leg. Another devastating blow crashed into his jaw. She let rage fill her, fueling the machine of her aggression. Her fists hit him over and over. Bone and cartilage snapped. Blood flew. His eyes rolled up.

The man fell backward, unconscious even before he tumbled over the railing overlooking the stage below. His body smacked against a table with a sickening thud. The legs of the table broke apart, turned to toothpicks. The man's limbs twitched then went still.

"Cruz, you okay?" Wolfe asked.

Skylar reached down to her prosthetic foot and snapped it back into place. "Never thought I'd appreciate losing that leg in Afghanistan." She rotated the prosthetic, testing it. "Still works."

"Good. We need to get out of here."

Skylar recovered her pistol then handed Alex his weapon. Breners was crouched, Alex's hand clenching his collar. The scientist's eyes were wide and his face pale. He appeared frozen in fear.

"Don't hurt me!" he cried.

"That's not part of the plan," Wolfe said. "You're coming with us."

"That wasn't part of the plan either," Skylar said, indicating the carnage. She used her phone to snap a couple of images of the dead men. "Leave him."

"Everything's blown to crap already," Wolfe said. "Might as well take him. See what he knows. Better than letting the Turkish police have him."

"Who are you people?" Breners asked as Wolfe forced the guy to stand on his own. "What do you want?"

"Right now, we just want to get the hell out of here," Skylar said.

Wolfe grabbed Breners by his shoulder and forced him down the stairs.

"How far is your ride?" Wolfe asked.

"Left it right outside the exit behind the stage," Skylar said as they reached the first floor. She'd stolen a motorcycle from the tangle of parked mopeds and bikes outside the Bazaar. "Can't fit more than two people, though."

"Then we'll find something else."

"Please, let me go!" Breners pulled against Wolfe's grip and started to break free. Skylar grabbed his upper arm hard and yanked him back toward them.

A loud crack echoed through the bar. At some point, someone had closed the front doors, probably to keep the gunmen in. But those doors flew open now. Three men stormed inside, tattoos curling around their bare arms just like the Russians upstairs. But instead of pistols, these guys carried AK-47s.

"Get down!" Skylar said.

She dove for the cover of the scattered tables and chairs, shooting blindly at the three men, and then dragged herself into a booth along the wall.

Wolfe and Breners were hiding behind a table flipped on its side, both flat on the ground. The three gunmen unleashed a torrent of fire. Rounds tore into the table, sending up a shower of woodchips.

Trying to escape that relentless gunfire was like trying to run through a thunderstorm without getting wet. Another bout of suppressing fire slammed into their positions. These people wanted Breners and whatever he carried bad.

She peeked out from behind her shelter. Bullets pounded her booth as one of the Russians stood to run, attempting to flank them. She dropped to the floor and aimed just beyond the corner of the booth. The position didn't give her much of a vantage, but she caught sight of the guy's legs.

More than enough.

She fired. Rounds sliced into the man's leg. He tumbled forward, sliding across the floor. The guy might as well have been a fly in a spider's web now. Three more rounds into his side kept him on the floor for good.

That left two more. But if these guys had an ounce of intelligence, they had backup rushing into position outside the bar. Wouldn't be long before Vector Team was surrounded.

Hard to win a shootout when you were the fish inside the barrel.

Time to get the hell out of here.

The exit behind the stage was no more than ten, fifteen yards away. To get there, they would cross a veritable killing field through the Russians' firing lanes. But a couple seconds' distraction might be just enough to make it to that door.

Skylar signaled to Wolfe and pointed to the exit. He nodded.

Deafening gunfire raked their position. Her heart thudded against her ribcage, threatening to break loose and sprint across the floor by itself.

She had one magazine left. Needed to make this count. Skylar unleashed a spray of wild covering fire. Wolfe ran with Breners, and she followed at a dead run. Bullets sliced through the air. Shrapnel exploded around them as the automatic gunfire tore the tacky tourist bar apart.

Wolfe and Breners made it out the door.

Skylar slipped out a few seconds after them. Bullets sparked against the metal door as it closed behind her.

"Help me with this," she said, motioning to a dumpster on wheels. Wolfe helped her push it in front of the door.

Breners was seated against the brick alley wall. Looked like he might be frozen in shock again. Next to him was the Yamaha MT-07 motorcycle she'd stolen earlier. She had left it here for a perfect getaway. But she hadn't counted on a third passenger.

The Russians pounded against the blocked exit door.

"We need to find another ride," Skylar said. "Get him up, and let's go!"

"He's not going anywhere," Wolfe said, his voice flat. "He's dead."

Skylar wanted to send a fist straight through the brick wall. This mission could not get any worse.

And then, of course, it did.

Police sirens screeched, coming in from multiple angles. The whole damn city was probably on alert.

"What do we do with him?" she asked.

Wolfe hesitated. "We have to leave him here. No other choice."

Skylar wasn't going to argue. She hopped onto the motorcycle and started it.

A moment later, Wolfe got on behind her and grabbed her hips. "Let's get out of here."

The engine whined, rear tire squealing before the bike shot forward. They cut between the cars filling the street, heading north to escape the congestion downtown.

They weren't the only ones.

Another engine roared behind them, rising over the sounds of traffic.

"We got followers!" Wolfe yelled.

A quick glance in the side mirror showed a black Toyota Land Cruiser peeling away from the Irish pub. Another followed.

Skylar pushed the two-cylinder engine to its limits, winding between slow-moving cars. Wolfe's grip on her tightened. Any other time, she'd crack a joke about keeping his hands to himself.

At least the press of traffic would hold the Land Cruisers back, giving her ample time to get away.

But when she noticed people screaming and diving into doorways or even toward the street, she looked in the side mirror again.

The Land Cruisers were racing down the sidewalk. They plowed through tables and chairs on restaurant patios and crushed potted plants.

Collateral damage meant nothing to them.

Ahead, blue and red lights flashed. Vehicles in the opposing lanes swerved aside to clear a path for a pair of police cars. As Skylar barreled toward them, one of the cars stopped in the middle of the lane. Two officers spilled out, brandishing weapons.

Skylar hooked hard to the right then jumped the curb. Scanning the urban terrain, she saw a park where only few people strolled the paved paths. She took the bike off the sidewalk and onto the grass. They raced up a slight hill. Soil sprayed up in a rooster tail from the bike's rear tire.

Gunshots exploded behind them. She didn't look back to see whether it was from their pursuers in the Land Cruisers or the cops. Frankly, it didn't matter. She needed to lose them both.

When she crested the hill, she turned slightly, glancing back to see the Land Cruisers racing up the green behind them. One of the police cars gunned it into the park, catching up. An officer was firing out the passenger window at the SUVs.

Bullets punched into the rear Land Cruiser. Spiderwebs of fractures spreading through the side windows. The glass broke apart in a spray of crystalline pebbles. But that didn't deter the driver. Nothing short of a bullet to the head would stop him.

"Hold on!" she yelled to Wolfe.

She hit the hand brakes hard, sliding the bike around a concrete fountain in front of the InterContinental Hotel at the edge of the park. The first SUV tried to alter its course. It skidded, tires scraping for traction on the slick pavement. But the turn was too tight for the four-wheel drive vehicle. It crashed sideways into the fountain. Concrete chunks flew and pipes bent, water spraying everywhere.

Skylar directed the bike toward the patio of the hotel. A few guests watched, frozen by fear, until the chatter of a rifle exploded from the remaining SUV.

A bullet hit the bike, metal ringing.

That was too damn close.

Guests sprinted inside, screaming. Skylar took the bike between the tall manicured bushes surrounding the patio then cut between a pair of large decorative pots.

Ahead, three more police cars blasted away from the street and tore over the park to cut them off. The SUV ignored them, still churning after Skylar and Wolfe.

A woman in a caftan ran right in front of the bike, shrieking. Skylar cursed. If they wanted to get out of this without more bodies stacked up around Istanbul, then she needed to do something drastic.

She aimed the bike for a set of stairs at the end of the patio. The bike whined as she revved the engine, testing its limits. She held her breath, jaw gritted, teeth grinding together. Her vision tunneled to the narrow world in front of her. Every obstacle clicked into her mind as she charted a clear path with reactions honed by thousands of hours of flight time in the cockpit of her old SuperCobra attack helicopter.

She drove straight up the stairs. The bike's suspension groaned with each bumping step, metal scraping against concrete. It felt like Wolfe might crack a rib if he held on any tighter. The bike shot up from the top of the stairs. It hung in the air for a second that bled on into its own eternity.

Then the bike landed heavily on the sidewalk with a heaving jolt.

She tightened her grip on the handles, desperate to control the motorcycle as it bucked, suspension protesting noisily against the abuse.

A deafening crunch of metal against concrete burst behind them, followed by a loud pop that sounded suspiciously like an axle breaking.

"SUV's done for," Wolfe said. "Cops couldn't follow. Nice driving!"

Skylar pulled a tire-screeching ninety-eight degree turn on the sidewalk then took them back into traffic. They joined the throngs of other motorcycles and scooters splitting the lanes once again, disappearing into the anonymity the crush of traffic provided.

Eventually, the sirens faded beneath the normal clash of honking cars and the throaty bark of ill-maintained engines.

"Where to now?" Skylar asked.

"Head west, following E80," Wolfe said, his voice ringing through her earpiece over the traffic noise. "We've got a plane waiting for us at Hezarfen."

"Got it."

They merged onto a highway, trading the mixture of modern glass buildings and towering stone minarets for rolling hills filled with lush green trees.

The adrenaline of the chase subsided, and with the wide road ahead, Skylar considered their mission. A simple intercept and observe had turned into a wild shootout and car chase.

"If this crap isn't on the international news in ten minutes, I'll be shocked," she said.

"Command isn't going to be happy."

Skylar cursed again. "They pull our funding, we're out a job. I can't deal with that again. First the Marines, now this."

"If they cut Vector now before we figure out what in the hell just happened, we're going to have bigger concerns than where our next paycheck is coming from."

Skylar understood his point. But the painful memory of waking up after losing her leg still haunted her. More painful than losing the flesh and bone was learning that she couldn't serve the country she loved any longer.

All this chaos, and they hadn't even achieved what they came for.

"We never even found out what Breners had," she said.

"No, we didn't," Wolfe said, sounding smug. "But we will."

"How? You want to go back and search the bar before we

leave Istanbul? That place will be crawling with police and military. Not to mention those Russians."

"No need to go back. I got the package right here."

"What is it?" she asked, leaving another obvious joke untouched.

"It's a small plastic vial filled with *something.* I grabbed it off Breners before we left the alley. We need to get this back to Maryland for the science team."

She took a deep breath, held it for a beat.

"You mean I just drove us up a damn staircase with a potential bioweapon in your pocket?"

"It's secure."

Skylar accelerated, zipping between cars. At least that was one small victory despite this mess.

The only question was whether it would be enough to shield them from the shitstorm that was about to descend on them.

3

FREDERICK, Maryland

COLONEL ABRAHAM KASIM, Vector Team's director, struggled to make sense of the Istanbul report. He reached for his coffee mug before remembering it was regrettably empty. Then he adjusted his reading glasses and searched through the papers on his desk in case he had missed anything to explain the mess his field agents had made.

Vector's operations center was housed in a nondescript office building on the main campus of USAMRIID, the United States Army Medical Research and Development Command. The other officers, scientists, and administrators in the surrounding buildings knew almost nothing about the small facility labeled Hazardous Material Disposal Unit or about the six-man team that worked there.

Three decades had led Kasim here, to the formation of this experimental covert group. It had taken him a lifetime of tracking nefarious government research groups and bioterrorists to plead his case to Brigadier General Heidi Liang, the commander in charge of USAMRIID. Six months ago, she'd signed off on Kasim's proposal, and Vector Team was born. While other government agencies were limited by pesky things like law, protocol, and diplomacy, Vector operated in near anonymity. They could react quickly, without deliberation, to risky threats where other intelligence agencies or military units were prohibited from rapid response.

Vector was the tool the United States needed to combat the burgeoning threats in the biological warfare arena.

Or at least, that had been the idea.

After just one tumultuous mission, he feared the demise of his life's work.

He needed to submit at least a summary of the report sprawled across his desk to Liang. She was the only individual in the US government who had even the remotest idea what Vector was up to. Even if what she knew amounted to little more than the snippets of need-to-know information Kasim sent her.

But she also controlled their funding and their future.

Kasim was supposed to somehow bridge the divide between showing her Vector was useful while keeping her in the dark about their exact operations. The less she knew about the particulars, the better. Kasim had leveraged a lifetime of trust in achieving that kind of discretion with her.

He had no intention of screwing the whole thing up by telling her their first mission had been nothing but a useless bloodbath.

But the attack in Istanbul was plastered across every cable news outlet, paper, and blog. Liang was going to start demanding answers.

He needed something, *anything* to report that would amount to more than a body count and a bunch of question marks.

He shuffled through the papers again and reread each line. There was no light at the end of this tunnel. No clue that explained what exactly had brought the Russians, Chinese, and Breners together.

Why had the Russians so desperately wanted to stop the trade between Breners and the Chinese? How had they known about the handoff? What was Breners handing off, and how had he found his buyers?

It was going to be a long night. And there was a voice in the back of his mind that wasn't helping his focus. He had told his wife, Divya, that he would make it home tonight before she went to be bed. That he would be in time for a late dinner, maybe a glass of cabernet sauvignon from the bottle she'd picked up for them six months ago at a local winery and had since gathered dust.

That had been a foolish enough promise. He had known he couldn't keep it even before everything hit the fan in Istanbul.

With the kids grown and out of the house, he sometimes wondered why Divya hadn't left too.

The door to the operations center cracked open, and Kasim looked up.

A slender man walked in wearing thick-framed black glasses and a gray knit cap pulled down over his ears. Leo Morris was the team's lead analyst, plucked from the ranks of white hat cyber operations in the National Security Agency.

Morris had a laptop under an arm, showing off a tattooed lion pouncing across his dark skin. Kasim assumed the tattoo had something to do with Morris's first name, but he hadn't ever asked to confirm. Whenever Morris emerged from his own windowless basement office to join him in the operations center, they had far more important things to discuss.

"Tell me you've got good news," Kasim said.

Morris shot him a bemused look then pulled out his wireless earbuds. Kasim could hear tinny music bleed out. "What was that?"

Kasim combed his fingers through his beard. This guy was

going to turn the last strands of black gray by the end of the week. "Istanbul?" he prompted. "Cruz and Wolfe will be back soon, and I want as much information as we can get before they touch down. We need to tackle this thing running."

Morris took his glasses off, breathed on the lenses, and wiped them clean on his T-shirt. "They got the sample Breners had, right?"

"They did. And our science team will take care of it. But no matter how many experiments they run, they're not going to be able to tell me who Breners was talking to or why those Russians interrupted their meeting."

"Oh, so you want to know who the Russians are. Maybe the Chinese dudes too. Right?"

Morris cracked his characteristic grin. The one that Kasim knew meant, *Why do you ever doubt me?*

"Go on," Kasim said.

Morris pulled a seat over from their conference table and joined Kasim at his desk. He popped open his laptop. A picture on the screen showed a man in the green dress uniform of the People's Liberation Army, the single star on his epaulet signaling he was a major.

"Han Shing," Morris said, tapping his knuckle on the screen. "This is one of the guys Breners was meeting with. Found him with our image recognition database."

Kasim skimmed the file. "He looks like nothing but a middle-level bureaucratic officer. What department?"

"Security."

"A Chinese security officer meeting with a scientist from Latvia in Istanbul. What's the catch? Is Shing involved in bioweapon development?"

Morris scrolled all the way through the file open onscreen. It was barely a couple of paragraphs long. "There's not much we've got on this guy. Maybe he's not important, or maybe he's been flying under our radar. But I couldn't find any affiliations related to biodefense or bioweapons development. Except for this."

Kasim read the last line in the file Morris had indicated. "He was registered for the Biodefense World Summit, just like Breners. The PLA isn't just sending no-name bureaucrats to this conference for fun. How about the man with Shing?"

"The pic Alex sent didn't match anything I had." That grin of Morris's crossed his face again. "But I found a way into the Summit registration files. Yan Zhi. Again, not a ton of info. He's PLA, but I don't know much else. I'm thinking maybe a babysitter or muscle."

Kasim grabbed his coffee cup, ready to gulp it down before he remembered, once more, that it was empty. He set it down with a sigh. "Well, who do they work for?"

"Both directly report to a Lieutenant Colonel Liu Qi." Morris pulled up a file with a picture of a gray-haired man. "This guy has ties all over the place. Most recently known to be working in... here it is... biodefense and security. Specifically, the Academy of Military Medical Sciences."

"Good. Let's put in a monitoring request for Qi. See what he's up to."

Morris scrolled for a moment then frowned. "Well, that's going to be hard."

"Why's that?"

"Just three days ago, Qi was killed in a one-vehicle traffic accident."

"And three days ago, I wouldn't have thought anything about it." Kasim traced a finger around his coffee mug. "But after everything that just happened, that sounds suspiciously like an assassination."

"Maybe. Which brings me to the Russians."

"Were those guys Foreign Intelligence Service? Main Intelligence Directorate?"

Morris closed his laptop and spread his hands. "Not that I can tell."

"Then are we talking Mafia?"

"Couldn't find a single facial recognition match."

"Mob or intel officers, how did Russia know about this? For that matter, what do they know about Breners and that sample?"

"Might as well be asking the wall," Morris said. "I don't have—"

The phone on Kasim's desk rang. A red light glowed, signaling it was an encrypted line.

He gestured for Morris to leave. "Keep digging. I need answers."

As Morris left, Kasim knew he wasn't the only one demanding answers. He picked up the phone with deliberate slowness.

"Kasim here," he said.

"What in the hell did Vector do in Istanbul?"

It was Liang. He had been dreading this call.

"You know I can't—"

"You assured me your team knew what they were doing. And then I see the news. A shoot-out in a bar? A car chase? Tell me that wasn't your people."

He could practically feel the heat radiating off her through the phone. "I can't tell you that."

"Abraham, I'm doing my damndest to keep my mouth shut about this. But the National Security Council is already investigating this as a potential terrorist act. If they find even a hint that you were involved..." She paused. "That's it. I'm canceling Vector's funding. Consider this mission scrapped. The whole thing needs to be shut down before we both end up at a congressional hearing getting reamed out by a bunch of lifelong political hacks."

"General, you can't do this." His fingers tightened around the phone.

"You know exactly what I can and can't do. The program's over."

"We've got actionable intel." An exaggeration, to be sure. But it was all he could offer. "Give me time to follow it up, make this right."

Liang sighed. "You helped me get where I am, and I was happy to give you Vector. But you know that I can't risk the security of this country."

"One chance, Heidi. You know me. You know I have this." He knew it was a cheap shot. Capitalizing on their friendship. "Just one more shot."

There was a pause on the other end.

"If I see another international disaster and I even suspect Vector's involvement, I'm shutting the whole thing down," Liang said.

"Thank you," he said, but she had already disconnected the call.

Kasim leaned back in his chair. That cab sauv was not moving from its spot on the shelf tonight.

He only hoped the rest of the world would remain just as undisturbed. The last thing he needed was another disaster on his plate.

Lisbon, Portugal

Renee Williams could still smell the slightly fishy odor clinging to the shirt she wore under her laboratory coat. She had considered going home to shower after visiting the docks to collect her field samples. That smell would be clinging to her tightly coiled black hair for the rest of the day, but she couldn't wait to start her new experiments.

Those freshly acquired samples held nearly invisible clues that she was eager to investigate. From deadly pathogens to nutrient-supplying microorganisms that supported rich plant life, she could unveil key indicators to environmental health through a few laboratory experiments.

Only a couple months ago, she had uncovered a microorganism in samples just like these that no other scientist had ever identified. Now, if she could confirm the same organism existed in these samples, she could support her latest findings and secure her role as a discoverer of new life.

Today she was a postdoctoral researcher at the University of Lisbon, but this project might be her ticket to a tenure-track faculty position.

She sat on a stool in front of a biosafety cabinet in one of her university's microbiology labs. Across the stainless-steel surface inside the BSC, she had spread a dozen filters that had been used to collect air samples over the Atlantic Ocean along the Iberian Peninsula and just north of Morocco.

Each sample was housed in a small plastic screw-top container. She reached under the glass partition of the BSC with gloved hands and unscrewed the first. Using a pair of stainless-steel forceps, she withdrew the paper filter.

The circular disc of paper appeared like nothing more than a drip-coffee filter. But if she looked under a standard microscope—or even better, a scanning electron microscope—she would see a world teeming with squirming microbes.

The door to the room opened, and another researcher entered.

"I can't wait to see what's in these little buggers," Paulo Reis said with a slight Portuguese accent.

He carried a stack of agar plates and slipped them under

the glass visor into the BSC. Then he plopped into the seat next to her, giving Renee a smile.

"You're going to be famous," he said, using his gloved hands to open one of the agar plates.

Renee cut the filter into two slices, letting the first drop into the agar plate.

Paulo replaced its lid then opened another plate for her to deposit the second piece of the filter.

"Famous is an overstatement," she said with a slight laugh. "I mean, how many people are going to read these papers?"

"Hopefully, the faculty search committee in our university. This might be enough for them to consider you for a position running your own lab."

"You think?"

Paulo nodded, safety goggles jostling over his deep brown eyes. "I know. You have discovered something quite unusual. Unique. It's worth a grant. If not one from your country's National Science Foundation then at least from the European Research Council. Universities across the world will clamor for you."

It was hyperbole, but Renee grinned as she cut another air filter. "I can only dream. An NSF grant alone would be nice…"

"But?"

"A European position might be better."

"Ah, just one and a half years doing research in Lisbon is enough to make you fall in love with the better continent, huh?"

She looked at him, heat rushing to her face. "I don't mind staying here longer, that's for sure. A certain somebody has convinced me it's a decent place to live."

He winked. "A certain somebody is glad you think so."

There it was. Hinting at something more. She might as well put him on the spot.

"You know, I was looking up long-term visa options," she said.

"Oh?"

"With all the work trying to jump through hoops for an employer-sponsored visa, sure seems it would be a lot easier just to find someone willing to marry me out here. You know anyone?"

Paulo's face took on a decidedly red tone. "I mean…"

That was the sort of joking—but not totally joking—remark they made with each other. She didn't really think he'd propose on the spot, but Renee couldn't help herself from needling her research partner.

She batted her eyelashes at him from behind her safety goggles. "What about your friend Alberto? Is he single?"

Paulo laughed and slid another fresh agar plate toward her. The whir of the BSC's air-filtration fans filled the silence between them.

"Alberto is not good enough for you," he said. "You will have to keep looking."

Renee stifled a sigh. She and Paulo had spent many weekends exploring Western Europe together. But her time in Portugal had always had an expiration date when her post-doctoral fellowship in Lisbon ended. She was sure there had been suggestions of something more to their friendship, but that was as far as they had let it go.

Both were determined to make a career for themselves in academia. Trying to find a job as a professor in a university was hard enough; trying to find *two* open positions in a single place was nearly impossible.

There was an unspoken agreement between the two of them: furthering their relationship would only result in certain heartbreak, even if she liked to flirt with the idea of it.

"Well, if I'm not going to get someone to put a ring on my

finger, then I'll need a good faculty position," she said. "Which means I need that grant."

"No problem for you," Paulo said.

"I don't know. There *is* one thing I'm worried about." She pictured their advisor, the middle-aged man who ran the lab. "I need more first-author papers. Nobody's going to give a grant to someone who isn't the lead author on at least a few good science papers."

"What about that last paper you submitted to the aerobiology journal?"

"That's the thing," she said, placing a filter on the agar plate. "Dr. Estacio put *his* name as first author instead of mine."

Paulo sighed. "He does that."

"That's not right. You and I did the work. I wrote the paper."

"I know, I know," Paulo said. "He has a bit of what you might call a big head."

She replaced the lid on the agar plate. "I'm not getting a faculty position if he keeps taking credit for my work."

Paulo prepared another plate. "You should talk to him. He might act like a big boss, but he gets scared easily."

"What do you mean?"

"He does not like confrontation. If you march in there and tell him you deserve to be first author, he will say, 'Oh, yes, you're right. I made a horrible mistake.'"

"Doubt it."

Paulo grinned. "Trust me. When I got tired of him magically becoming first author on my papers, that's what I did."

"And it worked?"

"Once."

"I need at least *three* first-author papers."

Paulo shrugged then wrote the date on the agar plates with

a black marker. They removed the plates from the BSC and placed them in a refrigerator-sized incubator.

"What can I say?" Paulo said, closing the incubator door. "Someone will surely recognize you are the brains behind this work, and when they do—"

A loud shout cut short his words. It sounded like it had come from outside the lab.

"What was that?" Renee asked.

"Maybe someone got hurt," Paulo offered.

They left the culture room, entering the main lab. A few graduate students and other research assistants were at the lab benches, working between microscopes and other buzzing instruments. Most had paused and looked toward the door to the hall.

More shouts—angry shouts—exploded outside. She couldn't quite make out the words.

"Sounds like it's coming from near Estacio's office." Renee paused by the door. "Someone's pissed at him."

"That is not the way I suggest talking to him."

She stifled a laugh. "Any idea who would be so angry?"

"No, but I would suggest you don't talk to him today."

The conversation outside seemed to have ended, and the voices quieted.

"No kidding. I'll save it for later. Maybe I'll call it a day and go back to writing the next paper."

Renee peeled off her lab gloves then started to open the door. Before she left the laboratory, she heard five loud bangs that cracked through the hall like thunder. Her ears rang, adrenaline flowing in cold waves through her vessels.

She stepped back into the laboratory, letting the door close silently.

Paulo looked at her, just as shocked. Two of the graduate students screamed. A handful of them had ducked for cover behind the lab benches.

Another loud bang.

Renee knew those sounds all too well from living on her family's ranch in Texas. Back when her dad took her out to the fields for target practice, a favorite pastime of his.

"What was that? An explosion?" Paulo asked.

"Gunshots," she said simply.

4

FREDERICK, Maryland

SKYLAR WALKED with Wolfe through the empty corridors leading to Vector headquarters. The metallic odor of spent bullets and oily exhaust fumes still clung to their clothes. She was ready for a shower, but neither she nor her partner wanted to delay meeting with Kasim.

If she needed to start looking for a new job, she might as well find out sooner rather than later.

Down the hall, she saw the nondescript door leading to the operations center.

She had experienced her fair share of spittle-filled, vein-popping, furious diatribes from her gunnery instructor in Officer Candidate School. She knew how to take a dressing down from a superior in stride. And she would be lying if she tried to say her mouth hadn't gotten her in trouble with her commanding officer more than once.

She was—or had been—a pilot. Kind of came with the territory.

But none of those experiences evoked the dread she felt marching toward the debriefing with Colonel Abraham Kasim.

Somehow, Wolfe looked as steely and cool as ever. That same jaw-clenched, eyes-forward expression he wore whether he was studying a briefing, stalking a scientist through Istanbul, or escaping an unexpected attack from a group of Russian hitmen.

The guy was like ice.

She was still trying to figure out what drove him. What had pushed him into the CIA then into Vector. During their training, he had always said it was a sense of duty. A need to help those who couldn't help themselves. But she sensed that was a cop-out answer.

There was something deeper there. The same kind of invisible, unspoken wounds she was used to seeing in her brothers and sisters returning from deployment.

Whatever it was that kept this guy up at night, he sure didn't let it show.

"How do you do it?" Skylar asked.

He raised a brow. "What?"

"This." She gestured toward his face. "You look like you're a middle-level manager walking into the weekly nine a.m. sales meeting, already prepared to be bored out of your mind. You're not worried about Vector?"

He shook his head then paused in front of the door to the operations center. "I've got too many other things to think about than whether this team stays funded or not. The Russians, China, Breners. All the people's lives that might be at risk if we mess up. Trying to figure out what was in that sample."

Skylar had trained with this guy for months, yet there was still so much about her partner that was a mystery.

"You don't show it," she pressed.

"You ever see a picture of one of those pro surfers taking on a world-record-breaking wave?"

"Sure."

"You think they're not imagining that wave smashing their body and board? That there isn't some voice in the back of their head asking what happens if all that water sucks them away in the undertow? Or about slamming into the razor-sharp coral just under the water's surface?"

"Sounds about how I felt when I was in the cockpit of my bird."

"Exactly." Wolfe wrapped his fingers around the door handle. "You know that everything's on the line. But all you can do is look forward and keep your balance. No matter what happens to us, I already started this mission. I'm finishing it, whether I'm part of Vector or not."

When Skylar looked into his eyes, she didn't have a single shred of doubt he would make good on his word.

"Then count me in," she said. "I'm not sitting this mission out."

They entered the operations center, ready for whatever came next.

ALEX AND CRUZ sat across from Kasim at the conference table in the operations center. Morris, the techie, had his laptop open at the other end of the table.

Kasim's eyes exuded a quiet anger over the reading glasses perched on his nose. Without breaking eye contact, he folded those glasses and hung them from the pocket in his suit jacket.

"I want to know how you let a simple surveillance and intercept turn into a shoot-out and a car chase," Kasim said. There was a cutting edge to his voice.

No, Alex thought. Not just an edge. A whole chainsaw.

"We—" Cruz started.

"You know what, on second thought, I don't want to hear it," Kasim said. He held up his finger and thumb, indicating a space no more than a couple of millimeters between them. "We were this close to losing everything. The mission. Vector. Your sample."

"But we didn't," Cruz said. "We IDed Breners's friends, and our scientists have his sample now."

"And yet we're still no closer to figuring what's going on," Kasim said. "We've got to fix this."

"We're still in business, though, right?" Alex asked.

"For now." Kasim sighed. "Commander Liang gave us one last chance. Only because she believed me that we had some actionable intel. You two are lucky we've got Morris."

Morris glanced up from his laptop with a smirk. "Very lucky."

The analyst tapped on the table's surface. The faux wood fizzled away to reveal a spread of images on what was actually a large touchscreen computer. The pictures showed the men they had encountered at the bar, including Breners, the Chinese, and the Russians.

"We still don't know why the Russians were there or who they were," Morris said. "But we've got some hits on the other guys."

Alex listened attentively as Morris went over Shing's history, along with that of their supervisor, Qi.

"We have confirmation that Qi was involved in China's biodefense initiatives," Kasim said. "Maybe he was trying to purchase the sample from Breners, and the Russians heard about it. Qi reportedly died in a one-car traffic accident three days ago."

Cruz jerked her thumb at the pictures of the Russian hitmen. "Think they were involved in that too?"

Morris shrugged. "No evidence either way."

"Does Qi have any prior connection to Breners and EnviroProct?" Alex asked.

Kasim gave Morris a nod. The analyst tapped on the table so that Qi's picture expanded. Next to the image of his face was a document in Mandarin.

"EnviroProct was working on a contract with Qi," Morris said. "It's vague, but we know it had something to do with studying human health issues. They wanted to test for a variety of microorganisms and contaminants that might be spread through water, air, or other environmental means. There were discussions with Breners about a new product called Aerokeep they were supposed to present at the Biodefense World Summit in Istanbul."

Kasim tapped on the screen. It showed a map of China with a couple of red dots near Beijing and Shanghai. "Apparently, EnviroProct brought prototype devices in China for a demo recently."

"And this vial we got from Breners… you think maybe it's something they found in their prototype devices when they were working over there?" Cruz asked.

"Could be," Kasim said.

"Maybe we were wrong about why Breners set up that meeting." Alex pointed at the red dots. "Maybe EnviroProct wasn't selling something to China."

Cruz finished his thought. "He wanted to warn them about whatever he found."

"Not a bad guess," Morris said. "Before you guys got here, I uncovered an internal email at EnviroProct from Breners's boss. Seems like someone wanted them to keep a lid on all this. I'm going to forward it to you now."

Morris's fingers flew across his keyboard, and an email popped up on the conference table.

"This was sent five days before the summit," he said.

· · ·

DR. BRENERS,

*We are not biologists. Cease investigating these microorganisms imme-
diately. Do not contact our clients without our consent on matters that are
not specifically outlined in the contractual terms of agreement. This is a
waste of company time and resources.*

Sincerely,
Martins Lapsa

"IF I HAD TO GUESS, someone got to Lapsa and threatened him
to drop the studies," Morris said.

The pieces of the puzzle weren't yet perfect. But Alex
could see them taking shape.

"I'm assuming this microorganism Lapsa referenced has
something to do with the sample I took from Breners," he said.

"It would appear that way." Kasim dragged his finger
across the table so the image zoomed in on the date. "One day
later, Breners sent the first email we intercepted to his mysterious contacts, who we now believe to be Shing and possibly
Qi."

"Can we ask Lapsa what's got his panties into a bunch?"
Cruz asked.

"Afraid not," Kasim said. "The man died from a heart
attack two days after his email to Breners."

"Heart attacks are easy to fake," Alex said. "Russian mafia
and intel officers know plenty about that."

"Being from Latvia, you can bet Breners knew that too,"
Kasim said. "Latvia's had to fight off their fair share of post-
USSR Russian influence, both covertly and overtly. Can't count
the number of times anti-Russian Latvian activists and politi-
cians have faced attempted or successful assassinations. The
guy probably put two and two together and realized he'd found
something he wasn't supposed to find in China. Whether he
was trying to sell this sample to his Chinese contacts or simply

doing the right thing and warn them, I think we now understand why he was so secretive."

"And it all went to crap anyway." Alex couldn't help but feel morose, remembering how Breners had died right in front of him. It had been bad enough when he'd believed the scientist was selling secrets. He felt an extra pang of remorse knowing the guy might have been a decent human being after all.

Morris was typing on his laptop again. He paused then leaned closer to the screen. His brow furrowed over his thick-rimmed glasses.

"Something wrong?" Cruz asked.

"Uh, you know I'm not big on coincidences," he said.

Alex straightened in his seat. "Go on."

"It's been less than a day since Istanbul, and now there's something going on Lisbon."

Kasim twisted Morris's laptop to face him. Alex could practically see the color drain from his face.

"Active shooters. An ongoing attack on a university lab." Kasim looked up at Alex and Cruz. "You two aren't keeping anything from me, are you?"

Alex held up his hands defensively. "You know everything we do."

"Damn it." Kasim pushed his chair away from the table and stood. "Morris, monitor the situation. See if you can figure out what's going on. Whether this has anything to do with Istanbul, Liang's going to want to know if we caused it. I'm praying that's a no, but like Morris said, coincidences are cheap cover for conspiracy."

Alex couldn't just watch another disaster unfold, especially if this was somehow connected to his actions in Istanbul. "What can we do?"

"You're sitting tight until we can figure out what Breners

was trying to give the Chinese," Kasim said. "I can't afford you causing any more trouble."

Alex hated being sidelined. He understood that Kasim was worried for the team's future. But he had a feeling things were going to get a lot worse before they got better.

Whether Liang liked it or not, Vector would be very busy, very soon.

Lisbon, Portugal

Renee crouched behind a desk facing the door to the lab with Paulo by her side. They had shoved another lab bench piled with equipment against the door with the help of their colleagues. It seemed like a paltry defense to keep out the gunmen. The other eight lab workers were sheltered around her.

More shots rang out around the building. Shouts exploded between the staccato bursts of gunfire. From somewhere else on campus, another salvo rang out. Screams blasted from down the hall, followed by the smack of footsteps and then bodies crashing against the floor. It sounded like the university had erupted into a warzone.

Renee flinched at another sustained burst. Cries and curses rose from the others in the lab.

She turned to Paulo. "Where are the police?"

"They said they're on their way," Paulo replied, putting away his phone. He squeezed her hand. "Shouldn't be long. We'll be okay."

"It's not okay!" a lab assistant said as she cowered behind another bench. "The police should already be here."

"This isn't right," Jameson, a post-doc researcher, agreed,

scraping his fingers through his hair. "Oh, God, this isn't right."

"Why are they doing this?" a French scientist named Bianca who was crouched near Renee asked, her voice rising. "What did we do to deserve this?"

"I don't know," Renee said. "But we need to be quieter."

A low rumble shook through the building. Dust fell in tiny columns from the ceiling, and a couple of round-bottom flasks fell from the shelves. They crashed to the floor in a spray of glass shards. A few of the researchers shrieked.

The voices in the hall suddenly went quiet.

Renee looked at the others and held a finger over her lips. But the tightening tentacles of dread worming through her insides told her it was already too late.

Footsteps clattered right outside.

Then someone rammed into the door. Another heavy thud, and one of the boxes of equipment on the bench they had placed in front of the door fell off, tumbled to the floor. More frightened screams escaped the researchers. One of them, a dark-haired woman named Liesel, began praying loudly in German.

The voices outside grew louder, excited. More of the people out there slammed into the doorway.

"Keep them out!" Paulo said. "Come on, help!"

He pushed another lab bench in front of the door with the help of a few colleagues. The door continued to shake as they got it into place. Then Renee and the others loaded the bench with everything from chairs to computers and lab equipment.

More gunshots burst outside the building.

Where are the police?

Renee looked over her shoulder toward the windows. Their fifth-floor lab overlooked a tree-filled avenue separating them from the main campus. The glow of fire bloomed from the broken windows of the psychology building across the street.

A low boom thudded across campus. Then a ball of fire erupted from the Institute of Education, oily smoke rolling into the sky. Farther to their south, pillars of smoke climbed into the blue sky.

"What in the…" she let her words trail off.

They were burning it all down. Why would anyone terrorize the university like this?

"Hey, they stopped," Jameson said.

"Maybe they're leaving," Bianca offered.

Renee turned back to the door. It wasn't shaking anymore, but if she strained her ears, she thought she could hear whispering voices outside. She couldn't understand what they were saying, but a gut instinct told her she didn't want to be anywhere near that door.

"Paulo," she whispered. "We need to get out of here."

She ran to the window. After unlatching it, she tried pushing it open. But the window was restricted to opening only a one-inch gap.

"I got it," Paulo said. "Stand back."

He grabbed a fire extinguisher from its place near the chemical shower and bashed it against the window.

Glass shattered, leaving a few jagged teeth along the frame. Renee knocked them out with a small metal box where they kept microscope slides.

Another boom erupted somewhere on campus, trembling through the walls of the lab.

"What do we do?" Bianca cried.

"We leave before we end up like that," Renee said, pointing out the window toward another ball of fire clawing up from a building.

Frederick, one of the lab assistants, shook his head. "No way. Not out that window."

"They're going to blow this place too," Paulo said. "And you heard the gunfire out there."

"Follow us," Renee said to the others.

The people outside the door had gone silent. That nagging voice at the back of her mind told her she could no longer wait. She lifted herself out the window and dangled on the frame, kicking until she found a foothold on the window frame below.

A warm summer breeze curled around her, and her stomach felt light.

Don't look down.

But she had no choice. She lowered herself to the window below, trying to control her breathing.

Paulo stuck his head out from the lab. "You okay?"

"Yeah, but hurry!"

He ducked back in, and she heard him trying to urge the others.

They refused to go.

She traced her toe down the bricks and the ledge near the next window below her. When she adjusted her weight, fingers searching for a new handhold, her foot slipped.

"Renee!" Paulo called. "Hold on!"

He descended toward her.

"I've got it!" she said, jamming her toe back into her foothold.

Her palms were wet with sweat, and she desperately wanted to dry them on her shirt. But she didn't dare.

Just four more floors to go.

Paulo scaled down the wall beside her. He was an amateur rock climber, and this was nothing for him.

"Get your foot right there," he said. "And—"

An explosion rocked through the building. Glass and fire exploded from the windows above, followed by a swirl of black smoke and anguished screams.

Renee nearly lost her grip, her muscles locking into place, mouth going dry.

"The lab," Paulo said, voice weak.

Renee fought to prevent herself from hyperventilating, adrenaline making her shake. "We have to keep going."

Gunfire roared from above. More screams. Was that Bianca? It sounded like her voice.

Renee struggled to focus on the climb down, each foothold and handhold harder to find.

Paulo coached her down to the third floor. Then the second.

A shout exploded from above, and she looked up. A man with a black mask peered out the window, pointing at them.

Another masked man joined him at another of the lab's windows, smoke still drifting out in tendrils. The man leveled a rifle out at Renee and Paulo.

"Let go!" Paulo pushed off the wall, arms cartwheeling, as he plummeted toward the bushes below.

Renee couldn't do it. She was locked in place, held there by her terror.

The crack of gunfire rang out from the rifle. Bullets seared through the air around her head.

At last, she kicked herself off the wall, aiming for the bushes near Paulo. Then she fell. Branches and leaves broke around her, enough to cushion her fall. Her feet slammed against the ground, knees buckling, pain jolting up through her bones.

"Come on, it's okay," Paulo said, already rising to his feet. "You did a good job. We can do this."

He grabbed her hand, forcing her to run through the trees to the road. Dirt and grass kicked up around them, bark flying where rounds punched into trees.

Every step sent a thunderbolt of agony through her ankles and knees. Paulo loped alongside her, favoring his right leg.

Somewhere, police sirens wailed.

Finally.

They ran into the street and ducked behind a line of parked cars. Bullets punched into the metal. The bastards weren't giving up.

Paulo clenched her hand tightly. "Are you okay?"

Renee nodded. "You?"

The rumble of a car engine cut him off. A black Mercedes SUV raced down the street, headed straight toward them. Renee yanked on Paulo, turning him around, and they sprinted down the other direction.

But another Mercedes was racing toward them from that direction, too, brakes screeching as it stopped to block their path. The rear door flew open, and two masked men lunged out, rifles pointed their direction.

Renee looked for another escape route. Between the men rushing down the street and those in the lab building, there was nowhere to go without being cut down in a hail of gunfire.

Paulo squeezed his fingers around hers. "I'm sorry, Renee."

"Me too."

She braced herself for the incoming bullets to lance through her body.

This is it.

5

IN THE FEW seconds before her impending death, Renee's mind raced. She had spent her life devoted to uncovering new scientific knowledge, content to work behind the screen of her computer and the lenses of a microscope. What had she done wrong to lead her to this point?

Maybe she should have stayed in Texas like her parents wanted.

But Paulo gave her hand another squeeze, reminding her that there were moments in her brief life that had been worth living. That even now she could find solace in her contribution to humanity's understanding of the world. Especially since she had done that with someone as brilliant as Paulo by her side.

Now she was going to die by his side. It seemed like such a waste.

Seconds passed. She heard only footsteps and distant pops of gunfire. She winced with each cracking shot.

But not a single bullet hit her.

Eventually, she opened her eyes to see four gunmen stalking down the road toward her and Paulo. One held his hand up, motioning for the other attackers inside the building to cease fire.

With them was someone she hadn't expected.

Dr. Estacio.

Blood ran from his nostrils and a cut along his forehead. One of the gunmen pointed a rifle at his back.

"These are the two you told us about?" a gunman asked in a thick accent she couldn't place.

Estacio nodded. "That's them."

A surge of emotions flooded Renee. Her knees went weak, head dizzy. She clenched Paulo's fingers tighter, drawing strength from his grip. He squeezed back, his whole body trembling. Whatever these people wanted, whatever they were planning on doing with her, she wanted it to be over.

"Are you telling the truth?" the gunman asked, prodding Dr. Estacio's back with the rifle.

"Yes, it was them. They did the work. They wrote the paper. You want them, not me."

"You stole the credit, then?" the gunman asked. "Your life depends on the truth."

"That's right. I'm sorry. Please, please, don't shoot."

"I won't shoot them," the gunman said. "But you are worthless."

He fired, and Dr. Estacio collapsed. The other three men rushed Renee and Paulo, their rifles trained and ready. The incoming sirens grew louder, but with every step closer those men took, the hope of some heroic rescue grew more distant.

"What do you want?" Renee managed.

The lead terrorist growled, "You."

The first gunman hit her stomach with the stock of his barrel. All the air rushed out of Renee's lungs.

"Renee!" Paulo tried to put himself between her and the gunman.

Another man punched him in the gut, and he doubled

over. Then the men dragged them toward the Mercedes, right past Estacio's body.

Renee flailed, trying to break free. Another blow against the back of her skull sent a wash of pain through her. She saw stars in her blurred vision.

The gunmen reached the SUV and tore open the rear door. They secured Renee and Paulo's wrists together with plastic zip cuffs then gagged them with rancid cloths. One of the men lifted Renee and threw her into the cargo space. Paulo came next, landing heavily beside her.

Then the men slammed the door, and seconds later, the SUV raced off.

———

FREDERICK, MD

EXHAUSTION PULLED at Alex's eyelids. He had taken a short nap on the flight from Istanbul straight to Frederick. But that wasn't enough to make up for the toll the past day had taken on his body.

But even as his brain begged for his bed back in his Baltimore home, the last thing he wanted to do was sleep. He couldn't close his eyes until he had some idea of what was in that sample vial. He waited in the corridor outside Vector's BSL-4 containment laboratory. Even in the hall, he wore the full space suit like the two scientists working beyond the glass windows.

Slow, plodding footsteps sounded from behind him. Cruz was marching toward him, awkward in her suit.

"You sure you don't want to take a break?"

"I want to be here for this," he said.

"I'm just as good at watching things as you are," Cruz said.

"And trust me, that nap was worth it."

"I need to know what's going on." He gestured toward the two scientists inside. "And right now, they look… confused."

His partner stepped closer to the window.

The science team was composed of John Park and Freya Weber. Park was an MD/PhD Harvard-trained biologist whose second home away from the BSL-4 lab was whichever hot zone around the world currently threatened to become an outbreak. When Weber wasn't in the lab, she spent her time fine-tuning her computational models of disease spread.

Park was pipetting tiny aliquots of the sample they'd recovered from Breners into individual cone-shaped wells in a plastic plate. Behind him, Weber stood in front of a genetic sequencer. The monitor beside her showed a series of color-coded peaks. Each peak represented different nucleotides—the building blocks of the genetic material of whatever was in that sample.

"How can you tell they're confused?" Cruz asked. "Seems like they know what they're doing."

"I'm not so sure about that," Alex said. "First, they were doing gram staining as if the sample contained bacteria. Then they did a bunch of polymerase chain reaction runs like they didn't believe the genetic sequencing results the first few times."

"Don't they usually look at these samples under a microscope first?"

Alex nodded. "They did. I watched them perform scanning electron microscopy. That's powerful enough to see bacteria or even a virus."

"And?"

"From here, whatever they were looking appeared to be big."

Cruz gave him a blank look. "How big?"

"Fractions of a micron."

"Sounds tiny."

"Not in comparison to a virus, which is on the scale of tens to hundreds of nanometers. The *thing* they were looking at is nearly one hundred times larger than that."

"So bacteria, then."

Alex shook his head. "That's what I thought, but that doesn't explain why they're rerunning PCR tests and genetic sequencing."

They watched Park and Weber inserting the next batch of samples into various machines for analyses. Each time the science team seemed perplexed by the result, pausing to consult with each other over their private lab comms, a knot twisted in Alex's gut.

The vial they had retrieved from Breners had less than a milliliter of liquid in it. Inside that droplet of liquid, the number of tiny microorganisms or viruses or whatever was drifting around in there would be finite.

Eventually they would run out of samples to analyze.

Cruz paced around beside him. She didn't have the extensive scientific background that he did from his training as a biotech-specialized analyst and intelligence officer in the CIA. But after being medically discharged from the Marines, she had been a quick study. He could see the gears turning in her head.

"What are you thinking?" he asked.

"Maybe this isn't a virus or bacteria."

"I had the same idea," Alex said. "They already tested to make sure this isn't some strange chemical-based weapon mixed in with viral or bacterial DNA. The NMR and XRD tests came back negative for synthetic materials and chemical residues—nothing but organic matter in there."

"Okay, science boy. But what if this is a fungal spore or something?"

"Negative on fungi." He pointed at an image on an SEM

monitor. The screen showed a pill-shaped object. "And the sample doesn't look like any fungal spore we've ever seen."

"But… I don't know, maybe I didn't get as much sleep as I thought. Maybe I'm just talking nonsense, but I get the feeling we need to think outside the box on this one."

Sweat trickled down the back of Alex's neck. Standing so long in the suit was getting to him, but Cruz's conversation had started to help clear the fog clouding his thoughts. It sparked a memory, an obscure topic he had studied once.

"You know what? Just ignore me. I don't know a bacterium from a hole in the ground."

"No, I think you're on to something," he said. He pressed an intercom button. "Quick question when you've got time, Doctors."

Weber looked up from her machine then walked over. She hit the intercom button inside the lab. "Still no concrete results. Sorry."

Her father had been a US soldier stationed outside of Ansbach, Germany, and her mother was a local. When she spoke, she still had a slight accent that hinted at a childhood spent in Bavaria. Alex had filed that information away, a bad habit left over from his days at the Bureau. You never knew when the smallest scrap of intel could become useful. Like right now, with the half-remembered research he'd just recalled.

"I know," Alex said. "I've been watching."

Weber cracked a smile behind her visor. "I feel like a seal at the zoo in here. Hard to bring my A game when I'm expecting you to throw me sardines for a job well done."

"I can bring the sardines if that's what you need," Cruz said.

"What I need"—she looked over her shoulder toward Park —"what we *both* need is a break. And I'm not talking about the kind where you grab a coffee and some gossip."

"What about this? Cruz had a crazy idea, but it's starting to sound not-so-crazy to me," Alex said.

"Oh?" Weber visibly perked up.

"What if it's not a virus or bacteria?" he asked.

Weber slowly shook her head. "It's not synthetic. It's not—"

"I know," Alex said. "I've been watching your analyses and tracking the results. But there's one thing we haven't tested for."

"An alien disease?" Weber tried. "Believe me, I've considered it."

"Well, kind of," Alex said.

"You're not serious."

"I'm serious, but I'm not talking about flying saucers and green men."

Weber paused, looking at Park as he fussed with one of the computers. "Fine. I'm listening. At this point, I'll take anything you got."

"A couple years ago, I read this thing on a new type of bacteria. Only, they weren't really bacteria. They were arc—"

Weber cut him off. "Archaea. Yes, that's right. Single-cell organisms that look like bacteria—but their genes and metabolism are more like eukaryotic cells."

"Exactly," Alex said. "I don't know much else about them, but maybe it's a start."

"If you had suggested this at the outset, I would've said you were insane. Archaea aren't dangerous. There have only been a few studies suggesting a loose correlation between them and gut microbiome health. Would your guy Breners be running around with a little organism that can occasionally *maybe* cause a bad case of constipation?"

Alex sighed. "I realize this is a long shot, but at least it's a shot."

Weber tapped on a computer nearby the intercom. The

monitor was visible through the window, revealing a series of academic papers. "Says here that we might have better luck using matrix-assisted laser desorption ionization time-of-flight mass spec to identify specific rDNA sequences in some human-associated archaea."

"So, uh, you're saying I might be right?" Cruz asked.

Weber gave her a slight nod. "We'll know in a couple of hours. Now, unless you two have got more brainy ideas for us, I suggest you go snag a coffee and wait out these results. We aren't going to be any faster with you staring at us."

Alex hesitated, but Cruz gently tapped on his shoulder. "Come on. You heard the expert. Coffee time. Doctor's orders."

6

Sᴠᴇʀᴅʟᴏᴠѕᴋ, Russia

Cᴏʟᴏɴᴇʟ Sᴇʀɢᴇɪ Pᴀᴠʟᴇɴᴋᴏ dug into the pocket of his suit and pulled out one of his two passports. This one showed his military rank. The other, the one he left in the pocket, identified him as a mere civilian employee of the Fourteenth Directorate of the Russian Radiation, Chemical, and Biological Defense, or RHkM.

Both showed the same picture of his square face and bald head, his jaw set in tight-lipped seriousness. The slight gauntness to his cheeks and sallowness under his eyes were lingering evidence of the horrible sickness he'd once endured as a teenager. But though he had long-since recovered from that illness, it had inspired his current career trajectory.

Pavlenko was a master of disease.

His civilian passport and a corresponding internal ID card allowed him to enter the Soviet-era pharmaceutical compound in Sverdlovsk. It gave him a layer of anonymity in the Fourteenth Directorate's center of operations. But the military ID was the only way to access the corridors surrounding the BSL-4 laboratories, previously known as Zone One.

That was the true heart of the Directorate's research operations.

"Welcome, Colonel," said a woman sitting at the desk in front of the decontamination chamber. A German shepherd patiently sat beside her, its tail swishing over the floor in a steady beat. It gave him a sniff.

Equal parts guard and living pathogen detector, the dog had been trained both to subdue unruly visitors and sniff out various diseases. That was a crucial measure in case a technician tried to exit after an improper decon process or an accidental contamination incident.

Pavlenko had seen the brutal side effects of a leak before. He was glad to take every precaution to prevent it again.

The woman examined his ID, though she had seen him nearly every day for the past seven months. Pavlenko didn't mind. Better that his people were diligent and disciplined than sloppy and lax. She hit a button under her desk that released the locks to the decon chamber.

Sliding doors retracted with a metallic groan, and Pavlenko entered. He donned his shoe covers and disposable gloves first and then entered the next anteroom, where a mist sprayed over him. Next came another white-walled space where he dragged a coverall up and over his body, cocooning himself inside it before putting on the white ventilated positive-pressure suit with its independent air blower and large visor that made him feel like an earthbound cosmonaut.

The air supply hissed, filling the suit, and he walked through the last anteroom before being released into the white-washed corridors beyond.

Only one other person traversed the hall. Wearing the same bulky suit, the man he walked toward was unidentifiable by sight. But Pavlenko knew only one other person would be here right now. Someone he needed to meet with privately.

There was no better way to ensure a message remained secret from prying ears than to enter one of the most secured and dangerous facilities in the world. The pathogens within these walls were capable of ravaging the entire population of Moscow within a week. That was more than enough to dissuade all but the most foolhardy visitors—and that was if the strict security measures outside failed to convince them to stay out.

Lieutenant Colonel Yuri Levin turned to face him. The man gave him a perfunctory salute. Even in the oversized suit, his belly protruded slightly, a testament to the time he spent working behind a desk and groveling to government bureaucrats.

"Have you had your tour?" Pavlenko asked.

Through his visor, Levin shot Pavlenko a look. His round features were screwed up in confusion as though he didn't understand the question.

With a frustrated huff, Pavlenko motioned to the tube from his suit's blower and crimped it with a squeeze. The whoosh of the air stopped.

Levin did the same.

"Now you can hear me?"

Levin nodded, his big suit jostling.

"First time in a suit," Pavlenko guessed.

A bead of sweat rolled over Levin's bulbous nose. "I am not used to them."

Pavlenko was pleased to hear that. The people who worked for him should never be too comfortable around him. Like the woman outside the decon chamber, he wanted those he depended on to remain vigilant about his rules and directives. Putting them in a position where their life relied on carefully following detailed regulations was always a good reminder for people like Levin. As an added benefit, he always found people were more obedient when they were operating with the implied threat of an ax at their necks.

"You have already had a tour?" Pavlenko asked again.

"Your assistant scientist, Dr. Yunevich, showed me the developmental labs."

"Impressive, aren't they?"

"Very."

Levin turned away from Pavlenko and toward the expansive glass windows. Beyond the glass were enormous stainless-steel bioreactors, gigantic drums feeding the microorganisms within them at a scale that left him feeling breathless with awe.

"These will ensure a prosperous future for us," Pavlenko said.

Levin tried to stand a little straighter, puffing out his chest. The only thing puffing out was his belly.

"One where Russia is no longer a laughingstock of the world," Levin said. "While others will fall, we will fill the void they leave behind. There will be many opportunities for us if we succeed."

"We will have a future that our fathers only dreamed of," Pavlenko said.

Most importantly, it was what *his* father, a member of the former Soviet Union's Biopreparat, had dreamed of.

"I'm certain of it," Levin said. But he backed away from the window as if merely looking at the bioreactors would poison him.

"Yes, so long as we all do our part."

"You do not need to worry about me," Levin said. "Field operations and security are fine. All you must do is work safely and quietly in your labs."

Pavlenko did not take Levin's bait. "I saw that Colonel Qi died in an accident days ago. That was very good. But what happened in Istanbul?"

"Breners and his contacts were killed. They won't be a problem anymore." Levin hesitated before continuing, his skin pale beneath the perspiration beading over his face. "Our reports also indicate that Lisbon was a success. Estacio's lab is destroyed, along with all their samples and internal data. The cover's holding. No one seems to realize it was just the one lab we wanted. They're even blaming it on radical terrorists."

"What about Dr. Estacio? I want to speak with him."

Levin shifted in his bulky suit.

"Answer me," Pavlenko said.

"According to the men I contracted for the operation, he was not actually the one we wanted. He is dead now."

Pavlenko's fingers curled into a fist. "I told you this was not a job that we should hire out."

"You are not in charge of field operations," Levin said, voice raising. "Do not forget your role is these labs, where the general put you. And *I* am doing exactly what General Dmitriyev ordered."

"By the sounds of it, you failed. I don't want hired guns making decisions about which scientists I need to talk to. That affects my scientific mission."

"They merely acted on your instructions. You wanted the man who wrote that paper—it wasn't actually Estacio." Levin prodded Pavlenko's chest with a finger. A dangerous gesture for more than one reason. "We retrieved two researchers, a man and a woman."

"Where are they?"

"We took them straight to the facility in Kaliningrad."

Pavlenko wished he could talk to these scientists in person. But Kaliningrad would have to wait. His duty was here in Sverdlovsk for now. "Did your hirelings bother to get the names of these researchers?"

"These are the individuals responsible for the research

you're interested in. If we had taken Estacio instead, we would not have the people you wanted."

"I doubt you can understand what constitutes the research I am interested in, but I hope for your career's sake that you are correct. You did not answer my question."

Levin took a step backward, quiet for a moment. "I have done my part. I trust you will do yours."

"I have. The first batch is ready for deployment."

"You are sure it will work?"

Pavlenko hated that question, especially from an insolent man like Levin. "If I wasn't sure, I would not tell you that it was ready."

"It's just… this seems unorthodox."

"What?"

"Your whole plan. We could contaminate water treatment plants or make dirty bombs with your weapon. But instead—"

"Trust me, Levin." Pavlenko gestured at the bioreactors. "This will work. We don't need to worry about customs and border patrol. Walls will not stop us. No laws can hold us back. We do not need a single person to step foot in the countries of our enemies for this to succeed. In one fell swoop, we can infect the entire world, and there is nothing they can do about it."

"I hope you're right."

"I *know* I'm right. The world will soon be a different place. And *we* will be its rightful heirs."

***

KALININGRAD, Russia

A HEADACHE THROBBED behind Renee's eyes. Her brain felt as if it was pressing against every part of her skull. She pulled herself into a sitting position. Blinking, she used a hand to shield her eyes from the glare of white lights.

Whatever she was seated on was soft. A bed, maybe.

Where was she?

Distant memories slowly swam through her mind. She seemed to remember someone inserting a needle into her arm then stuffing her into a box. Somewhere cramped.

She blinked again, trying to stop the stabs of pain plunging through her pupils.

As the shapes around her started to coalesce, she heard another voice.

"Renee, are you okay?"

Paulo.

"I…" She swallowed hard, her mouth dry, tongue sticking to the roof of her mouth. "I think so." She pressed a palm against her forehead. "You?"

Paulo was seated across from her in another bed. They were surrounded by four white walls and a single stainless-steel door, almost as if they were in a hospital room, but without any of the equipment.

"I'm hurting." He trundled across the room, plopping down next to her. "I think they drugged us… I remember nothing until now."

"Me too. How are we going to get out of this?"

Before they could continue their conversation, the lock clicked on the door.

Renee shrank against the wall. Paulo gripped her hand, and she took comfort in that touch.

The door opened, and a man walked in. He had a pistol in a holster strapped across his chest, and black tattoos snaked around his muscled arms.

"Come with me," the man said, his voice thick with a Russian accent.

When they hesitated, he tapped the side of his gun.

"Do not be difficult," he said.

Paulo stood, still holding Renee's hand. "We are in this together."

"How very touching," the man said. "Move. Now."

He led them out of the door and down a hallway with white tiles and walls. A distinct odor like cleaning products and astringent chemicals wafted over them. It reminded Renee of the smell of their lab back in Lisbon.

The lab that was now nothing but ash and rubble.

She shuddered, thinking of her lab mates and Dr. Estacio.

The Russian man looked back at her as he walked. "So you want to know how you are getting out of this?"

Renee's stomach dropped, and fear tingled through her with its icy fingers. Of course. They had been listening in on her and Paulo.

The man gave her a shrug. "It is simple. You are not getting out."

Renee wanted to wake up, to find out this was some horrible dream or maybe just a prank that had gone much too far. Her body felt like she was recovering from the worst hangover in her life. That was a reminder enough that whatever was happening to her and Paulo right now, it was all too real.

But despite what that man told her, maybe, just maybe, there *was* a way out of this. She and Paulo were scientists. They could outsmart a thug with a gun.

Right?

All down the hall, she noticed other doorways like the one that had led to their room. How big was this place?

"Where are you taking us?" Paulo asked.

The man stopped and turned. He slammed his fist hard into Paulo's stomach. The researcher crumpled, holding his abdomen, gasping for breath.

"Paulo!" Renee dropped down beside him, holding him as he struggled to breathe.

"You do not ask questions."

Renee helped Paulo back to his feet, her pulse thundering past her ears. She wrapped an arm around her friend's shoulder and let him lean into her.

Paulo managed to walk with Renee's help, and they followed the man through another doorway. This time, the space opened to a catwalk overlooking a large warehouse filled with shipping containers and forklifts.

No one appeared to be working in the place, except for a pair of men near an exit. They cradled rifles, looking up at the catwalk as Paulo and Renee passed by. She paused, trying to look into an open container below, but she couldn't see anything.

"Hurry up," the Russian man leading them said.

He pushed open a set of double doors. The halls in here were filled with people in scrubs and white coats. They passed windows revealing laboratories stocked with equipment Renee recognized for genetic sequencing, microscopy, and biochemical analyses. But this stuff was more than she had ever laid eyes on in all her years in academic research.

A few of the people inside those labs looked out at her and Paulo. Deep, dark circles hung under their eyes, and most appeared pale, as if they hadn't seen the sun in weeks. One man's face was covered in bruises. A woman had a long wound on the side of her head that looked like it had been stitched up by Dr. Frankenstein. All averted their gazes quickly, like they were expecting someone to punish them for merely existing.

What is this place?

Renee couldn't believe that yesterday she had been stressed out because of a paper authorship conflict with her advisor.

And then, in one night, everything had changed. She had no idea what would happen next. No control over her life, her choices. It made her want to start screaming, to make a break for it and damn the consequences. Instead, she let the Russian herd her through another doorway.

The lock clicked shut behind them, and they found themselves in an anteroom with white coveralls, surgical masks, gloves, and booties.

A voice sounded over the intercom with a slight hiss of static. "Put on your personal protective gear."

The voice didn't belong to the man who had escorted them to the lab. It wasn't as deep, and the Russian accent was less pronounced.

Someone else was watching them.

Renee hesitated, looking around the room for a camera. She spotted a black half-globe in the corner above the rack with coveralls.

"Do not make me ask again," the voice commanded.

Renee fought through her aching muscles and the confusion muddling her brain, fumbling to put on the protective wear. Once she and Paulo were done, the door to the anteroom opened, letting them into the next room. Inside was a laboratory with equipment much like their lab in Lisbon. Standard microscopes, sequencers, PCR machines, and chemicals lined the benches and shelves.

"Do you see the device on the center lab bench?" the voice asked, ringing over the speakers.

Renee tried to ignore the unsettling sensation of being watched by an unknown captor. She walked toward the lab bench. This one was clear of equipment except for a small device about the size of two soft drink cans.

"This one?" she asked, pointing at the lab bench with a gloved finger.

"That is correct. Does the device look familiar to you?"

When Renee hesitated, Paulo answered, "No. Should it?"

There was a pause that made Renee's pulse race. She wondered if Paulo had given the wrong answer. If that

Russian man waiting outside would come in here and gun them down.

The silence dragged on.

Renee tried to swallow, but her tongue seemed to cling to the roof of her mouth. She focused on taking deep, slow breaths, eyes locked with Paulo's as she fought the panic swelling through her chest. Paulo clenched his gloved hands together, wringing his fingers.

The voice finally came back over the speakers. "You are certain you do not know what this device is?"

Renee thought about lying. She could tell him she knew exactly what it was. This person, their overseer, seemed to expect them to know.

If they couldn't identify this device, would they serve any other purpose to these people? Would she and Paulo be thrown back in that room to rot—or worse?

She pictured the Russian man with his gun. The frightened looks on the workers' faces in the halls. Clearly, they had been brought here for a reason. This overseer must have thought she and Paulo should know what this device did.

And why would he think that?

Renee could only think of one reason, recalling what Estacio had told those gunmen before he had been killed. This must have something to do with their research. The project that she and Paulo had been working on.

The device itself had several ports along the curved sides and gaps that traced its circumference. From what she could see, inside was a mesh grating and a white, papery material. Possibly a filter, which reminded her of the ones she used for her research.

"This collects samples of airborne microorganisms," she said, trying to sound confident. "It's a sensor, an aerobiological detector."

"So you do know what it is," the overseer said. "Good."

Paulo gave her a questioning look, one brow raised.

She leaned in closer to the device. At the bottom was an inscription, a trademarked word that traced around half of the device: EnviroProct.

"Dr. Estacio was working on this project," the voice said. "And now you will be too. I'm told you'll be instrumental in our success. And if you aren't, we will find others."

"What are we supposed to do?" Renee asked.

"You'll be troubleshooting this device. Think of yourselves as white-hat hackers."

Paulo looked at Renee, cocking his head as if he didn't understand the phrase.

"Those are hackers who help detect and repair vulnerabilities in software or machinery so black-hat hackers—the malicious—can't get in," Renee said.

"She is correct. I want you to figure out any vulnerabilities in this system. I want to know what it would take for a microorganism to go undetected."

Now Renee was confused. "You want us to make it work better?"

"I did not say that. You will analyze the device. Understood?"

Renee stared silently at the device, wondering why someone would want to figure out a way to bypass this machine. The only answers she could think of chilled her to her core.

7

FORT DETRICK, Maryland

SKYLAR ENTERED Vector's operations center. The low hum of computers and the tap of a keyboard greeted her. Morris was at one corner of the small room, working at his laptop. He took out one of his earbuds and raised a hand in a brief hello, but he didn't bother turning around, too focused on whatever he was working on.

"First here, Cruz?" he asked then gulped from a neon-colored can of an energy drink.

"Always," she said.

"Kasim's been trapped in meetings all day. Sounds like they keep getting pushed back with every new detail coming out of Lisbon and Istanbul. The DNI is spooked, and the NSC is scrambling for answers. They don't have a clue what's going on."

"At least we're not the only ones in the dark, huh?" she asked.

"Not in the slightest."

She was glad that the Direction of National Intelligence and the National Security Council apparently didn't know about Vector's involvement in Istanbul yet. It gave them time to get back in the field and unravel this conspiracy before they got too mired down by external agencies investigating *their* activities.

She pulled out a chair at the table in the center of the room and sat, tapping on the table's touchscreen surface. The fake wood pattern gave way to a spread of images organized in virtual folders. Ones of those images was a map of Europe. Red circles glowed over Lisbon and Istanbul. Tapping those spots revealed a slew of news articles related to the incidents. Another tap on a different tab revealed classified intel outlining various terrorist groups and government organizations the NSC had identified as potential actors in the two attacks.

She read the profiles of each of these suspects, ranging from remnants of Al-Qaeda fueled by Saudi oil interests to Russian mafia associates aligned with former KGB elements to disgruntled members of the Chinese Communist Party.

"We're completely lost, aren't we?" Skylar asked.

"Lost? Who's lost?" Morris asked, finally turning around his seat.

"No one knows who these people are."

He grinned. "*They* don't."

"You're telling me you do?"

"I mean, I'm working on it. I've got some leads."

"Glad to hear it," Skylar said. "One day back, and I'm already tired of conference rooms."

The door opened. Curly brown hair bouncing, Dr. Weber entered with her usual buoyant gait. Her thin, short frame was a marked contrast to Wolfe, who was a full head taller. Dr. Park came in last, still dressed in his white coat over khakis and a green collared shirt. If Skylar didn't know better, she would've thought he was just an unassuming family practice physician hanging around his suburban private practice. As they settled into the table around Skylar, Kasim entered.

"I swear you all will be the death of me," he said. "Meeting after meeting, I've had to sit there and deflect and lie to people I've known since I joined the Army."

"Is Vector still on this op? Or does Liang think we had something to with Lisbon too?" Skylar asked.

"Cutting right to the point." Kasim paused just enough to make Skylar's nerves jitter. "Yes, Vector's still got the support of USAMRIID. But we're dangling by a thread."

Skylar let out a sigh of relief.

"We need results," Kasim said. "Knowing what was in Breners's sample would be a good start, along with why he was trying to give it to Shing. Liang's got more questions for us, and if she's got questions, others will too. Park, Weber, let's hear what you have first."

Weber dragged her finger across the table. The screen shifted to show a black-and-white magnified image of a pill-shaped microorganism.

"This is our culprit," Park said. "We confirmed it isn't virus or bacteria but rather archaea."

"What's an archaea?" Morris asked.

"Single-celled organisms that look kind of like bacteria but more complex. They're more mutualistic in nature too. For instance, there are a variety of archaea that inhabit human and animal gastrointestinal tracts."

"But researchers have never identified archaea pathogens," Weber said.

"Then how did this get weaponized?" Kasim asked.

"That's the most confusing part." Park tapped on the screen, and the image vanished, replaced by long chains of nucleotides representing the genetic content of the archaea. "As far as we can tell, this wasn't weaponized at all."

"What do you mean?" Wolfe asked.

Weber spoke this time. "We performed a basic bioinformatics database search, comparing the genetic data we recovered from the archaea in Breners's sample with established archaea sequences."

She tapped on the screen, and another microscope image appeared of the pill-shaped archaea.

"This image isn't from our sample," she said. "This is from a 2016 scientific paper in the *Journal of Gastroenterology*."

"Same archaea?"

"That's right. We're looking at *M. smithii*, the most common gut methanogen."

"Help me out here," Morris said, frowning at the image.

"It's just a microorganism that produces methane. These are one of the most predominant ones in the digestive tracts of humans and animals."

"They make gas?" Skylar asked.

"Yes, something I'm sure Morris is all too familiar with," Weber said. Morris shot her a feigned hurt look. "But in all seriousness, this is an extremely common archaea and is fairly well characterized. Our sample is nearly identical with this one."

"Why would Breners risk his life giving a common gas-producing bug to those guys in Istanbul?" Skylar asked.

"It's *nearly* identical. We found a single gene alteration that might be a clue," Park said.

"While it could be a normal mutation, given the circumstances, we think it might've been introduced through a lab-induced genetic modification," Weber added.

Park dragged his finger across the table so that the microscopic images of Breners's sample were side by side with those of the normal archaea.

"The cell wall of Breners's archaea is nearly twice as thick as those of the archaea native to the human gut," Park said. "These cells walls also express different levels of surface proteins around the outside of the archaea as a result, giving them a slightly different molecular footprint, if you will."

"What's the advantage of those walls being thicker?" Skylar asked.

"Thicker cell walls generally mean higher survivability in inhospitable environments," Park said. He sounded like one of Skylar's old professors, the biology lecturer so boring that he had nearly made her drop out of school. She forced herself to focus. "Archaea are naturally hardy microorganisms, found everywhere from salt lakes where no other life can survive to hot springs and underwater vents and volcanoes. They've adapted to nearly every environment on Earth, not to mention microenvironments inside of larger organisms."

"A thicker cell wall would also help the archaea survive, for example, a dirty bomb," Weber said. "Or maybe they're planning on dumping the archaea in a water distribution facility."

Skylar hated the feeling of not quite getting it. "But even if these archaea have been genetically engineered to survive harsher environments, what's the point? Does it cause some kind of disease?"

"Nothing that we've identified," Park said. "Without more samples, there's not a lot else we can figure out."

Kasim ran his hands through his graying hair. "We need more than that. Please, Morris, tell me you've got something."

Morris rubbed his hands together. "I think so."

ALEX DESPERATELY HOPED Morris had a better lead. Finding a slight variation on a seemingly innocuous archaeon could not be the only thing Vector achieved after what he and Skylar had endured in the past forty-eight hours.

Morris took a swig of his energy drink. "Qi, Shing, and Zhi are dead ends. Literally." He glanced over his glasses at Skylar and Alex. "I couldn't find anything definitive enough for you two attack dogs to go after."

"Tell us what you do know," Alex said, swallowing his annoyance at the techie. When Kasim had approached him with the Vector project, he'd assured Alex that the team would be the best of the best. But surely there was someone better than Morris.

Morris's fingers danced across his keyboard. "It was easier to find information about the attack on Lisbon."

"You know who's responsible?" Kasim asked.

"I don't know *who* did it. But I think I know *why* they did it." He used a stylus to trace a circle around the University of Lisbon campus then marked the buildings that had been attacked. "I tried to find a pattern, if maybe these attacks were selectively targeting specific facilities for some perceived political or economic reason. That's the story on the news, anyway."

"And?" Kasim asked.

"On the surface, they weren't."

"These were all random?" Cruz asked.

"No, I didn't say that," Morris said.

"I'm guessing the whole radical Islamic terrorist thing is a cover-up," Alex said.

"Ding! You get a cookie," Morris said. "And I got to say, after what Park and Weber just told us, I'm more sure than ever that I'm right."

Another tap from Morris, and a list of research groups popped up on the screen. Under each research group were the records of all the employees and students associated with the various labs.

"I didn't have to search too hard for this," Morris said. "Now, these terrorists didn't only attack labs. They hit the library and a dining hall too. But that all looks like smoke and mirrors to me."

Alex studied the lists. A heavy weight dragged through his insides as he read name after name. Next to each was a status, either "Deceased" or "Alive." A quick count showed nearly thirty people had died in the atrocities.

"I cross-checked all these researchers with reports from area hospitals and the university's crisis response team database," Morris said. "I found the status on damn near everyone except for two people."

Another click, and all the names disappeared, leaving only two: Renee Williams and Paulo Reis.

"Williams and Reis were members of Dr. Carlos Estacio's lab. I think this is the lab the attackers were actually targeting."

"Tell us why you think that," Kasim said.

"Estacio's group studied aerobiology."

Park perked up. "You're kidding. Isn't Breners's company involved in that arena? Did he have ties to Breners or EnviroProct?"

"I don't know yet," Morris said. "But I haven't exhausted all my resources."

"What about their lab's research papers?" Weber asked.

"That's the low-hanging fruit," Morris said. "I checked there first but didn't find any projects sponsored by EnviroProct or anything co-published with them. I'm going to find out if there was a nondisclosure agreement or something with Breners's company that wasn't public or, uh, near-public record. That requires a deeper dive."

"Okay, so we don't have a solid tie yet," Alex said.

"No, but Williams and Reis's absence struck me as odd," Morris said.

"I saw pictures of the labs in the news," Kasim said. "Several were turned to rubble. Are you sure they're not just missing or…?"

He let the words hang in the air, but Alex knew what he was asking.

"No matter how many dogs you send into that campus looking for bodies, you're not going to find them." Morris pressed a button on his keyboard with a flourish and a video played. "This is a CCTV recording just outside the Biological Sciences building. That's where Williams and Reis worked."

Alex watched two figures crouch behind a line of cars on the street.

"Those are our guys," Morris said.

Four masked gunmen emerged from an SUV, herding another man in front of him. There was blood all over his face, and he was holding up his hands in a pleading gesture.

"And that's Dr. Estacio," Morris said, indicating the hostage.

A flash of gunfire, and Dr. Estacio fell.

Alex braced himself as the gunmen advanced on Williams and Reis. Instead of shooting them, however, the gunmen dragged the scientists back to one of the SUVs and then drove away.

"They were kidnapped," Cruz said. "Why?"

"I don't know *why*, but I think I know *where* they went," Morris said smugly.

"Let's see," Kasim said.

"Fortunately for us, Portugal has a comprehensive system of speed and traffic cameras." Morris seemed proud of himself for uncovering all this. It was indeed a remarkable feat, surpassing Alex's initial expectations. But he couldn't help thinking of all the lives that had been lost in this single incident. The analyst sounded like he was talking about a movie or a video game, not an actual event with a real body count. "Took half the computational power we have available, but I tracked those SUVs. Image analysis picked them up again at this spot just across the border into Spain, just outside of Badajoz."

Images of an SUV driving into the gates of a private

airport appeared. A semitruck with a covered trailer followed them through the gates.

The view shifted as Morris loaded up the next set of CCTV cameras. The truck parked next to a cargo plane. A ramp stretched from the open rear hatch of the plane, and people unloaded long, metal boxes from the truck's trailer onto the plane.

Alex noticed Cruz recoil from the sight.

"You okay?" he asked quietly.

"Caskets," she said. "Just like the ones we send our people home in."

"That's right," Morris said. He took another gulp from his can of over-caffeinated sugar water. Alex was just as addicted to caffeine, but he wasn't sure how Morris drank that garbage. A good coffee, especially a well-done espresso, was worlds better. But so long as those atrocious drinks kept the analyst pumping out intel like this, he wasn't going to argue the merits of that particular beverage. "But I have no reason to believe these are filled with people. I mean, except for two of them."

"Which ones?" Alex asked.

"Wait for it," he said.

A bald man wearing a dark T-shirt got out of the SUV. The image was grainy, but it was good enough Alex could see a tattoo on the back of his left arm.

"Is that like the ones we saw in Istanbul?" Cruz asked.

"Maybe," Morris said. "I couldn't really enhance this image to confirm it."

"It's tenuous at best, but that gives me a little more reason to believe that the Lisbon and Istanbul incidents were connected," Alex said.

"Oh, definitely," Morris said. "Now keep watching."

The man went into the back of the truck, disappearing for twenty seconds. When he appeared again, he led a group of six men carrying the last two caskets onto the cargo plane. The rear ramp closed after them.

"If I had to guess, Williams and Reis were in those caskets," Morris said.

"Guesses aren't good enough," Kasim said. "Got better evidence?"

"Does a gut feeling count?"

"We're really scraping the bottom of the barrel here," Kasim said. "Hell, we're turning the whole barrel over and shaking out the crud between the cracks. If Commander Liang knew this was the evidence we're using to make decisions, she never would've given us a second chance."

"Good thing she doesn't know," Cruz said.

"It's definitely a long shot," Alex said, imagining the two young scientists trapped in those caskets. "But what else do we have? Morris, you know where this plane went?"

Morris nodded and showed them a map of Europe again. He zoomed in over a small piece of land bordering the Baltic Sea, crammed in between Poland and Lithuania.

"Russia's only ports to the Baltic," Alex said. "It was cut off during the collapse of the Soviet Union, and they're still hanging onto it."

"You know for sure that this plane went there?" Kasim asked.

"The pilot altered their flight plan a couple times, but I tracked down each change," Morris said. "They finally landed outside Kaliningrad. Tracking those caskets was a little harder in the city."

"Fewer cameras?" Cruz asked.

"More, actually," Morris said. "But harder to access. I found a truck delivering metal caskets to a warehouse belonging to a company called Mark-Logistik on the Pregolya River at the center of Kaliningrad's port."

An image of the warehouse showed on the table.

Alex looked at all the shipping containers stacked around it. "If they get Williams and Reis into one of those containers, we might lose them."

"Yup," Morris said. He drained the rest of his energy drink then crushed the can.

"Can you access Mark-Logistik's shipping and receiving logs?" Alex asked.

Morris tossed the can into the trash. "I tracked shipments going out as early as at 1400 hours local time in two days."

"That's not much time," Cruz said. "If that's when they're sending out Williams and Reis, we need to go now so we have time to survey the place and intercept them."

"We have no concrete evidence that this has anything to do with Breners's samples," Kasim said.

"But we do have two kidnapped scientists whose lives are at stake after a devastating terrorist attack," Alex said. "I'll be damned if we let that go unpunished."

"If someone wanted these two bad enough to stage a terrorist attack, they must have some big plans for them," Cruz said.

Weber had been silent for most of this conversation, but she spoke up now. "The fact that Breners's company was involved in environmental analyses and these two scientists did aerobiology research is reason enough for me to believe this is all connected somehow. Aerobiologists study the spread of microorganisms and other organic particle transport through the air. Sounds a lot like something Breners and EnviroProct would be interested in."

Alex was more than ready to go. This was it. This might be their only chance before the whole trail went cold. "If we don't leave for Kaliningrad now, we might never find our missing link."

Kasim steepled his fingers together, looking between each of them. Alex could nearly taste the tension in the air.

"I'm trusting you two to get in there quietly and figure out what is going on," Kasim said. "But know that Liang is watching us. If this looks like it's going to go bad or if we're barking up the wrong tree, you have to abandon the op whether you find those scientists or not. Understand?"

"Understood," Alex said. He understood, all right, but he didn't agree.

8

Kaliningrad, Russia

Renee didn't dare glance out the observation window of the laboratory. She could feel the eyes of that big tattooed Russian man on her back. The last thing she wanted was to attract his attention and invite him to drag her or Paulo out of the lab again, furious at them for not working hard enough or fast enough or just because he was bored.

She had seen what happened last time.

Paulo bent over the lab bench to examine the pieces of the EnviroProct canister that he had taken apart. A yellow and red bruise circled his swollen eye. Fresh scabs barely held back the blood that had flowed from the wounds across the side of his face.

"Are you sure you're okay?" she asked Paulo.

He gave her a forced smile. "I will be. Especially when you and I are out of here. Where should we go first?"

She whispered to him so they wouldn't be overhead. "We never made it to Florence. You promised me we would go."

"I want nothing more than to be in Florence right now." He traced his hand over hers. "Just keep imagining what it'll be like when we're in Tuscany. Think only about that."

"Those discussions better be about the device," that detestable voice said over the speakers.

Renee straightened and focused on the EnviroProct canister.

The guard outside was nothing but the muscle. An enforcer. While he yelled at them periodically, he didn't seem to actually know what they were doing or what kind of experiments they were running.

But the voice, the overseer, that came intermittently over the speakers embedded in the ceiling? He understood. This unknown man demanded results in a calm but threatening tone, promising retribution if they didn't fully cooperate.

At first, Paulo and Renee had tried to prolong their work as much as possible, doing the bare minimum. They had thought that if they slowly teased out details of these EnviroProct aerobiological detectors, they could buy enough time for someone to rescue them.

But as the hours had worn on, the initial hopes of someone magically showing up to whisk them away had evaporated. Maybe no one knew she and Paulo were missing. Worse, maybe they did know, but they didn't want to risk lives and resources to find a pair of no-name scientists.

The overseer had also told them they were on a deadline, though he would not say when that deadline was. Only that if they did not meet it, they would both share the same fate as his previous "employees."

She winced, thinking of the images that their mysterious overseer had forced them to watch on a monitor in the lab. The slideshow told them exactly what had happened to those poor souls. If she did survive, she would never be able to erase those horrific tableaus of torture and death from her mind.

"Renee?" Paulo asked in a soft voice.

She let out a long breath. "I'll be fine." She paused. "We'll both be fine."

He offered her a weak smile. "I know."

She could tell he didn't really believe her by that sorrowful look in his eyes.

All she and Paulo had right now were each other. If no one was coming for them, they would need to find their own way out. There had to be an escape.

Each time they had been transported between the bathroom or their bunkroom, she'd had time to quietly observe the facility. The place was filled with good hiding spots because of all the shipping containers. She'd seen a couple of exits, and the large warehouse doors regularly opened for delivery trucks. With only a handful of guards patrolling the place, they might actually have a shot at escape if they could hold out a little longer.

The overseer's voice boomed over the speakers. "You are not working fast enough. I've ordered someone to help."

The door to the lab cracked open, and Renee recoiled. Paolo stepped in front of her.

But instead of the big tattooed Russian storming in to beat them, a woman with gray, frizzled hair and a white coat stepped in. A reassuring smile spread over her face, the very last thing Renee expected to see.

She walked toward them, her hands open in a clear gesture she wasn't there to harm them. "They sent me in here to help you," she said with a French accent.

Renee didn't buy it. For all she knew, this older woman was a spy.

"I know you're scared." She spoke in a low voice. "I was— and still am. I will be honest. I am not sure if we will get out of this, but the only thing that I do know is if we don't work, we die."

She didn't even try to offer false reassurances.

"Who are you?" Paolo asked, still keeping himself between this woman and Renee.

"I am Dr. Coline Aubert."

Sudden recognition hit Renee. "Oh my God. I've read your paper on aerobiology over the Mediterranean. Why are you here?"

Aubert gave her a nod with a sorrow-filled expression. "I was on sabbatical. Or what I thought was a sabbatical, in Moscow. Halfway through my six-month stay at a government lab, some men blindfolded me and took me here."

"What about your family?" Renee asked. "Isn't anyone looking for you?"

"I don't know," Aubert said. "All I do know is there are maybe a dozen other scientists and researchers like us in this complex. And no one has come for any of us."

The door to the lab opened, and the tattooed Russian leaned in. "Less talking and more working. Or—"

"Yes, Markov," Aubert said. "I'm sorry. It's my fault. I get lonely and chatty. You know how it is."

"I will break you," Markov said. "Work."

Even Paulo shivered, and Renee could not help but look at his wounds again. They'd probably scar, permanently marring the bronzed skin around his temple.

After Markov disappeared again, Aubert ushered them back to the lab bench. But this time she didn't wear her comforting smile. Up close, Renee could see the crooked, swollen shape of her nose indicating a recent break.

"We must get to work. It is the only way to survive, understand?" she said.

Paulo and Renee both nodded, returning to the lab bench.

But if no one had come for Aubert, a world-class scientist from a top university in Paris, what chance did Renee and Paulo have?

These Russians must have some terrifyingly powerful connections.

"Tell me where you are with this," Aubert said. "Maybe we can all work together and buy ourselves some more time."

Renee leaned over the lab bench. She hoped the overseer would be pleased to see them discussing these technical issues. And she was thankful for Paulo's efforts because she could barely keep focused.

Paulo pulled up a technical drawing of the device on the computer. A few files, including this one, had been given to them by the overseer.

"The device is way more advanced than the ones we use— *used*—at our lab, but I can tell this one collects air samples." He motioned to the filters inside. "The series of filters separate microorganisms of different sizes. There's also a tiny water tank that gathers condensation from outside the detector. It hydrates the samples on the filters, washing them down onto this."

Paulo held up the circuit board and handed it to Renee.

"Take a look at it under the scope," he said.

She put the small device under a dissecting scope. On top of the circuit board she saw hundreds of small reservoirs.

"Those little wells you're seeing detect bacteria and other cells inside the water," Paulo said.

"How?" Renee asked, turning away from the scope.

Aubert moved in to look.

"The sensor detects changes in electrical conductivity of the water as the water droplets evaporate," Paulo said.

"You can tell all this just by looking at the device?" Aubert asked.

Paulo tapped on the computer. "No, not at all. But when Renee and I were in Lisbon, our supervisor, Dr. Estacio, had me redesign our own collectors. I came across this paper in the Proceedings of the National Academy of Science that used a similar technique with sensors a lot like this one. It takes advantage of bacteria osmoregulation as the water droplets evaporate."

Renee began to understand how the device might work. "The osmoregulation proteins in the bacteria respond as the water evaporates by taking in more water and ejecting salts and other charged molecules. That changes the conductivity of the droplet."

"Bacteria all have their own osmoregulation channels and respond uniquely to changing environments," Aubert said. "These detectors must be able to track those changes, identifying which bacteria might be present in the sample."

"You think osmoregulation is enough to identify individual species?" Renee asked, looking at the older scientist.

"Probably not," she said. "But the device can also isolate the samples. An analyst could always retrieve them like we do and take them in for genetic sequencing."

"Still, that process only starts when this thing detects a microorganism using osmoregulation," Paulo said. "We have to think up a way to get a microorganism *past* that kind of detection."

Renee picked up the sensor with its circuit board and tiny wells. An answer came to her mind, but she hesitated, unsure whether she should reveal it yet or not. She wondered when the overseer expected a definitive solution, and as she did, she tried not to let her eyes linger too long on Paulo's injuries. She vowed to put on a good show for their overseer so the evil man didn't turn them into another of those pictures she'd seen.

Revealing her idea might make her, Paulo, and now Aubert seem more useful, keeping them alive that much longer. But she had no illusion that it was just their own lives at stake.

If the overseer was simply trying to improve this detector, he certainly wouldn't be kidnapping researchers to perform this work in a hidden lab.

No, the overseer had something far more nefarious planned. He wanted to know how to bypass this device. From her and Paulo's work, she knew sensors like this existed to protect people. To warn them of potentially dangerous particles or pathogens.

And now Renee had a pretty good idea of how a dangerous pathogen could bypass this advanced device.

"No more delaying, Dr. Williams," the overseer called over the speakers. "I can see that you are thinking. Let's hear it."

"And if I don't?"

"Whether you choose not to share your ideas with me because you think you are being noble and brave or you are merely clueless, I encourage you to reconsider. You saw what happened when we had to fire our last researchers."

Renee gulped. If she died in here, then no one could warn the outside world what these twisted people were trying to do. No one could stop them. They would just bring in someone else to replace her, Paulo, and Aubert. Her only hope was to stay alive a little longer, buying them time to escape so she could tell someone what she had seen.

Aubert gave Renee a comforting squeeze of her shoulder. "We must do even what we hate to survive."

"Fine," Renee said. "Fine. The solution's simple. I'll tell you everything."

SVERDLOVSK, Russia

PAVLENKO ENTERED the office of General Vitya Dmitriyev with a newfound confidence. That had been a very productive conversation with Dr. Williams. The general looked up at him over a pair of reading glasses resting on a nose reddened by burst blood vessels. He took a sip from a glass of amber liquid then beckoned Pavlenko to take a seat.

"Do you care for a drink, Colonel?" Dmitriyev asked.

Pavlenko knew the drill. A drink would muddle his mind. Such fogginess would not help him in either his discussions of complex scientific topics or to avoid the dangerous political tightrope act that every conversation with Dmitriyev entailed.

But to refuse a drink from the general was tantamount to throwing a full glass of vodka at his face.

"Please," Pavlenko said, settling into the seat.

Dmitriyev stood and turned to the bar behind his desk. He poured a generous helping of Old Kenigsberg, aged four years, into a snifter.

The choice of beverage did not speak to the fortunes behind Dmitriyev's oligarchical connections nor his taste for the finer things in life. Far from it. The alcohol was a mere seven hundred rubles, roughly ten American dollars. And in Pavlenko's opinion, it was repulsive.

Serving that swill came with a clear message.

First, the general didn't want to waste good alcohol on Pavlenko. Second, he had chosen a liquor whose origin Pavlenko was very familiar with.

Dmitriyev held the snifter up, letting the amber liquid glow in the ceiling light. "They say this is Kaliningrad's finest." He passed it to Pavlenko as he sat. "But for all our sakes, I do hope that there are better things coming out of that impoverished shithole. Such a city, especially one that distills drinks like these, hardly seems Russian. I hope that I may soon be proved wrong."

He raised his glass, and Pavlenko met it in a toast.

"May great things flow once more from Kaliningrad," Dmitriyev said.

Their glasses clinked together. Pavlenko downed the astringent liquid in a single gulp, matching Dmitriyev.

"Putrid, no?" Dmitriyev asked.

"It is acceptable," Pavlenko said, biting back his disgust.

"Acceptable is not good enough. I have high standards. Don't you?"

Pavlenko tried to remain stoic, calm. The general was supposed to know only that Pavlenko was working on a secret project that would topple the economic might of their rivals. Even this man wasn't meant to be privy to the kind of work that Pavlenko performed. Loose lips were not good in the business of bioweapons, but Pavlenko had a suspicion that Levin had leaked details just to get in Dmitriyev's good graces.

"A position opened up in Moscow that may suit you," Dmitriyev continued.

"Oh?"

"A cabinet-level position."

"I was not aware that there was a vacancy in the president's administration."

A wicked grin cut across Dmitriyev's face, his finger tracing the rim of his glass. "The minister of the Health and Welfare Department is also not aware that his position is opening. But he will find out very soon."

Pavlenko tried not to let his eagerness show. A ministry position was a chance to finally get the ear of the president. A chance to repair his family's legacy after his father's failures. It was a position of power, in both government and industry. Life as a minister offered unfettered access to unimaginable wealth, all while having a hand in steering the direction of the country.

"Why me?" Pavlenko asked.

"I am told your work is important," Dmitriyev said. "And that you have a gift when it comes to human health. That you are very dedicated to your field of medicine."

Pavlenko wasn't sure what that meant. Maybe an insult. He chose the diplomatic response. "I am passionate about what I do."

"Passion is necessary, but confidence and aptitude are just as important," Dmitriyev said. "I am also told that Lieutenant Colonel Yuri Levin may be qualified for the position. He expressed his interest."

That all but confirmed Pavlenko's fear that the sniveling suck-up was politicking for Dmitriyev's favor. "Levin? He is hardly a man of science."

Dmitriyev poured them each another glass of cognac. "As I said, I am interested in results. If it takes a man of science or a man of… Levin's talents… then so be it."

Another gulp. The burning liquid slid down Pavlenko's throat, the heat of it mixing with the anger in his gut.

"In three weeks, we'll begin oil price talks with OPEC," Dmitriyev said. "That means I need results in two weeks."

"Two weeks?" Pavlenko shook his head. "That is far too soon."

"My advisors told me you're a man of great ingenuity. Were they wrong?"

"What you're asking is impossible. Four weeks is more tenable."

"In four weeks, we may no longer have room in this great country for colonels who bring no value to the motherland."

"You must be patient."

"How patient is your wife? She's waiting for you in Moscow. And what about your two daughters? Seven and nine, yes? Such pretty little girls. They must be anxious for their father's return. Maybe he's been gone so long that they worry he will never be back."

Pavlenko's teeth ground together, the muscles in his arms trembling. He could not fail them. He would not lose his children. Not like his father had lost him.

"We need to have the dominant hand before negotiations are complete. That is the only way to guarantee the revenue Russia needs." Dmitriyev leaned forward, that demonic smirk spreading over his face again. "And from what I hear about your project, we may have the opportunity to emerge as a new economic superpower in health and medicine. All of that depends on you. Two weeks."

"I cannot give you everything you want in two weeks. That is not the way science works."

Dmitriyev narrowed his eyes. "Do you know what happens when things do not meet my expectations?"

Pavlenko said nothing.

Dmitriyev stood, picked up the bottle of cognac then dropped it into a trash bin beside his desk, never taking his eyes off Pavlenko. The glass shattered, and the smell of pungent alcohol permeated the air.

"I do not mind throwing things away that I no longer have use for," Dmitriyev said, easing back into his seat.

Pavlenko recalled what the kidnapped researcher had told him. A way to avoid the prototype EnviroProct Aerokeep devices. It would take several weeks to roll out a new design for their weapon, if not longer. But the Aerokeep devices were not yet being deployed everywhere around the world. While they had been installed throughout Europe, the deaths of Shing, Zhi, Qi, and Breners had ensured EnviroProct never finished putting up more than a handful of test sensors in China. Those few detectors weren't enough to disrupt his plans.

"I can offer a compromise," Pavlenko said. "I will give you half the globe now. That's enough for you—and OPEC—to see what we can do. But I need more time for the second stage."

Dmitriyev raised a brow as if considering the offer. "I'll accept your terms. But if the outcome isn't satisfactory, you and your family will regret this deal."

"Do not worry," Pavlenko said. "I will not fail."

Dmitriyev dismissed Pavlenko with a trite wave. "You know my standards are high. Meet them."

Pavlenko had to hold himself back from slamming the general's door shut when he left. He wanted to shout out the man, to scold him for rushing this project. Military men like Dmitriyev did not dictate the speed at which science operated.

But Dmitriyev did dictate Pavlenko's—and his family's —fate.

He had no choice. He waited until he was down the corridor from Dmitriyev's office and in an empty stairwell. Sucking in a deep breath, he fished his phone out from his pocket and called his comrades stationed in Western China.

"Initiate deployment immediately."

With those three words, so began the resurrection of Russia's might, led by Colonel Sergei Pavlenko. He would accomplish what his father never could.

The world would be brought to its knees.

9

KALININGRAD, Russia

BY THE TIME Alex and Cruz finally reached Kaliningrad, Morris had scrounged up confirmation that Mark-Logistik had scheduled four trucks to leave the shipping facility by 0800. They needed to intercept Drs. Williams and Reis before these people shipped them elsewhere and determine what, if any, connections those researchers had with the archaea.

Alex and his partner had spent the day scouting the port in dark, oil-stained coveralls. They had lurked between the monotonous gray faces of the Soviet bloc-era buildings interspersed with red and yellow cranes that loomed over container ships.

The docks had been filled with trucks, forklifts, and workers. The stench of oil clashed with the salty air and distinctly fishy odor. Now, with darkness bathing the port, only the gurgle of a few distant truck engines churned over the call of gulls and the gentle lap of water against the monstrous ships at the docks.

While a few truck trailers were stationed in front of the massive doors near the front of the Mark-Logistik facility, no vehicles had left since Vector's arrival. Nearly a half dozen men seemed to be guarding the trucks. Getting in through those doors there wouldn't be easy.

In contrast, only a handful of men had come and gone through the building's back entrance. It was adjacent to a lot where a few semitrucks were parked next to empty shipping containers.

Alex and Cruz had also scoped out the security cameras outside Mark-Logistik. Several guarded the front of the building, two at either end of the loading dock, and one right above a back door that led into the alley. From their observations, they had discovered all the doors leading into the warehouse were locked with a card reader. Alex guessed the security inside would be even tighter, but that only mattered if they could get in without someone spotting them on the external cameras first.

He waited in front of one of the semitrucks. A few yards away, Cruz hid behind a dumpster.

Mark-Logistik guards had been out in pairs every hour on the dot to take regular smoke breaks and do a lap around the back of the building all day. Alex had hoped that the nightshift continued that trend.

He checked his watch. No one had taken a break in the past two hours.

The longer he waited, the harder his heart pounded. He thought of the images of Renee Williams and Paulo Reis that Morris had shown them. The post-doc researchers looked painfully young to his eyes. Just a couple of kids, really. Maybe they were still trapped in one of those caskets, stuck inside this warehouse. They would be terrified.

Worse, if he and Cruz didn't find them, they would lose

any hope of figuring out what had gone wrong in Istanbul and Lisbon.

The back door clicked open.

"Here we go," Cruz whispered over the comms. "I see two guys walking out now."

Alex peeked out from in front of the truck cab. The flick of a lighter sparked in the darkness, followed by the orange glow of cigarettes. Usually this was the time when the men would wander away from the door then take a walk around the perimeter.

That would be a perfect opportunity for Vector to jump them, steal their IDs and key cards, and then waltz into the facility.

Two people come out of the warehouse. Two people go in.

Simple and efficient.

But these guys weren't moving from the door. They leaned against the brick wall and began an animated conversation, punctuated with what Alex could only guess were angry curses.

"What's going on?" Cruz whispered through Alex's earpiece.

"Don't know."

"Maybe I can convince them to move."

"How?"

Cruz merely shot him a smile. "Trust me."

Alex wasn't yet sure he could.

SKYLAR'S HANDLE on the Russian language was limited to some rudimentary vocabulary and basic phrases she'd picked up during deployments in Kyrgyzstan. Enough that she could understand some simple conversations but not enough that she could join in. That didn't quite give her the capability to blend in like a local. To complicate things, there weren't many tourists in Kaliningrad. Those who frequented the city's bars and plazas were in the old town to the north. Foreigners wandering the docks would be as strange as a shark taking a hike in the desert.

On the other hand, a drunk dockworker would not be so suspicious. She could fudge just enough Russian to play that part.

She started walking down the road past the trucks and back door. The voices of the two guards carried into the still night as they argued boisterously, making wild hand gestures. The smoldering ends of their cigarettes looked like fireflies in the darkness.

With a meandering gait, Skylar slowed as she strolled down the middle of the street in plain view. She paused, pretending as though she was having trouble lighting a cigarette. The two guards didn't even look up, too caught up in their own conversation.

What's it take for a couple of bozos to give a lady a little attention?

Subtlety was dead for tonight.

She whistled, leaning over so she stood like a dying tree half blown over by a windstorm.

The guards looked up. The one on the left slid his hand down to his waist. The bulge under his jacket all but confirmed he was armed. She had no doubt the second man would be too.

One of the guards spoke, his voice coming out gruff and aggressive.

Skylar couldn't quite understand every word, but she got the gist.

What do you want?

"You have…?" she asked in Russian, imitating the use of a lighter. She hoped her inebriated act would be enough to smother her terrible vocabulary and accent.

The guard who had started reaching for his pistol relaxed

and laughed. He started away from the doorway, shaking his head.

Skylar did her best to give him an endearing smile, keeping her eyelids half closed, mind whirring.

It wouldn't do any good if she knocked this guy out, and the other ran back in to tell his buddies. She needed both guards.

Come on.

The first guard continued toward her, a grin on his face. He had apparently bought the whole routine, hook, line, and sinker.

Might as well push it further.

Skylar beckoned the second guard, puckering her lips and giving her best impression of a barfly looking for a good time with a couple of big, strong men. She hated playacting like this. But every second they were stuck outside of the Mark-Logistik warehouse was another second closer to losing the already cooling trail they were following.

She sucked up her pride and blew the other guard a wet, disgusting kiss.

The second guard laughed, said something in a low voice to his friend, then joined the first.

Just a few more feet.

One of the men held his light out to her.

Skylar stumbled backward, pretending she couldn't maintain her balance. She landed on her backside, rolling enough to sell a tumble, while preparing herself for what came next.

The second guard laughed, and the first took a step toward her, reaching down to help her.

Both these men had to have at least an extra fifty, sixty pounds on her. No way was she taking them down if this became a standing boxing match.

She took the hand of the first guy. Then rocked herself backward, using the motion to swing him off balance.

As he fell forward, she slammed her boots hard into his abdomen.

The guard let out a rattling gasp, all the air expelled from his lungs. He flew over her. His head slammed heavily into the asphalt with a sickening thud, his body immediately going limp.

Not likely dead but thoroughly knocked out.

The second guard stood frozen, gawking. His mind finally seemed to process what had happened. He lunged forward, reaching for the weapon under his coat at the same time.

Adrenaline was already pumping through Skylar's vessels. Her vision tunneled on the angry Russian, his nose scrunched into a snarl. She kicked a foot out and swept one of his legs out from under him.

The man sprawled forward, cutting a nasty gash in his chin. Only halfway out of its holster, his gun clattered on the asphalt. He scrambled for the dropped weapon.

Skylar brought her heel down on one of his hands. Bone crunched, cartilage cracked, and the man opened his mouth to let out an agonized yowl.

That's not going to work.

Skylar rolled on top of him, locking an arm around his neck, silencing him. Using a combination of momentum and strength, she twisted so her spine was back on the ground.

Didn't matter that he weighed more than her or that his biceps were damn near as big as her chest. On the ground like this, she had complete control. She used her left hand to lever her right arm tighter around his neck and squeezed her legs around his waist, locking him in place. His eyes bulged. The vessels on his forehead grew larger. He flailed, trying to peel off her arms, but she only tightened her grip.

Sweat poured over her forehead. Her muscles strained. Jaw gritted.

Go to sleep, you ugly bastard.

Finally, he stopped gasping. His eyes rolled up. Limbs went slack.

Panting, Skylar pushed herself up. Wolfe was still crouched behind the truck cab twenty yards away, his gun in his hands in case she needed backup. She gave him an ironic bow that he did not appear to find amusing.

She beckoned to him with a hand signal and took the wrists of the man she had just knocked out, starting to drag him away from the bay, back to the dumpster where she had first been hiding.

But before she had taken him more than a couple of feet, the door to the building opened with a clang again. A third guard strode out.

He spotted the first man, still spread-eagle on the asphalt past the trucks, and started straight toward him, his fingers wrapping around the gun holstered at his hip.

10

ALEX WATCHED the third guard rush out of the warehouse. After the man reached the first body and checked his comrade's pulse, he paused, aiming toward where Cruz had gone. He started to backpedal toward the building as if his nerves and caution had got the better of him. With one hand holding the pistol, he reached toward his waist with the other. His fingers wrapped around a radio.

There was nothing else Alex could do. He drew his suppressed pistol and fired.

The low whoomph of the shot punched through the still air, the sound echoing off the nearby warehouses. The guard's radio clunked to the concrete, and the man stumbled backward, his hands grasping at his chest. His eyes locked on Alex as his mouth opened, lips moving silently like a landlocked fish.

Twice more Alex fired. Rounds punched straight through the man's chest, and the guard collapsed backward against one of the big tires of the semitruck behind him.

Cruz emerged from where she had retreated, stowing her own sidearm when she saw the third man was done. Together, they quietly dragged all three guards toward the dumpster.

They patted the trio down for key cards and ID tags. Blood covered the clothes of the guard Alex had shot, so he stole the leather jacket and slacks off one Cruz had knocked out, exchanging them for his grungy coveralls. All the guards they'd observed throughout the day had seemed to gravitate to this same wardrobe. Dark jacket. Jeans or black trousers.

Definitely not the blue coveralls Vector had been wearing all day. He gestured for his partner to get changed too.

"That definitely was not how I would've handled the situation," Alex said in a low voice, straightening his jacket.

"Worked, didn't it?"

"Riskier than it should've been." He still wasn't sure whether he admired her move or was pissed at its brazenness. "Definitely not something I learned in Agency training."

"Sometimes you can't play things by the book." Cruz tried on the other jacket that wasn't covered in blood. It was far too big. "At least I didn't go in guns blazing."

"I didn't want to, but the guy didn't give me another choice," Alex said. "Either that or he was going to warn the whole damn place."

Cruz tied her hair up and took the knit cap off one of the guards, pulling it tight over her head. With the guard's clothes, she looked a little like a scarecrow wearing a boat sail. But at a passing glance, she wouldn't look as conspicuous as she would wearing those dingy coveralls. If she kept her face down, someone watching the back door's camera might not give her a second glance.

Alex gathered the guards' sidearms. He emptied the rounds in the chamber of each pistol then ejected the magazines, tossing the bullets and the weapons into the dumpster.

It wasn't a perfect way to conceal the weapons if someone was determined to recover them, but it would buy Vector more time.

"This time, let's be a little quieter," he whispered. "Ready?"

His partner nodded.

They strode back between the trucks outside the facility and walked straight up to the doors. A nervous sweat trickled down Alex's back. This was it. Time to see what these people were hiding in this secret facility tucked away in this dark cesspool of a port. He fished one of the key cards out of his pocket and waved it up to the RFID reader next to the steel door.

The door unlocked with a click, and Alex pulled it open, taking a deep breath. He slipped inside, mindful of the slight weight of his holster under his jacket, fingers twitching, ready to reach for it should someone jump them on the other side.

But instead they were greeted by an eerie quiet. A few dim lights hung from chains attached to the ceiling of the nearly four-story tall warehouse. Stacks of shipping containers were lined up in even rows. A crane on rails lay dormant above a flatbed truck parked just inside a closed rolling door.

Somewhere water dripped onto concrete, the splash echoing in the cavernous room.

Alex didn't like the way the sound carried. It meant they needed to work extremely quietly.

He and Cruz took a few more tentative steps into the facility. They clung to the shadows to avoid any CCTV cameras.

This place was enormous, and they did not have the luxury of time. Someone was bound to discover those three guards knocked out and tied up outside eventually. As much as he hated splitting up, they had to cover as much ground as possible quickly.

He motioned for Cruz to take the stairs up to the catwalk as he covered the ground floor.

Alex snuck between the shipping containers, mindful of the cameras he spotted at the corners of the warehouse. Most of the containers were locked closed, but he saw a pair down the row with their cargo doors hanging open. He would start there before trying to crack the others open.

Before he made it halfway down the line, a door on the second floor opened. Alex shrank back against a shipping container, peering around the corner.

He held his breath, slowly reaching for his pistol.

Three men walked down the catwalk. One wore a black T-shirt. His muscled arms were covered in tattoos. One of those tattoos was an unmistakable Cyrillic A, just like the men in Istanbul. He stood a head taller than the other two and walked with a self-assured swagger, a pistol holstered at his hip. The second man wore a leather jacket and a scowl like a bulldog.

Those two prodded another man in a white lab coat.

Lab coats definitely didn't belong in a normal shipping warehouse on a grungy port like this.

Alex squinted, trying to get a better view of the prisoner. Even from his vantage, the guy appeared to be shaking. He wondered for a brief second if this was the infamous Dr. Paulo Reis. If maybe they had already spotted their first target.

But the prisoner stepped beneath an overhead light, revealing that he had blond hair and pale skin. He was a marked contrast to the picture Alex had seen of Reis, with his dark hair and olive complexion.

Still, the sight of those two men with guns and the frightened scientist only cemented the notion that the events in Istanbul and Lisbon were connected. This was one piece of a much larger conspiracy that they were only beginning to delve into.

Alex couldn't hear their conversation clearly, but the Russians seemed to be arguing. And they were headed right toward where Skylar was hiding.

She had squeezed herself into a doorway about thirty yards away from the men. There was no other cover on the second floor. He guessed she would have already slipped through into the room beyond, except the doors opened outward. As soon as she opened it wide enough to escape, the guys marching toward her would spot her.

She was caught between two bad choices.

Alex raised his pistol, ready to take down the biggest of the three men. He prayed they just went into one of the other three doorways between their position and Skylar's.

Come on. Make this easy.

Twenty yards before they reached her.

He didn't relish shooting these men. Surrounded by metal walls and shipping containers, he might as well take the suppressor off for all the good it would do. The sound from a single shot would bang around in here like a firework, calling every Mark-Logistik guard into the warehouse. That would significantly diminish their chance of success.

Not to mention a prolonged gunfight wouldn't go unnoticed by Mark-Logistik's neighbors.

Getting the Russian authorities involved was not going to end well for Vector.

With one hand maintaining his pistol's aim, Alex took out his phone with his other. He snapped a few photos of the men.

"Command, Vector One," he whispered. "Got some suspects here, plus a prisoner."

"Received, Vector One," Kasim called back. "Will relay results soon."

The yelling grew louder, and now Alex could hear them more clearly.

"You have not been helpful, and now you think you can sabotage the work we gave you." The man with the tattoos pulled out his pistol, jabbing it toward the man in the lab coat. He spoke English with a heavy accent.

"Please, I promise I am doing what I can." The guy in the lab coat backed against the railing, raising his hands in front of his chest in a defensive gesture.

"It's too late," the man with the gun said. "You have failed too many times. We warned you. We warned all of you what that means."

"No, no, no," the scientist said, shaking his head.

A flash of light then an explosive gunshot that echoed wildly in the space. Alex blinked, his eardrums ringing with the gunfire. Cruz used the momentary distraction to slip into the door she'd been hiding in front of.

The scientist toppled over the railing of the catwalk. His body smacked against the concrete floor below with a wet thud.

Who the hell are these people?

SKYLAR PRESSED her back against the inside of the door. She stifled the voice in her head telling her to go back out into the warehouse. The voice telling her to take those Russian bastards down before they could find Alex and execute him like they'd done to the scientist.

She fought to control her breathing, willing the electricity firing through her nerves to subside. Alex would be fine. Had to be fine. He said he wanted to do this quietly, and she had to trust that he would.

She just needed to focus. Figure out what was going on here. Find Reis and Williams.

Her eyes took a moment to adjust to the glow of a streetlight through a window at the back of the room. Four cubicles separated the space, along with two closed offices on either side. The cubicle closest to her was filled with boxes of dog-eared papers.

No glowing computer monitors. No lights. No signs of life.

She ducked against the wall of the cubicle.

Then in as low voice as she could manage, she asked, "Wolfe, you okay?"

There was a single tap on the mic.

She let out a low sigh, her nerves starting to settle.

A single tap meant 'yes,' but he couldn't talk. No mystery there. Those men must still be out there. He'd be sheltering in place. In the meantime, she would be stuck in this room.

Might as well see what's here.

She prowled around the cubicles. The two offices on either side of the central space had big glass windows in the scarred wooden doors. A peek through one revealed an office empty except for a few flattened cardboard boxes against the wall.

The second office looked more lived-in. A computer sat on the desk, and there was a coffee mug beside it. A wrinkled coat hung over the back of a well-worn leather chair.

Maybe that computer had documents useful for their investigation.

She entered the office, moving first to clear a closet beside the desk. The door creaked open slightly to reveal nothing more than a few dented filing cabinets.

After stowing her pistol, she turned on the computer. It hummed noisily as it booted, fans whirring. A box blinked across the screen with what looked to be a request for a username and password, but all the words were in Russian.

Skylar took out a small device and plugged it into a USB port.

"Command, Vector Two," she whispered over the comms. "Requesting computer access."

"Copy," Morris called back. "Ooh, this should be fun. It might take a few minutes for my programs to crack this, but I'll get you in."

She waited with bated breath, listening for the telltale click of the doorknob outside. The USB-transmitter meant she wouldn't have to use any Mark-Logistik networks to transfer data from this computer, so Morris could avoid tripping any digital alarms. So long as the tech analyst did his job right, the Russians would never know Vector had stolen anything from the PC.

"While you're waiting, we IDed one of the guys in Wolfe's picture," Morris continued. "Couldn't find anything on the scientist or the guy in the leather jacket, but the dude with the tattoos is Pyotr Markov."

"Should I know who that is?" Skylar glanced at her phone to see the images Wolfe had sent Command.

"Probably not. He was a former corporal in the Russian Ground Forces before getting discharged. No indication why. As a civvy, he got picked up for suspected murder, but charges were dropped. Apparently, he now works with a military contractor group called Archon."

"Are they behind this?"

"No idea," Morris said. "Our friends in Langley think Archon is a relatively new, small-time group of guns for hire. They supposedly don't have official ties to the Russian government, but they seem to have a habit of providing muscle for private companies. For instance, during last year's protests in Moscow, Archon members were suspected of masquerading as nationalist sympathizers and roughing up the dissidents."

"Nasty," Skylar said.

"Yeah, not great guys. But I don't see anything connecting them to bioweapons. Maybe Markov's just providing security. Either way, stay out of their way. They don't seem super friendly."

"I figured that out," she said.

Skylar retreated to the closet with the filing cabinets. A simple lockpicking tool was more than enough to bypass the pin and tumbler locks. As soon as she was in, she started sifting through the files. One by one, she lifted papers from their folders and laid them out on the cabinet. Morris had installed an app on her phone that provided real-time translations of printed text. She used the app to scan each paper.

The translations from Russian weren't perfect. Many provided a jumble of words that didn't make a hell of a lot of sense. But she pieced enough of that garbled language together to see she had found a trove of shipping records and accounting files. The shipping records provided dates of goods arriving and leaving, tracking each shipment by the crate and shipping container. The destinations included ports across the world, from Singapore and Shanghai to New York and Rotterdam. None of these files listed the contents of those containers.

Morris's voice sizzled over her earpiece. "Bam! We're in."

Skylar left the files on the cabinet and returned to the computer. The monitor flickered into a desktop with dozens of icons.

"Can't read a damn thing," Skylar said.

"Hold up," Morris said. A moment later, the words shifted to English.

"This another one of your programs?" Skylar asked.

A low laugh came over the comms. "Nah, I just changed the language settings. Don't worry, I'll revert 'em when we're done."

"No trace, remember," she said.

"Don't need to tell me."

"I will anyway. Do I need to do anything on this end?"

"Not a thing," Morris replied. "I'll start copying whatever looks interesting. Once I'm done, all you need to do is remove the transmitter."

"Copy."

She returned to the files, relaying more images back to Detrick. The minutes ticked by in tedious monotony. Even the constant edge of having to listen for an intruder no longer seemed so exciting.

Pull out a new folder. Snap an image. Transmit. Repeat ad nauseam.

"Found anything interesting?" she asked Morris.

"Shipping logs. Couple of bank accounts, definitely worth mapping out the incoming and outgoing wire transfers later." There was a brief pause. "Let's see… The inventory seems to mostly consist of construction equipment and agriculture supplies. You think that's code for bioweapons?"

"Not my department," she said.

"We can send that to crypto later for analysis, but they may be shipping exactly what they say they are. That could be more than enough cover to conceal any biological agents… or even people."

"What do you—"

The click of the doorknob echoed through the office.

Skylar jammed her finger against a button on the CPU, forcing the PC to power down.

"Hey, wait, I just need one second to—"

"No time," she said over Morris's protests.

The door opened all the way, letting in the light from the warehouse. Footsteps sounded outside the office.

She yanked the USB transmitter out. The cubicles would provide cover, but to get there, she would have to run straight in front of whoever had just entered the office space. That left only the closet with the filing cabinets. She retreated inside the closet and gently closed the door.

A few seconds later, a loud groan escaped whoever had just dropped into the chair at the desk. The man began muttering under his breath as the computer hummed to life again.

Ideally, this guy wouldn't be on the computer for long.

After a moment, the man outside pounded his fist on the desk, and she nearly jumped out of her skin.

"*Angliyskiy?*" he asked aloud. Then again, louder and angry, "*Angliyskiy?*"

Her heart dropped through her chest. That was a Russian word she knew well.

English.

Morris hadn't had time to change the language settings back.

ALEX WAS CROUCHED in the shadow of a shipping container. The man Morris had identified as Pyotr Markov hadn't left the scene of the execution. Markov had sent his comrade into another corridor. The guard had returned with five men and women dressed in ratty coveralls, each of them carrying cleaning supplies. Even from his vantage, Alex could see bruises on their faces. The way they shuffled, their heads bowed low, gave the impression they were here against their will.

Prisoners? Slaves? The thought made him sick.

"Clean this mess," Markov had said in accented English as he pointed at the catwalk where the scientist had been shot.

"You, take his body away," Markov said, pointing at two prisoners. "I do not want to see it anymore."

The pair of men in coveralls lugged the body up the stairs and through another doorway.

"You, clean here," Markov said to two of the remaining prisoners, pointing at the catwalk. Then he gestured at the last woman standing near him. "You go clean up down there."

The woman took a bottle of bleach and a cloth down the

stairs to the warehouse floor. Alex retreated just beyond the corner of a shipping container. The woman walked toward the row of containers, coming within maybe twenty yards from him. But she never looked up, instead wiping at her eyes with the back of her hand.

The spot where the scientist had fallen was near the end of the row. With a long sigh, the woman knelt and began cleaning the puddled blood.

"Already done up here?" Markov asked, examining the catwalk where the other men had been cleaning. He leaned over the railing toward the woman, a sadistic smile plastered across his face. "Don't you go anywhere. I expect all that mess to be gone before I get back."

He escorted the other prisoners back through the door. Alex was left alone in the warehouse with the woman. Her sobs grew louder as she scrubbed the floor.

This whole ordeal had wasted too much time. He wanted to investigate the containers and then move on. They needed to be out of here before daybreak.

He considered approaching that woman. He wanted to help her. To free her and her companions, if he could. But if she screamed—or if he had misread the situation—then this op would be over.

She didn't seem like a threat, and she seemed so wrapped up in her terrible situation she wouldn't notice him sneaking around.

But it was too risky. He vowed to help her and the other prisoners once he and Cruz were done with their intel grab. That was the best he could do for now.

While the woman scrubbed the bloodstains, Alex snuck into the first of the open shipping containers at the far end of the warehouse.

A few seconds passed as his eyes adjusted to the darkness inside.

What in the hell?

Stacks of what looked to be long, slightly curved pipes peppered with tiny nozzles filled the container. At the far end of the container sat a heap of tires.

He looked for a label on the equipment, something to explain its purpose. The pipes evoked a memory of a familiar object, but he couldn't quite figure out where he'd seen them before.

Deeper into the container, he brushed a gloved hand over the bumpy metal pipes until he spotted an engraved serial number. With his phone, he took a picture. Beneath the number was a name: Agrotechnika.

"Command, more images headed your way," Alex whispered into his mic.

"Got 'em," Morris called back. "I got cut off with Cruz, by the way. You might want to check on her."

"She can handle herself," Alex said as he probed the recesses of the shipping container, searching under the pipes and behind the tires.

Nothing else stood out.

"Vector One, I got a hit," Morris said. "You're looking at linear irrigation equipment. Serial number matches up with the company's products. Agrotechnika is a legitimate manufacturer of agricultural machinery."

Alex wasn't sure what to make of that, but this definitely wasn't the smoking gun they were looking for. Maybe the contents of the other shipping containers would provide better insight. He slunk to the open doors of the next container. Before he entered, he stole a glance toward the empty catwalk. There was no sign of Markov, but he could still hear the woman sobbing.

Maybe he was going about this all wrong. If he offered to help her, she might provide the intel he was looking for—or at least point him in the right direction.

No, trying to talk to her would be a mistake. He wanted to help, and now he was looking for any excuse to do that.

Keep your head in the game, Wolfe.

He ducked through the open door of the next container. More linear irrigation equipment was lined against the walls.

There was only one other unlocked shipping container. Almost halfway there, he heard one of the doors on the catwalk open again. He froze.

Light spilled out of a corridor as Markov strode out. He leaned over the railing of the catwalk.

"You are not finished yet?" he said to the woman.

"There's so much."

The woman's voice had a slight accent. Italian, maybe?

"You hurry, or there will be a bigger mess," Markov said.

"Yes, I am trying. Please. Do not hurt me more."

More?

Alex fought back the heat rising through his chest. As much as he wanted to throw Markov over the railing and save that woman, there were more lives outside of this warehouse relying on Vector's success.

Markov gave the woman a dismissive wave then disappeared into another doorway.

The best thing Alex could do to help this woman—and all the others who might be imprisoned here—was to uncover whatever organization was responsible for their imprisonment.

He squeezed into the next half-open shipping container.

His mouth went dry.

Simple metal caskets were stacked against the container walls, secured into place with nylon straps. These were just like the ones Williams and Reis had been transported in.

He quietly unstrapped one of the caskets then sucked in a deep breath. Maybe these were all empty. Maybe they had just been used as cover to transport the kidnapped scientists here.

Or maybe they were being recycled and reused for something else. His pulse accelerated as he lifted one of the lids, cracking it just enough to see what was inside. He expected to see vials of unknown substances or maybe hard cash. Possibly smuggled lab equipment for pharmaceutical manufacturing.

Instead, he saw a pair of wide-open eyes staring straight at him.

SKYLAR NEEDED out of this damn closet.

The man outside had called someone else in to fix his computer. With two of them, Skylar was even more conscious of every breath she took. She couldn't tell if the Russians suspected someone had been tampering with their computer. The only words she easily recognized were the curses.

In her experience, bioweapons businesses attracted two types of people. First, the smart, dogmatic ones behind the scientific developments and strategic deployments. Second, the hired muscle that provided security, drawn into the scheme purely because they'd been drooling over the substantial sum of money required to keep these highly illegal operations hush-hush.

Usually the mercenaries working in unscrupulous places like Mark-Logistik had enough brains to figure out how to pull a trigger, but they weren't winning a chess tournament anytime soon. Still, the shadowy leaders behind the operation generally beat a strong sense of paranoia into the dullest merc. Any good bioweapons program had to fly under the radar of not only foreign actors snooping on their turf but even their own government regulators.

The first guy probably would not have called in backup if he thought the English settings on his computer were nothing but a glitch.

Nah, these guys knew something was up.

And the only reason they hadn't sounded the alarm already was because they probably thought they'd screwed the pooch. Mr. Russian Office Worker probably didn't want their boss to know he accidentally downloaded a virus when he was surfing for X-rated videos.

He and his buddy would want to fix the issue themselves. Because usually when people messed up at a place like this, they got fired.

Like, gun-to-the-head fired.

Skylar didn't give a shit if that was what happened to these guys after the execution she'd seen in the warehouse. But if they found her in the closet, she had a feeling their reluctance to sound the alarm would go right out the window. Along with her dead body.

Maybe she could—

The door to the closet suddenly opened. A man with a gut like an inner tube stood in front of her, cigarette poking out of the corner of his mouth and a pistol at his hip. The guy seemed to be preoccupied, operating on autopilot. He started to reach toward the filing cabinet, at first not even noticing Skylar standing beside it.

Before his fingers hit the cabinet, he froze, mouth dropping open. The cigarette hung precariously over his cracked lips.

Skylar's fist flew up before she could come up with anything resembling a plan. Fist met chin in a devastating blow. The man's teeth snapped together with a resounding crunch, cigarette chomped in half, embers flying as it flipped away.

She thrust the heel of her hand against the man's Adam's apple. Felt the crack of cartilage giving away, heard its whiplike snap.

Skylar landed another hit in the middle of his chest that sent him falling backward. The back of his head thudded against the desk. Skin split into a red gash, and the man went down, fingers grasping at a throat that could no longer breathe.

The second man stood from his desk and reached for a radio sitting beside the computer. Skylar kicked it away. The man picked up the coffee mug and pitched it at Skylar.

She twisted just enough that the mug missed her face, breaking against the wall instead. Shards and coffee flew, spraying back at her.

Her eyes narrowed on the panicked Russian. She was a predator, unstoppable, living off momentum. Her only advantage was the electric paralysis of shock muddling the guy's brain.

The man had to be nearly twice her body weight, muscles rippling under his T-shirt. No tattoos on this guy, though. Couple of scars on his face. Details she took in as adrenaline etched the images across her brain.

With one of the man's hands sliding toward his hip, she lunged atop the desk. The man took out his pistol, and the barrel rose toward her. She swung another shattering kick, aiming for his wrist. The guy's fingers splayed, and the pistol flew into the wall behind him before clanging against the floor.

His eyes never left hers.

She might be a predator, but he was too.

The man's nose wrinkled into a snarl, and he leapt straight at her. When his weight smashed against her, she braced herself. She may as well have been trying to stop a derailed train. Her body crashed into the wall. Plaster cracked, and dust spilled over her. Sharp pain cut up her spine into the base of her skull.

He grabbed her face, thick fingers wrapping around her head, then slammed her back against the wall. More plaster gave way. Stars flickered across her vision.

Skylar could taste blood, and dizziness threatened to overwhelm the dregs of adrenaline keeping her on her feet. Her stomach lurched. The man grappled with her, throwing her to the floor. Her shoulder blades pounded the tile, and her teeth chattered together.

She squirmed on her back and tried to twist her legs around his and then twist again to throw him off. But the man was too heavy, resisting her efforts.

"Who are you?" he said, fingers squeezing tighter over her skull.

She imagined the bone giving out, fragments crushing her brain. But she gritted her teeth, saying nothing.

"You don't tell me, I will take you to the boss. He is not as kind as me."

While holding Skylar's head with one meaty hand, the man reached toward where his radio had dropped. He started to squeeze the call button.

Soon as he made that call, the whole jig was up. This place would go into lockdown. And her partner was somewhere out there, exploring the place alone.

This mission would be screwed.

Not going to happen.

She had one free hand. Fighting the pain of his grip, the weight of his body on her chest, Skylar reached out. She found the guy's manhood and squeezed as hard as she could.

The man let out a roar, rearing back. She wasn't worried about fighting dirty. No such thing when her life depended on it. She followed up with a fist rocketing into his kidney. Tight muscles met her blow, resisting.

With a shove, the man launched her away from him. She hurtled backward against the cratered wall. Fresh waves of fiery pain coursed through her body, but now was not the time to let a little thing like that stop her.

Her adversary's face was still red with pain. He was nearly doubled over, keeping himself upright with one hand braced on the desk. Their eyes locked for a moment, and then he lurched toward his pistol. Wheezing, he fell to the ground and scrambled for the weapon.

Skylar blinked through her pain, pulled up the bottom of her pant leg, and drew the blade in the hideaway sheath on her prosthetic calf. The man reached the gun at the same time and raised it toward her.

But she hit him first, landing an elbow just under his ribs. The knife blade punched through the man's wrist. He lost the gun again, yelling and falling backward against the desk. The computer tumbled off and broke against the floor. He threw one arm around her body and twisted so she was smashed between him and the desk.

A sudden crack split the air. The desk collapsed, wood fracturing into splinters.

Flames of pain swept through Skylar's chest. Her ribs screamed from the weight of the man pushing down on her. He slammed his good hand into her side. Each impact felt like she was fighting a wrecking ball. But through it all, she focused on her fingers tight around the knife.

That was all she needed, a finely sharpened blade engineered to do one thing.

Gulping for air, she used what little strength she had left to send the knife straight under the man's chin, up through his mouth. There was a slight resistance, a sickening protest of bone that soon gave way.

Warmth spilled over Skylar's hand.

The Russian stopped moving, but his deadweight continued to press against her. She could barely breathe or get any leverage. Last thing she wanted was for this man to kill her after he was dead.

Cruel irony.

With a massive effort that depleted her last reserves, Skylar shoved his body off hers. His corpse crushed the remnants of the splintered desk.

Skylar gasped for breath. Each sharp intake of air that pushed her lungs against her ribs felt like a thousand needles stabbing into her chest.

Damn it. Probably bruised something. Maybe a fracture.

She lay there for a few seconds, recovering her breath. Focusing on gentle, shallow gasps.

A voice called over her earpiece, and it took her a moment to recognize the speaker through the haze of pain.

Kasim.

"Vector Two, heard a commotion over your mic. Status?"

She reached one trembling hand up. Her finger gave the mic a single flick.

"Copy," Kasim called back. "Morris needs more data from that computer. Will you have access to it again?"

She pushed herself to a sitting position. Knives churned in her side.

The computer lay busted beside the dead man. Its case had been cracked open. She was no computer geek, but the broken board hanging out of the case like the guts of a wounded animal didn't look functional to her.

It was brokedick.

She tapped two clicks on the mic.

No.

"How about more pics of those folders?" Morris tried.

One click on the mic.

I can handle that. In fact, that might be all she could handle until the pain subsided and she caught her breath again.

She pushed herself to her feet, nearly falling with the effort. Her hand smacked against the wall to brace herself. She felt like she'd been trying to ride a 'roid-addled bull.

But that was just the first ride. The rodeo was far from over.

12

ALEX STARED at another face in yet another casket.

Dead. Just like the others.

The bodies appeared to have been starved. Nearly skeletal, their flesh drawn tight over their bones. They wore coveralls or scrubs, all dingy clothes like the prisoners he'd seen.

Who were these people? Where had they come from?

Why were they all dead?

He didn't have time or ability to perform an autopsy on them, but he searched the bodies as best as he could, studying their rigid, cold flesh.

Besides their malnutrition, there were other horrifying commonalities. Many were covered in lacerations. Some had unhealed burns. A few seemed to have broken bones. Each had bruises on the back of their hands and small injection sites indicative of an IV port.

Had these people been slaves, worked to the point of death and then killed via lethal injection? Or had they been part of some twisted scientific experiment? He took more pictures, each filling him with a deep-seated pity for the poor soul that had ended up like this, then sent those images to Command.

He had only examined six of the caskets. But he had a feeling every casket in this shipping container contained similar contents. There was no need to check them all when he suspected even darker secrets lurked in the depths of this facility.

After pushing the casket lid into place, he turned back toward the opening to the shipping container.

The sight there caused him to stop in his tracks. He inhaled sharply, hand instinctively flying toward his sidearm.

This time, the person staring at him wasn't dead. It was the Italian woman he'd seen scrubbing the floor.

She took a step backward, her hands up in a defensive gesture, eyes wide. Locked not on Alex but on the caskets.

Her mouth opened in what Alex feared might be a scream. He ran at her then clamped his hand over her lips. The warmth of her breath soaked his hand as she yelled into his palm.

"Quiet," he whispered, looking up at the catwalk, waiting for one of those doors to open again.

He pulled her into the shipping container. She pounded at his arm, nails scraping at his hand.

"I'm here to help," he said. "Please, they can't know I'm here."

She stopped flailing, but she held his hand in a viselike grip.

"I just need you to trust me. Otherwise, neither one of us is getting out of here alive."

Her hands fell to her sides, but he could still feel her muscles tense like she was preparing to sprint away.

"Look, I don't know what's going on, but I came here to figure it out. Do you understand?"

She nodded against his hand. He didn't dare let go yet. She might fear punishment from her captors if she cooperated with him. After what he had seen so far, he doubted very much that she believed a strange man lurking around a shipping container could save her.

"I've got backup," he said. "But maybe you can help me. You think you can?"

She remained still, sweat dripping over her forehead.

"I need your help. Please. That way I can help you."

Another nod, not nearly as emphatic as before.

"Thank you. Do you know what this place is for?"

She hesitated then shrugged.

"You're a prisoner?"

Nod.

"There are more prisoners here?"

Another nod.

"Have you heard of a woman named Renee Williams?"

She shook her head.

"Paulo Reis?"

Another no.

He gestured to the caskets. "Do you know who these bodies belong to?"

She nodded.

"Were they prisoners?"

Another nod.

"Test subjects?"

Nod.

Alex wanted to ask the woman more, to find out exactly what she was doing besides cleaning up spilled blood, but he heard the click of a door above them, followed by heavy footsteps.

The woman started to squirm again, desperate to be free. She let out a quiet whine.

He knew what that meant. If the guards found her shirking her cleaning duty, she might end up in a casket too.

"I'm going to let you go," he said. "But please pretend like you didn't see me. None of this ever happened. If you don't do that, I can't help you."

He let go. This was the moment when any trust he had built in those few seconds of interaction paid off. An enormous gamble. One that might make or break this op.

She turned to face him, eyes brimming with tears. Her mouth opened, and he feared for a second that she was about to betray him.

That he had made the wrong choice after all.

His fingers found the metal grip of his sidearm, ready to fight his way out of this place if she sounded the alarm.

But instead of yelling, she mouthed two words silently, but clear enough for him to understand.

Thank you.

With that she rushed back outside the container. He heard the squelch of the wet cloth against the concrete again.

"Vittoria!" That was Markov.

"I am finished!"

"Good." More plodding footsteps. They sounded as if they were coming down the stairs then across the floor. "You are very slow."

"But it is thorough," she said. "Like you asked. No one will know."

Alex peeked out from the shipping container enough to see the Russian looming over Vittoria. He clenched her upper arm, yanking her up from the floor.

"Back to work now," he said.

He dragged her away, and she stole a glance back at Alex. Her eyes met his for a fraction of a second before she disappeared behind another container with the Russian. There was no mistaking the fear in her eyes.

That was a look he'd seen before. One that had burned into his memory.

It said *Help me.*

Turning aside from the painful memories, he willed himself to focus on what he had to do next. It was the only way to help Vittoria. To help all the others whose lives might be at stake.

Alex listened for the door upstairs shutting again before leaving the container. Finally, he was alone with the shipping containers. This was his opportunity to see what else they hid. But after everything he had seen, he had a feeling that the truth he so desperately needed to uncover wasn't in these containers.

It was behind the door where Vittoria had been taken.

That was where he needed to be.

"Vector Two, Vector One," Alex whispered in the mic. "Following a lead, floor bravo."

"Copy, Vector One," Skylar said, kneeling over the dead Russian with the collapsed trachea. Half a smoldering cigarette was laying by his face.

Her ribs ached. She was still hoping they weren't fractured, but the pain made her wonder if an X-ray would reveal a small crack or two. Not that it made a difference now. A Marine didn't leave a live firefight because of a little discomfort.

She searched through the smoker's pockets, but all she found was a key card that looked like the ones they'd stolen from the guards outside. No identification. No bank cards. Nothing else. This was a man who wanted to stay anonymous. If he wasn't in covert ops, he was probably a merc.

The big man that had damn near smashed her to death was another story. In his pockets, she had found two passports. One looked like a typical Russian civilian passport. The other provided his military rank: *leytenant*.

An actual lieutenant in the Russian Ground Forces.

The translation app on her phone revealed he was assigned

to a brigade in the Nuclear, Biological, and Chemical Protection Troops. That cemented any suspicion that the Russians were directly involved in this operation.

A lieutenant in the Russian Ground Forces was unlikely to be the meanest shark in this sea.

This company-grade officer might've been organizing day-to-day operations for Mark-Logistik, but there was no way a mere LT was the brains behind whatever was actually going on here. He was just a peon in a much more complex covert operational unit. She had a feeling if she and Wolfe continued probing around Mark-Logistik, they would find a ladder up the NBC Protection Troops leading to whatever armchair warrior admin was leading the org.

"Vector One, stumbled on an LT in the NBC," she said. "Already in deep shit. Two hostiles down. Is the warehouse clear?"

"All clear," Wolfe replied.

"Command, Vector Two," she called. "Office clear. Got any specific requests?"

"I have some serious data blue balls," Morris replied. Skylar tried not to curse the analyst out. Easy for him to make a damn joke when he was sitting comfortably back in Detrick. "Can you find me another access point?"

"Will do. Over."

She escaped the confines of the office with her pistol drawn, just in time to see Wolfe on the catwalk about twenty yards to her right. He signaled for her to check out another door between his position and hers then slipped into the last door on the catwalk.

She crept to the door that he had indicated. A small window in the door revealed a narrow corridor. No one was walking the hall or sitting at the desk she saw at the opposite end. Empty, hopefully.

She slid the key card she'd taken from the guard outside over the door's electronic lock.

A red light blinked.

No go.

A cold sweat trickled down her neck. She tried again. The door stayed locked. She got a creeping feeling that maybe these people were onto Vector, watching them.

No, she was just letting paranoia get the better of her. Had to stay cool. Maintain operational calm.

She tried the lieutenant's key card instead of the guard's.

This time, the lock clicked with a satisfying thunk of metal.

Skylar nudged the door open enough to listen for any signs of activity inside.

All quiet.

She pushed inside. The air was heavy with the smell of bleach. Humming fluorescent lights revealed white tile flooring. White doors with numbers lined the hall. She would have thought this was a hospital if it weren't for the small RFID locks next to each door and the keyed deadbolt lock above their handles.

This place was more prison than clinic.

At the end of the hall was a desk. It had a single computer and a pair of folders.

Perfect.

She headed toward the desk. Halfway down the hall, she heard the flush of a toilet, followed by the click of an unlocking door to the left of the desk. The door started to swing open.

Not this again.

She didn't have time to retreat or hide.

Instead, she rushed straight at the doorway. A man walked out, tattoos crawling up the side of his neck. He spotted her and immediately reached for the gun hanging over his shoulder.

No time to do this quietly.

She brought up her suppressed pistol. Fired straight into the man's chest. The noise of the gunshot thudded off the walls.

The man stumbled back into the bathroom. His fingers grasped uselessly at the chest wound.

Skylar's heart pounded, pulse drumming in her ears. She rushed around the desk and aimed her gun at the guard, waiting for him to lunge up at her.

The color was already draining from his skin as blood pooled around him

If anyone was in the warehouse, they definitely would have heard that. Suppressors minimized the noise of a gunshot but couldn't silence it completely. Good chance that noise had carried into another corridor.

"Vector One, shot fired," Skylar said.

There was a single click on the mic from Wolfe to let her know he'd heard.

The computer displayed a series of CCTV images. A few showed the trucks at the loading bay attached to the warehouse. Other views displayed the stacks of shipping containers where Wolfe had been. Another revealed the parking lot out back where she'd entered. The last few cameras showed a corridor in front of what appeared to be a lab bustling with workers.

She put her pistol back in its holster and skimmed through the folders at the guard's desk.

Pictures of faces stared back up at her. Each printout seemed to be some kind of profile.

Behind her, the dead guard's radio crackled. A voice spoke over it. Sounded like they were calling someone's name.

She thumbed through the papers. Her translational app revealed details, showing where the people lived and where they worked. One thing became clear quickly: these people were almost all scientists or researchers of some type.

The radio came to life again. Same name as before.

Skylar looked at the dead guard. "After everyone I've already taken out tonight, you're the bastard who's going to get me in trouble?"

She turned back toward the file folders, flipping them over. They each had a single-digit number on them. A few files, showing different people, had the same numbers.

It took her a moment to realize what those numbers corresponded to.

The same voice called over the radio again. More urgent.

"Vector One, sky's going to fall," she said

She placed her gun on the desk in easy reach. The last two files were each labeled 9. That was the door closest to her. And the pictures on those files were strikingly familiar.

Renee Williams. Paulo Reis.

The people they'd come for were right next to her.

She patted down the dead guard as more voices clamored over the radio. She heard shouts outside on the catwalk. One of the CCTV cameras showed a pair of guards running down the lab corridor.

Getting out of this place was going to be a hell of a lot harder than getting in. But at least now, the only thing that separated her from her targets was a single door.

She took a set of keys out of the guard's pocket, along with his key card.

Inserting the one labeled 9 into the appropriate door with the key card in place over the RFID reader, she unlocked the door, ready to nab Williams and Reis.

"I'm here to—"

She stopped, staring into an empty room.

Where did they go?

She heard people knocking on the door to the prison wing. Voices called what she presumed was the dead guard's name. A quick glance back at the screen showed two outside with pistols in hand.

Someone twisted the handle, and she raised her handgun, ready to stop them.

The door didn't budge.

Whoever was trying to enter didn't appear to have authorized access. Just like the first guard's key card that she'd tried.

That meant their next move was to alert the lieutenant. That wouldn't go over very well.

Time to move, she thought. But the question remained: *To where?*

13

KALININGRAD, Russia

FOLLOWING Vittoria had been the right call.

Alex found himself in a corridor with expansive windows lending views into a large room filled with laboratory benches. Microscopes, sequencers, incubators, and all manner of equipment covered the benches.

Wooden crates were stacked against the walls inside the big lab. Either someone had just moved in here—or they were moving out.

The end of the corridor split off into a T-intersection. He heard voices down one of the arms but couldn't make out the words. Sounded like one of them might be Markov.

He advanced down the hall, sticking close to the doorways in case someone headed his direction. The entrances to the lab he had found so far were unlocked. They would work for a quick getaway, especially with the commotion he had heard outside on the catwalk after Cruz's warning.

"Vector Two, any sign of our targets?" he whispered.

"Found confirmation they were here. But I haven't seen them."

Alex's thought immediately returned to the bodies in the caskets. Were they too late?

"Where are you?" he whispered.

"Prison wing. Leaving soon as I can."

Alex crept into the big lab. He spotted a computer next to a gene sequencer. If there were any data that could help uncover the biological mystery of whatever was going on here, that would be the computer he needed access to. He powered on the computer and stuck in one of the USB transmitters.

"Command, Vector One. Plugged in, gene sequencer."

"Copy," Morris said. "Science team is gonna crap their pants when they see this."

Alex started toward the lab's exit. He wanted to see what else was going on, leaving Morris to do his magic with the computer.

But as he nudged open the door, he heard the distinct crackle of voices over a radio, followed by shouting. He closed the door again and ducked back inside, watching from behind a laboratory bench.

Markov and two other guards escorted a group of prisoners toward the warehouse. Maybe ten or more in total. Among them was Vittoria. They were split up in pairs, carrying metal canisters the size of propane tanks for a grill.

Large Dewar flasks, Alex realized.

Those flasks would be filled with liquid nitrogen or dry ice to preserve biological samples for transport.

"Vector Two, party headed your way," Alex said in a low voice to Skylar.

A single click on the mic answered him.

He stood when he saw the last of the prisoners exit onto the catwalk then slipped into the hall. Where were Vittoria and the others headed? He considered following them. Maybe they were bound for those caskets too.

But while Alex wanted to go after them, that wasn't what Kasim had sent Vector into Kaliningrad for. They needed answers. They needed Williams and Reis. All these other lives would have to wait, as much as it pained him.

Pausing by the T-intersection, he listened for the sounds of anyone else on either side.

All he heard was his own racing pulse and the whoosh of air flowing through the ducts overhead.

He took the left hallway first. Windows ten yards wide revealed the equivalent of a BSL-3 laboratory with big biosafety cabinets and an anteroom to suit up. Definitely not something normal for a shipping warehouse in the middle of a rundown Russian port city.

Before he investigated further, he cleared the other hallway. Just another BSL-3 laboratory. One wall was lined with silver hoods for cell culture. Metal cylinders each nearly three feet in diameter and twice as tall were lined up in a row in the center of the room, connected by a tangle of silver pipes.

A casual observer might think the place was a fancy brewery, but Alex knew whatever was growing in those big bioreactors was far more dangerous than a cold beer.

He took pictures of everything he could. This was potentially damning evidence that Mark-Logistik in Kaliningrad was a cog in this post-Soviet Biopreparat war machine.

But images of a suspected bioweapons lab weren't what he wanted. He needed the actual bioweapons and the people behind them to prove definitively what in the hell was going on.

"Vector One, I scraped everything I can from that sequencer," Morris called over the comms. "You got more for me?"

Alex rushed back to the lab where he'd left the USB transmitter and plugged it into another computer.

"Command, new prey," he reported.

Now that he had done his recon on the layout of the laboratory wing, he performed a more thorough search of the first lab, sifting through the drawers in the lab benches. He found plenty of pipette tips, tubes, and reagents for assays. Nothing unusual as far as a lab in a random port warehouse goes.

He heard a door swing open and loud voices calling in the hall outside the lab again.

"Vector One, we need a way out," Wolfe called in a whisper. "Getting messy."

There was another bang, like a door being slammed open.

Alex was so close to finding something; he couldn't abandon the search now. There had to be something more that would shed some light on the archaea.

At the back of the lab sat a pair of large metal containers for storing samples in liquid nitrogen. As he unscrewed the lid of one, tendrils of cold mist poured out. He used a pair of nearby thermal gloves to remove a rack of six-inch-wide metal boxes from inside the container. Liquid nitrogen dripped off the metal, rolling and evaporating as it hit the floor.

The last few droplets of nitrogen hissed away, and he opened the metal boxes within the rack.

Every one of them was empty. Not a single sample.

A search of the second liquid nitrogen container revealed it was just as empty.

Then he recalled the Dewar flasks the prisoners had been transporting. They must have removed everything already. He halfway considered gowning up and examining the BSL-3 labs, desperate to obtain a sample, some evidence of what it was these people were working on.

But his internal debate was interrupted by the sound of more shouts followed by a single, ringing gunshot.

Frederick, MD

Kasim paced in the operations center of Vector HQ. For a few long moments, the only sounds were the taps of Morris's fingers across the keyboard. Wolfe and Cruz had maintained relatively tight radio discipline, transmitting comms only when necessary.

That meant they were proceeding through the op with quiet professionalism, but it also left Kasim in constant suspense. He had spent years working with teams running covert ops. Waiting in near silence, especially when the only comms they received were ominous reports of missing targets and gunfire never got any easier.

All Kasim could do was steel himself and hope his two talented operatives pulled this off. Their careers with Vector were far from the only thing on the line tonight.

"Still no confirmed sighting of Williams or Reis?" Kasim asked.

"No." Morris took out his earbuds, letting a fast-paced tune bleed out. "The only evidence we have they were even there are those bios Cruz found."

"Who are the other prisoners?" Kasim asked.

"Mostly scientists and researchers. Some apparently went to Russia under a long-term sabbatical plan. Others were reported missing in their home countries after going on vacation in places like Thailand or China."

"So what the hell are we dealing with? Some kind of scientist trafficking ring?"

This was unlike anything Kasim had ever seen before. Good thing he'd already told Divya that he was away for a business trip. He had made it clear to his wife that he wasn't going to be home tonight—or possibly any night over the next week. Every time they thought they were close to an answer, they only ran into more questions.

The door opened, and Park rushed in, white coat fluttering behind him. He didn't bother with as much as a cursory greeting. He set his laptop on the table and flipped it open to face Kasim.

"That genetic sequencing data Wolfe sent back is gold," Park said. "Look."

His screen showed two different lists of nucleotides, *G*s, *A*s, *T*s, and *C*s spanning the screen.

Kasim adjusted his reading glasses. The two lists looked identical.

"What am I supposed to see?" he asked.

Park clicked on a button. Red rectangles highlighted subtle differences in the chains of DNA. "The top sequence is the archaea sample that Wolfe and Cruz took off Breners. The bottom sequence shows the sequencing data transmitted from Kaliningrad."

Kasim squinted at the screen. He didn't have the expertise that Park did in microbiology, but he hadn't gotten this position through his administrative and bureaucratic navigation skills alone. "Sample one, the Breners strain, is innocuous. But if I'm following this, the Kaliningrad strain is a genetically modified version."

"Exactly," Park said. "I can say with ninety-nine percent certainty that the Breners strain was adapted from the Kaliningrad strain. It has all the same chromosomes we found in that first sample. But these differences you see don't match anything we've got in our databases."

"You're saying you have no idea what these changes in the archaea's DNA does."

"Afraid not," Park confirmed. "I can't imagine it's anything good."

"That much is clear. I want you and Weber to see if you can model what those genes do. If they engineered archaea as bioweapons, these genes might map to another existing pathogenic organism or virus. That'd be a hell of a lot easier than making up their own genetic sequences to do something that doesn't exist in nature, right?"

"Our thoughts exactly. Weber's already on it."

"Good."

He expected Park to take off. The guy spent more time in the lab than most people spent breathing. He rarely left those sterile chambers when he was at work, except when Kasim ordered it or he had something to share. Instead, Park stood by the table, staring at the computer and rubbing the stubble on his chin.

"Tell me what else is on your mind," Kasim said.

"Modern research hasn't definitively revealed any diseases caused by archaea before."

"I understand that."

"That means we have no existing cure for an archaea-originated disease. No vaccines. No natural immunity."

Kasim felt the heavy weight of dread drag through his insides. "Then what you're saying is that when they deploy it, we have no way to stop it."

Park's face was pale. "I'm afraid that's right. A disease based on archaea would be completely unstoppable."

14

SVERDLOVSK, Russia

PAVLENKO WAS SUITED up inside a BSL-3 laboratory, surrounded by some of the most talented scientists in the Fourteenth Directorate of the RHkM. He strolled between the researchers lined up at the lab benches. They began the process of using gene editing techniques to modify his weaponized archaea according to the recommendations he had squeezed out of Williams and Reis.

By suppressing a single cell membrane protein, his team would ensure that the archaea would never be identified by EnviroProct's Aerokeep pathogen detection equipment. The bioweapon would effectively be a ghost. While epidemiologists prepared for a litany of nightmare scenarios of spreading pathogens, no research papers suggested a pandemic caused by archaea.

He could not wait to prove how foolish they all had been.

"How long will the genetic modifications take?" Pavlenko

asked one of his scientists, a woman named Dr. Natalia Yunevich.

She faced him, her voice muffled between her mask and visor. "The genetic modifications to this strain of the archaea will be complete by the day's end."

Pavlenko smiled beneath his own mask. These were results Yuri Levin could never offer Dmitriyev no matter how much he tried to win favor with the general.

Unfortunately, this new strain of archaea would only be used for the second deployment of their weapon. General Dmitriyev's time constraints had given him no choice. The first batch had already been deployed successfully in China. But unlike China, Europe had far more EnviroProct Aerokeep devices deployed throughout the continent. Researchers and government agencies there would have a much better chance of tracking down the weaponized archaea to his facilities. He couldn't allow them to do that.

"After we have a fully modified strain, how long until we can culture a new batch?" Pavlenko asked.

"We do not need to culture a completely new batch," Yunevich said.

"Explain."

"Instead of breeding new archaea, we can carry out these genetic modifications on the ones we already have. This will take only a matter of days rather than months."

"Very good, Yunevich," Pavlenko said. "Remind me that you deserve a promotion as soon as we deploy this second batch."

"I will certainly not forget."

That would keep them on the schedule he'd promised Dmitriyev. He turned away from the benches filled with scientists and exited the lab, enduring the tedious decontamination processes on his way out.

He headed toward his office to share the good news. The

general would be pleased to learn that Pavlenko could make good on his promise in a way that did not compromise the security of their operation.

As he turned down the hall, Levin marched straight toward him.

"Colonel, I was just looking for you at your office," Levin called. "We need to talk. Now."

Pavlenko ushered them into his office and closed the door. Levin didn't bother to sit.

"Someone has infiltrated Kaliningrad," he said. "Several of Archon's men—and one of our own—are already dead."

Pavlenko's face burned with an intense fire. Levin was lying. This couldn't be true.

"How could someone find our operations in Kaliningrad?" Pavlenko asked.

"I don't know," Yuri said then narrowed his eyes. "Perhaps it has something to do with those new researchers from Portugal you wanted. Maybe they were tracked."

"No, no, it can't be." Pavlenko didn't like the way Levin glared at him. Already the duplicitous man was compiling a story that would lay the blame on Pavlenko. Should this mission fail, should someone outside of Russia discover what they were doing, Levin was setting the stage so that Dmitriyev would readily believe it was all Pavlenko's fault.

That would not be acceptable.

"And who hired the kidnappers?" Pavlenko said. "Who vouched for Archon?"

"It is not Archon's fault," Levin said, pacing with his hands on his belly. "They come recommended from the Directorate. You saw the media blaming the attack in Portugal on radical terrorists. These men did as you required." He paused, standing in front of Pavlenko's desk. "But I will make it clear to Dmitriyev that you were the one who risked our cover by bringing these scientists in."

"That is where you are wrong. Thanks to those scientists, we have solved a significant problem in deploying the archaea. But that is not your concern. You are the one responsible for field operations and security. So tell me, what is going on in Kaliningrad?"

Levin was silent, his face turning red.

"Lieutenant Colonel Levin, I expect an answer." Pavlenko jabbed a finger onto the desk for emphasis. "Who is in Kaliningrad? Who killed our men?"

"I don't know."

"And Archon doesn't know either?"

Levin's nose twitched, and his fingers balled into fists like he was going to pounce on Pavlenko. But the man was all bark, no bite. Right now, he seemed to have even lost his bark.

"Then I have a simple solution," Pavlenko said. "We are already preparing for the last stage of archaea deployment. Move all our scientific operations from Kaliningrad. That includes scientists and hostages. Scrub all the data they leave behind. Make sure there is no trace of the archaea there."

"Where do we send them?" Levin said.

"Straight to the last deployment site," Pavlenko said. "Prepare the Mark-Logistik container ship. I want it sailing when the sun is up."

"That is a lot to accomplish in very little time," Levin said.

"Thanks to you and Archon, we have no choice. Find whoever is threatening our operations. We must know who they are working for. Then kill them."

"Fine." Levin squared his shoulders, standing taller. "Just know that I am not doing this for you. I am doing it for the motherland."

"Cut the false patriotism. You are in this for yourself and no one else. Don't pretend otherwise."

Levin opened the office door. "No one will know we were

ever in Kaliningrad, but Dmitriyev will know it was I who saved your failing operation."

"You better hope he believes you. Because if you fail and he does not, you may want to put on a few more pounds of insulation to survive the long winters in Siberia."

KALININGRAD, Russia

WITH AUBERT and Paulo's help, Renee carried a crate of supplies down the stairs toward the main floor of the warehouse. The rumble of a truck engine swept through the massive open door. Already she saw a few caskets piled inside the open shipping container on the truck's trailer.

Markov lumbered between the dozen or so other scientists and technicians trailing after Renee. He shoved one man, and the scientist nearly lost the box of lab samples he held.

"Hurry!" Markov said. "We are leaving, and if you do not keep up, you will end up like Sullivan!"

Renee felt weak at her knees. The image of one of their fellow scientists lying on the floor outside the laboratories was still a raw wound in her mind. When Markov had judged the scientist wasn't packing lab samples fast enough, he had executed the man.

No warning. He had just torn out his weapon and fired.

That had been motivation enough for the rest of the scientists and technicians to do exactly as the man had said. They had been pulled from their prison cells, labs, or wherever else they had been working to help the Russian guards load up the shipping containers and trucks.

Renee, Aubert, and Paulo hoisted their cargo into one of the shipping containers. Two Russian guards inside moved the crate to the back of the container between a stack of metal caskets.

"What's going on?" Paulo asked Aubert.

"I don't know," she said in a hushed voice. "I've never seen them so worked up."

"Maybe we'll have a chance to get out." Paulo turned to Renee, giving her a ghost of a smile. "Remember Tuscany."

From up on the second floor of the warehouse, someone began yelling. Renee couldn't quite see what was going on from her vantage behind the rows of shipping containers. Paulo wrapped an arm around her protectively, pulling her in close beside him. Aubert stepped in front of both of them. She leaned past the containers to look up at the catwalk.

"Careful," the woman said. "They're yelling at two of our technicians. Oh, no, they're—"

She didn't need to finish her sentence.

Renee could hear the sound of fist meeting flesh and the agonized screams of the technicians.

"What are you doing?" Markov asked them, coming around the side of another container. "Get to work!"

He grabbed Renee by the back of her neck and shoved her. She sprawled forward. Pain washed through where her knees cracked against the concrete. Paulo tried to stop Markov. But the big Russian hit Paulo with a hammering blow right in the scientist's stomach.

"No," Renee said. "Stop!"

Markov towered over her, his lips curled back, fire in his eyes.

"Don't hurt them," Aubert said. She crouched next to Renee, helping her to stand. "We are working. Please!"

Renee limped next to Aubert, and together they hoisted Paulo to his feet. He could barely breathe, still recovering.

Markov opened his mouth to speak but suddenly stopped. A voice crackled over the radio, speaking in what Renee assumed was frantic Russian. Markov listened for a second then began yelling at the other guards. Renee noticed them immediately pick up their pace. Markov took another step toward Aubert, Renee, and Paulo.

"We're getting back to work," Aubert said. "Markov, you don't need to hurt us."

He raised a hand as he marched toward Renee. Paulo, still wheezing, tried to strike him, but a rough backhand from Markov sent him reeling.

"Paulo, no," Renee said. She tried to scramble toward him.

"You are coming with me," he said. His fingers tightened around the back of Renee's collar, and he dragged her back toward the truck. She struggled against his grip, thrashing, but couldn't free herself.

Another guard wrapped his arm around Aubert and pressed a gun against her temple, screaming at her in Russian. He guided her after Renee.

Paulo pushed himself upright again, his eyes narrowed. He used the shipping container to steady himself and started toward them.

"Leave… her… alone," he said. He lurched toward her, and she reached out toward him.

"Paulo," she said.

He started to hobble toward her, but another guard wrapped his arms around him. The Russian pulled Paulo back.

"Hold on," he said, eyes glimmering with a wet sheen. "Florence, Renee! I promise!"

"You've still got work to do," the guard said.

Tears started to blur Renee's vision as Markov hoisted her into the truck trailer. To her left, another guard injected something into Aubert's arm then pushed her backward into a casket. The guard secured the lid and turned toward Renee.

She fought against Markov, but the man wrestled her into another casket. Every time she tried to push herself out, he shoved her back into it. There was no getting past this beast of a man.

He grinned as she tried to battle his raw power. "You think you are strong like a tiger. You are nothing but a housecat."

He jabbed a needle into her arm and depressed the plunger. A biting pain spread from the injection site, followed by a dizzying numbness. Markov disappeared over the edge of the trailer. She could hear him shouting commands as the world spun.

A deep exhaustion tugged at her consciousness. Everything around her began to fade. The casket lid came down over her.

Paulo.

His name swirled in the darkness of her mind. She strained to stay awake, to figure out what had become of him.

But then came the gunshots. One after another.

Renee feared she had her answer.

15

KALININGRAD, Russia

SKYLAR WAS STILL CROUCHED near the desk in the prison wing when her earpiece crackled.

"Vector Two, status?" Wolfe asked over the comms.

"Alive."

"What's happening? Who was shot?"

"The Russians are forcing the scientists to load up their trucks," she said. "There was some kind of struggle."

"Any sign of our targets?"

"The camera resolution isn't good enough," she said. "I couldn't see them."

More yells exploded from the warehouse. On the CCTV monitor, she watched the guards in front of the prison wing door run off. Looked like they were headed to the lieutenant's office to get him to open the prison wing. This was her chance to move.

She shut down the camera system and deleted the surveillance program, along with all the recorded footage from the evening. That might help buy Vector some extra time. After hurrying out of the prison wing, she rushed straight for the end of the catwalk to the stairs.

The wide-open, twenty-foot-tall warehouse doors at the other end of the building let in a cool breeze. A pair of trucks had been backed into the space, their engines rumbling, spewing the stink of burning diesel. One had an open shipping container on its trailer. A group of maybe eight guards watched over another half-dozen prisoners. They were loading big plastic containers and crates into the shipping container.

Yells rang out from the offices. The guards must have discovered the dead lieutenant.

She took the stairs down two at a time. In her hurry, she nearly stepped on a man in coveralls sprawled across the floor at the bottom of the steps. Next to him was a broken metal container.

"Vector One, found one of the gunshot victims. Guy in coveralls with a Dewar flask."

Skylar hadn't seen what had caused the guards to shoot the man, but by the frantic gestures and loud yells targeting the other prisoners, she guessed it had something to do with the prisoners not working fast enough.

The Russians seemed as anxious to leave this place as Skylar was. Only problem was they seemed to be leaving with the people and things she and Wolfe had come for.

A group of three guards left the offices. Instead of going to the prisons, they went to another door that Skylar hadn't explored yet. This time when they came back out, two of them carried AK-47s. One of the men, a guy with tattoos roping down his arms, was barking orders at them. The guy had too many non-reg tattoos to be an officer in the Russian military like the LT she'd killed.

When he turned, Skylar recognized his face from the image her partner had sent Command.

Markov.

He took his armed comrades through the door where Wolfe had gone.

"Vector One, three contacts headed your way," she whispered. "Markov and two others. Running in with heavy hardware."

Skylar peered around another shipping container, careful to stay in the shadows. From her vantage, it was hard to make out the faces of the prisoners in the brief glimpses she had.

"Command, we got enough data from the labs?" Skylar asked. "Our time here is running out."

Kasim's voice sparked back on the channel. "More is always better. Do you have eyes on Reis and Williams?"

She watched the prisoners, squinting. One of the men had fresh bruises covering his face. His features were swollen, but if she imagined him without the injuries, he might pass for Paulo Reis. The dark hair seemed to match.

"Possible affirmative on Reis, negative on Williams. We clear to make a move for him? Might not have another chance. They look like they're prepping for transit, and the Russians have already cut down at least two other prisoners tonight."

"Do you have an opening?" Kasim asked.

"Not exactly," Skylar whispered. "But I've got a feeling when we do, we're not going to have time to ask again."

Her boss paused. "The science team wants better samples. We still don't have a damn clue what those archaea actually do. And we also need to know where those weapons are going. Intel takes priority over extraction."

Skylar watched the man she guessed to be Paulo Reis shuffled along the concrete. "Might not have that intel in this facility anyway."

"Vector One, your opinion?"

"I'm with Vector Two," her partner whispered. Skylar felt a

brief flare of gratitude that Wolfe had her back, and then he continued, "We might not have much more time."

"What do you mean?"

"Things are about to get hot in the labs. Really hot."

ALEX HAD ALREADY SIPHONED the data off half the computers in the lab. Any one of them might have the data the science team needed to determine what the archaea weapon actually did when it entered the human body. But he wanted to be one hundred percent certain.

Once they left this place, there was no coming back. As he waited, he worried the trigger-happy gunmen would come bursting into the lab at any moment. He wasn't foolish enough to think he could defend himself with nothing but a pistol, not against all the armed guards running around now. Fortunately, this lab was filled with common chemicals used in biological and chemical research. And in the right hands, those chemicals could be deadlier than a magazine full of bullets. So while he waited for Morris to pull data from the machines, he rushed around the lab, scrambling to find everything he needed.

The chemicals he found were normally kept far apart in different flammable chemical cabinets for a damn good reason. He placed them strategically on the lab benches near the entrance, all in open view.

One that Alex was only too happy to exploit.

Pounding footsteps and shouts outside the lab told him time was up.

He ducked behind a lab bench, holding his suppressed SIG Sauer. He watched three men rush into the lab corridor, just as Cruz had warned. The first of the men was Pyotr Markov, carrying an MP-443 pistol. Flanking him, the other two men carried AK-47s.

Markov gestured for one of the gunmen to follow him and left the other to guard the door to the lab wing. That meant Alex wasn't sneaking out without the Russians noticing. Markov and the other gunman ran down the corridor. They disappeared out of Alex's sight as they headed toward the T-intersection that led to the BSL-3 lab and the bioreactors.

He considered lining up a shot on the remaining guard. The man had his rifle shouldered, ready to fire. The bulkiness beneath his jacket suggested body armor. The wire-reinforced glass windows were likely made of ballistic glass—a preventative measure to contain any lab accidents. Also effective at stopping small arms fire.

If he tried to shoot the guy from here, he might as well just start tossing glass beakers against the door and singing the national anthem for all the good it would do.

Markov and the other gunman soon returned. The head merc was holding something rectangular, slightly larger than a phone, in his left hand.

Alex couldn't quite see what it was, but Markov didn't give him much of a chance to figure it out. He kicked in the lab door, and both gunmen rushed in, their gun barrels roving over the space.

It was now or never.

Alex fired at the four-liter glass bottle he had set on the lab bench by the door. The bottle exploded in a spray of glass shards, and liquid spilled over the counter. A second clean shot tore through another plastic bottle, and the contents gushed out.

As the nitric acid and ethanol mixed, an unrestrained chemical reaction ripped through them. What was left of the bottles exploded in a spray of glass shards and melted globs of plastic. Tongues of brilliant fire erupted from the benchtop. Black smoke rose in a miniature mushroom cloud, and a wave of heat rolled through the lab, washing over Alex.

Both the gunmen started yelling. Unfortunately, their bodies had blocked Markov from the worst of the explosion. While flames roared over the men, Markov merely dashed back out into the hall. One of the burning guards squeezed off a burst of rounds in a panic, bullets lancing into the wall behind Alex.

As the two Russian gunmen tried to pat out the fire dancing over their clothes, Alex fired. Rounds punched into their body armor, knocking the wind out of them. Then he managed a headshot that brought the first gunman down.

The other man was clearly fighting against his pain to stay upright, skin blistering and peeling. The astringent smell of strong chemicals and burning flesh filled the air. The remaining gunman let out an angry cry as he unleashed a wild spray of bullets.

Alex dove behind the lab bench as a fusillade tore into the cabinets around him. Wood and plastic sprayed from each impact, sending a shower of debris over him. The deafening rifle fire was joined by the blasts from a pistol, hammering Alex's eardrums.

Markov had turned the corner around the lab bench to flank Alex. He lunged behind another to block the incoming fire.

The man with the rifle stumbled toward Alex from the other side. He fired into the man's legs. The Russian yowled and tried to adjust his aim, but Alex's next shot went through his throat. The mercenary crumpled to the floor, and his rifle clattered away.

Alex dove for the weapon then leaned around the corner to take down Markov. But the Russian had disappeared.

Where the hell did you go?

Alex tried to listen through his damaged hearing. Fire licked up from the cardboard boxes lining the bench nearest the door. Dark swirls of smoke began to fill the room, and Alex searched for movement within the ominous fog. His eyes started to water with the acrid smoke, a deep cough threatening to wrack his lungs.

He saw a silhouette move in the murk and fired. Each shot shuddered up his arm. The crunch of glass and crack of wood was just barely audible. He blinked through the streaming tears in his eyes, moving toward the doorway.

Markov had seemingly vanished. Was he dead?

Another plastic bottle of ethanol broke from the searing heat, and a wave of flames rolled toward the ceiling.

He didn't have time to search for a body. He needed to leave now.

"Vector Two," he said, voice scratchy. "Get our targets. Go."

A single click on the mic.

The chemicals roiling in the air tore at his nostrils. He felt like glass daggers were being drawn through his trachea and into his lungs. Coughs erupted from deep in his chest. He pulled his shirt up and over his nose, backpedaling toward the door to the lab.

Then he caught movement again to his left. A shape barreled toward him from the rolling tide of smoke. He managed to swing his weapon around. Didn't have enough time to aim before he was knocked off his feet.

His head slammed against the floor, vision blurring. The dizziness already sweeping through him from the smoke inhalation grew worse. His gun fell from his grip.

A heavy weight pressed down on his chest.

Markov had a knee against Alex's sternum then pressed his gun underneath Alex's chin. He grimaced at the touch of the cold steel.

"Make a move, and I shoot you now," Markov said. "Who are you? Who do you work for?"

Alex said nothing. The flames behind Markov climbed up

the wall, devouring more of the laboratory supplies. They were growing closer to other containers full of reagents—bombs waiting to go off.

"Tell me who sent you!" Markov said, pressing harder.

His world threatened to go dark. Blackness crept around the edges of his vision. He struggled to breathe between the caustic smoke and Markov's weight on his chest. His mind screamed at him to move, to shove the man off and get away.

But a voice deep behind that panic, the one drilled into him by years of training, was stronger. It knew the wrong move now was fatal. That reacting too violently, too quickly, would only end with a bullet through his brain.

Patience, even now, was the better option.

"Talk to me!" Markov struck Alex in the jaw with the handle of the pistol.

He tasted blood. Markov was angry. But there had to be a good reason he hadn't outright killed Alex. Especially after those gunmen had tried. Maybe he thought Alex was already his. No longer a danger. That the information he could extract from him was more valuable than simply taking his life. Which meant whoever was in charge of Markov wanted that info too.

Good, Alex thought. *The bastard doesn't know who we are.*

"Are you deaf?" Markov yelled.

Before Alex could answer, one of the bottles of isopropyl alcohol on a nearby shelf erupted. The spreading fire set off other searing blast.

Markov flinched from the flames coursing over his back. This time, it was his body that shielded Alex from the brunt of the fire.

Alex twisted out from under Markov, pulling on the man's wrist. The gun went off, exploding next to Alex's ear. Hot pain shook through his eardrum, the ringing in his ears now worse than before.

But he was still alive. The bullet had only grazed past.

Another two damaged containers of IPA exploded in the spreading conflagration, clouds of fire and smoke clawing at the ceiling.

The laboratory had turned into a scene straight from hell. And only now did Alex realize how odd that was.

The sprinklers should've come on by now.

He didn't have long to consider why.

Flaming ceiling tiles fell and cracked against the floor next to him, sending up a wave of embers. He rolled out of the way and scooped up his gun.

Markov was already moving, scrambling to recover his own weapon when more balls of fire flared around him. The man disappeared somewhere behind the wall of flames and smoke.

Alex fired a few shots to cover his retreat then ran out of the lab. Through the lab window, he saw Markov backlit by the inferno. The man locked eyes with him, swinging his hand up. Alex ducked, firing into the window, desperate to get off a shot even a millisecond faster than his adversary.

But, as Alex had suspected, the glass was too strong. It spiderwebbed but didn't break.

Markov grinned, blood trickling down the side of his face. Instead of a pistol, the Russian held what appeared to be a small remote.

It suddenly clicked why the sprinklers in the lab hadn't worked. Why the fire had gotten so out of hand. The sprinklers and alarms had been turned off intentionally. Markov and his associates *wanted* this place to burn. Alex had just started the festivities early.

Markov pressed the remote.

A deep rumble welled up from the other corridors of the laboratory wing. The building shook. Glass shattered. Metal groaned and snapped. A monstrous roar filled the corridor, nearly sucking the air from Alex's lungs.

Then came the wall of fire.

16

THE WHOLE WAREHOUSE SHOOK. Skylar ducked as rusted pipes in the ceiling fell loose from the blasts, swinging precariously. One dumped water into the middle of the warehouse floor. A pile of crates on the catwalk tumbled off and broke open, spilling laboratory glassware over the concrete.

Screams rose from the six prisoners near the back of the trucks at the warehouse door. A few of them dove for cover, but the others seemed too beaten down to be afraid anymore.

By Skylar's count, eight guards still roamed the area. Three carried rifles. The others wore holstered sidearms. She peered around the corner of a shipping container as one of the trucks rumbled away. Another backed in to take its place as the guards recovering from the blast yelled frantic orders at each other. A few of them lifted metal caskets into the back of the trailer.

None of them ran away to investigate the explosion, which told Skylar these guys probably expected it. The explosions were no accident. Maybe a self-destruct procedure?

That made getting Williams and Reis all the more important.

Another series of rumbles tore through the building. Flaming debris burst into the warehouse from the other corridors. One explosion tore the door from the office where she had killed the lieutenant. Burning papers sprayed into the place like hellish confetti, embers and ash falling all around. Smoke began pouring into the warehouse.

Flames or not, her mission hadn't changed.

"Vector One, sitrep?" she whispered over the comms.

No response.

"Vector One?"

Son of a...

"Command, can you reach Vector One?"

"Negative," Kasim called back. "Vector Two, what's going on?"

A tide of panic roiled at the back of Skylar's mind, threatening to overwhelm her. Fires, explosions, and Wolfe had gone silent, maybe... No, she couldn't believe it. Not yet.

"Not sure," Skylar called back to Command. "Everything's going to hell here."

A deep boom resonated from somewhere else in the facility.

Damn it, Alex Wolfe, where are you?

Her mind kicked into overdrive, the same feeling she had once experienced when enemy fire rocketed toward her chopper. Emotions disappeared. There was no time for thinking through scenarios. Her priorities were clear. Didn't matter if she liked it or not.

Reis needed to be extracted first. Then Williams and then Wolfe.

Time to move. Now.

She used the confusion of the blasts to move forward past the containers. The three guards with the rifles were waving on the prisoners near the back of an open trailer.

Now or never.

Her first shot leveled one immediately. The other two

barely had time to swing their rifles around, searching for the source of the gunfire amid the crackle of fire consuming the rest of the building.

One of the guards spotted her, turning her way. But by the time the Russian had his rifle aimed, she had already sent three shots into his chest. He fell backward, no longer moving.

The third gunman let loose a spray of rounds that sparked against the shipping containers and ricocheted off the concrete floors. Other guards started drawing their sidearms, dropping the caskets they had been hoisting into the trailer. A few of the prisoners scattered, sprinting for safety, blocking the firing lanes.

The place would quickly become a killing floor.

Skylar sent the last few rounds from her magazine into the last Russian with a rifle. Her slide locked back.

She moved to a new shipping container, changing magazines. A fire burned in her ribs from the exertion. It seemed like every accelerating beat of her heart was making the pain worse.

Can't let it stop me now. Just move and shoot.

Skylar had the advantage of surprise and chaos. She was the lioness selecting her prey from the stampede of antelope.

The Russians shouted to each other and spread out to new firing positions. Five left, plus anyone Wolfe might have let live in the laboratories before they started going up in flames.

She heard gunfire then a scream. Leaning around a container, she saw a prisoner lying sprawled over the floor. Dark spots spread over the back of his coveralls where bullets had plunged into his back. A Russian cursed, kicking the prisoner's ribs, his pistol still aimed at the dead man's spine.

A painful knot twisted in Skylar's gut at the sight of the cold-blooded execution.

You son of a… she raised her pistol.

Three shots brought the Russian down.

Just four of these bastards to go.

Sweat trickled down the back of Skylar's neck. Smoke started to cover the ceilings, its acrid scent biting and harsh. She held back a cough, knowing that the pain might make her black out if she let it loose.

Outnumbered, she couldn't stay in one spot for long.

Footsteps and shouts echoed against the walls and shipping containers, making it difficult to pinpoint her next target. Half the voices and footsteps belonged to the prisoners. Smoke cast the warehouse in a gray fog.

She ran down the length of another shipping container and stole a glimpse toward the exit to the warehouse. The open warehouse door was just forty feet from her position, past another pair of shipping containers and the truck. Another prisoner was running alongside the truck, fleeing toward freedom.

Then a rash of gunshots.

The prisoner tumbled forward and skidded across the concrete.

There were only four prisoners left that she'd seen. Four prisoners, four guards. And now those guards were shooting at anyone who wasn't them.

Reis and Williams would be in danger if they weren't already down.

Skylar fought to control her breathing, wincing at the stabbing pain in her sides. "Vector One, need backup in the warehouse. Lost track of targets. Four hostiles left!"

There was still no response.

Come on, Wolfe.

She listened for a click on his mic, something to tell her he was okay. But she had to swallow her fear when she heard pounding steps headed her direction. Another prisoner rushed past the shipping container she was hiding behind. It was a man.

Reis?

She reached out toward him, and he twisted her direction, shock painted across his face. Then rounds lanced through his side. He crumpled in a messy heap.

A pang of nausea swept through her.

No, no, no, was that it? Had she failed?

She twisted around the container just enough to fire on the guard that had cut down the prisoner. He let out a surprised curse before bullets stitched his chest then his head.

Checking the lanes between the containers, she ensured no other Russians were headed her way. Then she rolled the prisoner over, studying his face.

Middle-aged, dark skin, graying hair. It wasn't Reis.

He might still be alive, along with Williams.

Three guards left. Three prisoners.

"Vector One, do you read?" she tried again. "I could use more eyes."

"We're not getting anything from him," Kasim called back instead.

Another explosion rumbled in from the laboratory corridor.

The sound of more shouts filled the warehouse. The trucks' engines growled to life, and the vehicles lurched forward, one after the other, dragging the last trailers out from the loading bay.

She advanced toward one of the vehicles, running from the shelter of a crate to a collection of steel drums then another shipping container.

Wolfe, Williams, Reis, where the hell are all of you?

One of the Russian guards followed the truck out. He roved his pistol's aim back and forth, sweeping for targets.

Just near him, Skylar saw movement. Another prisoner trying to make a break for it. Running from beyond a shipping container, straight toward the open warehouse door. But thanks to the shipping container, the prisoner couldn't see the Russian heading to intersect him.

And as the man ran, Skylar recognized the battered face.

Reis.

She only had a second to react, drawing a bead on the Russian. If she missed, if the guard survived, Reis was dead. Their mission would be in flames, just like the building. Sure, Williams might be alive, but Skylar hadn't seen her yet. Far more likely that the other scientist had already been killed.

So these shots had to count.

She squeezed the trigger. Once. Twice.

Slide locked back. Empty again. No more chances.

The Russian stood for a second, and Skylar's stomach lurched. Had she missed?

Reis was still running straight ahead. As soon as he cleared that container, he'd be directly in the Russian's line of sight.

"Doctor Reis!" Skylar shouted, trying to draw his attention, trying to stop him.

But her voice was lost in the roar of the flames, the rumbling of the trucks' engines, and the shouts elsewhere in the warehouse. He ran straight out into the open.

No!

The Russian's gun was pointed at Reis. The scientist froze, exactly the wrong instinct.

Skylar was already jamming a new magazine into place. She started forward, hoping maybe, just maybe, she might draw the Russian's attention away from Reis.

Instead, the man slumped to a knee, his weapon falling from his grip. His mouth dropped open before he collapsed sideways.

She had gotten him after all.

The man's death was enough to break Reis from his shock. He started forward like he wanted to be on the last truck even if it cost him his life.

Two guards left.

They would be panicking now, and the young scientist was going to draw them toward himself. Toward *her*.

She sprinted at Reis. He saw her coming and sped up.

"Stop!" she yelled.

But of course he didn't. He had no idea who was friend or foe in all this chaos. Desperate, heedless of her injuries, she dove for his ankles. He sprawled forward, and she twisted, using her body weight to keep him down. More agony bellowed up through her injured ribs. She bit back a cry of pain while aiming her handgun back down the aisles between the shipping containers.

"Here to help. Where's Williams?" she gasped.

There was a flash of movement down one of the aisles. Looked like the coveralls of a prisoner.

"What?" Reis managed, voice coming out in a croak.

"I'm trying to help you and Williams," she said. "Where is she?"

"I don't... I... the truck."

Another jolt of movement. Shapes running between the aisles. The crack of more gunfire, followed by a scream.

Two guards left, lurking in the smoke. Only two other prisoners running around in here. What were the chances one was the woman she wanted to save?

"Talk to me, Reis. I'm trying to save your ass."

"They already took her," Reis finally spit out. "They took her and some others in that last truck. Those caskets. We have to help."

"That's what we're here for." Skylar looked up at the loading bay. The last truck was trundling along the road alongside the pier, heading off wherever the Russians had taken the others.

"Command, Vector One, this is Vector Two. I'm at the

warehouse door. Got one target. Other is leaving in a truck. Caskets, like before."

She started dragging Reis back to the shelter of a container, but he fought against her, struggling to get free.

"We have to get Renee," Reis said.

"Listen to me," she said. "Quit fighting. I'm trying to help."

The message didn't seem to sink in.

In the distance, the wails of sirens pierced the noise of the raging fire.

The authorities would be here soon. She imagined they would sweep this under the rug, a tragic chemical explosion at a port manufacturing facility. Everything would be explained away in the Russian state propaganda networks.

And if she and Wolfe stuck around, Vector would disappear just easily as the true story of what had taken place here.

"Vector One," Skylar called into her mic. "Got Reis. We need to leave. Now. Please respond!"

Come on, Alex. Please!

But instead of hearing a tap over the mic or her partner's voice, she heard the distinct click of a pistol hammer drawing back. One of the Russian guards appeared from beyond a shipping container, running right at them, his weapon drawn.

17

ALEX COUGHED, smoke billowing behind him as he stumbled out onto the catwalk. His head pounded with an unholy fury. His lungs felt as though they were on fire. The blast must've knocked him unconscious, but he had no idea how long. His ears still rang. Cruz's words had sounded muddled, but at least he could finally hear them. Embers floated everywhere. He blinked, trying desperately to fight the dizziness from over-taking him.

"Vector Two, I'm here," he said.

Eyes watering, he saw movement at the loading bay door through the screen of smoke. Looked like his partner dragging someone with her.

Then he saw the Russian barreling toward her. Alex aimed and fired a burst of rounds. The man tumbled, momentum alone carrying him forward. Cruz winced at the gunshots then looked up at him.

"Thanks, Vector One," she said. "Still one guard left, and Reis says Williams is in the truck, getting away. We got two more prisoners running around in here."

"I'm on my way," Alex said.

He ran down the catwalk, headed toward the stairs. Figures ran beneath the smoke pouring in from the corridors.

The stairs were just ten feet away now. He squinted through the enveloping smoke. A burning sensation crept through his lungs, and he struggled to breathe, trying to stay low.

Then he heard shouts somewhere below. Sounded like a guard yelling at a prisoner.

He rushed down the stairs, remembering the promise he had made to Vittoria. He couldn't stand by as all these lives were needlessly destroyed.

"Vector One, lost visual on you," Cruz called. "We need to leave now to catch Williams."

Screams came from Alex's left, somewhere beyond the smoke.

"Go," he said. "I'll catch up."

He ran toward the screaming, pushing through a cloud of smoke. The flames had spread from the corridors now and were eating through the crates stacked against the walls. More booms resonated through the warehouse.

One of the blasts caught Alex from behind. He stumbled forward then fell hard against the concrete. He managed to maintain control over his weapon and pushed himself up, gasping for air. His head pounded worse than before.

Somewhere behind him, he heard the creak of metal giving way. The support beams were starting to fail. Burning ceiling tiles crashed atop shipping containers. Alex shielded his face with his arm as embers sprayed him. He heard panicked footsteps somewhere to his left and ran toward them.

He rounded a corner past a shipping container. Two prisoners cowered against the side of another container. A man he didn't know and Vittoria.

"Come with me!" he shouted. "We're getting out of here."

From the opposite end of the row of containers, the last

Russian guard appeared through the smoke. His gun was leveled at the prisoners. Another boom coursed through the building.

The guard instinctively ducked, and one of the prisoners stood, starting to run. The guard fired a wild shower of bullets. Alex shot back, and the guard collapsed.

The prisoner that had tried to run was lying flat on his stomach. Alex ran to him, checking the man's pulse with two fingers against his neck.

Gone.

"Vittoria, we're leaving," Alex said, turning to her. "Like I promised."

The woman looked up at him, her face awash in pallor. She tried to stand but let out a pained moan then sat back down, one hand holding her abdomen.

Alex hooked a hand under her shoulder and pulled her up.

She let out a scream of agony. "No, no, it hurts."

Another ball of fire rolled into the warehouse from one of the corridors, black smoke pouring out with it.

"We need to get you out of here," he said.

She leaned against him, one arm over his shoulder, and they hurried toward the loading dock. With each step they took, she whimpered in pain. She tripped, falling to the floor beside a pile of scree before they had even made it halfway to the door.

"Leave me!" she screamed.

"We're getting out of here," Alex said. "I promised."

He bent to scoop her up. Gunfire exploded from above. Rounds smashed against the floor and containers near him.

He looked up, training his handgun toward the catwalks, firing blindly in response.

Markov stood on one of the catwalks, his clothes singed. Smoke swirled around him.

Alex fired at the Russian, but the man was already running

to the catwalk's stairs. Before he could make it, more of the ceiling gave way. Smoldering debris dumped into the center of the warehouse, blocking the path between Alex and Markov.

He reached down again toward Vittoria, ready to carry her to safety. If Cruz caught up to that truck and got Williams, then they could be out of here in a matter of minutes. He'd get Vittoria to the medical assistance she needed.

He could still save her life.

But when he started to put his arms under her, Vittoria's head tilted limply over her shoulder.

Alex didn't have to check her pulse to verify what he could already see in her glassy eyes. She was gone.

If only he had been faster, then maybe they could have avoided this. They could have gotten the intel they came for and escaped sooner, leaving these people's lives intact.

This wasn't the first time he'd let someone die. That he'd failed.

He wanted to yell, to curse. To find Markov just so he could fill the man with lead again and again.

But he couldn't let his anger stop him. There would be time to mourn the dead later. Now he needed to focus on saving the living.

SKYLAR RAN ALONGSIDE THE PIER. Pain shuddered through her ribs with every step. Reis was trailing her. He seemed to have finally gotten the clue that she was trying to help. Or maybe it was just the promise that they were going after Williams.

The truck rumbled south toward where a couple of the larger shipping container vessels were docked. Already, the early morning dockworkers were gathering around the burning Mark-Logistik facility. Sirens screamed in the distance. The blue and red lights of police cars descended toward them from the east.

"Vector One, authorities are going to be here in five!" she said, nearly breathless.

"Copy," Wolfe called back. He sounded bad. Like he'd been smoking two packs a day for forty years straight. "I'm out of the warehouse."

"We're on foot, headed west toward some container ships."

The semitruck lumbered slowly through the pothole-pocked roadway along the pier, its lights glaring in the dark. Smaller sedans swerved out of its way.

"I'll grab our car," her partner said.

They had left their Audi south from the facility. Skylar would have run straight for it, but she didn't want to lose sight of the truck. But now, as her chest heaved, the pain in her ribs growing worse with every breath, she wished she would have taken the chance.

A handful of cars were parked beside one of the warehouses ahead. Workers filing into the building for an early morning shift. As she watched, a small, red car pulled into a nearby spot. The driver got out, yelling into a cellphone, gesturing wildly at the truck that had sped by.

"We need a ride," Skylar said, pointing to the car.

"You want… to steal it?" Reis asked.

"You want to save Williams? Then help me."

They ran toward the car. The dockworker was still staring at the truck, shouting into his phone. He didn't turn toward Skylar until she was just a couple of feet away from him.

"*Spasibo*," she said, yanking the keys from his hand, pushing the guy backward.

He took a step toward Skylar, angrily yelling, but a wave of her gun convinced him to stay put. She jumped into the driver's seat. Reis opened the door to the front passenger seat and pushed a few empty cigarette cartons off it.

The engine came to life with an unhealthy grinding sound. She threw the car into reverse, the vehicle squealing out into the road, then pushed the gearshift into first. They took off.

Ahead, the truck laid on its horn. It slammed straight into a car in front of it, grinding the vehicle sideways. Skylar did her best to dodge one of the unfortunate car's quarter panels tumbling over the asphalt.

But she couldn't avoid all of the debris. Something clanked against the underside of her sedan, followed by a long scraping sound.

She kept her foot pressed on the pedal. "You said Williams was in the trailer, right?"

"I think so," Reis said.

"You think or you know?"

"I'm pretty sure."

"How many others were in there?"

"Three or four," Reis said. "Maybe more. I really don't know. They put them in those caskets they used to bring us here."

"But they're not in the truck cab, right?"

He gave her a confused look. "I... I wouldn't think so."

She caught up to the truck and started to pull alongside in the opposing lane. Dim streetlights flashed by. Another car ran headlong toward them, forcing her to brake hard and swerve behind the truck again.

"Hang on," she said, accelerating alongside the truck again when the car passed.

She pushed the pedal to the floor. The weak four-cylinder engine probably wasn't strong enough to carry four adults going uphill, but the truck wasn't exactly a Formula One racecar either.

She managed to pull parallel with the cab.

"Duck and cover your ears!" she said to Reis.

He bent down, his head toward his knees. She leaned over

him with her handgun. The first shot shattered her passenger window. Safety glass crumbled away in crystalline pebbles.

The car hit a rivet in the road and jerked to the left. She regained control with one hand, fighting to prevent the vehicle from shooting off the side of the road. Aiming with one hand while driving a car that was falling apart wasn't easy. But she'd handled worse in her bird. Compared to piloting a helicopter through a war zone, this was a walk in the park.

The truck driver was still alive. He turned toward her then yanked hard on the wheel. The move forced Skylar to turn hard to avoid being crushed. The car already had two tires in the junkyard, and there was no way it would survive more than a glancing impact from the truck.

When the semi came closer, trying to smash into her again, she had to take the vehicle straight off the road, bouncing on the gravel and trash alongside it.

"Screw you!" she shouted.

She fired again. Bullets punched into the door of the truck. The semi suddenly jerked hard to the right.

A round must have hit the driver. Skylar whooped.

The truck was halfway off the road now. That gave Skylar enough room to get her car back onto the asphalt. She continued firing. Reis flinched with each shot. The truck swerved left then right.

Definitely hit him.

The truck recovered for a moment, straightening out even as it slowed, and then turned hard right. The trailer swung violently behind it, tilting, threating to topple entirely.

Skylar yanked on the handbrake. Her tires bit hard into the asphalt. The smell of burning rubber filled the vehicle.

Somehow, the dying driver managed to keep the semi and trailer upright and continued toward a freighter. Even from here, thanks to the lights on the dock, Skylar could see the crew crawling up the gangplank to the freighter as a crane lowered a container onto the deck.

Skylar pushed the beater to its limits.

"They're going to escape," Reis said. "You can't let them take Renee."

"They still have to load that container onto the ship," Skylar said. "We got time."

"I don't think so. Look." He was pointing at the gunwale of the ship.

The glow of the lights around the ship's superstructure revealed the silhouettes of gunmen lining the vessel. She saw the muzzle flash. Then she heard the chatter of automatic gunfire. Sparks exploded in front of the sedan, and she braked hard, swerving.

Rounds punched into the car's hood. Steam vented up from the wounds in the rusted metal. Reis scrunched into his seat, hands over his head.

Skylar spat out a curse. Driving straight down that dock was suicide.

She pulled a hard U-turn and tried to retreat down the dock. The engine chugged, letting out a belching gasp. The grinding from the drivetrain grew worse. Black smoke poured out from under the hood.

More gunfire rattled against the back of the car, and the rear window fell away in a shower of glass pebbles.

"Go, go, go!" Reis said. "What are you waiting for?"

"I'm trying," Skylar said.

The smoke pouring from under the hood grew worse. Skylar couldn't see where they were going, driving nearly blind back to the road.

Bullets peppered the vehicle, hitting more sporadically.

Almost there.

Then they slammed into something. She flew forward, ribs hitting hard against the car's wheel. No airbags in this piece of crap. Her chest erupted into blinding pain. She would have screamed if all the air hadn't been knocked from her lungs.

Reis crashed against the dashboard. His head hit with a loud smack. He leaned back, groaning and massaging his temple.

Skylar fought against the pain and turned to see behind them. Flashes of gunfire burst from the ship like miniature strikes of lightning.

Men rushed down from the gangplank with weapons brandished.

"What do we do now?" Reis asked.

"Run."

18

ALEX SAW the flare of gunfire from a freighter. That was where Cruz must be. His partner was a lightning rod for violence. The engine of the BMW 7 Series growled as he accelerated toward the pier, navigating past the trail of wreckage left behind from what he assumed was Cruz's handiwork.

He kept the headlights off to minimize his visibility, relying on the dim glow of the sporadic streetlights. It made driving riskier, but he didn't want to draw any undue attention. Already, the first police cars had made it to the Mark-Logistik warehouse, and the spectacular fire had drawn a considerable crowd as early-morning laborers abandoned their duties to observe the unfolding disaster.

With all the commotion, Alex had no doubt that the gunfire would draw the authorities in next. A few of the people he zipped past were pointing at the ship. He had no idea what in the hell these gunmen were going to tell the police. But he had a feeling the connections of whoever was running this bioweapons program ran deep within the local government.

That made it even more imperative that he and Cruz got out of there immediately.

"Vector One, you close?" she called, sounding strained.

"Almost there," Alex replied. "Running dark."

He took a hard right when he made it to the dock with the freighter. Two shapes hurtled toward him. Beyond them, a car burned. Black smoke rose from its crushed hood where it had hit a light pole. Nearly a dozen gunmen were firing from positions a few hundred yards away near the gangplank to the freighter.

He slammed on the brakes, twisting hard on the wheel so the car slid sideways before coming to a complete stop.

Cruz yanked the front passenger door open, jumping in. A man Alex assumed to be Reis spilled into the back seat. He took off again before either could shut the door, accelerating as he raced away from the docks.

"What about Renee?" Reis asked. "We can't leave her."

He started to open the back door.

Cruz turned in her seat and grabbed his wrist. "Don't."

"They're going to take her," Reis said. "I promised I would stay with her."

Alex looked in the rearview mirror. Reis's face was contorted in fear and desperation, his eyes wild with panic.

"You run back there by yourself, you'll die," Cruz said. "You won't be saving anyone."

"Then both of you go with me. You don't know what they'll do to her."

"I'm sorry, Dr. Reis," Alex said, turning the wheel to take a hard right. "We don't have the manpower. If we tried right now, they would slaughter us. Then there would be nothing we could do for Renee."

"We can't just abandon her," Reis said.

"We won't," Alex promised. "We'll get her back. But now we need to regroup."

He didn't slow until they reached A195 and took the highway. The early morning traffic had begun to pick up, and he slowed to blend in with the other cars and trucks.

As the first creeping oranges and pinks of the sunrise bled across the sky, he could still see the huge column of black smoke rise from Mark-Logistik.

"Command, Vector One," Alex spoke into his mic. "Leaving the city with target two. Target one is still MIA."

"Copy," Kasim called back. "Evac is ready and waiting."

Alex took them onto A229 east toward where an airplane would be waiting in Gvardeysk to take them away from this decrepit part of Russia.

"I think we're in the clear," Alex said. "Everybody okay?"

"Stupid question," Cruz said, holding her side.

"I mean, do we need to reroute our flight plan to a hospital somewhere friendlier than Russia?"

"No, I'll live," she said. "Just had a run-in with Markov. Bruised some ribs, I think."

He looked at Reis in the rearview mirror. "How about you?"

The man's face was covered in a mixture of ash and sweat between the bruises and healing cuts. His bottom lip trembled.

Instead of answering Alex's question, Reis had one of his own. "What's going on?"

"We were hoping you knew," Cruz said.

"I don't know a damn thing," Reis said. "That's what Renee and I told those people in that… that lab."

"You know why they took you there?" Alex asked.

"I couldn't say," Reis said, but there was something shifty about his expression. His eyes darted to the door handle again.

"What about that guy Markov?" Cruz asked. "He's from a group called Archon. What can you tell me about them?"

"I have no idea what Archon is, but Markov seemed to be in charge of the guards."

"That's it? He wasn't running the whole show?" Cruz asked.

"No, I don't think so," Reis said. "What about Renee? Are you going to call this in or something? Send in backup to save her?"

"If we're going to help her, we need to know what you know," Alex said. "Tell me about Markov."

Reis looked mutinous for a moment before answering, "He watched over us when they forced us to work in the labs, but someone else gave us orders."

"Who?" Alex asked.

"We never saw him. He just yelled at us through a speaker in the lab."

"You've got to know more than that," Cruz said. "Think."

"I don't know, okay?! They all spoke Russian. I probably know less than you. And I don't even know who *you* are!"

Alex met his gaze in the rearview mirror. "We help people, and we think those Russians in that warehouse have very different goals than us. That's all you need to know."

"You didn't help anyone," Reis said. "Of all the prisoners in that warehouse, you only managed to rescue me. You should have tried harder to get Renee."

In his mind's eye, Alex saw images of Vittoria and the other murdered prisoners. Reis was right about their failure. Vector had a long way to go toward rectifying the disaster Kaliningrad had become. "Look, Dr. Reis, things didn't go as planned. But if we're going to make things right, we need you to tell us everything that happened to you two, starting when they took you out of Lisbon."

"First tell me how you know who I am. How did you find us?"

Cruz growled. "Buddy, we aren't in the business of answering your questions. Clock's ticking. They're getting away with Williams. Speak fast."

"They raided our lab in Lisbon," Reis said in a rush. "After that, Renee and I tried to escape. They caught us, knocked us out, and I woke up inside a casket. Next thing I knew, they were carrying her and me into some kind of prison where they forced us to work with them."

"What did they make you do?" Alex asked.

Reis told them about his time in the lab. When Reis mentioned the EnviroProct device, Alex slammed his palm against the steering wheel. It was all coming together.

"Do you have any ties to EnviroProct?" Alex asked.

"No, I don't personally."

"Personally?"

"The professor Renee and I worked for is, or was, I think, a consultant for them."

Cruz shot Alex a knowing glance. This was news to them and Command.

"How well did he know the people at EnviroProct?" she asked.

Alex could tell she wanted to know if Reis or the professor knew Breners. But they had to hold their cards a little closer to their chests. They still weren't sure whether they could fully trust Reis.

"I don't know," Paulo said. "I really don't. There were only two times, I think, that someone from EnviroProct came to our lab for research. Dr. Estacio mentioned something to us about a nondisclosure agreement and said they were going to start a project that was supposed to be kept completely confidential."

"You didn't think that was odd?" Alex asked.

"Not really. We work with R&D companies pretty frequently. This one seemed to be about some high-tech stuff, so I wasn't surprised we were supposed to keep it quiet." He wiped at the ash covering his face. "How is this going to help you find Renee?"

"You're helping right now," Alex said. "What do you know about Estacio's plans with EnviroProct?"

"Not much," Reis said. "The times an EnviroProct representative came to our lab, all we did was present our own research to him. We didn't discuss their work."

"Who was this representative?"

"It was a guy named Philip or Francis, I think. He had a funny last name. Brewer, Bernard, maybe?"

"Felix Breners?" Cruz blurted out.

Alex winced. His partner might be good in a fight, but she had all the subtlety of a brick. Cruz wouldn't have lasted ten minutes at the Agency.

"Yes, that was it! How did you know?"

"Not important." Alex recalled that Morris hadn't come up with any ties between EnviroProct and Estacio. Was the researcher lying about this for some reason? "You mentioned an NDA. Did that ever get signed?"

"I don't think so," Reis said. "At least, I never signed anything, which I suppose makes sense because we never actually saw what EnviroProct was doing."

Alex wasn't a betting man, but he'd wager that Estacio had gone ahead with the project. Tenured professors were allowed to take on outside consulting gigs to pad out their salaries, as long as it didn't take up too much of their time. The poor bastard had probably thought working for EnviroProct was an easy way to earn a little extra cash.

Instead, he'd ended up with a bullet to the head. Estacio, the thirty dead students in Lisbon, Vittoria and the prisoners. This operation was already overshadowed by losses. And if Vector didn't figure what was going on—and fast—the list of casualties would only get longer.

Fort Detrick, Maryland

While Kasim downed coffee to keep him going, Weber had told him she didn't like anything that messed with her brain. No caffeine, nicotine, alcohol. Nothing.

At least, not usually. Her worst vice was the occasional bite from a dark chocolate bar—seventy percent cacao, nothing lighter. Nothing sweeter. She conveniently ignored the chocolate's caffeine content.

Instead of chemical stimulants, she relied on music. Her drug of choice was smooth jazz. And he knew from experience, a little Kenny G or Anita Baker meant she was hot and heavy in the world of science, her mind working on overdrive. Either she'd just gotten a break—or she'd hit a dead end.

He hoped, for their sake, it was the former. He'd been running into enough of his own dead ends.

"What's the situation?" he asked.

"Hello, sir," Weber said with a tired smile. "Park's still developing models to predict the function of the proteins translated from the genetic data to see if we can figure out what the engineered sequences do."

"Any luck?" Kasim asked.

"So far, it doesn't match anything we've seen before. This may be a totally new pathogen."

"That's insane," Kasim said. "Developing a brand-new pathogen could take years."

"Decades, even," Weber agreed.

"Someone's been working on this for a long time. We're not up against a bunch of amateurs."

"True enough. However they did it, the work paid off. These archaea aren't something we've got any analogue for."

Kasim felt like he was exploring a cave that just kept getting deeper and darker. Every time he thought they had a clue, a way out, it dropped straight down toward the bowels of the earth.

"You didn't call me down to talk about how impressive our enemies are," Kasim said. "Show me what you've got cooking."

She turned down the jazz and indicated her computer screen. "I've been monitoring our SARN systems carefully since we identified those Chinese officials Breners met with."

SARN was a joint program developed by a group of public health organizations, including the Centers for Disease Control, Canada's Public Health Agency, and the World Health Organization. USAMRIID had adapted syndromic surveillance tools from programs like the US's BioSense and Indonesia's Early Warning Outbreak Recognition system. SARN tracked symptoms and illnesses reported in clinical environments, allowing researchers like Weber to monitor potential pandemic situations and bioterrorism-related events.

"What do you see?" Kasim asked, settling into a chair beside her.

"There are a few different strains of colds and influenzas being reported in places like China, Saudi Arabia, and even some in our heartland. Pneumonia seemed particularly prevalent in China too."

"These are non-endemic?"

"Maybe. But still none of them are indicative of a potential outbreak."

Kasim leaned forward in his seat, examining the screen. "Something set off an alarm bell, though."

"This." Weber pulled up a folder full of de-identified medical records. "I've caught instances of gastrointestinal diseases in multiple clusters throughout western China, all occurring over the past twenty-four hours."

"What symptoms are we looking at?"

Weber scrolled through the medical records. "Complaints of stomach pain, diarrhea. Some vomiting."

"This isn't just an influenza?"

Weber clicked on her computer to show a few lab reports. "Initial tests from these first few clusters show negative on influenza. No known viruses. Most are being logged as potential food poisoning."

"Suspected but not confirmed."

"Right," Weber said. "No known cause from any clinical lab results so far."

"These are only twenty-four hours old." Kasim adjusted his reading glasses and scanned the reports on Weber's laptop. "Tests would still be out, right?"

"That's true. It could be a day or more before tests come back for things like stool symptoms."

Kasim leaned back in his seat. "If we're looking at GI symptoms, this could be a relatively normal *E. coli* outbreak. Maybe contaminated vegetables or meat from a packing plant."

"I would have come to the same conclusion if Breners hadn't given that archaea sample to us, and Skylar and Alex hadn't found those genetic sequences at the Kaliningrad facility."

"Coincidence isn't causation."

"I know, I know. We use science, not gut instinct, here. But there are no known diseases associated with archaea. Which means there aren't any standard clinical lab tests to detect archaea, either. The doctors in China wouldn't even consider it, so they would have no chance of treating it."

"Frightening to think about." Kasim paused. The ramifications of an untraceable disease sweeping through people like a reaper's scythe were chilling. For their sake, he prayed Weber was wrong. But he knew better. "How many cases have you identified?"

This time Weber opened a map of China. Red circles showed over several cities in the west.

"I found a little over three hundred spread throughout Xinjiang, Tibet, and Qinghai," she said. "I'm still doing some digging to track the spread. I want to know if this is airborne or point-of-contact or something else. Really, I just need the Chinese to collect more patient contact tracing data."

"And that all assumes it isn't just food poisoning."

"Which we should find out if China does its job on the contact tracing."

"You're relying on a notoriously cagey government to report data. We've been down this road before," Kasim said. "Not likely to be helpful."

Weber's perpetually sunny expression turned grave. "I know, sir. But what else can we do?"

Kasim let the thoughts percolate through his mind. If this *was* the archaea, if they'd already lost the game to their mysterious opponents, then he was out of options. "Just to play devil's advocate, give me your best reason why this isn't food poisoning."

"We know archaea occur naturally in human beings, and most of them are in the gut biome," Weber said. "Breners's archaea is derived from a gut-borne archaeon, so it seems simple enough to me that a disease caused by this bioweapon would originate in the GI tract."

"That's still all conjecture." Kasim tapped his knuckles on the desk. "I want something solid. Make sure you rule out all other potential causes, natural or otherwise, before we pin this on our suspect archaea. I can get Commander Liang to start allocating more resources our way if we've got more substantial evidence to prove this is the result of a bioweapon."

Weber nodded. "You got it. I have a feeling we'll need all the help we can get, if this is as bad as I think it is."

"And I have a feeling you're right. Any chance China would come to this same conclusion?"

"Unlikely. They never got the sample, so they don't know what to look for."

"Fair point. That seems to be why Breners was bringing it to the Chinese. Maybe Shing and Qi knew more about the archaea than we did, though. Maybe they were already in the middle of warning the CCP when all this went down."

Weber frowned. "And then whoever is responsible for the archaea sent a hit squad to stop them from acting on that intel."

"Are you seeing these symptoms anywhere other than China right now?" Kasim asked.

"Not yet."

"See if you can track its spread back to any Chinese biowarfare-related assets. While circumstantial evidence points to the Russians being involved, there are too many unknown layers here to rule out Chinese participation in this project. Those symptoms could very well be caused by a leak from a biomanufacturing plant."

"Wouldn't be the first time a bioweapon was accidentally spread in a local community," Weber said.

"Ask any of those old Biopreparat Soviet scientists. They had to cover up more than one disaster. Do you have any other leads I can track down to confirm your theory?"

Weber closed her laptop. "Unless Park comes up with something from the lab or we get a breakthrough on the epidemiological front, I don't have anything else."

"Cruz and Wolfe have custody of one of the researchers from Lisbon. Right now, it looks like Reis and Williams were asked to do some work on prototype EnviroProct pathogen detection systems. Something about searching for invulnerabilities, figuring out how a microorganism like a bacterium might evade the sensors."

"Interesting," Weber said thoughtfully. "I want to talk to him."

Kasim balked. She wasn't trained for interrogations or interviews like this. "Out of the question. We don't know if he's a trusted asset."

"Alex and Skylar are smart. But they aren't scientists. I need to talk to him." She jabbed her finger on the table as if to emphasize the point.

"Reis is a foreign national. We're supposed to be flying under the radar in the US. I can't just put you on the phone with a guy that, for all we know, could very well be a double agent."

"This is a scientific mission. You want scientific solutions, you need people who can understand science."

Kasim folded up his reading glasses and slipped them into his pocket. "You tell me what you want to know from Reis, and I'll send those questions to Cruz and Wolfe."

"I want a conversation."

"Weber. Come on."

She stared him down for a few seconds. She clearly didn't want to give up on this point. Kasim trusted her, but he simply couldn't afford to let the doctor make any kind of security misstep. Not with a potential bioweapon and millions of lives on the line.

Finally, she backed down with a sigh. "You win, sir. I'll prepare a list of questions, stuff I want to know. But if you want that guy to start talking science—I mean real science—at least let me listen in."

"That we can do," Kasim said.

Weber cranked the volume on her stereo again, the mournful sound of a lonely saxophone following Kasim out into the hallway.

19

Tallinn, Estonia

Skylar stared out the bedroom window of their suite at the Nordic Hotel Viru toward Tallinn's famous walls. The gray stone looked like it would be right at home around a medieval castle. A few spires from churches and towers inside those walls gave the place a picturesque skyline over the busy shops and restaurants below.

The fairytale charm of the city brought more than enough tourists from around the world to ensure Skylar, Wolfe, and Reis could blend in. A change of clean clothes and a little makeup on their injuries helped too.

Initially, Skylar had thought they might return to the States. But Kasim wasn't interested in immediately bringing Reis to American soil. They needed to keep him in the dark as they tried to understand his role in the unraveling conspiracy.

Not to mention being in Estonia had its benefits. It kept them close to Russia and Kaliningrad in case they needed to execute another infil op.

Flexibility was key, especially when they still hadn't located where that ship with Williams was headed.

She hoped they would get a call soon. Skylar was more than ready to get the hell out of this hotel.

The suite was luxurious enough. But who needed luxury? She had slept everywhere from under the trees during a rainy Washington spring for her Survival, Evasion, Resistance, and Escape training to the stuffy and cramped plywood B huts through deployment in Afghanistan.

She could survive perfectly well without the million-thread-count sheets and gold-plated faucets next to the shitter. Indulgences like that damn near disgusted her. Here she was in this hotel room, ordering room service, when she had just witnessed the deaths of prisoners forced to work for the madmen who might be responsible for the creation of a new bioweapon. Still more people were imprisoned by Markov and those Russian fiends. And if she and Wolfe didn't figure out what was going on, they might be looking at the deaths of hundreds, thousands, maybe millions more.

Her mission wasn't nearly finished. And sitting in this hotel wasn't getting them any closer.

"Seriously, Skylar, you got to eat," Wolfe said, joining her by the window.

She looked over her shoulder at the plate of food she'd left untouched.

"Can't," she said. "Not right now. How can you? You saw the same disaster I did."

Her stomach growled, telling her that she was wrong. But the guilt gnawing at the back of her mind wouldn't let her take another bite. It wasn't just the lives that had been lost. Kaliningrad, in her opinion, had been a devastating failure.

"I eat because I have to," Wolfe said. "We aren't helping anyone if we don't take care of ourselves."

"We're not doing a great job taking care of anyone," she said.

"Kaliningrad wasn't a total failure. We have Reis. The Detrick team has a trove of new data. I call that a partial win."

Even as he said it, she could see the doubt in his eyes. He flicked his gaze away, staring out the window instead of meeting her gaze.

"A partial win? You know as well as I do that doesn't count for much," she said. "Might as well break out the participation trophies for the Little League's worst team and tell 'em 'job well done.'"

"If you want a win, how about trying to get Reis to talk? I can barely get him to open his mouth."

"You tried the good cop routine with him," Skylar said. "What makes you think I can do any better?"

Wolfe pursed his lips like he didn't enjoy what he was about to say. "The guy is traumatized. He's dealing with shock, loss."

"That doesn't answer my question, partner."

Wolfe glanced down at her prosthetic. "He needs to hear from someone else who knows pain."

Skylar narrowed her eyes at him. "I've seen that look in your eyes too. You're like the guys I served with after half the squad got blown to shit from an IED. I'm sure you've got your own stories."

"I do. But they aren't what's needed at the moment. They aren't right for Reis."

"Are they right for me?" she pressed him.

"This isn't about me or you." He gestured to the sitting room. "It's about that man out there. The scientist who might have the one clue we need to move forward."

Skylar wanted to argue more or to get Wolfe to open up. Her partner was paranoid about his secrets. Must be a CIA thing. But he was right about this. Only one way through this mission. She followed Wolfe to the sitting room. Reis sat in a chair staring out the window.

Dark circles drooped under his eyes between the bruises and cuts. Alex had treated his wounds with antiseptics and bandaged his injuries. The researcher had been lucky nothing seemed serious enough to warrant a hospital trip.

Skylar wasn't foolish enough to believe that meant Reis would walk away from this ordeal without any scars. The deepest ones would be on his mind. Never again would the researcher feel safe, even in the comfort of his own home. He had learned what it was to have everything stolen away from him in an instant.

No matter what he did, life would never return to the normal he'd known before the attack in Lisbon.

She looked down at her prosthetic foot poking out from her jeans. *Damn it, Alex.* He was right.

"How are you doing?" she asked as she pulled up a chair next to him.

"Are you really letting me have an opinion on that?" he asked. "Or are you going to tell me I can't have my own feelings either? I can't contact my family. I can't contact my university, my friends. I can't go after Renee. And I can't get any of *my* questions answered."

"Look, I get what you're going through," Skylar said.

"Doubt it."

"You have no idea."

He glared at her, anger simmering in his eyes. "Tell me, then."

Skylar looked over at Wolfe. He shook his head.

She pulled up her pant leg, revealing more of the prosthetic. Reis's eyes widened. "The details are classified. You're just going to have to take my word for it that I didn't lose this to a hungry tiger. Things aren't always what they seem."

"You lost a leg. I'm sorry. I still want to know what we're doing in here instead of searching for Renee."

Skylar sighed. So much for trying to be soft and gentle with this guy. For making a personal connection. That might be Wolfe's way of doing things, but that was not how she'd been trained. "Okay, look… Dr. Reis? Paulo?"

"Call me whatever you want. My name doesn't matter. You can take that from me too. I just want to know where Renee is."

"And so do we," Skylar said. "That's why we need you to talk. Ever since we got here, you haven't been helping us with that."

He sat there silently, brooding, as if to prove her point.

"See? This isn't very helpful, Paulo. We're in a bit of a time crunch. Talk."

"Or what? You'll beat me like they did? Waterboard me? Threaten my family too?"

Skylar almost wanted to tell him 'yes' just to get his lips moving. But the threat was utterly empty. She and Wolfe weren't like those people. "No. You've just got to trust us."

"You haven't shown me a good reason to trust you. I shouldn't have told you anything to begin with, but I was in shock, okay? How do I know you're not just using me to kidnap Renee, like those other people did?" He crossed his arms over his chest. "Excuse me if I'm not in the mood to trust today. Especially killers like you."

"Killers? We saved your ass."

"And everyone else in that place died. I saw you in there. It wasn't your first time turning a gun on someone."

Skylar felt the hot grip of frustration curl around her insides. She wanted to slap Reis, but she held herself back. Her anger wasn't at him. It was at herself. Because Reis was right.

"You know what?" she asked. "You're not wrong. Things didn't go how we'd hoped. But we're trying to make that right.

To do that, we need to understand what you were working on in Kaliningrad and in Lisbon. Maybe there's a link. Something we're missing that will help us figure out where Williams is and what those Russians wanted with you two."

"You want me to talk?" he asked. "Tell me why you all are doing this. You're acting like it's just to save Renee and me, but there's more to it than that. Much more than you're letting on. I understand you two are like secret agents or something. American, based on your accents, but what do I know? Maybe there's an underground world filled with assholes kidnapping scientists and selling them to work in their secret labs."

Reis shook his head, brushing a hand through his long hair. It was matted down and oily.

"I go from one kidnapper to another," he said. "Give me some proof you're on my side. Tell me who you're working for."

"We can't do that," Alex said.

"Come on."

"That's not negotiable."

"Then I'm not helping," Reis said. "I need some assurance that you aren't going to turn around and kill me just to tie up loose ends. Without that, why should I talk?"

Maybe this guy thought he was doing the right thing, but it sure as hell seemed like he was acting like a petulant child. Talking nice wasn't going to work. He needed to see that they weren't screwing around.

Skylar tore her knife from the hideaway sheath around her prosthetic. The blade hummed from the quick motion, a mere millimeter from Reis's neck.

The color drained from his face.

"Cruz!" Wolfe shouted.

She ignored him. "Do you see how easy that was for me?"

Reis's eyes were wide, genuinely frightened.

She sheathed the knife. "If we wanted to hurt you, you

would've known by now." She paused to inhale deeply, calming herself. "Look, we're protecting you by not telling you who we are. If those people in Kaliningrad find out you know, you're going to be in worse trouble. Williams is going to be in worse trouble. The less you know, the better off you are."

Reis trembled, the defiant expression gone from his face. She saw only a scared man, worried for his future and about the woman he obviously cared for as more than just a lab buddy.

"I just want to know that Renee is going to be okay," he said at last. "And when we're no longer useful to you, I don't want either of us to end up dead on the floor of a warehouse in a foreign country."

Skylar looked at Wolfe. Maybe his way of dealing with people wasn't such a terrible idea after all. She decided to try a little gambit.

"He's right," she said. "We've got to give him something."

Reis perked up at that, surprise on his face.

"You know that the more we tell him, the more he's worth to the enemy," Alex said. "And we can't do this without authorization."

"I don't care," Reis said. "They want to kill me, they can. If I'm going to die anyway, I just want to know I'm actually helping Renee."

"Maybe we should call home," Skylar said.

Reis was frightened out of his mind. Locked up tighter than a bank vault. Completely out of his element, trapped with two people in a foreign country speaking a foreign language, even if he was fluent in it.

Maybe there was a way to warm him up. To speak in his own language.

Not Portuguese but close enough.

FREDERICK, MD

KASIM WALKED side by side with Weber to Vector's operations center, going over the rules for the call one more time.

"Okay, you know what you can and can't say," he said.

"I can say that I was right, and you all needed me to talk to Reis after all," the epidemiologist replied.

He didn't like being wrong, but he wasn't too big of a man to admit when he was. That might be the one reason Divya was willing to overlook his marriage to his work.

"Yes, you can say all you want about that after we're done with Reis," Kasim said. "But if you have any questions about whether you're cleared to say something on the call, wait for me to give you approval."

"Yes, yes, you got it."

Kasim knew the scientist was smart. One of the best epidemiologists in the country, if not the world. And while she was trusted with some of the most valuable secrets in biodefense, her role meant that she rarely came face-to-face with individuals outside her security clearance level. Weber was no field operative. Maybe this was a bad idea.

They settled down at the conference table in the operations center. Morris was waiting for them and handed them each a headset.

"You're on an encrypted line," he said. "I'll be monitoring for any interference or sign that anyone is trying to listen in. But your best bet is to keep this brief and to the point."

Weber nodded, fitting the headset over her ears.

Kasim did likewise, fighting down his misgivings.

Halfway around the world, Alex had lent Paulo Reis his earpiece and mic, setting up the other end of their connection.

"All right, channel is ready and locked down," Morris said.

"Dr. Reis, can you hear me?" Weber asked.

"Yes," a voice replied with a slight Portuguese accent.

"I've reviewed a few of your papers with Dr. Estacio. Your background in environmental microbiology is pretty impressive."

"Okay. Glad to know you can use Google and read."

Weber arched her eyebrows at Kasim. He could tell what she was thinking. This guy wasn't going to be easy.

"I'm sorry we have to meet this way, and I wish I could tell you my name," she said. "I'm a scientist too. I really enjoy digging into new fields, discovering all the things I don't know. That's the thing about a PhD, huh?"

"What's that?" Reis didn't sound amused.

"You specialize in one small part of this big world. The more you learn about it, the more you realize how little you— or anyone else—actually knows."

"That's true. I can tell you there's a lot I learned recently I wish I never found out."

Weber let out a soft laugh.

"I can imagine," she said. Her German accent seemed more pronounced. Kasim couldn't help wondering if that was playing the fellow European card to help soften Reis up. "It's much nicer to believe everyone on this planet lives in peace and gets their happily ever after. Quite startling to realize things are much darker than we imagined."

"Not really interested in talking about good and evil."

"Fair enough," Weber said. "Neither am I. I want to talk about science. There's nothing inherently good or evil about science, which is what I like about it. So let's talk about your research."

"Can you tell me why?"

Weber looked up at Kasim. He nodded. They had anticipated this question and ultimately decided they would hold no punches. They needed a lead, and Reis might be the key to moving this investigation forward.

"We're investigating the potential development of a new bioweapon."

She paused. Kasim hoped that that was sinking into Reis's brain.

"We're trying to stop it," Weber said. "I've been authorized to share some of the details with you. But we need your help."

"You're asking for my scientific advice?"

"If you're willing to provide it," Weber said. "We can't crack this without you."

She had claimed that the allure of a scientific problem would be too much for the talented scientist to pass up. Either he would want to prove he was intelligent enough to warrant the PhD following his name or the innate curiosity that had driven his career would be too much for him to resist.

"We uncovered a possible connection between EnviroProct and the people who kidnapped you," Weber said. "This connection consists of a single lab sample."

"Sample? Of what?"

Weber smiled at Kasim. He couldn't help smiling back. She really had been right after all.

"Usually, we expect biological weapons to come in the form of infectious agents, chemicals, or toxins we're already familiar with," she said. "The sample we obtained is unlike anything we've ever seen."

"Well, what is it?" Reis asked.

"We believe EnviroProct discovered this specimen in a test of their Aerokeep devices."

"Yes, but what is the sample?" Reis asked. "If it's not a known pathogen…"

Kasim could hear the desperation in his voice, the desire to understand exactly what the problem was. Weber was toying with him, drawing out the suspense. The young scientist must feel like everything in his life was in a tailspin, and now the only thing he had control over was finding a solution to this single intellectual problem slowly being laid out in front of him.

"The sample contained a microorganism which has no direct link to any disease known to man," Weber continued. "It was—"

"Archaea," Reis finished before she could.

Kasim blinked at how quickly the guy got it. Either he was very smart—or else he was in on the plot.

"Yes, that's exactly right," Weber said. "What do you know about archaea?"

"It's one of the specimens we catalogue."

"Who catalogs them?"

"My specialty—and Renee's, for that matter—is aerobiology," Reis said. "We investigate airborne seeds, pollen, spore, and microorganisms. We study how those things effect biodiversity as they travel on wind currents across the world. You'd be surprised how airborne bacteria carried away by a storm in Africa, for instance, might affect crop growth somewhere in Europe."

Weber was jotting down notes on a pad of paper. "And these studies involve archaea?"

"That's right. We only recently began investigating them."

"Did you ever suspect they might be infectious agents?"

Reis paused before answering. "No, but our lab wasn't interested in pathogens."

"Others in your field are, though."

"Yes, of course."

Weber was silent for a moment. Once again, she was drawing out the tension.

"Very, very few people in the world know what I'm about to tell you next," she said in an almost conspiratorial whisper. "I'm trusting you with intel that you absolutely cannot tell anyone else. The consequences could be devastating. Do you understand?"

Reis said nothing for a few seconds.

Kasim couldn't help but think of Commander Liang. If she knew what they had already revealed to an unvetted foreign national like this, she would probably ax the whole organization. But at this point, they were desperate. And the deeper Weber delved into Reis's knowledge of aerobiology and archaea, the more he realized they might need this researcher's help after all.

Whether he liked it or not, Reis was crucial to their mission.

"Yes, I understand," Reis finally said. "I will tell no one."

"We believe that the bioweapon I mentioned earlier consists of weaponized archaea," Weber said.

"Weaponized archaea?" Paulo asked, his voice cracking. "That is ridiculous. Archaea aren't infectious or dangerous."

"And as ridiculous as it sounds, I have reason to think it's true."

"Why would someone do this?" Reis asked. "How?"

"We're not sure," she said. She dropped her voice again. "The reason I'm telling you this is because we think this weapon was already deployed."

"You cannot be serious."

"There are already hundreds, if not more, cases."

"It's not a known infectious agent," Reis said, repeating exactly what Weber had told Kasim before. "We don't have vaccines or cures for archaea. None of this makes sense."

"You're exactly right," she said. "We're just as confused, but we're finding more and more evidence that these theories are far more than just idle conjecture."

The truth was that they had precious little proof, but Kasim didn't object to Weber's slight embellishments if it got the point across to Reis. "So maybe you can now see why it's so important for us to understand why these people kidnapped you and Dr. Williams. And maybe if we figure that out, we can figure out how to stop them."

There was a long pause. Kasim drummed his fingers over the tabletop.

"I'm not sure if this is helpful," Reis started. "But the last paper Renee wrote was about archaea."

"Go on."

"She identified a new strain, maybe even a new species. Something we'd never seen before, at least, right off the coast of Portugal. The paper was under peer review. We didn't realize it when it was submitted, but Dr. Estacio had taken credit as first author instead of her."

"Do you, by chance, have any data from that study?" Weber asked.

"I do not have anything on me," Reis said. "And I watched our lab go up in flames."

"Surely you kept something in the cloud or on your personal computer."

"Estacio was very careful to keep sensitive data like this locked down so someone else did not steal our discovery."

Weber must've felt the same sense of loss Kasim did, judging by the look on her face.

"There's nothing, then?" she asked.

Kasim stroked his beard as he waited for Reis's reply. He hoped this was not another road to nowhere.

"I might have an early draft of that paper in my university email account," Reis said. "It's possible you may find something useful there."

"I think you might be right," Weber said.

"If you really think this is going to help stop this bioweapon, I can share it," Reis said. "You know, if you had told me right away what this was about, I would have helped you all sooner."

Weber shot Kasim a knowing grin. "We appreciate your

cooperation. You must understand why we couldn't be so forth-coming before. My friends will help set you up to send us that data. Thank you, Dr. Reis."

There was some noise at the other end of the line as Cruz and Wolfe prepared a computer for him. A few minutes later, Morris gave them a thumbs-up to confirm he had received an encrypted email with the information Weber had requested.

"Let's see what they found," Weber said. Kasim followed her back to the lab.

It didn't take long for her to run a comparative analysis of the genomic data they had obtained from Breners's sample against the one that Williams and Reis were trying to get published.

"It's a one hundred percent match," she said.

"So the archaea Williams and Reis found months ago was the same as the sample Breners was trying to give to the Chinese," Kasim said. "What do you think that means, scientifically?"

"I don't think the archaea is naturally occurring. Other-wise, Williams wouldn't have been the first to report on it," Weber said. "If I were to guess, it was part of a test."

"Explain."

"If you're going to spend years and millions of dollars developing weaponized archaea, you won't want to simply release it when it's done and just hope that it spreads throughout your target environment. You probably want to make sure the delivery method works."

"You're saying it was a dry run. Out in the middle of the ocean or wherever Williams found it."

"That's what I think," Weber said.

Kasim was beginning to think this crazy idea might actu-ally hold merit. "It wouldn't hurt anything that way, but it would give whoever was in charge a chance to track environ-mental spread."

"Exactly."

"Strange to find it in the ocean. But it looks like they got it to spread fairly wide, especially if they were tracking down Williams, Reis, and Breners to prevent news of it coming out. Plus, the attack on Lisbon gave them two scientists that could help them subvert the Aerokeep systems."

Weber continued to write on her notepad. "If I'm right about this GI disease in China, then we know they're done with those tests. They've already moved onto deployment."

"I'm afraid you're right," Kasim said. "Question is: How are they deploying it?"

"Jury's still out on that," Weber said. "But I think I might have met someone who might be able to help, if you're willing to bring him into our fold."

"You're not saying…"

Weber put down her pen and nodded. "This is Reis's specialty. I want to know more, ask him more questions, and show him the epidemiological data, but I can't do that without your authorization."

Kasim sighed, trying to figure out how he'd sell this to Liang.

20

UNKNOWN LOCATION

RENEE WOKE UP TO BLACKNESS. Her head pounded like she'd run a marathon then rehydrated with vodka instead of water. She heard the rumble of engines, felt vibrations shaking through her body. When she tried to move her wrists, something plastic held them into place.

"Is anyone out there?" she tried.

Sweat trickled over her skin, soaking her clothes. The stench of her own body odor filled her nose. She blinked, hoping her eyes would adjust and the world would suddenly come into focus.

But no matter what she did, her eyes weren't the problem.

Her memories swam back, the last moments before she had been knocked out by an injection from one of those Russians. She could still see Paulo, yelling her name, held back by one of their guards.

While she was struggling to stay awake inside that casket, her mind fighting against the sedatives, the crack of gunfire had exploded. Then came the explosions. Screams. Curses. More gunfire.

She felt her insides constricting and choked down the sick feeling churning in her gut.

Was Paulo dead?

No, she didn't want to believe it. There were still too many things they'd promised they would do when they escaped. Too many places to go. Too much lost time to make up.

She needed to tell him that they shouldn't be scared of a relationship any longer. That even if their jobs sent them halfway around the world away from each other, they had to try. Because after all they'd gone through together, all they had seen, they owed that to themselves.

But now, she was alone.

Renee's thoughts drifted from Paulo to her family. Had they heard the news from Portugal? Had they tried contacting her only to find she was missing? Or did they think she was dead too?

God, she would give anything for just one phone call. One call to let them know she was still alive, and so long as she was still alive, there was hope.

Another bump jolted her against the restraints holding her limbs down. Her forehead smacked the lid of the casket. The collision sent a strike of pain through her sore body.

She wasn't sure how long she'd been sedated. All she knew was that exhaustion seeped through every aching bone. She wanted to close her eyes, to fall asleep and wake up somewhere else. Somewhere she wasn't enslaved by a demented criminal group forcing her to use her scientific knowledge for what she could only imagine was a truly malicious purpose.

The longer she listened to the gurgle of engines, the hotter it grew in the casket.

She tried counting each passing second. When she made it

past twenty minutes, even keeping track of time became too laborious.

The dry heat filled her casket. Her skull felt as though a gorilla was squeezing it. Her tongue stuck to the roof of her mouth and she struggled to swallow.

A voice in the back of her mind told her she was suffering from heat exhaustion. Maybe even a heat stroke, if things didn't change.

Why had these people taken her away from that strange warehouse facility only to let her die in this casket?

"Please, please, let me out," she said.

Her words came out in a pained whisper.

Then, at last, the engine stopped. Voices filtered in.

Next came the clunk of locks disengaging and the groan of metal shipping container doors. Her casket was lifted. It bobbed as she heard the sound of footsteps on metal. Then those footsteps sounded more like grinding or swishing instead of plodding boots meeting concrete. It was a familiar sound but one she couldn't quite place. The casket became even hotter, unbearable now. It felt as though the sun was cooking her alive inside this metal box.

The footsteps carried on, voices murmuring.

That was when she realized why those footsteps sounded so strange, yet so familiar.

It was the squishing, scratching sound of feet in the sand. Her mind was moving more slowly, lethargically. She could barely recall the memory of her and Paulo at Nazare, the seaside Portuguese town famous for its occasional world-record, hundred-foot-tall waves.

Two weekends ago, they'd been enjoying the *vino verde* at a lazy beachside bar, snacking on freshly caught seafood. Their only concerns were writing papers and getting them published. Competing for the next grant to continue their work.

That all seemed unimportant now.

Like giant waves crashing over a sandcastle, their kidnapping had washed away all worries of that seemingly safe existence in one instant.

Her only concern now was surviving the next few minutes.

Then the people carrying the casket lowered her. The lid opened.

Blinding sunlight tore into her retinas. She clenched her eyelids closed, but even that didn't stop the heat of the intense UV radiation scratching at her cells. Hot air sweltered over her body. She felt as if every droplet of water in her was evaporating through her skin at once.

"Release her," a voice said in English, accented in Russian.

Strangely familiar.

She heard the click of the restraints being released. Hands wrapped around her arms. They yanked her up and out of the casket. Someone set her roughly into the sand.

The hands let go. She collapsed, her legs numb, too weak to hold her upright. The hot sand embraced her. A scorching wind rasped at her skin.

"Water," she said.

Someone shoved a cold bottle of water in her hand, and she sipped greedily.

"Slow down," the familiar voice said again.

As her vision cleared, she saw a man crouched in front of her.

"You will make yourself sick drinking that quickly."

She lowered the bottle of water then used one hand to shield her eyes. The man in front of her wore a sweat-soaked collared shirt. His skin was pale, head shaved clean. He didn't look as if he had spent much time out in this unrelenting sun. Despite his size, the sallowness under his eyes made him look as if he'd been deathly ill long ago. Like maybe he still carried the scars of that sickness with him.

"Do you know where you are?" he asked.

She definitely recognized his voice, but her mind was still foggy. She took another sip of water, looking around. It seemed important to answer the man's question. Like this was a test— or that the answer to the question held some important meaning.

Beside her was the truck that had transported her here. Six men were unloading a second casket. Another six carried a third casket toward a large white building surrounded by golden sand. Strange tubular metal arms protruded from the building into another warehouse just a dozen yards away. Those arms stretched hundreds of yards from the warehouse like the arms of an octopus. They looked like a massive version of the machines she'd seen used to water crops on a farm.

Beneath some of those arms, patches of green grass grew. The ground there was darker, almost like it was soil instead of sand.

But beyond this little oasis, the world was desolate. Vast dunes rippled over the landscape, punctuated by huge red rocks.

"Desert," she managed, her voice hoarse. "Which one?"

"Does that really matter?" the man asked.

Finally, she recognized the voice. The derisive, demanding tone. "You were the one watching in this lab. The overseer. Paulo… where is Paulo?"

"He's gone," the man said.

"Gone?" Renee felt her knees go weak. She wanted to scream but couldn't muster the energy.

"Don't worry," the man said. "He's not dead. At least, I don't think so. Not yet."

He held out a hand to help her up. She didn't take it, trying to push herself up instead, her limbs trembling. But her body was too weak from the mixture of sedatives and heat exhaustion. She nearly collapsed before the man picked her up from under her shoulders, helping her to hobble forward.

"Dr. Williams, I am Dr. Pavlenko," the man said. "I'm a scientist, like you. But I specialize in a very different field, and that's why I need your help."

He guided her toward the white building, following the men lugging caskets.

Her mind was still moving slowly. Why wasn't she blindfolded? Why was he letting her see all of this? None of it made sense. Surely a man committing the crimes that Pavlenko was wouldn't want her to have any of this information.

"Why tell me this?" she asked.

"You're a very intelligent person, Dr. Williams," Pavlenko said. "I'm sure you can figure it out."

When the answer hit her, she stumbled again. Pavlenko kept her upright.

"You aren't letting me leave…"

"As I said, you're very intelligent. The world thinks you're dead, and you have nowhere else to go. Even if you ran, the Sahara is a hungry beast. She devours her meals quickly."

TALLINN, Estonia

ALEX WALKED along the medieval walls surrounding Tallinn's old town. He wore a pair of sunglasses, slim-fit jeans, and a black T-shirt that helped him blend in with the European tourists. Tables spilled out of cafes filled with people laughing and drinking. Canopied stalls sold souvenirs and cheap trinkets emblazoned with the iconic Viru Gate with its pointed red roofs topping the stone towers flanking the historic town center's entrance.

For the second time that day, he performed a routine security check. He didn't think anyone had followed them from Kaliningrad, but he would take no chances.

Staying in the hotel room without some kind of external surveillance routine was a good way to get unexpectedly cornered. And Alex had quickly learned that those Russians had a bad habit of reacting to dangerous situations with sudden and overwhelming force. Even Skylar's brutal warrior mentality might not be enough to protect them next time.

His phone rang, and he fished it out. The caller ID showed it was an unknown number. Likely encrypted, just like his own device.

"Yes," he answered.

"We're on a clean line." It was Kasim.

"What's the word?"

"Morris found something. Look, you and Skylar need to get yourselves to the airport. We've got a private flight scheduled in two hours."

"Where to?"

"Vietnam."

Alex had suspected somewhere in Europe, Russia, or even China. But he hadn't expected Southeast Asia. That brought back memories from his time in the Agency. Not all of them good.

"Why Vietnam?" he asked as he started walking back toward the hotel, keeping his eyes out for anyone following him or surveilling the hotel entrance.

"Morris uncovered an old Biopreparat program run by a man named Pavel Khovansky," Kasim said. "Successful scientist, rubbed elbows with all the right people in the USSR. But his project failed, and when the Iron Curtain came tumbling down, so did he. The guy pretty much vanished."

"Is he somehow associated with the archaea we found or Markov?"

"No, not that I can see. This guy died about a decade ago."

"I'm not in the business of chasing ghosts," Alex said.

"Right now, ghosts are all we got. Morris hasn't gotten any hits on that freighter in Kaliningrad."

"No surprise. We blew their cover. They probably changed their designation and are flying new flags."

"That's our guess," Kasim replied. "If anyone can find out where these people went, Morris can. I know he's young, but you need to trust him, Wolfe."

"I still want to know why they had that farm equipment." Alex watched a man and woman enter a restaurant. He thought he heard them speaking Russian, but they didn't give him a second glance.

"Our best guess is that it was used as a cover for their shipping logistics."

"Were they shipping anything to Vietnam?"

"Not that we know of," Kasim said. "We found some Biopreparat records from when the First Deputy Director of Biopreparat, Ken Alibek, defected in 1992. That included Khovansky's research on a project called Operation Groundswell. The project was active throughout the late eighties up until around 1990. There wasn't much on the project, but what we did uncover describes a bioweapon that causes symptoms very similar to the ones Weber is monitoring in China."

"Were they working with archaea back then too?"

"Possibly."

Alex paused, looking up and down a street filled with cars. He spoke in a lower voice. "You're sending us out to Vietnam when our enemies are probably still somewhere around Europe. I need more than a 'possibly.'"

"This is our best lead," Kasim said, his voice flat. Daring Alex to keep pushing against his orders.

"The Archaea domain wasn't even recognized until 1977." Alex walked past a small gelato shop with a line out the door.

"That's true, but early on, people really only classified the extremophiles as archaea. Not much was known about archaea like gut biome methanogens. The *M. smithii* that the Breners and Kaliningrad samples seem to be based on wasn't even sequenced until 2011. But the Groundswell records provide data on, I quote, a 'strange bacteria.' That, plus the symptoms are enough to draw some suspicion, wouldn't you agree?"

"I see where you're coming from," Alex said. He passed the entrance of the hotel. He would do one more loop, just to ease his own mind. "But I don't yet see the Vietnam connection."

"Groundswell was operating a chemical fertilizer manufacturing plant in the Ninh Binh province. I think they were using the location as a cover so they could blame it on the Vietnamese if things went awry."

Alex turned down another street, watching a pair of taxis pass. He was starting to see why the plant had caught Vector's attention, but his instinct was still to continue searching in Europe. If they were wrong—if the real threat was here—then they'd be too far away to do anything about it.

"Weber and Park said there are no known diseases caused by archaea, hence there are no cures for it. If this thing is already loose and spreading in China like Weber thinks, then there's nothing we can do to fight it," Kasim said.

"I don't like the sound of that."

"Thing is, in Ninh Binh, that Groundswell bioweapon they were manufacturing… rumors suggest it got loose. I don't know how. Water, air, maybe they were doing direct injection testing in the local populace."

The thought of that stoked a fire in Alex's chest. He tried not to curse as he passed by a group of tourists loading onto a bus. Making bioweapons was bad enough. But the revolting history of bioweapons programs unleashing their creations on unwitting populations as test subjects was enough to make him want to pull a Skylar and toss every one of the monsters responsible straight out the nearest window.

"Christ. What happened?" he asked.

"Hundreds of locals fell sick over the period of a couple weeks. About twenty-five percent died. No one was recovering from this thing. Then, one day, poof, they got miraculously better. No more deaths."

"Better?"

"Either the Russians fudged the numbers, or they had a cure on hand."

Alex turned a corner. "That wouldn't be the first time the Soviets screwed up and accidentally let loose a bioweapon."

"Exactly," Kasim said. "The same thing happened with the Sverdlovsk anthrax leak in 1979 and the 1971 engineered smallpox outbreak in Aralsk. They tried to cover it up, administering the antidote to all those unwitting accidental test subjects that didn't die, but the higher-ups in Biopreparat definitely weren't happy."

"If that's what happened in Ninh Binh, we might find someone or some clue that would lead us to a cure."

"You got it. I'll send you the location of the old manufacturing plant. I don't think it's operational, but you never know. I'm going to work my contacts to find you someone on the ground who can help you make inroads with the locals. We need everything we can get now. Because otherwise, if Weber is right, there is nothing stopping this thing from ravaging China and wherever else the Russians plan to deploy it."

"Understood," Alex said. "One last thing."

"Shoot."

"We taking Reis along?" he asked. "I don't do well babysitting when I'm on the job."

"He's going to the airport too. But he's not going to Vietnam."

"Where, then?"

There was a pause. "He's going to help us at Detrick."

Alex nearly stopped in his tracks. They had originally planned to take Williams and Reis into their custody for questioning then let them go. But Reis was in too deep, knew too much. Now Kasim wanted to bring a foreign national with no security clearance into their fold.

"I thought this was going to be more of a protective custody thing until we got this sorted," Alex said. "I hope you know what you're doing with him."

"I don't," Kasim said. "But Weber does. At this point, I'm in the mood to act first, apologize later. Because if the archaea are half as dangerous as Weber thinks, we need every hand on deck to stop it."

"That's a lot of pressure for Vector to handle alone. When are we going to bring in backup?"

"Right now, we're operating off shoestring evidence. We might have already used up our last chance with Liang in Kaliningrad, so I'm not itching to talk to her unless you bring me solid intel from Vietnam. As it stands, we'd be laughed out of the room for suggesting a bioengineered microorganism that isn't linked to any known human disease is somehow causing a few hundred people in China diarrhea and stomach pains. We need more. So right now, you and Skylar are it. You want to tell me you can't handle it?"

Kasim had him there.

"Of course we can." Alex entered the sliding glass doors of the hotel, finishing his surveillance route. "And this couldn't come at a better time. I've been dying for a good bowl of pho."

21

Ninh Binh, Vietnam

Skylar woke as the van she and Wolfe were riding in turned down a narrow dirt road barely wide enough for the vehicle. On either side, lush green rice paddies promised that if the driver wasn't careful, the van could easily meet its end in a bath of muddy water.

The hired van had picked them up from the Noi Bai International Airport outside Hanoi. Instead of taking a private jet into Vietnam, Kasim had sent them to Bangkok first, where they had transferred to a commercial airline.

The Vietnamese government still clung to a strong sense of paranoia against suspicious state actors looking to cause unrest. While the country's economy was booming in many ways, Vietnam maintained an iron grip on its media to quash any thought of dissent against the communist rule. While there were signs that those policies were changing, Kasim still insisted they enter the country as normal tourists. That would draw less attention than an impromptu last-minute chartered private flight brokered through his contacts in Vietnam.

Their job was to go in and out of the country quietly. No bloodshed, no gunfights. Just a basic intel gathering mission.

Just like Istanbul, she thought. She hoped this one would turn out different.

Skylar could see why so many tourists were drawn to this country. On either side of the rice paddies, steep karst mountains jutted up like the fins of a subterranean dragon. Lush green trees and ferns covered those picturesque mountains. She almost felt bad that Reis had been sent back to Fort Detrick instead of coming here with them.

"This place is a hell of a lot prettier than Indiana," Skylar said.

"You grew up in Bloomington, right?" Wolfe asked.

At first, Skylar was surprised he knew. But she realized she shouldn't be. Not when details like that had been logged in records like her official military personnel file. The guy soaked in details and intel like a partying frat boy downed Jägerbombs.

"Yeah, Bloomington," she said. "There are plenty of trees there but not all of this." She waved a hand to indicate their lush surroundings. "This is damn gorgeous."

"Always liked Northern Vietnam," Wolfe said. "You should see Sapa Valley. Or take a cruise in Ha Long Bay. Mountains just like these except on the water."

"I take it you've been. Work or pleasure?"

"A little of this, a little of that."

"Man, I really picked the wrong career path." She winked. "Up until now, of course."

"What? The Middle East and Central Asia didn't do it for you?"

"Those deserts *might* look good on the right postcard," she said. "But have you ever been in a place so hot that a camel spider used your shadow to keep cool?"

Wolfe laughed. "Tell me being stationed out of Kyrgyzstan was better."

"A little more color. But that's like trying to compare going for a jog at noon in the Phoenix summer to doing the Polar Plunge in Juneau in the middle of the winter."

"I take it you wouldn't go back."

"Not for pleasure. For work, always."

The van took a right alongside the paddies. They approached a series of wooden bungalows set on the left-hand side of the road. The thatch-roofed structures were nestled under the sheer cliff walls of the karst mountains.

"This you," their driver said over the thrum of the engine. He pointed down the curving dirt road. At the end, there was another set of buildings lining a tiled path. A painted wooden sign said Tam Coc Bungalow Hotel.

The van pulled up next to a line of scooters parked in front of an open-air restaurant and bar that served triple duty as the boutique hotel's check-in counter. The driver retrieved their grungy backpacks from the rear door. The bags had been suitably roughed up to look at home in any fifteen-dollar-per-night hostel throughout Southeast Asia.

"Thanks," Wolfe said, passing a few bills to the driver. The driver gave them a thankful smile then got back into the van, navigating it deftly back onto the cramped road along the paddies.

An aquamarine pool reflected the day's last rays of orange sunlight. Four young men and women waded around in it, cooling off after a long day of sightseeing, with bottles of beer in hand. It took only a few minutes to check in, passing over falsified passports for verification to a woman in her late thirties, before they were escorted to their bungalow. After giving them a brief tour of the room with its canopied bed and window unit air conditioner, she promised them made-to-order breakfast in the morning and footbaths whenever they got done sightseeing. Then she left them alone in their room.

"I dig the AC," Skylar said, collapsing in one of the beds. "Didn't expect it out here."

"It looks rustic on the outside, but they treat with luxury," Wolfe said. "All for thirty bucks a night."

"Kasim's going to like that."

"And no twenty-four seven desk service. No security cameras. It's quiet at night."

"Makes slipping out in the dark much easier."

"Exactly," Wolfe said. He checked his watch. "Our contact is supposed to meet us for dinner at a family-run place back down the road."

"They got hardware for us?" Skylar asked.

"That's the story."

Skylar felt naked without weapons. But flying straight into the country with a suitcase full of guns was a surefire way to end up at a forced labor prison living in a twenty-by-ten cell with ten other people and a hole for a toilet.

Not exactly where Skylar wanted to be when there was a mission to run.

After taking a few more minutes to enjoy the air conditioning, they started the long walk back between the paddies to the small restaurants and shops near the Tam Coc River. The sound of cicadas and frogs filled the air as the sun set, and Skylar swatted at the mosquitos swarming over them.

"If the Russians don't get us, these damn bugs will," she said.

"Better invest in some spray, because we got a long night ahead of us," Wolfe said.

The road to town was mostly straight between the paddies. Skylar noticed her partner peering over his shoulder, but there was nowhere for anyone to tail them unless they were swimming in the mosquito-infested waters.

Once they got into town, it was a different story. Tourists and locals alike sped by on smog-tossing scooters, their whining engines calling out in a clashing chorus. The sounds of karaoke from a bar bled into the street. Skylar searched for some sign of their contact as they navigated the scooters and a few stray dogs begging for scraps. But she had no idea who they might be looking for, and nobody stuck out.

"There's the place." Wolfe nodded toward a spray of short plastic stools and tables along the side of the road.

Just beside the stools and tables was an open doorway leading into a house. The aroma of cooking garlic, onion, and ginger drifted out. A pair of diners ate at one of the tables, digging into bowls of vegetables and noodles.

Skylar glanced at the sign above the plastic tables and chairs. Aroma Ninh Binh. It was the right place. But they were looking for someone who had come alone. Neither of the two backpackers chowing down on their cheap meals seemed like a fellow covert agent.

They kept walking, scanning the streets as subtly as possible.

"Something's wrong," Wolfe whispered.

Skylar looked behind them at the scooters blazing up and down the street.

Nearby, people were laughing as they shot pool at a nearby open-air bar. Two kids ran into a convenience store, waving a few bills as they made a beeline for the candy display. No one was following them. No one that she could pin as a contact.

"Shit, you think someone got to him?" Skylar asked.

"Don't know," Wolfe said. "Kasim said everything was clean. Our contact didn't have any ID on us. Just knew the time and location to meet. They should be there."

Skylar walked beside him as he ran a counter surveillance route. While she had been trained in the art, her expertise in combat had been forged in the skies over Afghanistan and

Iraq. She had always been more of the explosive firework type, while Wolfe spent his career swimming through the shadows.

At first, she'd thought their styles were too different, constantly clashing over how to proceed. But she was coming around to the idea that their strengths could actually complement each other. If she could just get the suspicious bastard to trust her...

She let him lead as they wound between the stores and restaurants. They looped back on their path as he glanced periodically at his phone, looking like a lost tourist. It was a good enough bit that Wolfe nearly had Skylar convinced he'd forgotten where he was going until he suddenly paused.

"I think we got eyes on us," he said in a low voice. "Don't look now, but when I signal, you head straight toward that store." He gestured toward a shop selling canvas prints of mountains, monks, and temples. "I'll head to our left."

He indicated a street with a single dim streetlight between the tangles of telephone and electric wires.

Skylar saw what he was doing. He wanted to keep her in the open, while he drew their tail off and ambushed them in the alley. He was the bait. A more vulnerable target in the dark, away from the main thrust of tourists wandering around the small town.

"Now," he said.

Skylar walked off, giving him a perfunctory goodbye. She headed straight to the store as if one of the canvases had grabbed her attention. Alex gave an exaggerated sigh to play the part of the exasperated boyfriend tired of being dragged to the fiftieth souvenir shop that evening.

He gave her a wave. She told him she would catch up, keeping her full attention on the shop.

She did her best not to look behind her, not wanting to make it too obvious that Wolfe had made their tail. Out of her left pocket, she slipped a compact mirror, keeping it low in front of her. Angling it just enough to watch her partner.

He continued down the dark narrow street. She waited to see their tail follow him.

But no one took the bait. Had they spooked their follower? Or was Wolfe wrong?

Skylar started to turn away from the paintings. Before she could spin, an arm wrapped over her shoulder. She felt the unmistakable press of a gun barrel against her side.

Shit.

"Thought you guys would throw me off, huh?" a woman said. She let out a small chuckle.

"Look, let's pretend you and I are friends," the woman said. "Walk with me, away from this place, and we'll go somewhere quiet we can talk. And if you try anything, you're dead. Then your partner's dead. And I'm gone. Long gone."

ALEX WATCHED a woman with long dark hair guide Cruz away from the shop. She made it appear as if she and Cruz were best friends. A passerby might think they were out for nothing more than a stroll and a laugh. But the way she had her right arm in front of her, holding a shemagh scarf over her hand, told him their relationship was anything but amicable. The scarf looked like the kind some of the locals wore to keep the dust out of their face when driving a scooter. Completely innocuous on its own. But Alex guessed beneath that scarf was a weapon. A gun or knife, judging by how cooperative Cruz seemed to be.

This woman had seen straight through Alex's feint. She knew what she was doing, which worried him all the more.

How had they had been followed all the way to Ninh Binh?

Were their false identities compromised? Was there a traitor at Vector?

Only one way to find out.

Alex started after the women, scanning for anything nearby that he could use as a weapon. Plenty of restaurants, a few food stalls. But even if he snagged a knife and closed the distance to get in range to use it, Cruz wouldn't escape a shot or a stab to the gut.

His best bet was to play into this woman's plan. She hadn't killed Cruz yet because she must want information. And she already knew Alex was part of Cruz's team, so there was no use pretending that he *wasn't* following her.

"Hey, ladies, wait up!" Alex called.

He jogged to catch up. When he was no more than ten feet away, the woman adjusted her right hand, prodding Cruz. That was enough to tell him he wasn't supposed to get any closer.

"So glad you could join us," the woman said, barely giving him a second glance.

She led them around a corner, past the last couple of souvenir stores and straight through the darkened doorway of a boutique hotel under construction. Tarps hung over the half-built brick walls. Trash was strewn about the wet dirt.

Perfect spot to take a couple of people you wanted to get rid of. Not far from the town, plenty of concealment. This wasn't the first time Alex had been in a spot like this. In fact, it was exactly the type of place he used to trap his own targets when he'd had jobs in the region.

Maybe this was a hit after all.

He scanned the area, looking for a hammer or something heavy he could defend himself and Cruz with. Nothing stood out.

This lady was good. She had no doubt preselected this site then cleared it.

Just like he would've done.

He lurked at the entryway. The glow of a dying streetlight bled in from behind him. Masked in shadows, Alex couldn't get a good look at the woman's face.

"Well, we're here," Alex said. "What now?"

"Who do you work for?" the woman asked.

"You seem to know what you're doing then you ask a question like that?" Alex asked. "Didn't peg you for an amateur."

"You…" She paused, saying nothing for a second. "Wolfe?"

The woman took a step forward. She let the shemagh scarf fall from her right hand, revealing a suppressed pistol aimed at Cruz's stomach.

"Damn, Wolfe, it really is you," she said. "What the hell are you doing here?"

Alex squinted, but the shadows prevented him from seeing her face properly. She took another step toward him. Then his memories erased the long hair—no doubt a wig—and the caked-on makeup that gave the appearance of more defined cheekbones and narrower eyes.

"Tracy Nguyen?" he asked.

"The hell is going on?" Cruz asked.

"That's what I want to know," Nguyen said. "I didn't think you worked for the agency anymore."

Nguyen had been an intelligence officer at the CIA at the same time he was. Their paths had crossed periodically. The last project they'd worked on together was dismantling an Indonesian pro-Islamic State network targeting sites of worship with abrin bombs in West Java. While he focused on bioterrorism threats, her focus was squarely on Southeast Asia. He had always thought she was just another desk jockey pushing papers at Langley.

"I don't," Alex said. "You?"

Instead of answering his question, she shrugged.

"You can't say."

"Can any of us?" she replied.

Alex was caught off guard by seeing a familiar face. Especially when that familiar face was on the other end of a gun pointed at his partner.

"Tell me, what do you recommend?" he asked, beginning their prescribed sign/countersign exchange. "I heard the *bun cha* is good here."

Nguyen shook her head. "The *canh chua*'s better. I know a place where they serve it with fish straight from the Tam Coc."

"Take me there. Stomach's growling."

Nguyen lowered her weapon slightly. Just enough so it wasn't pointed straight into Cruz's gut but not enough to signal that the sign and countersign exchange made her feel completely comfortable. The fact that she didn't trust them made him all the more suspicious.

This wasn't going to be easy.

"You don't mind if I…" She motioned toward Cruz, indicating she wanted to pat her down.

"You've got the damn gun," Cruz said. "Do whatever you want, but just tell me what the hell is going on."

Nguyen began patting down Cruz cautiously. She knocked on the hollow prosthetic leg. "Anything in there?"

"You can check it out."

Nguyen pulled up Cruz's pant leg to reveal the plastic and alloy prosthetic. Sure enough, she discovered a foldable knife tucked into Cruz's boot beside the leg. She held it up in the dim moonlight, the three-inch blade glimmering, then dropped it in the dirt.

"Picked it up at the gift shop on the way out of the airport," Cruz said, shrugging. "Don't like walking around naked, you know?"

Nguyen finished the pat down. "Sit. Hands behind your back, against that wall. No sudden movements."

"Look, I'm with him," Cruz said. "You already know who he is, apparently, and—"

Nguyen shot Cruz a look filled with cold steel. Alex remembered that same expression when one of their colleagues had screwed up an intel drop outside Jakarta.

"Listen to her, Cruz," he said.

"Fine." Cruz backed away, hands in a defensive gesture.

When Nguyen approached Alex, a thousand worries ran through his mind. Why was she so paranoid? Was she a double agent now? This wouldn't be the first time two former colleagues who'd gone off the radar faced each other on opposite sides of the playing field.

If he moved quickly, he could disarm her. She might get a shot off, but he could duck to the right. Uppercut straight to her elbow, break it. Another strike into her kneecap. She might expect it, so maybe a feint would work. Take a step with his right foot, but juke to the left instead.

But then again, if she was actually their contact out here, if she had the keys to the next stage of their operation, causing that kind of damage would not be helpful.

All he could do was let her take control. Trust her in a world where he'd been taught to trust no one.

Didn't feel right.

He sucked in a breath as she came nearer, patting him down with one hand.

"You can relax," she said, backing away. "Still hitting the gym, I see."

"Oh my god, don't tell me she's your ex too," Cruz said, rolling her eyes.

Nguyen laughed. "Trust me, he's not my type. Plus, you know the old saying about not crapping where you eat."

Finally, Nguyen lowered the weapon. She didn't holster it. Alex took a tentative step forward.

"Woah, now," Nguyen said. "Doesn't mean I'm good. Just… talk. I want to know what I'm doing here with you two."

"How much do you know?" he asked.

A scooter zipped by outside. Nguyen tensed, only relaxing when the whine of its engine droned away.

"Practically nothing," Nguyen said. "I was told to gather hardware and show up in Ninh Binh."

"And you show up ready to kill?" Cruz asked.

"I was expecting to *be* killed."

"Why's that?" Alex asked.

"Things have gotten complicated here," she said. "But I'm not authorized to spill those details to someone who isn't with the Agency anymore. Give me something better, Wolfe. Prove you haven't turned."

She had put him in a tough spot. Telling her who he worked for might not do any good, since very few in the US government knew about Vector. At this point, he had no way of knowing if he and Nguyen were still working for the same cause.

But she was the only one in the room with a gun. And one way or another, he was going to need to get his hands on one.

22

"WE'RE WASTING TIME," Skylar said. "We've got an op to run. Tell me why you think we're going to kill you so I know what the hell is going on."

"I'll keep it simple," Nguyen said. "I'm in the middle of long-term project dealing with triads from our friends up north and a very dangerous drug trade. We're talking about an environment where human life isn't exactly put on a pedestal. Assets I've been working with for months suddenly go dark or end up floating facedown in the middle of a rice paddy. Then I get a message saying I'm supposed to meet someone with a certain stockpile of gear at a certain restaurant at a certain time in a town in the middle of nowhere. Looks like a setup."

"Do we look like we work for the triads?" Skylar asked.

"You'd be surprised how little it takes to flip the people you thought you knew."

Wolfe held out his hands in a placating gesture. Skylar could see him playing it cool, keeping the emotion from his features. But she also recognized that slight glint in his eyes. She'd seen it enough by now to know he was ready to throw down if everything hit the fan.

"If this was a hit, a setup, we'd have come with a lot more than a pocketknife," he said.

"You know as well as I do that guns and knives aren't the only things that kill a field officer," Nguyen said. "I gave you something, you give me something. I'm supposed to be your supplier, your guide, and your translator. And I don't even know why."

"I'm not sure you want us to add more to your plate," Wolfe said. "Better off not knowing."

"When I'm told to suspend my operations, which are pretty damn important to me, and abandon an active investigation where I was inches toward flipping my new mark, I'm either being set up or else something much bigger is going on. Which is it?"

"Bigger," Skylar said.

"Like world-ending bigger?" Nguyen asked, brow raised. "Because if it's anything less than apocalyptic, I'm not going to be happy."

Wolfe sighed. "We need to get moving."

Nguyen looked between them. "I get the sense she doesn't mind exaggerating things, but that's not your deal, Wolfe."

"What's that supposed to mean?" Skylar asked.

"Former military, right?" Nguyen asked, looking her up and down. "I can tell by that cocky way you walk down a street. Like you're not afraid of a fight. Got the gait of a Marine." She paused. "That's not quite right." Then she grinned. "Maybe a pilot."

Skylar didn't like how easily this woman read her. She'd hit it right on the nose. "Anything wrong with that?"

Nguyen laughed. "Not unless you're trying to blend in. Watch Wolfe. The guy's big and tall, and somehow, even in little old Ninh Binh, he can make himself disappear. He gives off an aura that convinces your eyes to pass right over him. You might try watching him."

"You going to critique us or help us?" Skylar said.

"I'm still waiting for you to tell me what's up," Nguyen said.

Wolfe gave Skylar a look like he was staring into the bottom of an empty pint glass, wondering where his beer had gone. She knew what that expression meant. He was weighing the options, figuring out how much he could barter before he got what he wanted.

"Nguyen, I might not be working for the same boss, but our employer is the same," he said. "My department is working on bioweapon threats. A program from the Soviet era has roots in this area. That particular program may have been resurrected."

"And three decades after Biopreparat was shut down, you're telling me this thing survived?" Nguyen asked.

"More than survived," Wolfe said. "Problem is, we have no cure for this particular bioweapon."

Nguyen was quiet. Skylar watched the realization sink over her. "You think someone is going to use it?"

"We think they already have."

"Jesus, why didn't you lead with that?"

"You didn't trust us, why would I trust you?" Wolfe asked.

"Look, I'm still not one hundred percent convinced that this isn't some plot to take me out." Skylar noted that she still held her pistol at the ready. She'd jammed the barrel hard enough into her side to make Skylar's already bruised ribs ache. "Only reason I'm going to cooperate is because I remember you from our Langley days."

"I appreciate that," Wolfe said, "because we've got a whole lot of people relying on our success."

Nguyen finally holstered her pistol. "Fine. You ready to see the goodies I brought?"

"Thought you would never ask," Skylar said.

UNSPECIFIED LOCATION in the Sahara Desert

RENEE SAT on the edge of a cot in a small room. Besides the cot, all she had was a bucket in the corner and a million questions racing through her mind.

Plans of escape and promises of a future with Paulo, no matter how short, had given her hope at the last facility. She had heard the rumble of trucks and the blare of ships' horns from inside the labs there. She figured the warehouse was at least somewhere close to civilization. She had naively thought that if she could make it out of that building, she could run somewhere for help. Surely someone would have been willing to help her or at least alert the authorities.

But hope had no place here.

Her captors could leave the front doors unlocked, and she would have no real chance at escaping alive. Where would she go? Wander the desert until she passed out from dehydration?

She was completely alone, left to fester in her own spiraling thoughts, staring at the corrugated metal ceiling.

Then the door banged open, and she shot to her feet. An older woman was thrown into the room, and the door shut behind her.

"Dr. Aubert," Renee said, rushing to the woman's side. "Are you okay?"

She helped Aubert onto the cot. The older scientist massaged her temple. Blood trickled out of a new gash in her cheek. Renee had nothing but the coarse sheet on the cot to offer her. Aubert dabbed at the blood.

"They were not happy with my work." She gave Renee a soft smile despite the ugly wound. "Did they hurt you?"

"Not yet," Renee said. "I haven't even been let out of here, though." She paused. "Have you seen Paulo?"

"Oh no," she said. "I have not seen him."

Renee wanted to collapse, to curse and yell. But she held in the anger and fear. If Pavlenko and his cronies were watching, she didn't want to give them the satisfaction of watching her break down.

Aubert wrapped an arm around her. "We will get through this. You will see your family again. You will see your friend Paulo. We must get through this, do you understand?"

Renee nodded. "These people are absolutely evil. How are they getting away with this? Why hasn't anyone stopped them?"

"I don't know," Aubert said. "But we are still together. These people cannot escape scrutiny forever. If we can just hold on, someone will come."

"I hope so," Renee said. "But after everything I've seen, I have a hard time believing it."

"You must believe in something." Aubert readjusted her grip on the sheet and pressed it against the blood again.

Renee tore off a strip of the sheet and helped Aubert clean the wound. "It's hard to believe in anything when they've taken everything from us."

Aubert's eyes narrowed, the wrinkles deepening around her eyes. "Don't ever say that. They have not taken everything. So long as you're still alive, you have your mind. No matter how poor, no matter if a person is imprisoned, no matter if they take away all your rights, you still have that." She tapped the side of her head. "You're still free up there."

"I'd like to think that. But I bet these people know how to take that too."

She expected Aubert to have a retort, some sage wisdom she could impart to Renee and dispel that nihilism.

But Aubert was silent. A single tear rolled down her cheek, mixing with the blood.

"I'm sorry," Renee said. "I didn't mean to—"

The door swung open again. Markov entered with a wicked scowl on his face. His body took up the entire doorframe. His face was blistered and scabbed from what looked like bad burns. Bandages covered parts of his arms, concealing some of his tattoos.

"What happened to Paulo?" Renee demanded. "Tell me that he's safe!"

"He's safe."

"Where?" she asked.

"How should I know?"

"You said he's safe."

Markov grinned. "You told me to tell you that."

The exhaustion, the dehydration, the hopelessness, the brutality. It had all been too much. His cruel humor made her want to scream, to pound her fists into his ugly face.

"What do you want?" she asked.

Aubert wrapped her fingers around Renee's wrist. "Don't be rash."

Renee no longer cared. If Paulo was dead, if all she had to look forward to was a sandy grave in the desert, then so be it.

She shrugged Aubert's hand away and stood in front of Markov. Her forehead barely was level with his chest, but she didn't care. She stared up into his eyes.

"I told you before; I will tell you again," Markov said. "You are nothing but a mewling housecat."

"Tell me what happened to Paulo."

"Or what? You will scratch me?" He shoved her back into Aubert with a single hand then took another step toward them. "Dr. Pavlenko told me we made a mistake."

His fingers slid to the pistol holstered at his hip. Renee's pulse thundered through her ears, but despite the iron grip of fear clenching her insides, she forced herself to her feet.

She would not let this man kill her lying down. "And what was your mistake?"

She tightened her fists, trembling, hoping Markov didn't sense her fear.

"We were not supposed to bring both of you," he said coolly.

Renee gulped hard. There was little doubt in her mind what that meant. She was only a post-doctoral researcher, barely out of graduate school. Her experience was nothing compared to the lifetime of achievements Aubert could boast of.

Pavlenko's choice was obvious.

"Fine," Renee said. "Get it over with."

If Paulo was dead, then she would be joining him. She tried to steel herself, ready to accept her fate. At least she would no longer be working for Pavlenko.

Markov gave her his crooked grin and drew his pistol. He raised it and fired.

23

THE GUNSHOT WAS DEAFENING in the enclosed space. Pain speared through Renee's eardrums. Those next few seconds ticked by in brutal suspense. She expected the flames of agony to spread through her chest. To feel her life pour from the bullet hole in her flesh.

A few seconds passed, her ears ringing, before she realized what had happened.

Aubert lay sprawled over the cot. She had dropped the sheet, and her mouth hung open. The wall behind her was splattered with gore. That brilliant scientific mind, wasted.

"No," Renee said. She couldn't even hear her own voice.

Markov put the pistol away and beckoned for her to follow him.

She ignored him, dropping down to Aubert's side. She hadn't known the poor woman well. But Aubert had done her best to comfort her and Paulo, had offered them strength and hope. They had helped each other endure this madness.

And once again, the Russians had taken someone from her.

Renee wanted to be brave. To tell this man that she would no longer cooperate.

But seeing Aubert shot right in front of her destroyed any thoughts of rebellion. Images of tortured prisoners Pavlenko had shown her back in the lab flooded her mind's eye too. There were fates worse than death. If these madmen had spared her, then she feared what she would be forced to endure.

Chills ran through her body. She started to shake.

Markov put a big hand on her shoulder, squeezing gently. His voice cut through her muddled hearing. "This will be over sooner if you cooperate. If you do not, it will be so bad, you'll wish I had shot you too."

He guided her out the door and down a corridor. Other halls branched off around her. She heard a few angry voices. She turned slightly to see what was causing the commotion, but Markov cranked her head back.

"That doesn't concern you," he said.

There was a gunshot and Renee gasped, frozen. More scientists who shared Aubert's fate?

Markov pushed her forward, steering her away from the sounds of sobbing and cursing. She wanted to run, but Markov tightened his fingers around her upper arm. There was nowhere to go.

Markov's nostrils twitched, his face drawing close to hers. "I do not like this any more than you do. I do not like babysitting scientists. In fact, I am very, very bad at it. I am not known for my patience."

She could practically feel the heat radiating from his words, the frustration simmering beneath the veiled threats.

"Cooperate and obey," he said.

She nodded meekly. What else could she do?

He guided her into a laboratory that looked similar to the one in the last facility. The same cylindrical EnviroProct device was on one of the lab benches.

This nightmare just kept repeating. Only this time, Paulo wasn't here.

Another man was already in the laboratory wearing a white coat, bent over the device, examining its components.

Was this another prisoner assigned to work with her? Someone to replace Paulo?

Oh, God, if Paulo was being replaced, maybe he really was dead.

The man near the device turned.

It was no prisoner. It was Pavlenko. He didn't seem impressed or intimidated by Markov.

"Go find your master, dog," Pavlenko said. "Levin will no doubt have something for you to do."

Markov glared at Pavlenko, fingers clenching into fists. For a second, Renee felt like she had come between two grizzlies squaring off over a deer carcass. Markov finally relaxed his hands and left.

Pavlenko beckoned for Renee to join him.

"Do you know why I asked you to find this device's weakness?" he asked.

She shook her head.

"You are a smart woman. I know you've been thinking about it. After all, what else is there for you to do?"

She was quiet. There was a cold, calculating intelligence behind Pavlenko's blue eyes. A predatory gaze that set off all the alarms in Renee's flight-or-fight instincts.

"You intended to publish a remarkable paper," Pavlenko said. "You identified a microorganism I had selected specifically because most ignore it."

"Archaea," she said, her voice weak.

"You must imagine my surprise when I got word that someone had found *my* archaea from an air sample collection device off the coast of Portugal. And then they had the gall to claim it was a new species of archaea *they* had discovered."

"There were no other papers, no reports, no genetic data of an organism exactly like that one," Renee said. She felt like a zombie, mindlessly reciting answers.

"That was intentional," Pavlenko said. "Unfortunately, you were not the only one to discover my archaea. The other laboratory that discovered these archaea was much more advanced than yours."

The answer was glaringly obvious, literally standing in front of her face. "EnviroProct."

"Yes, a scientist there found it. Worse, he had a good guess about the purpose of this archaea. He didn't want to publish it like you did, but he planned to share his results, nonetheless. I had him stopped before he could ruin my plans."

Renee tried to follow the Russian scientist's speech, but she kept seeing Aubert crumpled on the cot, brains and blood and skull fragments sliding slowly down the wall.

"So I ask you again, why do you think I would go through so much trouble concealing the archaea from the public? You must have a guess. Tell me," Pavlenko said. He peeled back his white coat to reveal the sidearm holstered at his hip.

"It's a weapon."

"Good. I don't like intellectual dishonesty. You must be clear about your hypothesis and honest about your intentions to approach a research investigation appropriately."

"Honest about your intentions," Renee repeated. "Why did you bring me here?"

"You're a quick learner." Pavlenko grinned. "Your work is not done. You've provided good, usable information on how our archaea can avoid the detection of these EnviroProct sensors. But as we make those changes to our entire stock of archaea, I want you to work with my researchers to ensure the modifications are actually effective. Quality control, you might say."

"You can do that on your own. You don't need me."

"You're right. I don't *need* you. But while we are experts in developing these organisms, you're the expert at finding them. You've spent your career doing that. Spend a few days ensuring that with our newest developments, even you cannot detect the archaea any longer."

He opened a cabinet above the lab bench. It was filled with the devices and filters Renee had used when she was working in Dr. Estacio's lab.

"I've assembled all the collection systems you've ever used in your research. You have three days to test them."

"You're going to kill me anyway. Why should I do this?"

Before he answered her, he spoke a few Russian words into his mic. A woman in a white coat came in carrying a rubber mask with a small plastic bulb attached to it. The device looked like a bag valve mask used to help someone who couldn't breathe.

Renee backed away. But Pavlenko forced the mask over her face. The woman pressed Renee's arms against her side so she couldn't struggle. He squeezed the bulb. A white powder fluttered around inside it.

Renee held her breath, pressing her lips together as tightly as she could.

"You must inhale eventually," Pavlenko said.

Her brain screamed at her to resist, but her lungs were aching for oxygen. She tried to push the air out, keeping whatever poison was in that bulb from entering her system.

Darkness started to creep over her eyes. Her fingers twitched, her head feeling light.

She could not control it any longer and took in a deep gasping breath.

"Very good," Pavlenko said then signaled for the other woman to exit.

Renee expected to feel a sharp fire burning down into her throat. Maybe her nerves would start to give out or her heart would slow, her brain growing lethargic as her blood vessels no longer delivered oxygen.

But instead, she felt nothing. Nothing except for the fear of not knowing what came next.

"As I said, you only have a few days," Pavlenko said. "Then you will find out what the archaea truly do."

Could this be like Ebola, her organs slowly dissolving? Something like rabies, her mind growing paranoid as it fell apart, her body physically repulsed by the thought of a drop of water? Or a slow-acting nerve agent that would paralyze her as it shredded her nerves?

"If you don't perform satisfactorily, I will not provide you the antidote to stop what the archaea will do to your body," he said. "It is a fate so painful you will beg for a bullet to the head."

"How… how do I know there's actually an antidote?"

"You're a smart woman. I'll give you a clue."

Pavlenko gave her a final smile as he headed toward the laboratory exit. He paused at the door, held the mask up to his own face, and breathed in.

-24-

NINH BINH, Vietnam

NGUYEN TOOK Alex into town to rent a couple of scooters for himself and Skylar at one of the local tour operators. For the equivalent of an extra few bucks and a sizeable deposit, the man in charge of rentals was willing to overlook the regulations requiring him to keep a copy of their passport details.

The more layers of cover, the better.

Navigating between the highways and the small dirt roads around Ninh Binh would be much easier with a scooter than a car, not to mention more inconspicuous with the number of tourists and locals alike on the vehicles.

Nguyen hopped on the back of Alex's scooter. She directed him over a narrow road leading to the west out of town as Skylar tailed them. They traded the streetlights and headlights of other vehicles for the weak glow of the stars over the countryside.

"Where are we going?" he spoke over the whining engine and the rush of wind.

"Trust me."

"You know, it doesn't get any easier the more you say that."

He thought he felt Nguyen let out an exasperated sigh. "Thai Vi Temple. That help?"

He didn't reply.

"Thought so," she said. "It's back out under the mountains. Left everything for you guys there."

Alex didn't like being dragged to a new location outside the agreed-upon terms. Anyone could be waiting for them in the screen of trees on either side of the road or at this temple.

"No funny business, I swear," Nguyen said. "Just didn't want to drag all that hardware into town and let it fall into the wrong hands if things turned out differently, you know?"

He understood. It was probably what he would've done, too, given the circumstances.

"Been a long time since Langley," she said.

"For you or for me?" Alex said.

"Both of us. Although you disappeared before me."

He didn't answer, uncertain where this information gathering was going. At best, it was her professional interest, scrounging up info to back up the story he had told about looking for a bioweapon. At worst, she could be delving for intel to relay to Vector's adversaries.

If she had intercepted their real contact, pried them for information, and then...

He let the possibilities simmer at the back of his mind. Nguyen was right. Paranoia was good when paired with thoughtful caution. But he couldn't let it consume him to the point that he was unable to continue their mission.

They pulled down a dirt road lined on one side by shuttered restaurants and stores. Their headlights illuminated a few goats staring back at them from behind a rotting wooden fence. Four scooters were parked near a stone gate with large wood doors that looked big enough to drive a truck through. Nguyen told them to park next to the other scooters.

"Someone else here?" Alex asked.

"One is mine. The rest are from the temple workers." She gestured to a pair of small wooden houses farther back along the road. "That's where they live."

They parked the scooters next to the gate. The main doors were closed, but two smaller doors on either side were open. Those doorways took Alex, Skylar, and Nguyen to a stone-tiled plaza where a two-story pagoda stood to their right. Straight ahead was a temple with a tiled roof lined with carved dragons backed up against the mountains.

Skylar paused just beyond the gate. "You sure this isn't a mistake, Wolfe?"

Nguyen pulled out her pistol. Alex tensed, ready to lunge at Nguyen. But the other operative held the pistol by its barrel and handed it grip-first to Skylar.

"Don't make me regret this," Nguyen said. She strode ahead to the temple without looking back at them. The message was clear. She bought their story and gave them her trust, and now she wanted them to return the favor.

Alex followed her under the arches over the temple's entrance.

The scent of incense simmered from offerings in front of golden statues depicting the gods. Nguyen took them between the altars then out a back exit. A short gravel pathway led to a trail winding up the side of the mountain and disappearing into the trees.

Alex listened for the crack of branches or crunching gravel. Any indication someone else was after them.

Sweat trickled down his back, the humidity clearing only slightly as they climbed the snaking pathway. They finally reached a small cave built into the mountainside. A single Buddha statue rested inside, legs crossed, smile illuminated by a pane of moonlight. Nguyen directed them inside then flicked on a penlight.

"I'm… just going to stay here," Skylar said, pausing at the entrance.

The cave wasn't deep, but Alex understood her caution. She didn't fully trust Nguyen, and she wasn't about to let anyone who might be out in those woods surround them.

Alex followed Nguyen past the Buddha. She used a small flashlight to drive away the darkness.

"Weren't you worried one of the temple caretakers would find your cache?" Alex asked. "I would've thought somewhere in the woods would be safer."

"Not at all," Nguyen said. "Too many hunters and curious kids. Sometimes the best place to hide something is in plain sight. I can come in and out of this place looking like nothing but a religious pilgrim or just a camera-happy tourist. But if someone catches me, a nonlocal, spending a lot of time in a random spot in the woods, that might make people a little more curious."

"Curiosity? From whom?" Alex asked.

"Government officials, bureaucrats with nothing better to do than report potential dissidents. The triad types—and everyone that piggybacks off their presence in the area." Nguyen stopped, pausing by three stupas built into the side of the cavern.

"Not even the triads want to disturb a religious site like this steeped in superstition. Even the worst of them aren't grave robbers." Nguyen grunted, pushing aside a stone slab. "Fortunately, the monks who were buried here are long gone."

"Thought you weren't worried about grave robbers."

"*I* moved them." She paused, wiping the sweat off her brow. "Don't look at me like that. I'll put them back when we're done."

She pulled out a couple of seventy-liter hiking backpacks

from the stupa. She unzipped one, holding it open for Alex to examine.

"You've got everything in here," she said. "Suppressors, H&K Mark 23s for the both of you. Night vision goggles, extra magazines, and Interceptor Multi-Threat Body Armor System —I know it's a couple years outdated, but it's what I could get on the fly."

"I'll take it," Alex said, but he hadn't expected to be outfitted for a gunfight. "This was supposed to be a quiet op. You don't think this is overkill?"

"Better safe than sorry."

They lugged the bags to the cave entrance where Alex showed Skylar what Nguyen had procured.

"Believe me now?" Nguyen asked. She offered Skylar one of the gun cases with a suppressed pistol then motioned for her own weapon back.

Skylar handed it over and took out her new weapon, checking the chamber. "That's better."

"All I was told was to arrange the meetup," Nguyen said, "but I don't know what comes next."

"Goes without saying you're fluent in Vietnamese, otherwise you wouldn't be out here," Skylar said.

"Goes without saying, then you don't need to say it."

"You got some bite," Skylar said. "Here's the deal. In 1990, a bioweapon was accidentally released from what was supposed to be a chemical fertilizer manufacturing plant. A bunch of people got sick, then the Russians swooped in and made 'em all better."

"We want to find some of the survivors," Alex said. "They might know something about whatever was used to cure the victims."

"I can do that," Nguyen said. "But you're going to need to give me a few more details to help point me in the right direction."

Alex shared all they knew about the place while Skylar methodically checked their gear and the packs themselves.

"It's going to take a day or two to pull this together," Nguyen said. "That work for you?"

"Doesn't matter if it works for us," Alex said. "It's the world that needs answers fast."

"I'll see what I can find." Nguyen passed Alex a cellphone. "Clean unit. I'll call you when I find something."

She gave them a secured number, and they returned to their scooters, bags in tow. Next stop would be their hotel to reassess their equipment. Alex wanted to double-check for trackers and other devices. Even more than that, he wanted a nap. But there was no time for sleep. This night was just getting started.

FORT DETRICK, Maryland

KASIM SAT in front of a computer in Vector's operation center and reviewed everything his team had compiled on Dr. Paulo Reis. The scientist was young, just thirty-one. Born and raised in Lisbon. His father and mother still lived there in a four-bedroom flat. He had two younger sisters, one a nurse, another a doctor starting her first internship.

Apart from a couple of speeding tickets, the guy's record was as clean as anyone who had ever stepped into the most secured facilities of Detrick. Model citizen, bit of a nerd. No surprise. Besides rooting for Ronaldo and the Portuguese National team whenever the World Cup came around—which was expected of any upstanding and patriotic Portuguese citizen—his one and only true passion seemed to be science.

Every social structure that Reis had been a part of, including his family, orbited science. His friends were all from past or former laboratories Reis had worked at. He led journal clubs at his university, discussing recent advances in microbiology and related fields. And he had spent a total of four years abroad, studying or working in various academic labs ranging from Rice University in Houston to Utrecht University in the Netherlands.

He had a library's worth of published scientific papers to his name and appeared destined for a career as a scientific rock star. Reis's background would stand up to the most invasive security clearance check. Kasim felt more confident about involving him in Vector's work.

But even if there was a black mark on Reis's record, they might have had to overlook it. Weber and Park had become increasingly desperate to have a lengthy talk with the young scientist.

The door to the operations center opened.

Weber poked her head in. She carried her laptop bag strapped over her shoulder. "Ready."

Kasim joined her in the hall, and they traveled out of Vector's HQ.

"This kind of weather almost makes me wish I wasn't working in a lab," Weber said.

Kasim shot her a dubious look. "I severely doubt that. When's the last time you spent even an afternoon outside the lab?"

"I run the trails nearly every day."

"And you told me you run to clear your mind so you can make breakthroughs in the lab. Face it. You're all about the science."

Kasim gave her a knowing smile. None of them had been selected for these positions because they were masters of work-life balance. Everyone on Vector leaned heavily on the work side of that scale. The small moments they found between the tidal waves of work were fleeting at best.

Just like now.

Kasim let his smile fade as he led them into another building far from the Vector's headquarters. He had reserved a conference room at one of the National Cancer Institute Frederick Campus buildings. While he was ready to let Weber meet with Reis, he didn't want the young scientist in Vector's HQ yet.

They navigated hallways packed with researchers and administrators to a doorway where two Marines waited. The Marines checked their IDs then let Kasim and Weber into the conference room.

Paulo Reis sat at a large circular table. His ruddy complexion was beset by a library's worth of wounds and bruises written across his face. Two more Marines stood behind him. At a nod from Kasim, they exited, leaving Kasim and Weber alone with the exhausted researcher.

"Dr. Reis, it's good to meet you in person," Kasim said, shaking his hand.

"Good is not the word I would use," Reis said. "Kidnapped by would-be terrorists and now by the United States. The only thing that sounds good right now is going back to Lisbon with Renee. Where is she?"

"Rest assured, we're still searching for Dr. Williams."

Reis's eyes narrowed. "Searching? That means you lost her."

The guy was sharp, even if he was as dead-tired as he looked.

"I'm not going to beat around the bush, Dr. Reis," Kasim said. "This is a complicated situation with a lot of moving parts. We have our very best operatives and analysts working on it."

"But the truth is, there are some areas where we need help," Weber said.

"I am not helping you until you help Renee."

"I understand," Kasim said. "And I understand how angry and afraid you must be. Please, just give us a chance. I promise you—"

"I don't care about your promises."

"Dr. Reis, give us a chance to explain." Weber booted up her laptop. "We care about the lives of people like you and Dr. Williams, just as much as we care about protecting our country."

Reis didn't look any happier, but at least this time he didn't argue with them.

"Everything we're about to tell you must remain secret." Kasim pushed a badge across the table to Reis. "As of right now, you're officially a contracted foreign national security consultant. I had to pull a lot of strings to get you this kind of clearance. This also comes with a substantial fee for your services."

He pushed a prepared document across the table, numbers outlined that would make ten years of service in Reis's postdoctoral research position seem like a pittance.

Reis scanned the document. "I don't care about the money. What's missing from this contract is a guarantee that you will find Renee."

"You have our word."

"I recently found out someone's word isn't good enough," Reis said.

"I can eliminate the pay from your contract if that makes you feel better."

He meant it not as a threat but a test to see how Reis would react.

Reis stared at the numbers. "A pile of cash is not an antidote for infectious archaea, and it won't save Renee. You can keep the money." He signed the documents. "But if you need me to agree to all this so we can continue our work, then fine."

Our work. That was good.

"Officially, you'll be working with the National Cancer Institute as a visiting researcher," Kasim said. "We've arranged accommodations for you on base too. You'll have eyes on you at all times for your safety and ours."

"Accommodations? This sounds more like a prison."

"For security purposes, we need to keep you close. But I promise you'll be much more comfortable with us than with those Russians."

"Fine, fine," Reis said. "So when do I start?"

"Right now," Weber said. She turned her laptop toward him. "I told you that we believe the archaea has already been deployed. I think it may be causing a new disease I'm tracking through China. We first identified a few dozen patients with unexplained symptoms in Western China. Since then, I've come up with nearly four thousand patients with similar illnesses from our syndromic surveillance."

"China is sharing this data with you?" Reis asked. "Are you sure it's accurate?"

"They didn't exactly share it," Weber said. "And you don't need to worry about how we got it. We're seeing symptoms like nausea, diarrhea, and severe abdominal cramping. The Chinese are calling this Acute Gastrointestinal Syndrome or AGS. Health officials in the CCP have been working under the radar to figure out what's going on. They're considering shutting down entire cities and roadways as well as enacting flight bans and quarantines over the next few days."

"But this spread shows that it may be too late," Reis said, pointing at the map on Weber's screen.

"Very astute," Weber said.

"Why did they wait so long to do anything?" Reis asked.

"They didn't," Weber said. "When this disease hits a city,

we see hundreds of cases pop up almost instantaneously. This phenomenon appeared first in population centers starting from the western reaches of the Xinjiang province. Before we came to meet you, cases of AGS were already being reported in eastern Sichuan too. The rate of spread within these population centers is faster than anything we would have expected. It appears to be headed on a collision course with Beijing, Hong Kong, and everywhere in between in a matter of days."

Weber played a time-lapse video of China. Red dots representing the cases bloomed in the west then exploded in cities heading east.

"What I'm showing you now happened in a period of just over twenty-four hours," Weber said.

"Diseases don't spread this fast on their own," Reis said, the color draining from his face. "Do you think these are dirty bombs being released? Maybe someone poisoning waterways or food supplies in a coordinated attack?"

Kasim had to admit he was mildly surprised to see Reis shifting straight into problem-solving mode and asking the right questions, even if they were a little basic.

"I've considered it," Weber said. "But why would they release dirty bombs in this kind of pattern? Why not hit Beijing and Shanghai first, for instance, instead of less densely populated areas out west? Or why not release all the bombs or infect all water supplies at once, reducing the chances of their ongoing efforts being identified?"

Kasim pointed at the map on Weber's screen. "A more natural outbreak-type spread originating from a single city, too, could be mistakenly attributed to an illegal wet market infection or a mutation in a zoonotic disease coming from normal agricultural operations."

Reis narrowed his eyes, studying the screen as if he were starting to construct his own hypotheses.

"The pattern and timeline of infections defy all our normal

epidemiological patterns," Weber said. "It doesn't fit neatly into the scenarios you mentioned, nor does it fit a typical outbreak model."

"Do you know the mode of transmission?" Reis asked. "Airborne, physical contact?"

Weber shook her head. "None of the traditional modes of transmission between people fit this model."

Reis stared at the screen as the pattern repeated, over and over, showing the disease spread. "No wonder it doesn't fit. This disease isn't spreading between people."

"What do you think, then?" Kasim asked.

He pointed at the screen. "There's no way to stop it. Travel bans, quarantines. None of it matters. I can tell you exactly how this disease is spreading. But you probably won't believe me."

"Try us," Kasim said.

Reis met his gaze. "Sandstorms."

25

Ninh Binh, Vietnam

Skylar felt better with the weight of the pistol pressed against the small of her back. Her scooter bumped over the empty pitted highway, igniting a throbbing ache in her ribs.

She wore a loose-fitting rain jacket to conceal the weapon. Despite the humidity, the jacket wasn't entirely out of place. Ninh Binh was in the middle of its wet season. Clouds blotted the stars and threatened to spill over at any minute. Skylar could smell the oncoming rain. She hoped it held off until they were done with their investigation of the Operation Groundswell facility. Maybe, if things went well, they would be out in a couple of hours with confirmation that the bioweapons used here were the predecessors of the archaea strains. Even better would be if they could find some forgotten records with the cure to the engineered archaea.

Wolfe rode ahead, his headlight bobbing in the darkness. They exited the highway onto the pitted dirt side roads.

"We're about five klicks out," he said over the comms. "Kill the headlights."

They paused at the side of the dirt and gravel road then put on the night vision goggles they had stowed in their packs. After another kilometer of driving, they pulled off the side of the road and killed their engines. They traveled the rest of the way by foot, navigating through thick tangle of trees and brush, the world a sea of greens and blacks through the NVGs.

A few drops of rain splashed over Skylar.

So much for the weather holding out.

By the time the trek ended at a chain-link fence topped with razor wire, the rain was falling in a steady rhythm. Water seeped under her jacket and sluiced over the vines snaking through the rust-covered fence.

Skylar peered between the vegetation and chain-links into the facility beyond. She saw crumbling concrete buildings pounded by sheets of rain. Weeds sprouted from the fissures in asphalt lots spread between the structures. Puddles filled those cracks. A few rusted cars and vans were interspersed by trees, crates, a couple of shipping containers, and other debris.

"Doesn't look like anyone's been here in a while," she said.

There went any hope that they would find an active facility to help them link the modern archaea and the failed Operation Groundswell.

"At least it hasn't been turned into another chemical plant or sweatshop." Wolfe spoke loudly to be heard over the rainstorm. He took out a pair of bolt cutters then clipped part of the fence away.

They ducked through the hole he had created and started across the field toward the closest building. While the place seemed to have been left in a state of utter disrepair, it wouldn't be hard for the Russian government, or anyone else for that matter, to pay someone a few bucks to keep the place under watch. Abandoned property like this was just rife for a criminal enterprise to set up shop.

Just like the triads and other groups Nguyen had warned them about.

Dodging between the shelter of trees and the scattered debris, they reached the first structure. The doors to the entrance had since been removed. Inside, vines and trees pushed up through the broken concrete floor. Most of the ceiling had collapsed, doing little to protect them from the storm. Skylar led them through a hallway filled with decaying leaves and mud.

She peeked into each room they passed. Rotten and mildew-covered office furniture filled most of them. Then the corridor opened up to a much larger chamber in the middle of the ruined facility. Past the broken windows and cracked glass doors, broken pipes hung from the half-collapsed roof. Stainless-steel fermentation drums and bioreactors lay on their sides. The din of the rain pounding those metal machines filled the space with a violent cacophony. Amid the scree of rubble along the mold-covered walls, she saw pieces of air ducts and ventilation systems.

"No mistaking what this place used to be," Skylar said, struggling to be heard over the noise. "They were making *something* here."

They moved on from the fermentation and batch reactor facility and returned outside.

Lightning split in the sky, illuminating another concrete structure that loomed ahead. The crack of thunder rumbled over them. It resonated deep in Skylar's chest and through her bones. She prowled toward the structures. Her boots slopped through the mud, and she kept her eyes constantly sweeping the edges of the forest for movement.

"What's this place?" Skylar asked, when they entered the second building.

The building—or what was left of it—was long. Much of the roof had collapsed. Shorter concrete walls separated the space into stalls. They looked like stables, each filling with muddy water.

"I'm not sure," Wolfe said.

Rain streamed over piles of rubble and filled a few sun-bleached plastic buckets sitting in some of the stalls.

Then she froze.

"Look at that," she said, pointing into a stall.

Half-buried in the mud and smaller chunks of concrete, she had spotted a skull. Its triangular shape made her think it might have been a pig.

"Animal enclosures," Wolfe said. "They must've tested their weapons on animals."

Skylar felt sick at the thought of the countless animals that must've suffered at the Soviets' hands. But she expected no less from people who were willing to inflict a weapon like this on innocent humans too.

Wolfe climbed over the three-foot-tall stall partition and bent next to the skull. From his pack, he took out a knife and chipped away a few small chunks of the bone.

"Maybe there's still evidence of the Groundswell bioweapon on this guy," he said. "Might as well send some samples back to the science team."

Skylar continued down the row of stalls. Under a stack of rocks, another fleck of white drew her attention. She went into the stall, figuring she would make herself useful and collect another sample.

Lightning blasted through the sky. Another wave of relentless thunder shook through her. She removed a few rocks. A cold shiver crept down her spine. It wasn't from the cold rain. Rain splashed around a few small bones that she was damn near certain weren't from a pig.

"Take a look at this," she called over the pounding rain. She scooped away more of the mud.

Wolfe joined her. "Is that—"

"Part of a human hand, right?" she asked.

"Looks like it."

"They weren't just testing on animals."

Skylar took a few samples as Wolfe had done before searching through the rest of the stalls.

More than likely, after the Soviets had abandoned the Groundswell project, they had removed as much evidence as possible. But with as quickly as the original Biopreparat program had fallen apart, they might not have been as thorough as they should have been. Evidence of bioweapons research existed in other Soviet facilities, like the Vozrozhdeniya Island where Biopreparat scientists had pursued mass production of germ warfare weaponry near the Kazakh-Uzbek border. But Vector's search of the other research buildings and fermentation facilities revealed no other hard evidence of bioweapon production or human testing.

"I'm surprised this place hasn't been turned into something else," Skylar said as they circled back toward the hole they had cut in the fence. "Why didn't the Vietnamese government come in and clean it up? Why not turn this into a new factory, a place that *actually* produces fertilizer or something?"

"Good question," Wolfe said.

Skylar looked back at the facility. Another flash of lightning tore through the rain-swept sky. "The biggest disappointment is that we didn't find a damn clue about a cure."

"I hope that Nguyen is having better luck than us," Wolfe said. "Might as well find out."

They found shelter under the trees, and Wolfe fished out the phone from his pack. A moment later they had Nguyen on the line. Skylar listened in, standing close.

"I think I found someone," Nguyen said. "A woman who

was thirty-six in 1990. I met her son at a bar. He told me she was one of the survivors of a terrible disease that spread through her village around the timeline you gave me."

"Can we talk with her?" Alex asked.

"Already arranged it. Tomorrow morning, first thing."

Skylar was glad for the lead. It meant they could leave this haunted, crumbling factory of death.

FORT DETRICK, Maryland

"I'M GOING to have to ask you to repeat that," Kasim said.

Reis sat across from him and Weber in the secured conference room in the National Institute of Cancer building at Fort Detrick.

"The spread of this disease is being caused by sandstorms." Reis pointed at the map of China. "It's almost too obvious now."

"I don't believe it." Kasim turned to Weber. "Sandstorms? Is this possible?"

"Possible? Maybe. Likely?" She paused. "It's not something I would've considered. Then again, I wouldn't have considered weaponized archaea either."

"I realize it sounds ridiculous," Reis said. "I've been to many conferences in aerobiology and worked with colleagues who study the transport of microorganisms and disease vectors that originated because of sandstorms. Winds in Africa and Asia kick up billions of tons of dust from desert soil every year."

"And this is just a desert thing?" Kasim asked.

"There is no heavy vegetation or moisture to hold this dust in place in the desert." He mimed a wind blowing over the table. "The sandstorms kick it up, then all this microorganism-laden dust is transported literally wherever the wind goes."

"You're telling me a strong wind can transport a pathogen in a cloud of dust and then infect a couple of Chinese cities?" Weber asked.

"It's more than just a couple of Chinese cities," Reis said. "The map you showed me is a normal route for aerosolized dust coming from the Taklamakan Desert in southwest Xinjiang."

"If that's true, then the pathogen responsible for AGS is just traveling in the air," Kasim said. "People breathe it in as the winds carry this to them."

Weber reeled back in her chair, shaking her head. "This sounds like the work of an evil genius. They wouldn't have to worry about sneaking dirty bombs into the country. They don't even need sleeper agents stationed anywhere. Just release it into the air, and the wind does the work. It seems like a theoretically effective way to infect millions, maybe billions of people extremely quickly."

Kasim tried to imagine how a disease that spread on the wind would change the world. The mere thought of the damage that would cause to lives and the stability of countries made him sick.

"Do we know that it would work?" he asked. "Has anything like this been done before?"

"Can I show you something?" Reis gestured to Weber's computer.

She pushed it over the table toward him.

Reis brought up a peer-reviewed article in the research journal *Nature*, which examined a study in geophysical research letters from the year 2000. "I was initially interested in this field from an environmental point of view. For example, mysterious widespread coral bleaching in the Caribbean was documented as early as the 1980s. It wasn't until nearly two decades later that researchers found this coral death was caused by a specific soil fungus originating from dust in African deserts."

"Pardon me if I'm not worried about coral," Kasim said. "Do you have evidence that this dust transport can affect human health too?"

"Yes, absolutely," Reis said. "Take a look at this."

He showed them graphs reporting levels of airborne allergens over the east coast of Taiwan.

"In 2005, scientists tracked down fungal spores causing respiratory issues," he said. "These spores came all the way from sources like the Taklamakan and Gobi Deserts, traveling over mainland China to Taiwan."

Reis opened another study that showed a satellite image captured by NASA's Total Ozone Mapping Spectrometer-Earth Probe. A long red and yellow fan of color stretched from the Taklamakan desert over China. It encompassed Taiwan, Japan, North and South Korea.

"What you're looking at here is a seasonal dust-spread event," Reis said.

"It says 'June, 1998' here," Weber said.

"That's right. And it's the middle of June right now. This kind of dust spread is very common in summer months."

"Tell me, Dr. Reis," Kasim began, "these dust storms must travel high in the atmosphere."

"That's right."

"Wouldn't the extreme temperature differences between freezing conditions in high atmosphere and the heat of a desert kill off many of these microorganisms and pathogens?"

Reis shook his head. "The microorganisms that travel the farthest are adapted to extreme temperatures."

"What about UV irradiation?" Kasim asked. "How do they survive that?"

"We've found bacteria in our studies that are highly

pigmented or have thicker cell walls, defenses we think help them to withstand UV radiation," Reis said.

"Archaea may be the best suited of all these microorganisms for this kind of transport," Weber said. "They can survive extreme temperatures, and this might explain why the archaea we found were engineered to have much thicker cell walls."

Reis nodded. "A dust storm is nothing for archaea."

"This makes more sense than I want to admit," Kasim said. "I can see why these people chose to weaponize archaea. They can be transported by these winds over borders, and there's nothing we can do to stop it."

"And the microorganism is like a ghost," Weber said. "We don't test for archaea in the clinic."

"Even in my field, we focus more on aeroallergens, virus, bacteria, and fungi, even the dust itself, which can cause respiratory distress," Reis said.

Kasim talked himself through the sequence of events, testing it out. "This group of Russians, for whatever reason, wanted to deploy a bioweapon somewhere in the Taklamakan desert. They first mapped out the routes their archaea would travel. They used the innocuous version of the archaea in a test run to ensure that the microorganisms would survive the dust transport. Dr. Williams intercepted the unweaponized version of the archaea outside Portugal, and Breners also found it in an EnviroProct Aerokeep device near China."

"While we've seen AGS spreading in China, we haven't seen anyone affected by it yet in Europe," Weber said. "They tested the archaea spread over Europe, so when is it going to hit there too?"

"It's just a matter of time," Kasim said.

Reis brought up another paper on the computer. "I think you need to see this. It's not just Europe that would be affected."

Once again, a satellite image appeared. This one showed a

dust storm traveling from North Africa, originating from the Sahara. The heat map of the dust transport showed the particles traveling across the Atlantic to encompass most of North America.

"The monitoring devices Renee's samples came from were spread out through the Atlantic, including off the coast of northwest Africa, which indicates the pattern I'm showing you is the likely path of dust transport." Reis showed a second image of a wide swath of dust traveling from the Sahara toward Europe and the Middle East. "These patterns are typical of global dust transport systems from the Sahara during the summer."

"Good God," Weber said. "The next dust storm could infect most of Western civilization and the Middle East in one fell swoop."

"We're looking at an attack that will put billions of lives at risk and severely destabilize the global economy," Kasim said. "Only a few geographic areas will be unaffected by this disease, including Russia."

"We're not going to be able to do anything to stop it, are we?" Reis asked.

"We're not giving up yet," Kasim said. "There's got to be something we can do."

Weber studied the map on the laptop screen. "They can't just take a barrel of archaea and dump it into the sand, right?"

Reis shook his head. "They would need an enormous supply. Enough to contaminate a wide area—say a few square kilometers—so the winds picked up enough of it to have the kind of public health impacts we're seeing in China."

The cold fingers of dread cut through Kasim's insides as he recalled the images Wolfe and Cruz had sent back from Kaliningrad. He was beginning to realize how the Russians were deploying the archaea. "That's all we need from you for now, Dr. Reis. Thank you very much for your help."

"What now?" he asked as they stood. "Will you find Renee?"

"With any luck, we will," Kasim said, heading toward the door with Weber. "I think I know how they're distributing the archaea. The only problem is that the desert's a big place. It's not going to be easy to find them, and we don't have much time."

26

UNSPECIFIED LOCATION in the Sahara Desert

DARKNESS HAD long since settled over the desert, but Pavlenko could not retreat to his quarters to sleep. Not when his plan was so close to completion. He monitored the news from China and the reports from his science team while sipping from a cup of tea.

There was a knock on his door. Dr. Natalia Yunevich stood at the doorway. Apparently, he was not the only one finding sleep hard to come by.

"Come in," he said.

She settled into the chair in front of his desk. Dark bags hung under her eyes, and her brown hair, though it was tied back, was oily and stringy. He wasn't used to seeing her without her white lab coat. By the looks of things, she probably hadn't spent more than a couple of hours outside the lab recently.

"Did it work?" she asked.

"I'm reading through your reports on the genetic modifications." He scanned the computer monitor, where he still had a set of her data exploring the effectiveness of those modifications. "I'm sure you already know."

"I'm talking about China." She looked away at a map of Russia hanging in a frame on one wall. "Did EnviroProct's sensors interfere with our plans?"

"Your work is in the lab. Leave this to me."

"I would, but… my family is in Moscow. Yours is, too, no?"

Pavlenko pushed the keyboard away, clasping his hands together. Now he was beginning to see what had kept her awake.

"They are. Our families are safe."

"I want to believe you." Yunevich squirmed like she had something on her mind but was afraid to offend him. "I'm afraid for my family." She inhaled sharply, bracing as if waiting for him to lash out at her. "EnviroProct already began testing their prototypes in Asia in April. Right when we deployed the test archaea in the Taklamakan."

"And what does this have to do with your family?"

Yunevich folded her hands in her lap, wringing them together. "You know the repercussions if the Chinese catch on to the archaea."

"Do not worry about repercussions from Dmitriyev."

"How can you be sure?"

"China did not expand their contract with EnviroProct," he said. "There are no more functioning Aerokeep devices there."

Yunevich's brows scrunched together. She didn't look like she was convinced.

"Trust me," Pavlenko said. "You are not the only one who stands to lose everything if we fail. The only people who knew anything about the test—Breners and his Chinese contacts—are all dead."

"No more Aerokeep devices, no more scientists warning

about a strange new microorganism," Yunevich said. "You are saying that we will be fine."

"More than fine. The latest news from Beijing showed they are only just beginning to recognize this mysterious new disease, Acute Gastrointestinal Syndrome, in western China. They are publicly dismissing the danger of AGS, but my contacts said they are contemplating much broader shutdowns already."

Yunevich actually smiled. "Dmitriyev will be pleased to see that. No school, business, or public transit shutdowns will stop the archaea now that it's airborne."

"Nothing stops the wind," Pavlenko agreed. "Brilliant, isn't it?"

Yunevich nodded but said nothing. Pavlenko sensed her hesitancy. She was a talented scientist, but she had been reluctant to help him with this project. He had personally recruited her to the archaea program and had promised her she could always change her mind. She could quit anytime she wanted.

But what he hadn't told her—what even he hadn't realized when they initiated the program—were the repercussions for voluntary or involuntary departure from the 14th Directorate.

When one of Pavlenko's scientists, Ivan Stepanov, had resigned just this past February, Pavlenko had been disappointed to see him go. But somehow Dmitriyev had gotten word. Stepanov and his wife had tragically fallen out of the window of their tenth-story apartment in St. Petersburg two days later.

If that was the punishment for retiring from the program, they had no doubt the rewards for failure were worse.

"Are you still worried about China?" Pavlenko asked Yunevich.

"No, I believe you. But Europe will be more difficult. If only EnviroProct hadn't installed their Aerokeep devices across Europe in May."

"If they had waited just a month, we wouldn't have needed your last batch of genetic modifications," Pavlenko said. "But we've done what we must since. We will succeed."

He expected Yunevich to leave, satisfied with his reassurances. She made no such move. This was why he preferred his scientists to be captives, broken to his will.

"How much do you know about Operation Groundswell?" he asked, trying a different tack.

"I heard about it," she replied. "But it was a failure. That's all I know."

"That's all most people know." He tried not to let scorn bleed into his voice. The failed Operation was more personal to him than most realized too. "The man running the program had the right idea but the wrong execution. He was inspired by anthrax bacteria. The bacteria itself doesn't usually spread from human-to-human contact. But the spores enter through wounds, inhalation, or consuming contaminated food or water."

"Those spores are hardy," Yunevich said. "That makes them all the more dangerous."

"Precisely, but it is a well-known pathogen. There are many ways to detect and treat anthrax."

Pavlenko picked up his teacup only to find it empty. He offered Yunevich a cup and refilled his own from a pot on a cabinet behind his desk. As he did, he continued, "That was why my father focused on what he thought was a strange, new bacteria in the intestines of humans and animals. We now know it as archaea."

Pavlenko placed a cup of tea in front of Yunevich and sat.

She took one hesitant sip. "No cures. Nearly invisible to most laboratory assays. But EnviroProct threatened all that."

"They did. But our archaea are invisible again thanks to your work and the work of those scientists we captured. Even if EnviroProct's sensors remain deployed around North

Africa, Europe, and the Middle East, even if they continued to distribute their device to new locations, our archaea will go unnoticed in the dust-carrying winds traveling to the United States. We have won, and our enemy doesn't even know it."

"I hope you are right," Yunevich said.

"I am," Pavlenko said. "Once deployed, our second batch will take just ten days to reach the continental US. No one will have the ability to track the spread of the disease through the Aerokeep sensors. There will be little warning, nothing they can use to track the spread down to this facility. We can hit them again and again. We—"

His phone rang.

"Yes?" he answered.

"Pavlenko, you are awake."

He recognized the voice. Whenever Dmitriyev called unscheduled, something was wrong. The fact that the man was calling at this time of the night meant something was very, very wrong. He waved Yunevich off, and she scurried out of the office, leaving her cup of tea behind.

"Kaliningrad cognac is absolute shit," Dmitriyev said. "Disgusting."

Cryptic, of course. The man was more paranoid than even an FSB special agent operating in a hostile country.

"It was not as good as I had thought it would be," Pavlenko said.

"We are paying good money to keep our exports out of that city under control, aren't we?"

"You may wish to speak to Levin about security—"

"I'm speaking to you," Dmitriyev said. "At any good company, it is the chief executive officer who must take responsibility for every employee, from his highest-level managers to the janitors on nightshift. Your people are making mistakes, Pavlenko."

"This *mistake* hasn't changed the trajectory of our plan," Pavlenko said.

"The only thing I dislike more than failure is lies."

"We've made adjustments to keep on target."

"Are you certain?"

Pavlenko thought of the genetic engineering technologies they were employing. The work that Dr. Williams was contributing to. "Yes."

There was a beat of silence.

"It seems a new disease is happening in China," Dmitriyev said.

"Very unfortunate news," Pavlenko said. "I imagine the damage to their economy would be tremendous if they can't get it under control. Just think about what this might do if it spread through Western Europe, the Middle East, and the United States."

"Yes, that would certainly put Russia in a unique position. I believe our scientists are monitoring the situation closely."

"They are," Pavlenko said. "And I'm certain with Russian ingenuity we will rapidly contribute to the healing of both the economy and the general population. Our researchers are already studying AGS. They may even have an idea for a cure already."

"No one would question our scientific or economic superiority if that proves to be true. But I worry this may spread to Russia."

"I imagine our researchers have already thought of ways to prevent that. We just have to trust in our scientists."

Another pause. At least Dmitriyev seemed to finally recognize the power of Pavlenko's work.

"I would like to trust our scientists," Dmitriyev said. "But there is one thing still bothering me."

Pavlenko waited, silent.

"We have friends in North Vietnam," Dmitriyev said.

"Some of them just reported foreigners recently expressing interest in your father's old company there. Do you know why that would be?"

An iciness spread through Pavlenko's vessels. He couldn't believe it. Had these people actually connected his work to his father's? Were they closer to finding him than he had realized?

He took a deep, slow breath.

No, no, if these people were in Vietnam, that was a good sign. They were reaching for the ghosts of the past because they had lost the trail to his facilities in the Sahara and Taklamakan. They wouldn't waste their time snooping around a defunct Biopreparat site if they had a better grasp of what Pavlenko was actually doing.

And there should be no evidence to point from the site of Operation Groundswell to where he was now.

"Pavlenko?" Dmitriyev asked.

"I do not know why anyone would be interested in my father's old *company*," Pavlenko finally answered. "It was a ruined business, a failure. Something I do not intend to repeat."

"Very good," Dmitriyev said. Although by the tone in his voice, Pavlenko could tell Dmitriyev didn't believe there was anything good about the situation. "I still think we should stop these people from asking too many questions. I expect this situation to be handled. Your mess. You clean it up."

The line clicked off.

Pavlenko took a cigarette from a pack in his pocket. His fingers shook as he lit it, then he took a long drag.

An encrypted email appeared on his computer. Russia, like other competing nations, had cultivated their own network of operatives, agents, and certain criminal elements to ensure they had their own economic avenue into the Southeast Asia region. These groups often delivered news related to Russian interests, including monitoring the former Biopreparat site Pavlenko's father had managed.

There had only been a handful of times in the past when someone had shown interest in the place.

Twice it was nothing more than some adventurous backpackers who engaged in so-called dark tourism into places like Chernobyl, former chemical weapons testing sites in Japan, or other abandoned relics that humanity had tried to forget.

Another time it had been a group sent by a local investor to scout out potential sites for a secluded resort near the picturesque mountains of Ninh Binh.

Fortunately, the rumors and stories passed down by the locals kept most people far away.

But this email marked the first time he'd heard of foreigners asking specifically about survivors of the 1990 disaster, a memory that still haunted Pavlenko.

He recalled his father's outbursts the night it had happened. How he had yelled at Pavlenko's mother when she'd tried to comfort him. The sound of a glass full of vodka thrown against the wall. Pavlenko had been fourteen at the time. His father had always claimed they had moved to Vietnam to pursue agricultural chemical production, but the cagey way his father talked about work had led Pavlenko to believe something more was going on.

His suspicions proved true when a mysterious disease struck the local community—and his own household. He put a hand over his stomach, remembering the pain and the long hours writhing in bed. Death had seemed like a distinct certainty, even a welcome relief, before he had been administered a cure.

Soon after, his father had been demoted and disappeared altogether. Pavlenko and his mother were separated. He had been given a new name and left to be forgotten in an orphanage. It was during those years of abandonment that he had decided what to do with his own career.

He would finish what his father had started.

He had survived too much for all of this to collapse around him now. He dialed Levin.

"I need you in my office immediately," he said when Levin picked up. "Bring Markov."

He finished his cigarette then smashed it into an ashtray. He lit a second right before Levin finally entered with Markov. The Archon mercenary had bandages over his arm and looked like he'd been wrestling with a bonfire. But if he was in pain, Pavlenko couldn't tell by the way the muscled man sauntered in.

"You're too slow," Pavlenko said.

Levin started. "I was across—"

"No excuses. There's a situation."

Levin's eyes went wide with that shocked look he got right before he fished around for excuses to defend his failures. Markov had his tattooed and burned arms folded over his chest, appearing as though he was already bored.

"I've been made aware that foreign investigators are sniffing around an old Biopreparat site in North Vietnam," Pavlenko said. "They may be looking for us."

"I will send some of our people there," Levin said. "We can intercept them. I will gladly tell Dmitriyev once again that I gave the commands that saved our country from embarrassment."

Pavlenko wanted to slap the smirk off Levin's face. "How long will it take for your men to get there?"

Levin's smirk started to fade. "At least fifteen hours before they make it from here to Hanoi."

"And then a few hours before they can reach Ninh Binh," Pavlenko said. "By then, whoever is snooping around that site will be gone. If these were the same people responsible for Kaliningrad, they must be stopped immediately."

Markov raised an eyebrow. "We don't need to send anyone from here—or Russia, for that matter."

"I'm listening," Pavlenko said.

"Archon is more than just Russians," Markov said. "We are everywhere. Say the word, and I will have our men take care of your little problem."

Pavlenko tapped the end of his cigarette over the ashtray. Levin had never told him Archon fostered a global network of mercenaries. He had always assumed they operated only out of Russia. Judging by the shock painted on Levin's face, he hadn't realized that either.

He did not like trusting operations to a group that hid so much from him, even if they had come recommended from Dmitriyev and the Main Intelligence Director. He made a mental note to inquire more about Archon later. For now, there was no other choice. He could not let these foreigners interfere with his efforts. If they found his facilities in the Sahara or Taklamakan, everything he had worked for would be ruined.

"Fine," Pavlenko said. "Contact your associates in Vietnam immediately. Find out who these people are and stop them."

"It will be done." Markov snapped his fingers. "Like that."

27

Ninh Binh, Vietnam

THE MORNING SUN had just started to peek above the horizon, and a few roosters crowed to greet it.

After leaving their scooters a half-kilometer away at a small restaurant, Alex and Skylar did a security check around the little hamlet nestled into the woods where Nguyen had said to meet her. He and Skylar had never had a chance to get that hot footbath the hotel operators promised. But when Vector Team had tried to leave in the dark of the early morning, the woman and her family had already been preparing the hotel's small kitchen for breakfast.

The woman running the hotel hadn't been at all surprised to hear that Skylar and Alex wanted an early start to the day. She had assumed they wanted to visit a local temple perched atop a mountain to enjoy the sunrise, and he hadn't bothered to correct her. Before they left, she packed them a breakfast of pastries. The food was great, but the coffee she had given them was what kept Alex going after the late-night reconnaissance of the Operation Groundswell facility.

He was used to long workdays and nights, but training and discipline could only hold off the poison of exhaustion for so long. Only the hope that this meetup would provide the breakthrough they needed kept him going when the caffeine wore off.

Nguyen had sent him the coordinates of the small village outside Ninh Binh where she had located an older woman named Dai Thi Diu. Dai was supposedly a survivor of the 1990 leak.

After discussing logistics and potential exfil routes, Nguyen had promised to ensure Dai's neighborhood was clear when she arrived first. But Alex and Skylar double-checked the area themselves, walking around the cluster of tile-roofed houses by the gravel and dirt road.

Chicken wire encircled the properties. All the usual livestock meandered about the yards. A few dogs gave them curious glances and lazy barks, but he guessed the canines were used to humans doing early morning chores in the largely agricultural community. Fortunately, most of the people they had seen this morning were already working in the fields and paddies. The only person they had run into near the houses was a woman making incense sticks. She didn't give them a second glance.

They returned to the small house where Dai lived. A few more dogs ran down the street, barking between the roosters' crows and the morning songs of the birds.

Nguyen was waiting out front with a steaming cup of coffee in her hand. "Enjoy your morning walk?"

"Always good to get a taste of the local scenery," Alex said.

Nguyen lifted her cup toward them. "Dai made coffee."

"That was kind," Skylar said, eyeing the cup.

"Promise it's not poisoned," Nguyen said before taking a sip.

Alex would certainly not turn down his second cup for the day. He needed it.

They entered the house. The smell of coffee filled the air, intermingling with incense burning at a small altar. A few pieces of ragged furniture were laid over the creaking floor, and a cheap flat-screen TV hung from the wall.

Skylar circled the interior of the house, peering into the bedroom then the kitchen where the sounds of clinking glassware came from. Her old military training wouldn't let her settle into a potentially hostile environment without knowing every nook and cranny.

Not that Alex could fault her.

Nguyen called out in Vietnamese. A woman in her late sixties came from the kitchen with a tray of mugs and stainless-steel single-cup coffee filters. She wore a bright-pink coat and an equally bright smile.

When she started speaking, Nguyen translated.

"Please, have a seat," Nguyen said.

The woman set down the tray on a low table. She placed a coffee cup with a filter on top for each of them. After pouring hot water into the filters, she gave them a wide grin, accentuating the deep wrinkles in her darkened skin, a face marked from years of outdoor labor. The aroma of the coffee grew stronger as the hot water dripped through the filters into the cups below.

Dai began speaking.

"She's asking why you want to know about the Better Life Agricultural Company," Nguyen said. "That was the public name of the facility you're interested in."

"Straight and to the point," Skylar said. "I like that."

The old woman laughed when Nguyen translated Skylar's words.

"She said while she appreciates visitors, this isn't the first time someone's asked about that place," Nguyen said.

"Who else was asking?" Alex asked.

"Most of this is hearsay, but she thinks a group of Russians came by a few years ago. Then there were some Chinese investors. They tried to purchase the space, but the facility is on government- protected land now. Besides, no smart person would ever work on anything on that land."

"Why's that?"

"Curses the spirits."

Skylar gave the woman a skeptical glance, and Dai laughed.

"She doesn't really believe in them," Nguyen explained. "She's not as superstitious as some of her neighbors, but throughout the nineties, people wandering around that area got sick."

That piqued Alex's interest. It meant that some of the bioweapons developed at the facility had indeed leached into the local environment, striking out at unwary individuals like a silent, waiting cobra. The samples he and Skylar had taken from the site might be more useful than he'd realized.

"What happened to these people?" Alex asked.

Dai's expression grew solemn as she spoke.

"No one gets sick anymore. At least not recently. But when they did, they experienced the same thing from when she got sick. Abdominal pain, diarrhea, vomiting. An intense fever. Exhaustion."

She pulled no punches in her description. The terrifying and excruciating gastrointestinal disease she described matched the symptoms of AGS that Weber had been tracking.

"She suffered for nearly two weeks and thought she was going to die," Nguyen continued. "And then a Russian doctor showed up to their house, promising a remedy. The doctor gave her family a few pills, and hours later, she felt as though nothing had ever happened. Like it had all been a bad dream.

"The only reason she knew it was real was because some of her neighbors had died after a couple weeks or more of suffering. They never had a chance for funerals, either, with the Russians trying to hush things up."

"How'd they do that?" Alex asked.

"The company paid off most of the families. And then when a few of those families kept talking, they 'moved away.'"

"They were disappeared?" Skylar clarified.

Dai nodded.

"Good Lord, so why's she talking to us now about it?"

A tear traveled down Dai's cheek.

"The Russians have been gone for three decades," Nguyen said. "Rumors spread. No one cared. She doesn't want people to forget about what happened, especially now that the Chinese are trying to do the same thing with all their factories around the country."

"Fair enough," Alex said. This story also proved that if this bioweapon was related like they'd thought, then there was a cure. That was incredible news. But it didn't matter if they couldn't find out where the people responsible for the current iteration of the archaea had stashed this cure.

"Does she have any idea what the cure was?" Skylar asked.

Dai shook her head then motioned to their coffee, urging them to drink up. They removed the filters. Alex took a tentative sip. It was far better than he could have expected. Rich and bold. Dai gave him a knowing smile when he complimented it.

"Does she know anyone else who might have more information about the people who ran the place? Anyone who worked there?" Alex asked, getting back to the subject at hand.

Dai nodded.

"Who?" Skylar asked.

"Her brother was one of the few locals who worked in the facility," Nguyen said.

"Where's her brother now?"

Dai walked over to a set of squeaky drawers and rummaged through one. She returned with a handful of photographs, laying them out on the table. She pointed at one.

Six young Vietnamese men stood in a line with their hands clasped behind their back. They wore bland olive-green military-like uniforms. Behind them was what appeared to be a newly constructed version of the facility Alex and Skylar had scoured last night.

"Her brother was ten years younger than her. He was brought in as part of an economic development program that required foreign companies to hire locals if they wanted to set up businesses in the area," Nguyen said.

Then that lone tear that had rolled over Dai's cheek was joined by another.

"Her brother did not survive," Nguyen said.

"I thought her family was given the cure," Alex said.

"They were. Her brother took the same pills she did. But almost as soon as he took it, he started having trouble breathing and his skin turned red."

"Sounds like an allergic reaction to the medicine," Alex said.

"Dai agrees. The only other time she saw her brother like that was years earlier when their father had brought back shark liver as a treat for them. It was supposed to be good for their health, but with barely a bite, her brother had that same reaction. That time, they got him to the family doctor. But since the family doctor was busy trying to help people suffering from that gastrointestinal disease, they couldn't get to him in time."

Dai spread more of the photos in front of them, jabbing her finger at another. This one also showed the group of Vietnamese workers, including Dai's brother, posed in front of the gates to the facility, all wearing serious expressions. This time a group of Russians in suits and formal dresses was with them.

"Here is the boss of the plant, the evil man responsible for all of this."

Alex recognized the man's face from their mission brief. That was Pavel Khovansky, the Russian responsible for Operation Groundswell. But what the briefing hadn't mentioned were the other two individuals next to him.

Next to Khovansky was a woman and a young man who appeared to be in his teens. The similar bone structure and cold blue eyes pegged them as father and son.

Nothing in the brief mentioned Khovansky had a family. In fact, Khovansky's personal records had been scrubbed nearly clean. The man might never have existed except for the mere mention that he had once owned the Better Life Agricultural Company associated with Operation Groundswell.

Alex filed that information away in his head. Maybe finding a modern link to the people who'd run this place would be useful.

He was ready to ask Dai another question, but the room had gone quiet. And it wasn't just the room, he realized.

There were no more crowing roosters, no more barking dogs, no more singing birds.

Everything was silent, except for the alarms blaring in Alex's mind.

SKYLAR REACHED for the handgun holstered snugly against the small of her back, finding comfort in the pistol grip. She didn't take it out yet, but if Wolfe was spooked, then she feared it wouldn't be long before she did.

"Who did you tell about this meeting?" Skylar asked Nguyen.

"The only other person who knows about this is her son," Nguyen said.

Wolfe stood and stepped cautiously toward one of the windows. He stayed in the shadows, out of the orange glow crawling through the room.

Nguyen and Dai exchanged a few words.

"Who the hell is her son?" Skylar asked. "You said there was triad activity around here… is he…?"

Dai spoke angrily.

"He's not in a triad," Nguyen said.

"Where'd you meet him?" Wolfe asked, peering out one of the windows.

"He's the bartender at a small place not far from here," Nguyen said.

"You expected a random bartender to keep this quiet?" Skylar asked.

"This wasn't just a random bartender," Nguyen said. "I found Dai's profile in the medical records of those who were affected from the 1990 leak. Couldn't even find an address for her, but saw she had a son here. That's the best lead I could get in the timeframe you gave me."

"What did you tell her son?" Wolfe asked.

"Seriously, Wolfe? Almost nothing. I told him I had a documentary crew surveying old Soviet manufacturing sites. The guy wasn't an idiot. I needed a good, solid excuse."

"He must've tipped someone off," Wolfe said.

"No shit," Skylar said. "Guy's working at a bar getting paid pennies. Perfect opportunity for someone to pick up an informant for a few bucks."

"That was the only person who knew anything about this meeting," Nguyen said. "Are you sure you guys aren't just being paranoid?"

"Ask her when the roosters stop crowing," Wolfe said.

Nguyen grew pale when she heard the answer. "Only when the civets and badgers are prowling around."

"Seems like we got predators out there now," Wolfe said. "And I'm not talking about the kind with four legs."

Dai looked between them, a mixture of anger and fear on her face. Poor lady couldn't quite understand what they were all concerned about, but she was probably wondering what kind of dog shit these strangers had dropped on her doorstep. Skylar couldn't help but feel a little sorry for intruding like this on the woman's life.

But thousands, millions, maybe even billions of lives hung in the balance.

"You spot any potential hostiles?" Skylar asked her partner.

He looked back from the window. "Maybe. I saw movement in the field a few seconds ago. Nguyen, any idea what we might be up against?"

Skylar pulled out her Mark 23. Dai started screaming in Vietnamese. Nguyen had to hold her to calm her down.

"Triads out here are usually quiet," Nguyen said, gritting her teeth as she endured Dai's flailing. "Can't imagine you've got more than a couple people coming in for a hit, unless…"

"Unless they have a better idea of who we are and what we're trying to do," Wolfe said.

"Look, are you sure there's even someone out there?" Nguyen asked. "Maybe…"

She let the words trail off.

"I see more movement in the bushes across the road," Wolfe said. "And it doesn't look like the breeze. Maybe two or three people lurking in the paddies."

"If these guys have any brains, you can bet they'll be out back too," Skylar said. "Not going to be an easy out. I'm guessing they're watching our scooters. That's what I would do. Force us to hoof it."

"Not like we have any other choice," Wolfe said.

"I'll check the back," Skylar said, starting toward the kitchen.

Before she made it to the doorway, glass exploded from above, shards spraying over her. It took her a second to see that a round had thumped into a framed picture of Dai's family on the wall.

Another rash of gunfire punched through the walls. Dai screamed, and Nguyen forced her to the floor.

Skylar looked at Nguyen. "Thought you said triads didn't usually lug heavy hardware."

"They don't around here," Nguyen replied. She gritted her teeth, her body over Dai's. "You guys must have some bad people after you."

Dai whimpered, her eyes closed, words tumbling out of her mouth in a prayer.

"Wolfe, we need to leave," Skylar said. "But we aren't making it out front without getting cut down."

"What about Dai?" Nguyen asked, voice hitching up in worry.

Another crash of rounds tore through the walls and windows.

"She can stay," Skylar said. "They don't want her! And if we don't get out of here…"

"You think these people will be kind to her?" Wolfe demanded.

Nguyen said nothing, but the expression on her face told Skylar all she needed to know. Leave it to her partner with his soft spot for kids and old ladies when the whole world was in jeopardy.

But while he was thinking of Dai, she had to keep her mind on the mission. Every second they debated what to do was a second wasted. A second closer to death. She scooped up the photos Dai had shown. Dai started yelling, reaching toward her when she stuffed them into her pack, but another gunshot cracked through the broken window. Dai shrieked and ducked low again.

"Come out with your hands up!" a voice called. The accent was rough, maybe Vietnamese. Definitely not Russian.

"Screw that," Skylar said. "Wolfe, Nguyen, take her out the back. I'll cover."

He rushed toward Dai and Nguyen at a hunch, brandishing his pistol. He shepherded them toward the kitchen as another burst of gunfire speared through the windows and the wall.

Skylar popped up from another window. She fired off a quick burst at the flickers of movement in the long grass across the road.

The brief cover fire gave her a fleeting moment to survey her surroundings. Every flash of movement glared in her vision.

Two guys ducked at the edge of the paddies, using the bank as cover. Another was closer to the house, right behind a tree. She caught two more shadows moving in the brush outside, branches and leaves wagging from their quick retreat. All wore black fatigues and masks. Their initial surprise from her suppressing fire seemed to have frozen them for no more than a few seconds. A hailstorm of lead tore into the house, chiseling through the walls and blasting apart the windows.

Skylar ran low for the kitchen. Showers of splinters burst from every impact, glass fragments flying. Pictures fell from the wall. The small altar with its incense offerings cracked and broke. Stuffing bled from the furniture.

Rounds seared through the air past her, and adrenaline churned through her vessels, slowing time. She operated like a machine, finely tuned by training and experience.

One of the attackers kicked in the doorway. He leveled an AK at her, but she was quicker, sending bullets plunging into his torso. He fell backward, and his rifle clattered over the rock and dirt. Dust filled the air as more bullets slammed through the house.

She saw glimpses through the broken windows of the others charging her position. Another burst of rounds from her Mark 23 gave her the momentary cover she needed to make it into the kitchen.

With her pistol slide locked back, she discarded her empty magazine and jammed in a fresh one. Dai and Nguyen had already made it out the back door. Wolfe had gone with them.

Why the hell had he taken off without waiting for her? You didn't leave your partner behind, damn it.

She saw Dai's pink jacket between the thick trees and brush, running northwest away from the house. Skylar was about to run after them when she heard the crack of gunfire from only a few feet away.

28

SKYLAR DOVE behind the nearest thicket of trees. Leaves were torn off branches, kicked up from bullets ripping through the forest. Chunks of bark burst off the trees. She expected to feel those bullets scorching into her skin.

But nothing hit her.

She wasn't the target.

Three gunmen advanced through the woods just north of her, all with rifles shouldered. Now Skylar knew why Wolfe hadn't waited for her. She could still see flecks of Dai's pink coat through the leaves. They were drawing the attackers away. The gunmen had their sights set on the trio, giving Skylar a chance to catch up behind them unnoticed.

But already the enemy was moving fast, spreading out into combat intervals, putting about twenty yards between one another as they disappeared into the foliage. If she didn't know better, she might've mistaken them for actual trained military. Not the triad goons she had thought they would face.

Even as the forest swallowed them, Skylar used the constant rattle and bark of their rifles to navigate after them. They certainly weren't concerned about conserving ammo.

The only reason Wolfe, Dai, and Nguyen weren't already dead was because of how thick the trees were. But that also meant Skylar didn't have a clean shot.

She saw flickers of movement ahead as she ran. But she had to get closer. Much closer to make sure she didn't screw up this chance at an ambush. All she had was the one magazine left in her pistol.

Her heart hammered against her bruised ribs, a war drum leading her into battle.

She glanced back to check that the attackers currently storming Dai's house from the front hadn't joined the pursuit. It wouldn't be long before they realized no one was in the house. She wanted to be long gone by then.

The man closest to her bobbed and weaved through the trees. His black clothes seemed to melt into the early morning shadows. He paused for a second to let loose another burst of rounds that cut into the forest. That gave her the second she needed to close in on him. Just ten feet away, she fired a controlled cluster of shots. Bullets stitched into his back. He sprawled face-first into the tangle of vines and ferns.

She tugged the AK from his dead grip and kept running.

More gunshots through the woods ahead. The crack of the gunfire echoed between the trees. Skylar raced to catch up to the last two men. Her chest heaved with each struggling breath, her ribs protesting. She fought past the constant pain, thinking only of what would happen if she didn't stop those two men.

"Wolfe, catching up," she said over the comms between gasping breaths. "One target down. Keep running."

"Copy," he said.

"Might need some help. Got more coming soon from the house."

Leaves swatted her. Branches clawed at her face. Snarled roots and the dense low-lying vegetation grabbed at her boots.

But she could not stop. Could not let herself get dragged down by this forest.

Then she glimpsed the other two men again. One was far ahead. Maybe thirty yards, by now. Hard to tell with all the trees. The other was closer. Close enough to hear the branches snapping under his feet. He looked over his shoulder. Maybe he'd heard her. Maybe he was checking on his fallen comrade.

Either way, he hadn't seemed to expect seeing her. He dropped down low, kneeling behind a tree. His rifle exploded in a fusillade of rounds, forcing Skylar to throw herself to the side.

So much for stealth.

Shredded leaves and twigs pelted her. She fired back, but the second man sprinted away, disappearing into the trees.

Voices from the four or five men who had run into the house burst through the trees. Their shouts permeated the woods, sounding as if they were spreading out. Maybe their comrades had warned them about Skylar.

They would be on her in no more than a couple minutes.

And now she couldn't see where her initial target had gone. If he had any kind of military training, he would already be crawling for a new position, of which there was more than enough in this forest.

She shouldered the stolen AK and opened fire. Rounds split bark and drilled through the trees. She wanted to provoke him, to see if she could get him to show himself. Without seeing where he'd gone, she would be risking her life trying to find a new position. But staying put would be equally as deadly with the other pursuers advancing through the woods from the house.

Her gambit worked.

Gunfire exploded toward her as she ducked under the knotted trunks of a few conjoined trees. Skylar crawled on her belly to a rotting leg. Bullets thumped against it. She dragged herself under the erupting wood chips to another tree.

Then she drew herself up to one knee. Just fifteen or so feet from her position, the gunman was leaning out from behind another tree.

She fired. Rounds lanced toward him. At least one caught him in the shoulder. He dropped into the ferns, vanishing for a moment. The bolt locked back on Skylar's rifle. Without any other magazines for it, she discarded the weapon and started to draw her Mark 23.

Before she could even raise the pistol to finish the job, the guy blasted out from his cover, letting out an animalistic roar. His rifle had either jammed or he'd run out of ammo too.

The reason didn't matter. But his desperate fury did.

The man threw himself at her like a starving grizzly. She tried to squeeze off a shot, but he hit her hard under her ribs. The impact ignited her injuries, white-hot agony flaming through her body. They both went down in the leaves and brush. Her pistol flew from her hand, disappearing into the nearby foliage.

The man swung a heavy fist into her side, catching her ribs. She let out a scream, unable to withstand the pain rocketing up through the bruised bone in an electric shock.

Another heavy knee landed just under her sternum. Air whooshed up from her lungs, and she gasped, struggling for breath, no longer screaming. He pressed her into the wet earth as if he meant to bury her. Blood dripped across her face from the gunshot wound in the man's shoulder. His right arm hung uselessly by his side, but he pressed against her neck with his one good hand.

She tried to punch at his jaw, but he dodged it.

Taking on a guy with a bullet wound should have been easy. But the pain from her past injuries burst throughout her body like a chain of firecrackers. Her lungs screamed at her, still struggling to draw in oxygen.

More gunshots and voices in Vietnamese and Russian-accented broken English filled the woods.

"Alex, help," she managed, her voice so weak that she wasn't sure it could carry over the comms.

Soon it wouldn't matter whether she beat this man or not. She was going to be dead in seconds.

"NGUYEN, take Dai to the bus station," Alex said. "Get her out of here."

Nguyen rushed ahead with the older woman, and Alex veered off to his left. At this point, all he could hope for was that Nguyen got Dai out of here alive. This wasn't the poor woman's fight, and he regretted bringing her into it.

The least he could do was buy them some time. But he'd heard his partner's scream a few moments ago. And then, nothing…

He spotted one of the gunmen who had been chasing them. The man was still running after Dai and Nguyen, no doubt attracted by the flash of Dai's pink coat.

Alex pressed himself tight against a tree and waited. His single pistol was nothing compared to the firepower that man carried. But he had surprise on his side.

The man ran right past him, intent on Dai and Nguyen. It took only a few shots. The man staggered, gripping his sides, swinging his rifle around on Alex.

Alex never let the man fire. The gunman went down with bullets punching into his chest, the last bits of his life sighing out. Alex scooped up the man's rifle and sprinted toward where Skylar should be.

He heard yells coming from the direction of Dai's house

and thought he saw flickers of activity maybe fifty, sixty yards back, running toward him along a shallow stream. Even with the slight clearing around the winding stream, it was hard to see deeper beyond it into the trees.

"Vector Two, do you copy?" he tried at a whisper.

No response.

His heart accelerated with a wild thump, the fear of losing her to the woods and these men all too real of a possibility.

Where did you go?

He searched down the sights of the rifle, looking for some sign. Trampled vegetation. Bullet holes in the tree trunks. Blood, for God's sake.

He thought he heard the sound of a struggle somewhere through all the plants, but the shouts from the attackers moving in from their south masked any hope of listening to breaking branches or crunching leaves to find Skylar.

"Skylar, where are you?" he tried again.

Nothing but a grunt came back over the line.

His pulse raced past his ears, growing louder with each passing second. She must have gotten tangled up with the last gunman. Maybe she was injured, dying.

Dark thoughts blasted through his mind in a spiraling typhoon. She had to be fine. Had to be.

Finally, he found a path of trampled earth and crushed foliage—signs of a struggle.

Before he could follow it, one of the gunmen barreled through the brush. He carried his rifle, ready to unleash hell on his prey, but he was still gunning down the path where Nguyen and Dai had gone.

Alex cut the man down with three rounds. Those echoing shots gave the others warning enough that he was here. He heard them shouting, but they stopped rushing so heedlessly through the woods, instead disappearing into the brush to surround him.

One down.

Three, possibly four to go.

He fired off another burst into their positions then dropped low, sneaking toward another cluster of trees. Two gunmen advanced toward the last spot he had been. After gently lowering the rifle, he took out his suppressed pistol. He drew a bead on the farthest man.

Three quick squeezes of the trigger and the man went down.

Alex adjusted his aim to the closer one. The last gunman swiveled, appearing to search for the source of the shots. The man took a few steps like he was headed for new cover. Three more shots from Alex's pistol, and the gunman collapsed into the bed of leaves and plants not far from his downed comrade.

The remaining gunmen had gone quiet.

Skylar was still nowhere to be seen.

He tried to find the path he'd been following before those gunmen had stopped him. Before he could, another fusillade of gunfire dashed any hopes he had of finding his partner soon.

———

SKYLAR COULD NOT SUCK down a single full breath. Her vision swam, red with desperation and fury. The man seemed to grow heavier as her head grew lighter.

She could feel her life evaporating a second at a time. The gunshots, the yells that she'd heard moments ago might as well have come from ten thousand miles away. Everything seemed to be fading.

Everything except for the pain.

If she had been at full strength, she would have used her feet to propel herself up and twist him off. But she was too weak, too damaged.

The only thing keeping her alive was the fact that this guy had one useless, bleeding arm. The color was slowly draining from his face. His adrenaline and shock from the initial wound would be wearing off. The agony of that bullet twisting around in his muscle would hit him full force, a wave of electricity pulling at his nerves and activating all those primal instincts of survival that surfaced when someone was pushed to the edge. Instincts that overrode logic and convinced people who weren't used to living close to death to make rash decisions.

That was what she hoped for now. She used one hand to pry his grip loose around her neck, just enough to prevent him from crushing her windpipe. He focused all his strength on tightening his fingers.

That was all the opening she needed.

Twisting under his weight, she drew her right leg up. Not enough that she could use it to cause him any damage with a knee or a kick. But just enough to reach the thigh sheath strapped there.

Her fingers touched her blade's hilt, just barely slipping off. Every little movement, every extra effort to move under this man cost her an increasing tidal wave of pain from her ribs.

She gritted her teeth. His fingers squeezed tighter, grasping for the hilt, trying to get a good grip on it. The pressure on her neck was worse than ever.

Just a little more.

More gunshots exploded somewhere to her south and west.

"Vector Two, do you copy?" Alex's voice chimed over the channel again. She couldn't answer him.

She stretched a little farther. Something popped in her side, but she finally got two fingers around the handle then slipped the blade out. In one swift motion, she brought it up and slammed it home, straight into the side of the man's neck. Her attacker collapsed, clawed at the blade. She used the rest of her strength to push him off her chest. He thrashed before falling still a few moments later.

She rose to one knee. Her chest felt like she'd been hit by a rhino and then the two-ton beast had decided to sit on her for good measure. She desperately needed a moment to catch her breath and let the pain subside. But the other gunmen in the woods weren't about to give her that chance.

"Vector One, I'm here," she tried, her voice hoarse.

No response.

Footsteps crunched through the nearby brush. She thought he heard a click on her comms, but she couldn't be sure.

She crawled toward where she had dropped the Mark 23, the only weapon anywhere nearby with ammo. More voices yelled out in a mixture of broken English and some Vietnamese. They sounded like they were coming from every direction at once.

She combed through the roots and leaves as quietly as she could, looking for her dropped weapon while she monitored her surroundings, waiting to see the flash of steel from a rifle or another masked goon emerging from behind the screen of leaves.

There!

She found her pistol lying smashed into the bed of leaves and mud. Another man stalked through the forest about ten yards to her west. She scrambled for the gun and scooped it up. Glimpses of the masked gunman flickered between the trees as he cut between the foliage. His path was taking him closer to her. He was maybe ten, fifteen feet from her position now. She stayed as quiet and still as possible, catching him in her iron sights.

As the man drew near, she saw he was wearing a black T-shirt. Poking out from one of the sleeves she noted a big Cyrillic A tattooed along the back of his biceps, just like the man they had seen in Kaliningrad.

Definitely not a simple triad hitman.

When he finally reached a clearing in the trees, close enough that Skylar knew there was no chance she would miss, she fired.

The man went down in a heap of limbs. Skylar drew herself up slowly, using a tree as support. She kept her pistol raised for any more incoming threats.

Another rattle of gunfire shook through the woods. She heard a pained groan.

"Vector One?" she tried over the channel.

A silhouette shifted between the trees, headed her direction carrying a rifle. She brought her weapon to bear, ready to squeeze the trigger.

This better be the last damn guy.

29

SWEAT TRICKLED down Alex's forehead and matted the back of his shirt to his spine. The effects of the flagging adrenaline pumping through his body left his fingers shaky, but he kept the rifle pressed to his shoulder. The acrid odor of the spent rounds hung in the air, mixing with the heady smell of the jungle. His skin prickled, his vision still tunneled down the rifle's sights.

He almost fired when he saw one last person with a weapon aimed at him, but the ponytail of dark hair told him this was not a threat.

"Skylar," he said in a whisper. Somehow in that moment using her last name seemed too impersonal. Too cold.

"Alex... damn..." Her words came out in a wheeze, her expression softening. She turned the M9 away from him but didn't lower it. "Are there...?"

"I think we got all of them," he said. He used his sleeve to scrub his fingerprints from the stolen rifle then tossed it to the ground. "God, I'm glad to see you. I thought..."

He let the words trail off.

"You okay, partner?"

Skylar leaned down, wincing, and scrubbed another rifle lying nearby. "I'll live."

"Any others?" he asked.

She shook her heard. "We got lucky today. But they're going to send more."

"Dai isn't going to be safe here either," Alex said. "She can't come back. Nguyen took her to the bus depot."

"Are we going to keep looking in Ninh Binh? Maybe there's another survivor like Dai."

"Our cover here is blown," Alex said. "They'll have people at the Groundswell site and ears at every damn bar, hotel, and tourist trap. Maybe their interest will die down if we lay low for a while. But AGS has spread way too fast in China. We don't have the time to hide out here and wait."

Skylar limped toward him, and together they began the trek north. They trudged on in silence, the calls of the birds and buzz of insects returning to the forest.

They were safe again.

But the world wasn't.

"This was a bust," Alex said. "We wasted time, made that woman's life miserable, and what have we got to show for it?"

Skylar gave him a slight grin. "Well, we're still alive, and I've got those photos Dai showed us."

"Doesn't tell us anything about a cure." Alex swiveled around, looking for any sign of followers.

"We know now that Khovansky had a family," Skylar said. "And we know people really did survive the first outbreak. If this is linked to AGS and the archaea bioweapons, then we're on the right track toward a cure."

"But we're not going to save lives by just being on the path toward a cure or even confirming it exists." He couldn't help the frustration and anger rising in his voice. The sheer helplessness he felt in that moment was overwhelming. "We only help people if we find that cure. Otherwise, all those victims in

China and everyone else who's going to get hit by the next wave are as dead as the men we just killed."

Skylar shot him a glance. "Alex, you okay?"

"After that bloodbath? Not really."

"No, I mean, that look in your eyes…" She stared at him as they slogged from the woods into a sun-soaked clearing. "I've seen it before. Back in my squadron, when we got to the scene too late, only to find Al-Qaeda sympathizers had already scorched our boys on the ground. Or when my squad saw me after I lost the leg. We didn't lose anyone today, so what happened to you, Alex?"

He was silent for a few seconds, his boots slapping over grass and fallen branches. "Why'd you join Vector?"

She shot him a bemused look but humored him anyway. "After I lost the leg, I started to pick up a degree in biomedical engineering with my GI Bill payout. Thought I could learn how to help those engineers regrow flesh-and-blood legs. That way people like me could get that part of ourselves back. Stupid, isn't it?"

Alex shook his head, letting the simmering anger fade.

"Realized I wasn't cut out for lab work, but I liked the bits and pieces of science I picked up," she said. "Then Kasim found me right when I was about to give up on it all. Right when things looked the darkest. Don't know how he knew, but when he told me that I could still have a mission, I never looked back. What about you?"

A dirt road stretched before them with rice paddies on either side. Tall green rice plants stuck up from the water, waving gently in the humid breeze rolling over them. Karst mountains surrounded the paddies and a flat field just beyond.

Alex waited until they had walked a few minutes down that road to speak. It was something he'd never told anyone before.

"I killed my brother," he finally said, barely getting the words out.

He expected Skylar to curse at him or recoil. But she didn't. Her expression softened, a rarity in itself. "What happened?"

"You remember when that terrorist was sending anthrax letters in the early 2000s?" he asked.

"Yeah."

He looked out toward the mountains. "My mother was a journalist with the *Times*. She covered politics. We were living just outside DC in Silver Spring. Every day after I got home from high school, one of my jobs was to get the mail. Just a dumb chore. Something I could easily do."

Skylar said nothing.

"My little brother, Patrick, was just twelve at the time. Always tried to be like me. Wearing my clothes, listening to my music, reading all these scientific books and magazines because that's what I did. Annoying at the time."

"Sounds like a typical little brother."

"He was," Alex said. "Then one day I came home from school. I was pissed because my homecoming date cancelled on me for some meathead on the football team. Didn't get the mail. My brother was waiting on the next *National Geographic* or something." Alex let out a sad laugh. "He only cared about it because I did, of course. He was upset I didn't get the mail, and, Skylar, I can still hear him slamming that door to get it."

"Oh no," Skylar said before the rest of the story left his mouth.

"That was the day my mom was targeted. And Patrick... he was too damn nosy. He saw that strange letter, even though it was addressed to my mom, and..."

In his mind's eye, Alex saw his little brother with the letter. Saw the white powder. The news stories he'd seen, the ones his mom had told them about, had all come together in a blinding flash.

He had known right then and there what had happened to his brother.

"Doctors couldn't save him," Alex finally said. "I remember the look in his eyes when he was sick. That fear. That helpless fucking fear. I'll never forget it. And when he was gone, I knew I couldn't do anything else with my life. I wasn't going to let other people die because I shirked my responsibilities. Or because they were in the wrong place at the wrong time. There are people in this world who don't value human life. People would abuse nature and turn it against each other like those terrorists did. Like the Russians seem to be doing now."

"I don't know what to say," Skylar said. "But I'm sorry."

Alex couldn't say anything else, and frankly, he didn't want to.

The long, silent trek took them down a barren road where they passed only a few small groups of farmers working in the paddies. A couple men glanced up from their work but turned away just as quickly. For that, Alex was thankful. The fewer witnesses, the fewer people who were alarmed by their presence, the better.

They reached a small town with a couple of roadside food stalls and a convenience store near a single bus stop. This was their best option for quickly leaving the area without their scooters.

Ten minutes later, their "bus" arrived. The vehicle was more of an extended van than anything else, but it had four wheels and enough empty seats for the two of them. That was more than good enough for him.

"We're definitely not getting our deposit back on the mopeds," Skylar said as she found a seat.

It was an attempt to break the tension. He couldn't laugh. But he appreciated the effort and settled in next to her.

"Guess not."

Alex usually enjoyed his time in Vietnam. This time, not so much. He was ready to go.

They didn't bother returning to their hotel near the Tam Coc. He doubted their enemy had intel to track the two of them down there yet, but he still didn't want to take any unnecessary risks. Definitely didn't want to risk a shoot-out that might endanger the local families and tourists at the hotel.

Besides, everything they had left behind in their bungalow was disposable. Nothing more than some extra clothes to bolster their cover as adventurous backpackers. Kasim would coordinate with the hotel staff to dispose of whatever was left of their belongings, assuming someone else didn't ransack their place.

Mission protocol required they carry everything they needed at all times, ensuring that they were always ready for a clean exfil, including fake passports and weapons.

The bus took them into the more crowded streets of Ninh Binh proper. Narrow buildings with green and red roofs lined the streets. Handfuls of scooters and pedestrians negotiated the sparse traffic. He and Skylar got off at a stop near a crowded street market filled with carts and tables full of knickknacks, clothes, and food.

Few tourists came to this part of Ninh Binh. Alex could feel the curious eyes of some of the locals. The mud clinging to their clothes probably didn't help. He quickly made a few purchases to replace their ruined outfits, grabbing the first things that looked like they might fit. They snuck into a musty public restroom at the end of the market to change. Skylar's pants came up above her ankles, and her shirt appeared pasted on. She shot Alex a dismissive look.

"Remind me to bring my own change next time," she said.

They continued onward, throwing their muddy and torn clothes into a trash can.

As they walked past convenience stores, eateries, and shops,

Alex set up the arrangements for their flight out of Ninh Bình with Kasim, promising a full debriefing when they were safely in the air. They followed a pothole-pocked street along the Sông Vân River to where it connected with the much larger River Đáy.

At the intersection of these two rivers were the lush temple grounds where Alex had told Nguyen and Dai to meet them. He prayed that they had both made the journey safely, holding his breath when they climbed up a set of concrete stairs to a pagoda pavilion overlooking the two rivers.

Only when they walked around the pavilion did he finally let out a sigh of relief. Dai and Nguyen stood near the stone railing. They were alive. Both unhurt. They looked like nothing more suspicious than a younger woman helping her older mother to pay her respects as they strolled around the temple grounds.

Nguyen seemed equally relieved to see them.

"You still in one piece?" Nguyen asked as they approached.

"We are," Alex said. "Run into any trouble getting here?"

Nguyen shook her head. "Dai needs a place to stay."

"Figured the agency could take care of that," Skylar said.

"Whoever sent you guys can't?" Nguyen asked.

"They'll toss the ball right back into your court," Alex said. "Do what needs to be done to protect her. Safer for all of us. Her house is off limits."

Dai said something.

"She wants those pictures back," Nguyen said.

"Right." Skylar took them from her pocket. They were creased and bent but still intact. She snapped a few photos of each then handed them to Dai.

The woman scowled when she took them, tut-tutting at Skylar.

"Sorry," Skylar said. "At least they're safe with you now, though."

"What happens next?" Nguyen asked.

"Not exactly sure," Alex said.

"After everything we just went through, I was kind of hoping you had a better answer. I want to know we made a difference."

"So do we," Skylar said.

"We aren't stopping until we do," Alex said.

"Then that's it, huh?" Nguyen said. "You guys flying out of here, leaving us to pick up the pieces."

"When you put it that way... yeah," Skylar said.

"Sorry to leave you in a bind, but thanks for your help," Alex said. "I promise we'll make it worth it. Until next time."

Nguyen looked out over the river and then back at him. "Next time we meet on business, I just hope it's a little less eventful." Her gaze flicked to Skylar, and there was something in it that Alex couldn't read. "Although maybe our paths will cross again sometime when it isn't business."

Skylar cleared her throat, shifting from foot to foot. "Sure. Maybe." That brief look of discomfort quickly turned to straight-lipped seriousness. "Just as long as next time it isn't with a pistol pointed at my ribs."

"As long as you guys don't cause me any more trouble," Nguyen said.

"Can't promise that," Skylar said.

Nguyen gave them a slight smirk. "Then you two better get the hell out of here until you can."

FREDERICK, Maryland

ALONE IN HIS OFFICE, Kasim studied the photographs that Skylar had sent of Pavel Khovansky and his family, along with the full debriefing report. The cup of coffee on his desk had long since been drained. Night had bled into morning already, and though exhaustion tugged at the back of his mind, he could not abandon the data they had sent.

There had to be something more, something they were all missing. He couldn't believe they had hit a dead end in Vietnam.

They simply couldn't afford to hit a dead end. Not when the archaea might be headed toward the United States any day now.

His phone rang. It was Divya.

"Still working?" she asked when he answered.

"I'm sorry."

"That's a yes. God, Abe. I know you're doing good things, but…"

If only she knew what his work entailed, how many people he had saved. He hated that he couldn't tell her everything. "This is more important than anything I've ever—"

"You say that every time."

"Divya, I'm—"

"No pleading. No apologies. I think I'm going to take a trip with my sister. Hema wants to go to Italy. Just for a week. Her client cancelled on her, so she's got time now. Spur-of-the-moment kind of thing."

He wondered how much of that was true. Was it a cover? Was she meeting someone else? Could he blame her?

Best not to worry about that now. The world depended on him not worrying about that. But traveling to Europe was a bad idea.

"Don't go," he said.

"Why? You're going to come home? Or you want to take the trip with me?"

"It's not that. I mean, I do want to, of course. But right now, don't travel anywhere."

"Why, Abraham?" her voice carried an undercurrent of venom.

"It might not be safe," he said.

"I knew you would say that. It's never safe to you."

"Trust me. Just this once."

She paused. He really thought she might give him the benefit of the doubt. That she might delay the trip.

"I'm going," she said. "You want to join us, you can. You know we can afford it, and right now, more than ever, we need it."

"Divya, you've got to—"

The line was already dead.

He massaged his temple, his elbow propped on his desk. He hoped Morris was having better luck. Before he could leave to check on the analyst in the operations center, his phone rang again. He was ready to plead his case with Divya again when he saw it was an encrypted line.

Had Skylar and Alex run into trouble? They should have still been in the air.

"Kasim here," he said, trying to hold back the simmer of dread.

"We received some interesting reports." The cool voice told him it was Liang.

"Oh?"

"At least eight gunmen dead outside a small Vietnamese city."

"Gun violence is rare in Vietnam," Kasim replied. "But I'm guessing that's not why you're calling."

"You're right. But that's not what set off our alarms. It probably wouldn't have come across my desk if we weren't monitoring that particular location because of former Biopreparat activity in the area."

"Makes sense."

"I just hope that the two are unrelated." There was a tinge

of restrained anger in her voice. "It would be a shame to find out we needed to make some adjustments to our programs."

"Agreed," Kasim said, trying to bite back his tongue. Everyone was pissed at him today. But he'd learned long ago in his career that a good leader didn't try to be friends with everyone. They did what they had to because they had to.

He understood Liang's worry. She didn't want Vector to be exposed. Vector and the United States had no authorization by the Vietnamese government to execute clandestine or military operations like this within their borders. It had been risky enough enlisting elements of the CIA to aid in their mission.

If the States' involvement came to light, the political, economic, and military fallout could be disastrous.

"If someone we knew was involved in Vietnam, I'm sure they would have a very good reason," Kasim said. "Perhaps something involving current events in China."

Liang paused as if considering it. He assumed she had her own teams monitoring the outbreak in China. He hoped his message was clear.

"It sounds like my other teams might be interested," Liang said.

"I'm going to look into a couple things on my own. Perhaps we should circle back in a couple hours."

"Perhaps we should."

The line went dead. Kasim needed to make a decision, and soon. Vector worked best operating independently and covertly. But with all the lives at stake, both in the United States and worldwide, it was time to bring Liang into the fold. Vector's operations would no longer have the independence that their previous layers of plausible deniability provided. But if Vector couldn't stop this plot alone, that was a small price to pay.

Before he could ask Liang to get more involved, he needed to have some idea of what exactly he was going to tell her—and what he needed from her.

He called Morris, Park, and Weber to meet him in the operations center.

"I get the feeling we're running down the clock," Kasim said. "Liang needs a real lead. Everywhere Alex and Skylar go right now ends in disaster, which makes me think we're still just poking a very big, angry bear. Weber, Park, where are we at?"

"Current systemic surveillance shows fifteen thousand suspected cases of AGS," Weber said. "The disease is no longer just affecting the advanced age and immune-compromised demographics. We're seeing the first cases cropping up in healthy patients between eighteen and sixty. The numbers are on an exponential trajectory now."

"The doctors in China have tried everything from broad-spectrum antibiotics to antiviral drugs and just about anything else you can think of," Park said. "Nothing's working."

"The disease is spreading exactly how Reis told us it would," Weber added. "He predicted the path of the current dust transport models out of the Taklamakan perfectly."

"And still no evidence of community spread?" Kasim asked.

"None that I can tell," Weber said. "It appears to be noncontagious based on the contact tracing data I've intercepted."

"What's the mortality rate?" Kasim said, bracing himself as he imagined what horrors were taking place in China and how they might soon reach the United States' shores.

"Right now, we're seeing very few deaths," Weber said.

"No deaths? Is it not fatal?"

"I'm not sure I'd go that far," Park said. "It's a predominantly gastrointestinal disease. It could very well be highly fatal, but it just takes longer to kill a patient. In 1990, the first death in Ninh Binh was nearly two weeks after the initial patient reported symptoms. We're just now seeing potentially deadly symptoms in China, like internal hemorrhaging. A few

302 • ANTHONY J. MELCHIORRI

cases reported intestinal ruptures, which would invite a host of infections if the patient didn't succumb to internal bleeding first."

"Good God," Kasim said. "This is a ticking time bomb of a disease. It sounds terrifying."

"That seems to be exactly the point," Weber said. "This is the kind of disease that gives governments time to freak out."

"Please tell me you've got a cure brewing," Kasim said.

"Nothing yet," Park said, sounding defeated. "We could run some simulations on the computer model to predict treatment outcomes, but it's terribly inaccurate given how little we know about archaea. Might as well be throwing rocks trying to hit the moon. We need an actual sample of the weaponized version of the archaea to begin drug screening."

"Understood," Kasim said. He wished the scientists had better news to report, but he couldn't fault them. They needed better intel. Story of the day. "Morris, got anything for us?"

Morris flipped open his laptop. "I'm still trying to verify my sources, but I found something."

At a tap on Morris's keyboard, the table screen lit up with the photos Skylar had sent from Vietnam. The images showed the families of the Biopreparat workers along with portraits of the Russian scientists, military officials, and administrators in charge of the program.

"Khovansky was a colonel and fairly prominent leader in Biopreparat, but his programs never got off the ground. The USSR kicked him to the curb after the fallout in Ninh Binh," Morris said, absently scratching at his goatee.

Another tap on the keyboard. The image zoomed in on Khovansky's family.

"According to official records, Khovansky never had a son," Morris said. "The wife, yes. But the son... nothing except for this image. It seems like they took him from Khovansky as part of his punishment. But I found this image of a boy who was committed to a Moscow orphanage just a month and half after Khovansky's removal from Ninh Binh."

Morris called up another image on the screen. It showed a teenage boy in an oversized sweatshirt and dark brown trousers. He had a distinct, slightly crooked nose and wide-set blue eyes. Those features were beset by an almost sickly, gaunt look. The file corresponding to this image read Sergei Pavlenko.

Besides appearing like he'd just been released from a hospital, he was a perfect match for Khovansky's son.

"They took Khovansky's boy from him," Kasim said. "Changed his name and everything. What happened to the father?"

"No idea," Morris said. "For all intents and purposes, he and his wife were wiped clean off the face of the earth. But this boy was not. He joined the Russian Ground Forces and went on to earn a PhD from Saint Petersburg State University in Biochemistry. After, he started a career working for the Academy of Military Science in Moscow. That lasted for almost a decade before he left the government to lead an agricultural manufacturing and supply company, Agrotechnika. The very same company whose equipment Alex found in Kaliningrad."

Kasim felt the thrill of a puzzle piece clicking into place.

"Is the agricultural business a front?" Kasim asked.

"Seems like it," Morris said. "I can't definitively prove it, but check this out."

A new set of images popped up on the screen showing strange mechanical equipment that looked like the tentacles of an enormous metal kraken stretching over a desert. Morris had obtained them from a website from a company called Future Guard with an English tagline of "New Lands for New Generations."

"What is this?" Kasim asked.

"It's Pavlenko's newest company. They're supposed to be developing brand-new terraforming technology, and you'll never guess where their prototype facilities are located."

Kasim didn't need to ask. The image of the sand dunes answered his unspoken question. The sandstorms, the archaea. AGS, Agrotechnika. Khovansky and now Pavlenko. It all fit together, and the picture these fragments formed chilled him to the core. They had to stop this, no matter what.

30

KASIM AND MORRIS met with Reis in a secured conference room just outside Vector's main hub of labs. The Portuguese scientist didn't show an ounce of surprise when they told him about the terraforming angle. Then again, the researcher had probably been through enough over the past couple days that if Kasim had told Reis there was an ongoing alien invasion, the scientist would have accepted this new reality.

"I found it, but I honestly don't get it. How does the terraforming thing fit?" Morris asked, arching his brow above his glasses as if he couldn't quite believe Reis would embrace this idea so quickly.

"Of course," Reis said. "These people are using dust storms to spread weaponized archaea across the world. Terraforming is an excellent cover. Countries with vast deserts have always been interested in doing *something* with all that unusable land. And you probably know this answer better than I do, but how many people are monitoring for military threats out in the middle of the barren desert?"

Kasim could not help but smile. This guy was sharp.

"Let me guess," Reis said. "They are claiming they can

reforest the desert. Their tech can create new agriculture-friendly land that will combat world hunger and climate change."

"You just about nailed it," Morris said. He turned to Kasim. "Man, this guy's good. Why haven't we offered him a full-time job already?"

"Was that just a lucky guess, or have you had past experience with terraforming?" Kasim asked, ignoring Morris.

"Terraforming comes up in our research on dust transport from time to time," Reis explained. "Some researchers in our field are looking at both the positive and negative implications of terraforming, especially as it becomes less science fiction and more science fact. For example, the Chinese government is trying to contain the spread of the Gobi Desert by blocking the wind and stabilizing the soil, stopping dust transport. They created what they call the Great Green Wall by planting trees and grass, along with other measures. A terraforming effort like Future Guard's would fit perfectly into their initiatives."

"Looks like you should've been the one briefing us," Kasim said. "Morris has identified two nexuses where Future Guard has been pursuing these prototype terraforming facilities. Morris?"

Morris pushed his laptop toward Reis, showing first a map of China. He pointed at a spot in the Taklamakan Desert. "They have a facility here. Does this track with your dust transport models?"

Reis furrowed his brow, studying the image then turned on his own laptop. He jotted down the coordinates. In a few minutes, he had a simulation running that showed where his models estimated dust from that region would be transported across China.

"Let me see that," Morris said, capturing images from Reis's computer. He overlaid them back onto his own computer with the reports Weber had given them on the spread of AGS in the population. "It's a perfect fit."

"You said there were two facilities," Reis said. "Where's the second?"

Kasim nodded at Morris, and the analyst showed Reis the next set of maps.

"It's in the Tabelbala region of the Sahara Desert close to the border between Algeria and Morocco," Kasim said. "We used satellite imagery to pinpoint its exact location once we knew what to look for. I think I already know the answer, but does this fit your model too?"

A few minutes of tense work, and Reis nodded. That was an optimal location to seed the desert sands with archaea. Any microorganisms in those sands would spread through Western Europe and straight over the continental United States with the right weather patterns.

"If they released something here," Kasim said, pointing at the map, "how long would it take to make it to the US?"

"Just under ten days," Reis said.

"Damn," Morris said. "You know that ship we were trying to track down? The one with Williams on it?"

Reis's ears perked at the mention of her name.

"I found a ship running Iranian flags that made a stop in Algiers yesterday," Morris said. "It continued onward, but that was the only stop in Northern Africa. I tracked down its shipping manifest. Agrotechnika dropped off a shipment there for Future Guard. Transporting agricultural equipment would be a perfect way to disguise their bioweapon."

For a few long moments, a tense silence passed over the three men. They had no solid intel on when a bioweapon would be deployed from the Algerian location, but if the spread of AGS was any indication, the weapon had been released in China nearly two weeks ago. Kasim doubted that these people would want to space out the release of the bioweapon too much. Deploying from both locations in a limited timespan would ensure that the world had less time to find a cure.

"Reis, are there certain weather conditions that make dust transport more likely to reach the United States from the Sahara?" Kasim asked.

"Of course," Reis said. "Increased temperatures and minimal soil moisture produce the best environment for dust aerosolization. The US Naval Research Laboratory recently began tracking these dust storms to better predict when they would happen and cross the Atlantic. You might get the models from them."

Morris was already working on his laptop. "Think I found it."

"What do they say about the next sandstorm?" Kasim asked.

Morris scrolled through the climatology data and predictions on his screen. "I really don't like to admit this, but it's, uh, a bit too dense for me to follow."

"I got it," Reis said. He delved through the data and models, skimming through the software's prompts. When he stopped, he gulped hard, pushing the laptop back toward Kasim and Morris.

Kasim stared at the screen for a few seconds then locked eyes with Reis. "If I'm to believe this, we're expecting a tremendous Saharan dust storm in approximately thirty-six hours."

Reis nodded. "If I were going to release a weapon into one of these dust clouds, those would be the exact conditions I would target."

"We don't know for sure they're planning on releasing the agent yet," Morris said. "Just because they *could* doesn't mean we're all boned in the next thirty-six hours."

Kasim read over the data a second time, just to be sure.

"This forecast doesn't show another dust storm of that magnitude for another four or five weeks. They aren't going to wait that long after starting the spread of this disease through China."

"What do we do now?" Reis asked.

"*We* don't do anything," Kasim said. "I'm getting the commander involved. Wolfe and Cruz are going to need backup."

SAHARA DESERT, Algeria

DRESSED IN A WHITE PROTECTIVE SUIT, Pavlenko strolled between huge steel cylinders connected to a series of pipes and sensors. A dozen workers monitored the computers and gauges tracking the environmental conditions inside the bioreactors where the archaea were being cultivated. All the reports he had seen showed archaea reproduction and modification rates were at nearly perfect levels. A sight like this should have made him happy, but the news of Vietnam had rattled him.

He had just received a memo from Dmitriyev inquiring why all those Archon mercs in Ninh Binh had died, but no one could tell him who was responsible for their deaths. Levin and Markov were supposed to have handled the situation. Now it seemed to be spiraling out of their control. First Istanbul, then Kaliningrad, and now Ninh Binh.

Dmitriyev told Pavlenko that someone had to be held responsible. Someone had to be punished for this failure.

Pavlenko wanted to blame Levin and Markov. At the start of this project, Pavlenko was supposed to only be responsible for the scientific operations. It was not his choice to work with Levin. But as Levin proved he could not be trusted to handle anything more important than sucking up to Dmitriyev and changing the toilet paper in the bathrooms, Pavlenko knew he had to take matters into his own hands.

Especially if he was going to prove to Dmitriyev that he deserved a spot on the president's cabinet.

With Levin's repeated failures, he worried where the dogs pursuing him might strike next. How long before these stubborn people made their way to the Sahara Desert?

There was no more time to delay. Not if he wanted to meet Dmitriyev's deadline and stay one step ahead of the bastards chasing his operations.

Yunevich approached him with a tablet PC under her arm. "Everything looks healthy, sir. The archaea modifications were a success, and—"

"Dr. Yunevich, we need to immediately begin preparing to evacuate all the bioreactors. The archaea must be loaded into the dispersal units tomorrow morning."

Yunevich took a step back, gesturing at the bioreactors with her tablet PC. "But the genetic modifications have not been fully integrated into the entire batch. We estimate that only sixty percent of this batch has been properly modified, and the changes will take at least—"

Pavlenko gave her a dismissive wave. "I understand that we may no longer be able to completely conceal the archaea from EnviroProct's Aerokeep units. We have no choice. The whole point of subverting EnviroProct's detection systems was to ensure that no one had forewarning or evidence of the archaea traveling over the Atlantic Ocean."

"Yes, sir, and if we give it another week, we can still do that."

"We don't have a week," Pavlenko said. "Someone is after us. There is a projected dust storm tomorrow evening that will ensure proper spread of the archaea across the Atlantic."

"Yes, I've seen the projections. These conditions also seem

ripe for another storm in a month. Maybe we can hold out until—"

"We cannot risk it. I want the archaea deployed for tomorrow. As soon as it is done, we will scrub all these bioreactors. I want no trace of the weapon anywhere in this facility. Will that be a problem?"

"No, sir," Yunevich said. "Everything that is not deployed can be neutralized and incinerated. But…"

Pavlenko could tell exactly where her mind was headed. Her team had relied heavily on the researchers they had abducted to work for them.

"You worry about the laboratories," Pavlenko said. "I will take care of our personnel."

"Of course." Yunevich turned from him, relaying his orders to the other scientists and technicians in the bioreactor facility.

He left the facility and went through the decontamination room, peeling off his PPE and enduring the decon sprays until he was released into the corridor.

That took care of one problem.

But he had other pressing needs. His entire legacy was at stake. He would not share the same fate as his father. A man derided by the government he had loyally served.

He had improved on his father's research. The archaea were the perfect biologically engineered agent to advance Russia's economic and military might. And now the whole program was hanging on by a thread. All because Levin's hired security forces could not stop two spies from tracking them down.

He stormed down the corridors, passing by other labs then a warehouse filled with crates and dormant tractors. At the end of the hall, he saw two men with rifles cradled over their chests. They guarded the administrative quarters.

"Are Levin and Markov here?"

"They're in the armory," one of the guards responded.

Markov and Levin shared the common language of brute force and intimidating weapons. Confronting them in a space where they were surrounded by the violent machines that gave them a false sense of strength was not ideal for what Pavlenko had to say.

"Tell them to meet me in the BSL-2 labs in thirty minutes," Pavlenko said.

He marched to the laboratory, where he donned a white coat. Two of his technicians were working at a lab bench.

"Leave," he said.

One looked ready to protest, pointing at a plastic tray with samples. He had a pipette in his hand.

"I will not say it again," Pavlenko said.

Pavlenko waited for them to exit before he retrieved a small plastic vial from one of the liquid nitrogen storage tanks. He warmed up the vial between his gloved hands.

In that vial were a few micrograms of the weaponized archaea. The small droplet of cryopreservation media containing the archaea melted quickly. He deposited the vial inside a biological safety cabinet, where he used a pipette to transfer the liquid with the pathogen into a larger conical plastic tube with a few hundred milliliters of water.

The archaea would not pose a significant risk unless it was aerosolized and breathed in or digested. Still, working with it in this environment was highly dangerous for the average person.

Pavlenko, though, had long since been inoculated against the weapon, a holdover from his time in Ninh Binh. His inoculation had not come from a vaccine. Rather, he had been infected with the very vector that he planned to deploy today.

And as an added precaution, the cure that his father had developed in tandem with the biological weapon back in the late eighties still worked against the modified form today. The same pharmaceutical compounds had been developed to treat other diseases, which meant he didn't have to worry about building brand-new manufacturing facilities to produce the cure.

Almost no one except him knew that those pharmaceuticals would treat the disease the Chinese and the WHO were now calling AGS.

That knowledge was perhaps the most valuable asset he still had control over—and he planned to use it to his advantage.

Once the archaea sample was thoroughly mixed into the water, he aliquoted samples of the new mixture into a spray bottle. He took the bottle out of the laboratory and hiked up and down the main corridors of the facility, spraying the mixture into the vents blasting cold air through the halls.

A couple of technicians shot him odd looks, but he paid them no heed. He returned to the laboratory when the deed was done, placing the spray bottle on a lab bench.

He waited only a few more minutes before Markov and Levin showed up.

Levin walked in looking like a kicked puppy, and Markov strode behind him as though he had been the one to do the kicking.

"I heard what happened in Vietnam," Pavlenko began.

Levin opened his mouth to speak.

"I don't want to hear excuses. You both promised that the people following us would be caught and stopped. Neither of you have delivered, and we don't even know who they are."

"Archon *will* stop them," Markov said, his face set in grim determination beneath the bandages covering half his face. "Our people are still searching Vietnam, and we've circulated the description of these two individuals throughout our organization."

"You failed in Istanbul, Kaliningrad, and Vietnam. Why do you think your promises now would reassure me?"

Markov's eyes narrowed, and he gestured toward Levin. "It may be our men who died, but it was this imbecile who gave the directions. Let us operate on our own."

"His people are incompetent," Levin said. "And now he tries to make up excuses to pass the blame."

"You hired Archon and Markov," Pavlenko said, maintaining an air of calm. He refused to let them rile him up. "You both are responsible for this failure. And I share responsibility for trusting you. Neither of you will fail again."

"We won't," Levin said.

Markov glared at Levin. "*I* won't. Just don't let this ass-kissing bureaucrat stand in my way."

"No one will stand in your way," Pavlenko said. "But Dmitriyev demands that someone pay for the disasters."

Levin's eyes went wide. "Do not put this on me."

"Screw this," Markov said. Pavlenko noticed his hand inching toward the sidearm holstered at his hip. "I'm only loyal to Russia so long as the rubles flow. I don't need these threats."

"This is not a threat," Pavlenko said.

Markov's fingers rested on the grip of his handgun. "Then quit playing games. Tell me what you want. You want us to hunt down these people who took Paulo Reis? You want me to find out who was sneaking around in Vietnam? Free me from sitting on my thumbs in this desert and I will deliver."

"I don't want you to do that," Pavlenko said. "So far, chasing after them has resulted in nothing but disaster."

"Then what do you want?" Levin asked.

"One of you will be given over to Dmitriyev," Pavlenko said.

"I don't need to pay anyone with my life," Markov said, pulling out the handgun. He kept the weapon aimed at the floor, but the intent was clear. "I will make my own way if necessary."

"Why not you?" Levin asked, pointing at Pavlenko. Beads

of sweat rolled over his forehead. "Markov, let's take him into our custody. He's the one in charge of this operation. It's his failed science project."

Markov took a step toward him.

Pavlenko had anticipated such a response. These men had showed no loyalty to him. Loyalty, he found, ran shallow when threats of death loomed.

"I would not do that," Pavlenko said.

"Why not?" Levin said.

"Because if I die, everyone in this building dies."

Markov laughed and leveled his gun at Pavlenko. "Not if I shoot first."

"You mercenaries are too predictable," Pavlenko said. "You think I would threaten your lives and not come armed myself?"

Markov raised a brow but didn't lower his weapon. "There is no weapon in your hand, fool."

"But there is in the air. In the halls. Everywhere in this base. You've been infected with the very archaea we're unleashing on the rest of the world in that short walk from the armory to this lab."

"You're lying," Levin said.

"You will find out in a few days. First will come the cramps, the nausea. You might think you ate something bad. 'It's just a stomachache,' you will tell yourself. Then, slowly your intestines begin to shed their inner layer, the tissues separating. You feel the pain in your belly spread through the rest of your body. Infections wrack your nerves, and you can no longer sit up or walk. The agony is so great you'll wish you were dead. But it takes another week, two, maybe three before the disease finally takes you."

"You speak like you know from experience," Markov said.

"I do," Pavlenko said. "And I am the only person in this building with the keys to curing the disease."

Markov waved the handgun at him. "Tell us how to cure it, old man."

Pavlenko grinned. "Do not toy with me. You kill me, we're all dead."

"I will break every last bone in your body," Markov said, taking a step closer. "You think this disease sounds painful? I will shoot out your knees then crush your fingers and pry out every tooth."

Pavlenko had no doubt the man would follow through with his threats, but he did his best to feign indifference. "Then we will all die in pain. As will your men. And after Archon's losses, how many people will hire a group with a track record like yours? How many men will join up to replace them when they hear of how inept you all are?"

Pavlenko put his hand on the handgun, pushing it down from where it was aimed at his chest.

"Markov, if you are anywhere near as good as Levin seems to think you are, I will give you a chance to prove yourself," he said. "Prepare your men to take on our enemy. Protect our operations in this facility for the next thirty-six hours. If we are successful, I will send you out to hunt, and I will provide you the cure."

"It sounds as though you are hiring me," Markov said. "I assume my contract is good even if Levin's isn't."

"That's correct. If I die now, if you torture me, you do not get paid."

Of all the arguments Pavlenko offered, he expected that one to be the linchpin to convince Markov. If not, then Pavlenko prepared himself for a bullet to the head. This was his final play, his final effort to maintain some semblance of control.

A final gamble.

And it worked.

Markov turned the gun away from Pavlenko and aimed at

Levin. The lieutenant colonel took a step back, throwing his hands up defensively before Markov fired.

The gunshot resonated through the small space. Levin crumpled to the lab floor.

"Dmitriyev wanted someone to pay," Markov said. "Now someone has paid. I want that cure."

"Thirty-six hours," Pavlenko said, wiping flecks of Levin's blood off his lab coat. "I need your *loyalty* for at least that long. Then you and your men will be the first to receive the cure."

Markov gave him a diabolical grin. "It seems that me and my men are now working in hazardous conditions, necessitating a raise. Then I will guarantee you my loyalty."

"My word is as good as yours." Pavlenko held out his hand to shake Markov's. "You can count on it."

Markov seemed pleased. Money and guns, that was indeed his language.

Pavlenko watched him leave, knowing he had no intention of paying the man a dime. Markov deserved his impending death, and Pavlenko would take great pleasure in seeing his creation take the man's life after their mission in the Sahara succeeded.

31

FREDERICK, Maryland

KASIM MARCHED THROUGH FORT DETRICK. The summer sun glinted overhead with a cheery warmth belying the storm he knew would soon be raging across the Atlantic, devastating the United States.

He walked up the steps to the office building on Porter Street where the USAMRIID administration was housed. As he passed the other scientists and administrators strolling down the hall, he shared nothing more than a casual nod to say hello, never showing his urgency.

Liang's office door was open when Kasim arrived, but there was already another man in a suit seated in front of her desk. She looked up from their conversation when Kasim gently tapped on the door.

She dismissed the other man and escorted him out of her office. He gave Kasim a long look like he had been severely inconvenienced as Liang shut the door.

With a wave, she indicated for Kasim to take a seat. She settled into the chair behind her desk. She might've been shorter than most of the individuals who shared her rank—mostly because her equals were almost all male. But she didn't let either of those facts inhibit the air of command Kasim felt just being in her presence.

"I take it you found the lead you were looking for," she said. "What now?"

"I need Special Operations Group support immediately," Kasim said.

Liang leaned back in her chair. "What in the hell are you doing that you need CIA special ops? This is a scientific mission, is it not?"

"While we've got talent in the field and the lab, we need more."

"Tell me exactly why we need Langley involved," she spoke in a low voice. "I know why Vector exists, but I'm tired of mysteries."

Kasim took in a deep breath. "What I'm about to tell you will destroy any plausible deniability you might have otherwise had."

"But you think it's worth it."

"I wouldn't be here if I didn't."

Liang closed the blinds over the window behind her desk. "You open your mouth on this and we fail, it's both our careers down the drain."

"We won't even be talking about careers in ten days," Kasim said. "But if you want, you can tell everyone this conversation never happened. Point me to the sword, and I'll throw myself on it."

"That's the confidence I need to see," Liang said. "No, Kasim, you bring me in on this, I'm not turning back either. You don't need to compromise your field operator's identities or anyone else in Vector for that matter, but I'm not going to throw you under the bus. At least, not without me jumping under it with you."

"Thank you, Commander. Vector believes the outbreak of novel AGS in China is linked to a Russian outfit using desert sandstorms to spread a new bioweapon that is designed to cripple the economy through a lengthy and uncontrollable spread of the disease. There's no known cure—at least, no cure we have our hands on yet." He rotated his wrist, checking his watch. "And now, in less than thirty-four hours, we think they'll release that same weapon in the Sahara Desert."

Liang leaned back like she had just been hit with the verbal equivalent of a one-two knockout punch. "This will affect us?"

"Once this weapon is released in the Sahara, it will spread across Western Europe and North America. There is no amount of border security, no counterterrorism operations we can run that will stop it at that point."

Liang looked surprisingly calm. Too calm for Kasim's comfort. He worried she was about to laugh him out of the room or call this conspiracy preposterous.

"Kasim, I want to see the science. But—"

"We've done the math," he said. "We've got the models, the data to support everything I'm saying. What we don't have is time."

"You didn't let me finish. I want to see the science, but if what you're saying has a modicum of truth to it, I don't have time to review your work. I'm going to have to trust your judgment. And I know you didn't come with this to me without actionable intelligence. What's next?"

"We identified a facility in the Algerian desert where we believe this bioweapon will be deployed from. There is also a sister site in the Taklamakan Desert in China that appears to be the origin of the AGS spread in China."

She stroked her chin, thinking about it. "You can give me specific locations, I assume."

"I can."

"Good. How can we stop it? Should I request a drone strike?"

"Not going to work," Kasim said. "Bombing the facility risks uncontrolled release of the bioweapon into the desert, entirely defeating our efforts to stop it."

"But you think SOG support will make a difference."

"I do. My field operatives will be involved in any infil op too. We'll shut down the facility from the inside and take everyone there into custody. That gives us a chance to squeeze them for intel."

"I'll see what I can do. I need to share the data on the Taklamakan with our colleagues in China. They'll want to nip this in the bud, and this intel might broker some goodwill. Will that work with your plans?"

"It should, provided we don't tip off the Russians prior to our op in the Sahara."

"We won't. Where are your field operatives?"

"They just arrived in Ramstein. Ready for redeployment."

She gave him a thin smile. "You knew I would say yes."

"I hoped you would."

"Then tell them to get ready for an airborne infil. We'll do this quickly and quietly. Algeria is a go."

Kasim nodded. "Yes, ma'am."

"Before you go, clarify one thing. You said there is no known cure.'"

"That's right."

"Everyone in Asia who might already be infected by this is… God. If it gets loose before we can stop it…" She let her words trail off.

"We have good reason to believe a cure exists, but we don't know where it is or what it looks like," Kasim said. "That's another reason why we need this op to succeed. It's not just about demolition."

"Surely the Russians aren't so bullheaded to release something like this in the world without having a stockpile of medicine to combat it—or at least to have the manufacturing facilities ready to go so they can play hero."

"That would be my assumption. But you know what they say about assuming things."

"Let's assume nothing," Liang said. "But I trust you to get it done. Stop the deployment of this weapon and bring home a cure. Do that, and Vector gets whatever they need from here on out."

Airspace over Algeria

SKYLAR SAT in a red fabric jump seat inside the big belly of a C-130. The constant thrum of the massive plane's engines reverberated into her bones, reawakening old memories of riding in these big beasts.

This time, instead of being surrounded by nearly ninety men and women in ACUs headed into the Sandbox for their next tour of duty, the vast cargo hold was damn near empty except for a few crates to support the claim that the plane was on a routine air supply training exercise.

Alex sat beside her, wearing a sand-colored moisture-wicking T-shirt like the ones she'd worn throughout the Middle East and central Asian theaters of war. His khaki pants looked like they were part of a standard-issue ACU too.

The uniform she wore was not much different, though she had selected a black T-shirt instead of the sand-colored variant.

They each wore ballistic vests over the shirts and had four-eye night vision goggles attached to their helmets. Instead of going into their next op with nothing but sidearms, they carried suppressed M4A1s. The weight of the rifle made Skylar feel a little better about what they were literally about to jump into.

Their new armed friends helped too.

In the jump seats across from her were eight men wearing a menagerie of uniforms that made them look as if they had frequent-customer punch cards at the local army surplus store. But these guys were not the stolen valor types flaunting a fake military past they'd made up in their own demented heads. They were kitted out with suppressed M4s, M27s, and even an M249 SAW. Their choice of equipment spoke to their varied pasts serving as Delta Force operators, Navy SEALs, or Green Berets. All had been recruited by the CIA to train as officers in the Special Activities Center/Special Operations Group (SAC/SOG.)

Yeah, these guys were the real shit.

They had been activated for the mission and ready in a matter of hours, joining Alex and Skylar in Ramstein. While Alex and Skylar infiltrated the Future Guard facility, these eight elite warriors would provide fire support to help stop the deployment of the archaea.

So far, her time with Vector had been spent playing the game by Alex's rules. Now they were firmly in her territory.

The loadmaster of the C-130 stood near the rear ramp of the plane looking back at the paramilitary forces.

"Five minutes until drop," she said over her headset.

A small red light on the bulkhead shone next to her. She began to lower the rear ramp to reveal a sea of black. Only a few scattered lights pinpricked the blanket of dark desert beneath them.

"You ready for this?" she asked Alex over the comms.

"I'm ready for whatever it takes to stop these assholes."

"That's what I'm talking about."

The leader of the paramilitary operation officers, a man named Kirk Grayson, gave his weapons a final combat ready check before standing and making his way toward the rear ramp.

"Soon as we hit the ground, Reaper will set the perimeter," Grayson said, referring to their team's call sign. The man had a distinct Baltimore accent. "We won't advance until Vector gives the clear."

"Approaching target," the loadmaster said.

Skylar felt the familiar rush of adrenaline before an engagement, her pulse humming through her ears. Her mind shut out all other thoughts except those of the mission. She made her way to the rear ramp after the officers with Alex on her heels.

The quickest and quietest way to get into the Future Guard facility was an airborne insertion—they couldn't lug this much hardware by land without risking being stopped. And in the desert, without much cover, Pavlenko and whoever else might be cooped up in the Future Guard facilities would see or even hear them well before their arrival, deploying the bioweapon before she and Alex could stop it.

Lucky for her, she'd always enjoyed skydiving. But Alex's face looked white and drawn. She clapped him on the shoulder and grinned.

"You'll be okay, partner," she said.

He did his best to return her smile and sat up a little straighter.

The red light near the open ramp blinked then turned green.

"Jump!" the loadmaster said over their comms. "Go, go, go!"

Grayson did not hesitate, disappearing over the rear ramp. The void swallowed his men one by one. Skylar flipped down her NVGs, and at the loadmaster's signal, she flung herself off next.

Wind rushed past her ears and tugged at her clothes. All the heft of her equipment was suddenly lost to the unrelenting pull of gravity, making her feel nearly weightless as she plummeted toward the unknown below in a last-ditch effort to save her country.

32

Sahara Desert, Algeria

Renee Williams was pipetting another sample of the genetically modified archaea into small wells in a plastic plate. Next, she would apply antibodies that would detect specific surface proteins on the archaea. This would confirm that the archaea had been modified so not even EnviroProct's most advanced devices could detect this strain. The microorganism would be nearly invisible.

She hated herself for doing this work. She wanted to throw all these collection plates and samples into the trash.

But if she did, this madman Pavlenko would just kill her and find someone else to do his research. Just like he'd done to Aubert. And probably Paulo too.

She had vowed to stay alive long enough so she could find some way to sound the alarm about Pavlenko. Even if she couldn't escape, maybe she could get access to a computer with an external connection. Anything to warn the world about what existed in this den of diabolical science.

The pain roiling through her gut made her worry that her time was more limited than she had suspected. Her insides shifted and twisted constantly, and she felt the bite of nausea clawing its way through her stomach. She would soon know what this weapon could do to the rest of the world.

Her mother already suffered from lupus. What would the archaea do to her body?

She set the pipette down. Was she being foolish clinging to hope that she could somehow make a difference? She was a dead woman walking, nothing but a test subject for this unrepentant demon of a man.

No, she could not let those dark thoughts overwhelm her.

There was hope.

There was a chance, no matter how slim.

The door swung open, crashing against the wall. Pavlenko stormed in with a pistol tucked into his waistband and flecks of blood across his lab coat.

"Did you figure it out?" he asked.

"The archaea has been modified," she said, unable to bite back the defeat in her voice. "It's working."

"I'm not talking about that. It's too late anyway." She thought she detected a hint of worry in his voice, a slight look of uncertainty flashing in his eyes before he met her gaze again. "You asked before if there was a cure."

"I did."

"Are you not interested any longer?"

"Why would I be interested if I'm going to die here anyway? I'm not an idiot. You don't plan on letting me go."

Pavlenko laughed. "As I said, you're a smart woman. I can make sure your family suffers—or maybe, since you've been cooperative, I can help them when our archaea spread around the world. Would you like that?"

"You're lying."

"About helping your family or about this disease spreading?"

"Both."

Pavlenko picked up one of the vials Renee had filled with an archaea sample. "First, there is a chance I am not lying. A chance that I will help your family. Second, I can assure you the archaea will spread around the world. I have already done the research to confirm it."

Renee set down her pipette. "Someone will stop you."

"They will not. China is already suffering. Tonight, we release another batch into the Sahara. Based on your research, you must know what will happen next."

Renee didn't want to believe him. This must be another bluff. A terrifying one. But he didn't mean it, did he?

Cold dread wormed through her insides.

Of course, it wasn't a bluff.

This man had not lied to her since he'd introduced himself to her. She could not keep hoping that this was all just a nightmare. When Pavlenko said he was going to release a bioengineered weapon, he'd meant it.

"I can tell by the look on your face you know exactly what this means," Pavlenko said. "But you haven't answered my first question."

Renee studied the man. So self-assured, arrogant. He was intelligent, maybe a bit of a narcissist. Someone who had been let loose in the world of science with no conscience or regulations to stop him, doing what he pleased with biotechnology. A waste of intellect that could have been applied to better things. To finding solutions to diseases and helping others instead of taking lives.

"When you infected me with this *stuff,*" she started, "you inhaled a dose yourself. You're vaccinated—or if not vaccinated, you have a remedy. Something that kills the archaea."

"You win the prize. I got the disease as a child. I felt the pain. I know what you are going through now. And I was able to engineer these archaea so the symptoms last longer. Much longer than when my father created the first strain. They cause more pain. More suffering. And eventually, a terrible death."

"When will you give me the cure?" Renee asked, already imagining the clenching in her stomach growing worse.

"I have a different solution in mind." Pavlenko patted his holstered pistol. "We no longer need your help."

Her mind flashed once again to Aubert. To the blood and brain on the wall.

She thought about begging for her life. But she wouldn't give this monster the satisfaction. Couldn't beg for her death before he disposed of her.

God, there had to be a way. Maybe she could take that pistol from him, turn the tables somehow.

"Come on," Pavlenko said, reaching for his gun. "I don't like to make a mess of things in the lab."

SKYLAR SPREAD her arms and legs, controlling her descent. White dots blazed over her NVGs through a world of green and black. Each revealed the SAC/SOG paramilitary operations officers below her, thanks to the infrared tags on their own optics.

The closer she drew to the Earth, the more she saw the jagged outlines of a few rocky outcroppings. Among them, she saw the white outline of a rectangular facility with long spindly arms spreading from a warehouse behind it. All of it was dark, lights off to keep it hidden from the casual surveillance flight.

That was their target.

Future Guard.

The rushing wind tore at her clothes and harness. She twisted her wrist just enough to check on her altimeter. She was at six thousand feet. Drawing ever closer to the sands and rocks below.

Almost there.

At five thousand feet, she felt cold instinct honed by airborne training yelling at her to deploy the chutes. But she fought the urge.

This wasn't a normal airborne op. This was a HALO dive. High altitude, low opening.

They would not open their chutes until the last possible second to avoid anyone seeing their flaring chutes or showing up suddenly on any radar system that might be operating at Future Guard.

Four thousand feet.

A few of the IR tags below jerked suddenly. The officers were beginning to pull their cords, their chutes deploying.

Three thousand feet. She released hers. The drogue chute burst open first with a whipping sound, followed by the blooming main chute. Her harness wrenched her body. The weight of her gear suddenly yanked against her body, carried by momentum. Pain flared through her ribs, but she ignored it.

She hadn't bothered telling the docs at Ramstein about her injuries. Didn't matter right now. The clinics would still be there when the mission was finished.

She tugged on the left steering line, keeping herself on target with the Reaper team. The first two men had just touched down, their chutes collapsing behind them. The others hit, one by one, kicking up puffs of sand that shone in little white clouds on her NVGs. They were spread out below in a line a quarter mile south of the Future Guard facility.

As she approached the sand, she brought up her legs, performing a two-stage flare. Her feet hit the soft sand, her prosthetic leg landing with a soft *thunk*, vibrations running up it into her thigh. Another crash of fire bled through her chest, and she thought she heard a soft snap.

Yep, these ribs aren't gonna look good after all this is over.

She ran out the momentum, the chute collapsing in the sand behind her. She saw all eight Reaper officers already haphazardly stuffing their chutes into their packs. After shrugging off her harness, she did the same.

A whoosh and crunch of boots against sand from a couple dozen yards away announced Alex's landing. He started cramming his chute into his pack as soon as he could.

They pushed the big bags into the side of the sand dune, kicking sand over it and letting the wind help bury the packs. Hiding them would prevent the chutes from flying away again to help avoid discovery from any wandering security forces.

"Reaper, circle around from the south," Alex said. "Vector will hit them head-on."

"Copy," Grayson said, leading his men over the dark sand.

The wind whipped over Skylar, grit pelting her face as she and Alex crested the dune with their rifles shouldered. To their south nearly fifty yards, she saw the IR tags from Reaper setting up their shooting positions, ready to cover her and Alex's entrance.

Straight ahead was the Future Guard facility. One of the doors on the north side opened, light bleeding out. Four men and women exited wearing what looked to be long white lab coats.

Skylar flipped up her NVGs, pausing at the top of the dune. Alex joined her, dropping to his belly. She pulled out a pair of binoculars and scoped their position.

She waited for a second, wondering why these four scientists would be strolling out into the night like this. Her answer came a few seconds later. Three men dressed in black fatigues and carrying rifles marched behind the scientists, their weapons aimed at the scientists' backs.

"Reaper, Vector Two," she said. "I've got three hostile

contacts escorting four white coats. Looks like a possible execution setup."

"We don't have a clear shot from our position," Grayson replied. "Four of ours are circling around."

"By then it'll be too late," Alex said to Skylar.

"We could fire on those three gunmen," she replied. "But we'll blow our position. Might still lose a couple of those white coats."

The scientists huddled together. Even from here, Skylar could tell from the way they kept looking over their shoulders and shook, they were scared. The gunmen waved at the scientists, gesturing for them to keep advancing. They seemed to be toying with their captives.

"We have to help," Alex said.

"We *don't* have to," Skylar said. "We'd be sacrificing our cover."

Each second they hesitated, the gunmen grew closer to making their decision for them.

"Damn it, I can't let them die," Alex said.

"Once we shoot, there's no going back. We're risking everything to save four people."

Alex was quiet. The scientists kept walking up the side of a dune. Skylar's heart thumped more heavily. She moved her finger from the trigger guard, sighting up the first armed goon. She wanted the mission to succeed, but Alex's words rang in her mind. She had the ability to stop this. To help the people right in front of her.

Otherwise, she would watch them die. They would unknowingly sacrifice their lives so Skylar and Alex might have a slightly better chance of infiltrating Future Guard.

Damn, was she really letting Alex's mindset bleed into her like this?

There were three hostile targets. Just her and Alex with eyes on them.

Soon as one of those guards went down, the others would go crazy, even if they didn't hear the suppressed shot.

She wished she had more time to decide what the right move was. Whose lives was she saving tonight? But as the guards raised their rifles, the time for deliberation ran out.

"Where are you taking me?" Renee asked.

Pavlenko walked behind her down the corridor. The cold steel of his pistol barrel pressed into her neck, letting him know just how close he was.

"Outside," he said. "Let the sands deal with you. Easier to clean up."

She heard the distant pop of gunshots and winced, heart fluttering. "What's going on?"

She knew the answer. She had seen the other scientists who had been imprisoned and indentured here. It stood to reason she wasn't the only one being disposed of tonight.

But she wanted to hear him say it, willing herself to fight against the deep threads of fear winding through her body.

"Just keep moving," Pavlenko said. "Don't make this worse for yourself than it already is."

As they approached an exit, she thought she heard screams filtering through the door. Then more gunfire.

"They must be stubborn," Pavlenko said with a sigh. "Or maybe our men let them run into the dunes. They like to do that, you know? Give the people some hope. Let them think they might get away."

Renee was shaking now. She couldn't help herself.

"Don't be frightened. I will not waste my time or yours like that. I prefer efficiency. One shot, it will all be over. Very quick death. It's much more than you deserve."

She tried to slow her pace. Maybe she could surprise Pavlenko, grab that pistol, and crank it out of his hands.

But he was a full head taller than her. He might be a scientist, but he looked like a bear. As soon as she started to turn, he would fire. She was certain of it.

Her knees trembled with each step.

So much for believing that in a few days she might come up with a way to escape this hellhole. So much for Tuscany.

So much for her future, her family.

The door was only a few feet away now. Everything outside was quiet.

Pavlenko said something in Russian. He definitely wasn't talking to her. She assumed he had spoken into his radio, but there was no response.

He was distracted now, looking at the radio. She started to turn slowly.

"Don't move," he said.

She stared at the closed door, wondering what lay beyond.

Pavlenko spoke in Russian on the radio again. There was no response.

She didn't know what he had said, but the tone in his voice sounded urgent.

He started to move around her. She waited to see if his aim would stray, even just for a moment.

But that moment didn't come. He never got close enough. Instead, he nudged the door to the desert open. A harsh wind curled through the hallway. Renee shielded her eyes from the grit blowing in, looking between her fingers to see there were no lights outside the facility.

Just darkness.

"Come on," he said, motioning toward the door. "Markov's people are probably drunk again. Fools."

She stepped out. The sky was studded in white stars, and

her eyes adjusted to the moonlight, slowly soaking in the desert landscape. This would be the last thing she ever saw.

A wide stretch of nothingness and a few glimmers that had traveled light-years to be with her in this final moment.

Maybe, in a way, it was poetic. Beautiful. She thought of Paulo. Was he, against all odds, still alive, looking up at those same stars?

There were worse sights to see in the last moments of a person's life.

As her eyes adjusted to the darkness, she could just make out three lumps in the sand about twenty yards from her.

Bodies.

At first she thought these were other scientists like her, taken out to be executed. But when Pavlenko stepped out of the building, no doubt seeing the same thing she did, she could not mistake the single Russian word slipping out of his mouth for anything other than a surprised curse.

This might be her only chance.

Renee dove at him with all her remaining strength. Then came the crack of gunfire.

33

Alex peered through the optics of his M4 and squeezed the trigger again.

He refused to allow the scientists to get gunned down in cold blood. Not after all the other needless death they had witnessed in Kaliningrad and Istanbul. Watching their executions through the scope of his rifle was not something he could live with.

He hadn't been sure about what his partner would do. But she had backed his play.

All four scientists were now running from the scene, heading into the desert. Reaper had already sent two of their closest men to intercept the fleeing prisoners.

Alex had hoped they would have a few minutes before anyone inside the base realized something was wrong. He had been banking on the fact that the sound of gunshots was something they would have expected from the impending execution anyway.

But that hope had been ill-placed.

A cone of white light had bled into the desert. Another scientist with sandy brown skin and tightly curled black hair had been forced outside by a large man. The guy was dressed like he belonged in an office, not in the military like the other gunmen. But he aimed a pistol at the scientist with all the steady assuredness of someone who knew how to take a human life.

Alex barely had time to adjust his aim and fire.

Sand puffed where his bullets burst next to the man, missing their mark. The man fired off a couple of shots—toward the scientist, not the unknown threat in the desert—even as he jumped back in surprise.

Skylar joined in the attack with a burst of her own.

The man stumbled backward, aimed his pistol their direction, and fired blindly. None of his shots landed anywhere close to them. But the guy was already retreating to the door.

"I swear I hit him!" Skylar unleashed another salvo that sparked against the door as it closed. "Son of a…"

The scientist had fallen into the sand. She didn't appear to be moving.

"Reaper, Vector One," Alex called. "One of the hostile contacts went back inside. Prepare to engage."

He had no doubt alarms would soon be blaring inside Future Guard. It would not be long before they would face more guards armed like the executioners. Trying to survive a gunfight from their shooting position on a sand dune with no cover was a shortcut straight to mission failure. And every second that skirmish persisted was a second closer to the release of the bioweapon.

There was only one thing to do now.

"Let's go!" Alex said, sprinting down the sand dune toward the dead guards and the downed scientist.

Skylar ran beside him with her rifle pointed at the doorway.

They reached the fallen soldiers. Skylar scoured their pockets with one hand while keeping her rifle in the direction of the door. She worked like a machine as Alex rushed to the scientist.

Blood covered her white lab coat.

His heart sank.

Just another life lost to these people. He knelt by her, and he recognized the face framed by the messy blond hair.

Alex's thoughts turned back to Reis. All his promises to the researcher meant nothing if she was dead.

"It's Williams," he whispered to Skylar.

She walked toward him at a hunch, her rifle shouldered. In the fingers pressed against the rifle's handguard, she held a key card.

"Is she…" Skylar let the words fade.

Alex leaned in close, pressing his ear close to her mouth. To his surprise, he felt warm air blow out in a gentle breath. But it was too early to breathe a sigh of relief.

"She's still alive," he said. He peeled off the lab coat from her left arm, revealing a wound in her shoulder. "Just in shock, maybe." He pulled out a packet of blood-clotting gel from his trauma kit and sprinkled the granules over the wound before pressing gauze on it.

"We got to move," Skylar said, creeping toward the door.

"I know," Alex said. "It's just—"

Williams's eyes shuddered open. She pushed herself away from Alex, scooting back then wincing at the effort and grabbing her arm. "What—"

"It's okay," Alex said. "Dr. Williams, I'm Alex Wolfe. This is Skylar Cruz. Paulo Reis is really worried about you. We're here to stop these people, and then we'll get you back to him."

"Alex!" Skylar said, looking back from a small window in the doorway. "I see movement in there."

"I… Oh…" Williams seemed to still be in shock. She grimaced, pressing her good hand over the wound in her shoulder. "Pavlenko... that man... He's going to deploy the archaea. He's going to release it. You have to stop him!"

She started to stand then stumbled. Alex caught her with one arm.

Gunfire exploded somewhere to their south and east.

"Engaging hostiles," Grayson called over their comms. "Eight, maybe more contacts. Reaper Four and Five are moving to enter the facility."

"We got to go," Skylar said.

Alex looked between Skylar then Williams. More gunfire exploded around the facility, flashing like lightning, the sound cracking over them in waves. If the enemy caught her, she was defenseless.

He could not leave her out here. Not in the middle of the desert.

"I can help you in there," Williams said, teeth gritted. "I can help. Let me. Please."

That made the decision for Alex. Even Skylar seemed to relent at the scientist's determination. She slid the key card in front of an RFID reader, and the door's lock clicked open.

"Reaper, Vector One," Alex called. "Pavlenko is moving to deploy the weapon right now. We're en route to intercept!"

They positioned themselves around the doorway, then Skylar pulled the door open. Alex rushed in first, and another wave of gunfire exploded.

Pavlenko limped through the halls of Future Guard with an AK-47 he had taken from the armory. Pain flared through his thigh with every step. He fought to slow his breathing, battling the panic and shock threatening to dull his mind.

It's nothing but a single bullet wound, he thought. *I will not be defeated like this.*

He dragged his right leg behind him. His foot and calf seemed to be growing increasingly numb with each step. He clenched one hand over the wound in his thigh and gritted his teeth against a scream.

Gunfire rattled through the halls. His people or the intruders? Pavlenko didn't know, and that lack of knowledge burned in his brain. Four Archon soldiers stormed past him carrying rifles. He gave them time to pass before continuing toward the bowels of the facility.

When he heard the crash of gunfire behind him, he looked back. A bloody handprint was on the wall from where he'd been leaning.

Droplets and smears of blood followed him across the whitewashed tiled floor. A clear trail.

No, no, no.

He was too close to victory.

Whoever these fools were trying to fight their way into this place, he would not let them interfere with his plans. All he had to do was make it to the control center for the archaea bioreactors and let the linear irrigation lines spread the microorganism in the desert sands.

But each step he took, his mind seemed to grow hazier.

Had he lost too much blood?

He had to focus. Just finish this job. He could worry about his wound later. But if this operation was sabotaged, there would be little hope for his career, his life, or even his family's lives in Moscow once Dmitriyev heard what happened. He would not let them bear the burden of his failure like his father had done to him.

Another burst of gunfire sounded somewhere in the facility, echoing in the enclosed space.

He pulled out his radio. "Markov, meet me in the bioreactor room. Now."

There was a beat of silence then more gunfire.

Markov's voice finally called over the radio. "*Da.* Three minutes."

Pavlenko forced himself forward. Each step took more strength, more energy. He used the rifle as a cane. His entire leg had gone numb now, and all he could do was lean heavily against the wall to prevent himself from falling.

Another distant round of gunfire cracked through the halls.

He fumbled through his pocket for his phone and shot a quick message to Dmitriyev.

If you do not hear from me in two hours, assume the worst. Scrub all records of my activity. Destroy Future Guard.

That was a final failsafe, insurance that whoever was in here would be erased even if they managed to kill him.

He stuffed his phone in his pocket and continued hobbling down the corridor. One of the lab doors opened. Dr. Yunevich looked out, an expression of fear painted across her features. She tensed as if she was ready to run.

"What's going on?" she asked.

"Help me," he said.

She hesitated, her eyes scanning him up and down.

"Now!"

She scurried toward him. "You need medical attention."

"We need to release the archaea," he said.

"But the storm will not pick up until tomorrow morning. If we release it now, the archaea may migrate deeper from the top layers of sand. It may be less effective."

"I know what will happen," he said with a growl. "Even if it is only half as effective, the dust storm will still infect millions."

"Are you—"

"If Markov cannot stop these people, then it does not matter. There will be no archaea release, and everything we have worked for will no longer matter."

"If this doesn't work as we promised, Dmitriyev will destroy us all."

"You have two sons. A daughter. Your parents. Your brother. I have a family, too, in Moscow. What do you think Dmitriyev will do if we don't release the archaea at all?"

She offered him her shoulder. Together they hobbled toward the bioreactor room. All he needed was a good thirty, forty minutes to work. That would be enough time for him to change the world forever. Both the West and the East would be brought to their knees.

He would accomplish what his father never had. Even if he died tonight, his legacy would be secure.

"THE LABS ARE THAT WAY!" Williams said, pointing down an intersection.

Skylar ran to the intersection then peered around the corner. Two men ran toward her brandishing rifles.

Two quick bursts from her own weapon put them down before they could fire.

"Clear!" She waved for Williams and Alex to follow.

To the scientist's credit, the gunshot wound hadn't slowed her too much, especially after Alex had slipped her a painkiller.

Skylar had thought it was a mistake to drag the researcher along. But the woman was proving her worth. Having her lead them through the Future Guard facility cut down on the time they would have wasted trying to navigate the complex alone.

Another distant pop of gunfire echoed through the corridors.

"All teams, Reaper Four," a voice called. "Three more hostiles eliminated in the south wing. Running into heavy resistance. We've liberated a group of prisoners. Captured and secured six Future Guard technicians and scientists."

"Copy, Reaper Four. Reaper Actual, still outside," Grayson replied.

"Reaper, Vector Two here," Skylar said. "Following a lead toward the north wing. Requesting fire support."

"Copy, Vector Two," Grayson replied. "Soon as we can. Heavy fire holding us back right now."

In other words, Vector was on their own for now.

A rumble like massive generators coming to life shook through the walls from the belly of the facility.

"What's that sound?" Alex said to Williams.

"I'm not sure," Williams said.

Skylar's eyes traced the floor and walls. A trail of smeared blood and crimson handprints on the wall took them down the corridor.

"Must be Pavlenko," Skylar said, nodding toward the bloody marks. "I knew I hit him."

"He's definitely headed to the labs," Williams confirmed. "First set of doors down there is the wet labs. Past that is the bioreactor chamber."

"We've got to hurry," Alex said.

More gunfire burst down the halls.

"Vector, Reaper One," Grayson reported over the channel. "We're inside now but pinned down near the south and western entrances."

"North was clear when we made it in," Skylar called back.

"It's not clear now," he said. "You're on your own until we can get past these guys. Watch your backs."

Skylar felt a chill slice through the adrenaline firing through her body. They were cut off from their backup, and every exfil route was blocked by hostiles. The only reason they were still alive, still running down the halls was because they had slipped through before their enemy could mobilize all their defenses.

But she had no illusions their luck would hold out.

More voices called down another hall, headed toward

them. Sounded like four, maybe five people coming from the direction they were headed.

"In there!" Williams said, pointing at a door. She yanked it open before Skylar could clear it. Skylar and Alex followed her into a laboratory. The lights were still on. Equipment hummed on the lab benches.

Pipettes and plastic culture plates were scattered on a lab bench as if someone's experiments had been interrupted by their attack. As she scanned the room, she heard the clatter of footsteps outside, along with the clamor of shouting voices.

Williams crouched nearby behind a lab bench. Alex was next to the door with his rifle trained on the exit.

But in the farthest corner of the lab, Skylar saw a man standing frozen, his eyes locked onto her. In his gloved hands, he held a plastic conical tube that he dropped when she took a step toward him.

She put a finger over her mouth. "We're here to help."

"He's one of them," Williams hissed.

"They're here!" the man yelled. "In the—"

Skylar lunged at him, slamming the stock of her rifle into his head. He went down with a heavy thunk, immediately unconscious.

But it was already too late.

The clatter of boots in the hall suddenly stopped, then the door burst open.

34

A GUARD CHARGED into the room, his rifle aimed at Skylar.

Fatal mistake.

Alex lunged for the man and tore the rifle up with one hand. The Russian squeezed his trigger. Bullets stitched the ceiling. Dust showered them both. Two other men in the hallway instinctively fired, but Alex used the man he was struggling with as a shield. Rounds thumped into the man's body.

Alex wrapped one arm around the enemy's arms. He steadied his rifle on the man's shoulder and fired a wild burst at the two gunmen outside the lab. Rounds tore into the two attackers, and the Russians tumbled backward against the corridor wall.

More rounds lanced into the doorframe. The soldier Alex had used as a shield was nothing but two hundred pounds of deadweight now. Alex could barely hold him upright, and he shoved the body out the doorway.

Bullets chiseled into the dead guard as he fell, and before the enemies outside could realize their mistake, Alex leaned out with his rifle shouldered.

He sent rounds spearing through two men kneeling at the

far end of the hall. One went down immediately. The other recoiled from rounds slashing into his arm. He lost control of his weapon, and a spray of bullets plunged into the wall and ceiling. Broken ceiling tiles fell, and an overhead pipe burst, shooting out a cloud of steam.

Alex sucked in a breath, adjusted his aim, and fired through the spreading mist. The man went down in a heap.

"Clear!" he yelled back into the lab. "Move, now."

Williams and Skylar followed him as he traced the trail of blood Pavlenko had left. The thump and gurgle of the machinery rumbled louder as they turned into a much wider corridor. Ten-foot-tall plexiglass windows revealed a vast room filled with cylinders the size of a semitrailer standing on its end.

Those were the bioreactors. Each of the dozen tanks looked large enough to hold thousands of gallons of concentrated weaponized archaea.

More than enough to infect Europe and North America twice over.

A catwalk connected the top of the cylinders and traced around the room. Footsteps clattered down the hallway, heading toward them. More gunfire rang out somewhere else in the facility.

"Reaper, location?" Alex asked over the channel.

"Made it past the south entrance," Grayson called back, sounding out of breath. "Reaper Three and Six are injured."

Those two men represented a quarter of the SOG team. With the number of soldiers Alex had heard storming this place, he wasn't sure how long Grayson could survive without Alex and Skylar turning tail to help them.

"Keep them engaged," Skylar called back. "We just made it to the bioreactors."

Alex ran toward the antechamber leading into the vast room. Williams and Skylar rushed along beside him. As he approached, he saw shapes moving along the catwalk. One wore a white lab coat. Another scientist. The other was the man they had seen escorting Williams outside. He limped, leaning on the rail with a rifle slung over his shoulder.

"That's him!" Williams said. "That's Pavlenko."

"Good job," Alex said. "Reaper, we IDed Pavlenko in the bioreactor room, north wing."

Alex and Skylar crouched near the entrance to the anteroom. They pushed open the first set of doors. He motioned for Williams to stay back a few feet. He rushed past racks of laboratory coats, stacks of nitrile glove boxes, and white protective suits with Skylar by his side.

Ignoring yellow biohazard signs and other red placards in Russian, he moved past a set of decon showers. He didn't care if he exposed himself to any archaea that might've leaked from the pipes and bioreactors. At this point, his life was nothing compared to the millions resting on their success.

All the while, the thumping and gurgling of the machines inside boomed even louder. It sounded as though all the contents of those enormous bioreactors were being pumped somewhere—and he prayed that didn't mean the archaea was already dispersed in the sand outside, waiting to be lifted into the air by the desert winds.

Alex paused at the last door in the antechamber. This one led into the bioreactor room. "Williams, do you think you can help me turn this thing off?"

"Maybe," she said. "I don't really know much about this side of things."

"Me neither," Alex said. "But we've got people back home that might be able to help. Suit up and meet me in there when I give the all clear."

"I'm already infected," Williams said. "It doesn't matter if I suit up."

"You sure?" Alex asked.

"Positive," Williams said.

"Skylar, take point," Alex said. "Flash-bangs out. Then, once we clear the entrance, I'll secure Pavlenko. Cover me, and don't let anyone through this door."

"No problem." She jammed in a fresh magazine and slapped the side of the rifle to hit the bolt release. "Ready on your mark."

The rattle of gunfire burst from somewhere else in the facility, muffled by the anteroom doors and the grinding roar of the bioreactor machinery. Alex sucked in a deep breath, ready to finish this mission for good. They were seconds from finally taking down the man responsible for this despicable operation. A man who sought to wreak unknowable terror and pain over a world that wasn't prepared for the twisted weapons he had developed.

Vector had to succeed.

Because if they didn't, the death toll would be tremendous. Even if they found the cure, it would be hard enough to treat those in China already afflicted with AGS. Trying to ration the cure, whatever it was, among East Asia, Europe, and North America would undoubtedly lead to confusion and anger as governments wrestled over pharmaceutical supplies while their people died.

Russia would still come out victorious.

He pulled out a stun grenade. The pin came out with a click, and he kept the lever squeezed down. Then, he counted down with his fingers.

Three.

He wrapped his free hand around the door handle.

Two.

He inhaled sharply, fresh adrenaline surging through his vessels.

One.

He pulled open the door, tossed the flashbang. Skylar's flew out after his. They ducked back. Blinding white light flared in the bioreactor room. A resonating thud shook the door. The sound was loud enough to blast into Alex's eardrums.

Through the small window in the anteroom, he saw Pavlenko duck down on the catwalk.

Alex pushed the door back open, Skylar rushed out, rifle at the ready.

But two men rushed out from behind a stack of crates near her right, away from where the flash-bangs had gone off. Each carried a rifle.

Skylar dove toward the floor.

Then came the deafening roar of gunfire.

SKYLAR FELT the bullets scorch through the air just behind her. She landed on her side, her bruised ribs screaming in agony. Her elbow hit the tiled floor hard, and her finger squeezed the trigger of the rifle. Shots exploded into one of the bioreactors. A sickly yellow liquid gushed out from the puckered wounds in the metal, puddling over the floor. That fluid released a smell somewhere between fermenting beer and rotting fruit.

She dragged herself toward the cover of the bioreactor. Another rash of incoming gunfire cracked into the floor. This time, it seemed to be coming from Pavlenko's position. He seemed to have recovered from the flash-bang, or else it was just a lucky shot.

But before she could get a shot on him, the two men charging from the crates descended on her and Alex. They blinked and stumbled. Must have had just enough warning to look away when the grenades went off so they weren't completely blinded.

One of the two men pounced on Alex, and they fell away in a tangle of limbs.

The other attacker looming over her was a huge man half-covered in bandages, swinging a pistol toward her face. Part of his face was wrapped in gauze, but she recognized his cruel eyes.

It was the man who been running security in Kaliningrad.

Markov.

She raised her rifle at his chest, pushing herself backward with her feet, her head dizzy. Markov grabbed her arm and twisted it. Then he cranked her rifle from her grip. Head still ringing, she kicked his feet out from under him with her prosthetic leg. Markov landed hard on the ground next to her.

He somehow maintained his grip on his pistol but let off a couple shots that punched into the floor next to her face. Fragments of broken tile slashed at her skin. The whole world went silent, her ears ringing from the blast.

She started to push herself up, but Markov lunged on top of her.

She pressed her fingers across Markov's face, holding him back as he swung a fist into the side of her head. The pain split through her skull. She tried to land a knee into his abdomen to push him off, but she couldn't move with his weight pressing down on her.

In his left hand, Markov held his pistol, bringing it to bear on her. Skylar put every ounce of strength she had into keeping that wrist away, enduring the battering Markov doled out. Pain from every side. Sweat and blood. The stink of the bioreactor's contents spilling around them.

Through her damaged eardrums, she thought she heard another gunshot. Then suddenly the pistol whipped free from Markov's hand. Weaponless, Alex twisted Markov's arm backward.

Blood wept from a wound in the side of Alex's head. The second ambusher lay dead on the floor near the antechamber, along with Alex's rifle. Bullet holes marred the floor, and she saw more rounds punching into the concrete, preventing Alex from recovering his weapon.

Pavlenko was firing on them still.

But Skylar couldn't deal with him yet.

Markov turned on Alex and attacked him with all the ferocity of a wounded, desperate tiger.

Skylar pushed herself up to a knee. Her head swam, pain bleeding through every inch of her body.

Markov was nearly twice as wide as Alex, and he pushed her partner to the ground, squeezing Alex's wrists until he dropped his rifle.

The ringing in Skylar's ears started to wane as she stood to her full height, her nerves burning with the sheer effort.

Markov grunted then slammed another leg into Alex's chest before shoving him backward against the window between the lab and the hallway. Alex's helmet thumped against the glass, and a spiderweb of fractures fissured through the window.

He barely caught himself from falling, scrambling to recover from his own disorientation.

Skylar started to slip her pistol from her holster, taking a few steps backward to put more distance between herself and Markov. The Russian and Alex collided again in a terrible clash. She couldn't get a clean shot on Markov without risking hitting Alex.

Then Markov twisted Alex around, putting her partner between her and himself. He slammed his fist into Alex's face with a revolting crunch. Alex stumbled backward, but Markov grabbed his collar and delivered another devastating blow. Alex toppled.

Skylar tried to catch him.

Markov clearly anticipated the move. He charged, hands outstretched. His weight collided with her before she could get her handgun all the way up.

More pain exploded through Skylar's ribs, the air bursting from her lungs. Her fingers splayed uncontrollably, the pistol flying away.

She hit the floor again, the archaea goop splashing over her body. Alex started to push himself back up then staggered toward her and Markov, trying to draw his own weapon. Before he could, Markov picked up Skylar and flung her back into the antechamber. She slammed into the floor, struggling to breathe, and crawled away from him.

Alex tried to follow, but another spray of gunfire from the catwalks crashed into the floor near him, forcing him back into the cover of a bioreactor.

Markov slammed the anteroom door shut behind him and collided with Skylar in a storm of blows. Agony blasted through her chest. Every time she tried to stand, she was knocked backward. She reached for something to hang onto but only succeeded at grabbing a stack of glove boxes. They tumbled over her as she fell against the floor. Then Markov landed on her, pressing his knee into her abdomen. A sharp pain rammed through her gut.

The Russian mercenary pummeled her with his monstrous fists, slamming them into the side of her head.

She did her best to block the blows, but she could barely temper the strikes. Her vision started to go black, the taste of blood filling her mouth.

Markov picked her up like she was nothing more than an empty rucksack, hoisting her over his head. "You try too many times to kill me."

He threw her across the anteroom.

She crashed into a shelf. Lab coats and face masks spilled over her. She gasped, blinking, trying desperately to hold onto her consciousness. She fought past the overwhelming pain and tried to push herself up one last time.

Markov marched toward her, bloody but implacable. "You must learn that I cannot die. But I am certain that you can."

ALEX AIMED his pistol at the doorway to the anteroom where Markov and Skylar had just disappeared. His rifle was still lying in front of that door near Skylar's weapon, not too far from where the now-dead soldier had disarmed him. Pain traced up his leg from one of the injuries he'd taken in the brief fight. He started toward the anteroom at a limp when the crack of gunfire pushed him back again.

He pressed himself against one of the leaking bioreactors, risking a glance at the catwalk.

Pavlenko was still aiming at his position, firing a rifle. The man's aim was poor, and his stance was unsteady from his wounded leg, but the bullets seared dangerously close to Alex all the same. He couldn't leave the shelter of the bioreactor.

He needed to somehow bring Pavlenko down. His SIG Sauer was a reliable weapon, but the nearly forty yards between himself and Pavlenko made getting a clean shot a hell of a lot more difficult while dealing with incoming fire. He needed either to get closer to Pavlenko or to get hold of one of those M4s.

Hiding until Pavlenko bled out or ran out of ammo was not an option. Skylar needed help. He had learned to trust her to handle any normal attacker on her own. But she was already injured, and that monster of a man had turned them both inside out in a matter of seconds.

He peered around the bioreactor to see if Pavlenko had moved. Another rash of gunfire cut into the steel cylinder. More liquid sprayed over him from the holes, adding to the odor of rot filling the air.

Archaea drenched him. The gunshots blasting through the

bioreactors likely aerosolized the stuff. Everyone in this room must have been sucking down enough of the pathogen to kill a small city. Even if he made it out of Future Guard alive, there was already an expiration date on his life.

But right now, his life didn't matter. And although it physically hurt him to admit, Skylar's life didn't matter at this moment either.

The only thing that mattered was stopping Pavlenko. One way or another, he had to get to that man and prevent him from infecting the rest of the world.

Now or never, Wolfe.

He leaned out from beyond the bioreactor and fired up at the catwalk. Bullets struck the railing and the ceiling. Pavlenko ducked low behind a control console and fired back.

Rounds drilled into the bioreactor, more hot mist spraying across his face. He tried to retreat behind the bioreactor, but a heavy force thumped against his chest. Pain spread through his ribs. His breath whooshed out. He gasped, struggling to breathe, his hands fumbling where the bullet had thumped against his ribcage.

No, no, no.

Then, from the anteroom, he heard another spat of gunfire.

This was it.

First him then Skylar.

Vector Team had failed for the final time.

35

Renee had been cowering in the anteroom when Markov and the other man had ambushed Skylar and Alex. She held the pistol Skylar had dropped, aiming it at Markov, her good arm trembling.

She pulled the trigger.

He shuddered from the shots she had sent into his back, slowly turning toward her, his red face a mask of disbelief and fury.

She remembered how he had told her she was nothing but a housecat.

But even she still had claws.

She fired again. The recoil from the pistol was almost too much for her, but she managed another two shots. One punched through Markov's chest.

The second hit him in the head.

The man let out a long breath, like a final sigh before going to sleep. His fingers loosened, and his pistol fell to the floor. He lurched forward like a felled tree.

Skylar scooped up Markov's pistol then brought herself up,

leaning heavily against the wall. Blood dripped from cuts and scrapes across her face, her chest heaving.

"Are you okay?" Renee asked.

"Fine," Skylar said, gasping. She grabbed hold of one of the lockers to pull herself up straight. "What about Alex?"

Renee looked out the small window in the antechamber door. She saw Alex sprawled on the floor, surrounded by fluid from the bioreactor.

"Oh, fuck," Skylar said, hobbling to her side. "Vector One, do you read? Vector One! Alex, you do *not* have permission to die, damn it!"

She took her pistol back from Renee then nudged open the door to the bioreactor room a few inches. She started to lean out, but shots hammered her position, forcing her to draw back.

"He's not responding," Skylar said. "Stuck out there... God, it wasn't supposed to go like this." She turned to Renee. "Is there another entrance to this room? A better way to reach Alex or Pavlenko?"

Renee wracked her mind. She had been more concerned about her fate rather than studying where every door in the hall led. "I don't think so."

"We can't get to him then." Skylar's face was starting to turn red, sweat trickling between the rivulets of blood. She was pacing desperately behind the door. "I need you to cover me. Do you think you can do that?"

"What's that mean?" Renee asked.

Skylar pushed Markov's pistol into her hand. "At my signal, start firing at the catwalk. All I need you to do is keep Pavlenko's head down. I'm going to make a run for it."

Renee trembled. Adrenaline and desperation had driven her to fire the gun on Markov. Now, the cold itch of fear was creeping back into her. She was about to face a hailstorm of bullets and shoot back like she was some kind of soldier.

"Dr. Williams, do you understand what you need to do?" Skylar said, speaking slowly, her voice hoarse.

Her guts twisted around like Markov himself was pawing at her intestines. She felt the sickness threatening to overtake her. This was the same sickness that would soon strike her country, her family—and Paulo. These people had said he was still alive. She needed to get out of here and see it for herself.

"Yes, I understand," she said.

"Here we go."

Skylar's jaw clenched. She held up three fingers. When her last finger curled down, Skylar bolted out of the doorway.

Renee mustered every last drip of courage she had and leaned out. The rattle of automatic gunfire echoed in the chamber as Pavlenko swung the rifle around on Skylar. Renee could barely raise her left arm to steady her aim. Pain from her shoulder flared with the effort. But she could not let something as insignificant as pain stop her. She started firing wildly at his position. Every bit of recoil tugged at her damaged muscles in her shoulder. The agony grew worse, and she let out a barbaric yell that didn't sound like her voice.

All her shots seemed to go wide, but she just kept squeezing the trigger.

Fight the pain. Fire. Fire. Fire.

Pavlenko's aim strayed from Skylar. He ducked behind the command console on the catwalk then directed his weapon at her. The slide on her handgun locked back, but she kept squeezing for another moment. No more shots fired from the pistol. She ducked back inside the antechamber just as gunfire blazed into the closing door.

She had done all she could.

She just hoped it was enough.

Skylar sprinted across the wet floor. Her boots nearly slipped out from under her. Liquid continued to bleed from a couple of the massive bioreactors. The sound of engines pumping fluid between the intact bioreactors and through massive pipes in the ceiling roared through the space.

Her M4 was on the floor, lying in the middle of an open space. Gunfire from the catwalk exploded toward her in another violent burst. She dove for her rifle, sparks flying around her where the bullets hit the pipes and bioreactors.

As she recovered the weapon, she scrambled toward a stack of crates near the wall. All the while, Pavlenko's aim stayed hot on her trail. Her heart thumped against her ribs, threatening to break out and sprint across the slick floor.

Every muscle in her body seemed weaker than before, each gasp of breath causing a sharp pain in her side like someone was hitting her ribs with a jackhammer. But pain would not stop her. It had not stopped her when she'd lost her leg; she sure as hell would not let a couple of bruised lungs stop her now.

Not when so much was at stake.

More bullets chewed into the crates. Splinters flew across her face.

Soon her cover would be turned to sawdust.

She leaned out behind the cover, ready to let loose a flurry of rounds right back at that bastard Pavlenko.

Instead, she saw a sight that nearly stole her breath.

Alex strode up the stairs to the catwalk, held up by nothing but sheer determination.

"Vector Two, I'm going up," he called to Skylar.

"Copy," Skylar said, sounding like she was talking through a mouth full of blood. "Thought you were dead, partner."

"Not yet."

The impacts that had rocked through his body armor had thrown him onto his back, the air knocked out of him. His ears still rang from his head slamming the ground, his hearing only now starting to clear. But until there was a bullet in his heart, he had to keep forging ahead.

He kept his suppressed SIG Sauer out in front of him as he cleared the last step up the catwalk. The woman in the white coat beside Pavlenko turned toward him from the control console nearly twenty yards from Alex. Pavlenko had his rifle pressed against his shoulder and let out another salvo, aiming toward Skylar.

Thanks to his partner and Williams, Pavlenko hadn't even seen Alex when he had sprinted for the catwalk's stairs. The man still didn't see him now.

Alex aimed the pistol straight at Pavlenko. He didn't want to kill the man yet. The mad scientist might prove useful, so he sent a shot punching into the bastard's right arm. Pavlenko let out a pained cry, losing control of his rifle. The woman near him dove to the catwalk floor, her hands over her face. Pavlenko started to turn on Alex, but he sent another bullet cutting through the man's leg.

This time, the Russian dropped the rifle, his hands clinging to the fresh wound.

"All teams, Pavlenko is down but not dead," Alex reported over the comms. "Securing him now."

"Copy, Vector One," Grayson called over the comms. "Advancing toward your position now."

Skylar stood from behind the crates and limped between the bioreactors, her boots splashing over the floor toward the catwalk stairs. When she reached the top of the stairs, Alex marched toward Pavlenko, passing the cowering scientist. The woman stood and ran toward the stairs.

"You're not leaving," Skylar said, grabbing the woman by the collar and dragging her after Alex.

Pavlenko had dropped his assault rifle on the platform beside him. Alex kicked the weapon away, back toward Skylar. The Russian's lungs expanded in deep breaths. Blood stained the side of his coat and soaked through his pants, but he was still alive.

"Stop this machine," Alex said, pointing the pistol at Pavlenko's chest.

"Or what?" Pavlenko said, drawing himself to a sitting position. His words came out strained, but he grinned at Alex with bloodstained teeth. "You shoot me again?"

"This time, I'll shoot to kill."

"It's too late," Pavlenko said. "We already evacuated the archaea from these bioreactors. The desert is being irrigated with it as we speak."

"Then I'll stand here and watch you bleed out, you sick son of a bitch."

"You Americans, always with such bravado."

"I can shut down the machine," the woman Skylar was holding said. All eyes turned toward her.

"You can?" Skylar asked.

"And I will, if you help me and my family."

"Don't help them." Pavlenko wheezed and tried to stand, scowling at the woman. His legs gave out, and he slumped back against the console.

"Do it," Alex said, looking at the woman. "You have my word that we'll help."

Skylar escorted the woman to the main console, and the scientist hit a series of buttons.

From the stairs, he heard footsteps. Williams joined them. She held a pistol with its slide locked back in her good hand.

"Go ahead, shut down the machines," Pavlenko said. "But it doesn't matter. I've already succeeded."

The pumps in the room groaned to a stop. A few seconds passed. All Alex heard was the whisper of air·through the ventilation ducts and the drip of liquid from the damaged bioreactors.

"There was nothing left to stop pumping through those bioreactors," Pavlenko said, pressing a hand over the wound in his arm. The Russian grimaced as blood streamed between his fingers. His face was growing pale. "The archaea are already entering the irrigation arms. You lost."

"I don't believe him," Skylar said.

Alex moved toward the console.

While Alex didn't have an in-depth knowledge of bioreactor operations, the gauges he saw showed there was no pressure in the bioreactors. On the gauges for volume control, the red ticker pointed at zero liters.

"Is what he said true?" Alex asked the woman.

Tears streaked her face, and she spoke in heavily accented English. "I'm sorry. All the contents of the bioreactors have been transported into the pumps that feed the irrigation arms. The arms are already spreading the archaea to the sands outside. Once the winds pick up, the archaea will be gone. It was too late."

36

Pavlenko slid down the railing and sat on the floor, clutching his wound. That made Skylar want to lift him over the side of the catwalk and throw him to the floor. She might have done just that if her own ribs weren't burning with an unholy fire that would make the devil squirm.

"Shut down the arms," Skylar said. "We can do that, right?"

"We cannot control the irrigation arms from here," the female Russian scientist said.

"Tell us how to stop it," Alex said. "You're killing millions of people. Don't you feel even an ounce of shame?"

"Your country's stubborn policies have cost millions of lives," Pavlenko said, snarling. "You swing your military power around with little regard for the rest of us the world. I do not feel shame for equalizing the playing field and giving my comrades the opportunity to fairly compete in this world. I'm finishing what my father started."

"Bull," Skylar said. "You're doing this at the cost of *innocent* lives."

"And your trillion-dollar wars are different?" he asked.

"Pavlenko, if you have a shred of humanity, tell us how to turn this irrigation equipment off," Alex said. "Don't make this worse for yourself."

Skylar could feel the itch in the back of her mind. The SuperCobra pilot part of her ingrained through years of service. The part that wanted action, resolution. Not endless delays when the enemy contact was right in front of her, nothing but a trigger pull away from being removed from this earth forever.

"Spill it," Skylar said. "Tell us how to turn those damn things off."

She fired off a burst of rounds past his head. The rounds punched into the wall a few yards behind him. He recoiled, but that stupid, frustrating grin never faded from his ugly face.

"You will not kill me," he said. "You're going to save my life."

"Why in the hell would I want to do a thing like that?" Skylar asked.

"Because you—and everyone in this facility—are infected with the archaea," he said. "They were already floating in the air when you arrived. The first breath you took when you entered condemned you to death. And now you're covered in it. With a dose that high, you'll be bedridden in a day, dead within two."

"It's not my life that matters right now," Alex said.

"Ah, maybe it isn't. But mine does," Pavlenko said through gritted teeth. "No matter how desperate you are to stop this machinery, I am the only one here who knows how to stop the archaea." He winced, his face contorting in pain. When it subsided, he looked up at Alex again. "I have the cure."

Skylar aimed her rifle at the woman. "Is he lying?"

The scientist shivered, holding her hands out defensively. "No."

"I think they're telling the truth," Williams said from

behind Skylar. "He was infected a long time ago, but he survived."

"Fuck this. Enough games," Skylar said.

"Skylar—" Alex started.

She slammed the stock of her rifle into Pavlenko's head. He collapsed on the catwalk, groaning. She loomed over him, ready to hit him again if he didn't speak.

"Reaper, Vector One," Alex called over the channel. "Pavlenko's not talking, and we need to stop those irrigation arms."

"We'll find a way," Grayson called back.

"Don't blow them," Alex said. "That'll be just as effective at spreading the archaea as if they kept running."

She cranked her prosthetic foot back to kick Pavlenko in the groin, ready to inflict more pain on the guy even if it wouldn't get him to talk.

Instead, he pulled a pistol from beneath his blazer.

She had no choice but to fire. Rounds stitched up his chest, and with a final sigh, he went slack over the catwalk. His fingers uncurled, and the pistol clattered from his grip.

"No," the Russian woman said, sobbing. "You killed him. Without him, we don't know anything about the cure! We're all dead now!"

"WE CAN FIX THIS," Alex said, his mind already racing.

"Vector, Reaper Actual," Grayson called over the line. "All teams reporting hostiles are down. I repeat, no more hostiles inside the facility or near the irrigation arms. We're rounding up every other contact we've found."

"Copy."

Alex should have felt a sense of victory. But they were still no closer to completing this mission than when they had landed in the dunes outside. With every passing second, Alex felt any potential successful outcome slipping between his fingers like grains of sand.

He turned to the Russian woman. She had already helped them once. Maybe she would do it again.

"Do you know how to stop this?" he asked.

She nodded, her eyes fixed on Pavlenko. "My family... they'll kill my family once they hear about this."

"We'll protect your family," Alex said.

The woman considered it for a moment and then nodded. "I am Natalia Yunevich. My family lives in Moscow. I have three children, a husband. My parents live there. So does my brother. His family too. Guarantee you'll protect all of them, and I will help."

"Making deals with the devil," Skylar said. "I don't like it."

"It's the only deal we've got," Alex said. "Command, Vector One. Got a potential asset." He relayed everything as fast as he could. "I told her we'd secure her family."

"Odds are long, but I'll see what I can do," Kasim said. "But Wolfe, you do what you have to do. Understood?"

Alex didn't like that. He could see from the worry on this woman's face that she was legitimately concerned about her family. She knew the repercussions of working with the enemy. Her life was already forfeit. Maybe she had chosen this assignment. Maybe she had been forced into it, just as reluctant to work for Pavlenko as Dr. Williams or Dr. Reis. But her level of guilt didn't matter. Whether she was innocent or not, Alex needed her help. That meant he had to tell her what she wanted to hear, no matter if it was true.

Another promise that I can't keep.

"My superior confirmed we can save your family," Alex said, feeling the heat of the lie burn at his insides even as he uttered the words. "Twenty-four hours, and they'll be safe."

"Twenty-four hours," she said. "It must be faster."

"We can't do faster. Not like this. Cooperate or there will be no protection."

He felt Skylar look at him. She had heard what Kasim had said over the comms. She knew the promise Alex was making was in vain. Yunevich's family would be gone, disappeared whether she made it out of this place or not.

"Fine," Yunevich said, sounding defeated. "I can tell you how to operate the irrigation arms. You do not have to destroy them. Destroying them will only increase the spread of archaea."

"Thank you," Alex said. "You're saving countless lives. Your family will be proud of you."

He tried not to curse inwardly at himself for letting those words come out so easily.

She walked through the process, and Alex relayed the instructions to Grayson. Reaper had to enter another warehouse-like structure attached to the main Future Guard facility where the controls for the irrigation arms were housed. After following Yunevich's procedures, Reaper confirmed that the irrigation arms were turned off.

"How much of that archaea was deployed?" Alex asked Yunevich.

She motioned to a computer near the control console. "May I?"

"What are you going to do?" Skylar asked.

"I have to run the process flow reports," she said. "Otherwise I cannot tell you."

"Fine," Alex said. He kept his weapon trained on her, and Skylar did likewise.

Even Williams watched the woman with interest.

Yunevich's fingers shook with each prod of a key. As much as Alex wanted to follow along, his grasp of Russian wasn't good enough to figure out what she was doing. He may as well have been watching an obscure arthouse film in Japanese, but all he could do was trust that his false promises of her family's security would be good enough to ensure her motives were pure—or as pure as they could be for someone who was working in a bioweapons facility.

He found himself holding his breath, listening for the sounds of new equipment whirring to life or awaiting the bark of alarms.

But nothing happened. She finally looked away from the screen, taking a step back.

Her eyes were brimming with tears, her lips trembling when she looked at Alex.

"What?" Skylar asked. "What's going on?"

"The irrigation systems did stop, I promise," Yunevich said. "But not in time."

Alex could sense she was trying to lead with the good news. "How much of the archaea was released?"

"Nearly… nearly eighty percent of the batch."

Alex felt his stomach drop, his head floating away for a moment. The bioweapon was out in the world, and there was nothing he could do to stop it. They had barely made a difference.

Williams looked between them. "When is that storm going to hit?"

Alex twisted his wrist to look at his watch. "Six hours."

The wounded researcher winced, clutching her arm, but her eyes were lit up with something like hope. "I might have an idea."

37

"How do you clean these bioreactors between cycles or batches?" Renee asked Yunevich.

The scientist looked at her, confused. "There's an in-line cleaning system—"

Then the woman's eyes went wide as Renee watched realization pour through her.

"What is it?" Alex asked.

"I don't exactly know how these things work, but there are some labs back at my university that work with smaller scale versions for pharmaceutical development," Renee said. "They culture different cell types to produce different antibodies, and—"

"I appreciate the explanation," Skylar said, "But we're running out of time."

"Oh, okay, sorry," Renee said, trying to compose herself. "Between each batch, they have to run cleaning solutions to sterilize the chambers before they start a new population of cells."

"I don't see how cleaning the bioreactors would help us," Skylar said.

"No," Yunevich said. "But you're suggesting…"

The woman went silent, almost as if she realized she shouldn't be giving any more help to the enemy. She backed away from the command console.

Renee finished the explanation. "We could dump all the sterilizing agents into the bioreactors—or at least the ones that weren't damaged—then pump the solutions into the irrigation arms. If there's enough sterilization agents, we could turn the irrigation arms back on and blast the chemicals over the sand where the archaea are."

"You think it'll actually kill the archaea?" Alex asked her.

"I don't know, but it's better than nothing."

"What else do we have to lose?" Skylar said.

"If all those chemicals get picked up by the storm, is that going to be bad?" Alex asked.

Renee shook her head. "These chemicals are strongest when they're concentrated. They're already going to be less effective when we spray them out of the irrigation arms, and there's nothing else in the desert they're going to hurt except us."

"And when they're in a storm headed across the Atlantic?" Skylar asked.

Yunevich spoke this time. "The agents we use will be far too dilute to harm people. There are also neutralizing washes we use following the cleaning procedures. You could deploy those too."

"Let's do it," Alex said.

"My family will be safe, right? You will tell your government I cooperated? They must understand I never really wanted to do this. I had no choice. I couldn't refuse—"

"Focus," Alex interrupted her. "Start running the cleaning cycle now."

Yunevich worked the controls on the command console.

Renee wondered if she would use this opportunity to pump

more poison through the bioreactors and into the irrigation arms. But when the pumps began clanging and growling again, the distinct smell of bleach wafted in the air from a couple of the damaged bioreactors.

"Your team must re-open the irrigation arms," Yunevich said.

"Reaper, Vector One," Alex said. "We need to reactivate the irrigation arms."

There was a beat of silence as Renee watched him listen to the reply.

"Yes, I'm serious," he said. "We're attempting to neutralize the archaea already in the sand."

They let the machines pump the sterilizing chemicals into the irrigation arms for a good twenty minutes until Renee heard what sounded like a rush of air through the pipes overhead.

"We have no more sterilizing agents," Yunevich said. "I am switching to the neutralizing agent, and then it will be done."

It took another half hour to go through the process. During that time, Skylar reapplied an antiseptic solution to Renee's arm. Next came another layer of clotting gel and clean bandages.

Skylar gave her a pill that she promised would take the edge off, and by the time Renee's head started to feel lighter, the pain fading to nothing but a dull throb, the cleaning and neutralization process was done. Alex secured Yunevich's wrists with zip cuffs before leading the group down from the catwalk.

Renee wanted to feel safe now that it looked like her imprisonment in this horrific facility was over. But even if their efforts to stop the archaea in the Sahara Desert worked, there was another war being raged.

One that she and even these operatives couldn't stop.

A wave of pain pulled at her insides, numbed only partially by the pill that Skylar had given her.

The fight for their lives had only just begun.

"Reaper, Vector One," Alex said. "Got two passengers. Leaving the bioreactor room now."

He felt something tighten painfully in his guts as they marched down the corridor back toward the south exit. Maybe it was his nerves getting to him, or maybe the archaea were acting faster than anticipated. He wouldn't rule out anything yet, but there was one thing he felt certain about: even if they had neutralized the archaea that Pavlenko had released into the desert, waiting for the storms to pick up, there were still millions whose lives were on the line in Asia.

They needed that cure.

He wasn't foolish enough to think just because they had protected North America and Europe, they could walk away from Future Guard feeling as though the mission was a success.

Lives were still lives, no matter where they called home.

Even if he was thinking about solely the interests of the United States, a dramatic pandemic event like this spreading through China was bad for all their economic partners. And soon the winds carrying the archaea over China would reach Taiwan, Korea, and Japan, too, destabilizing more of the United States' military and economic partners.

"Are you inoculated against the archaea?" Alex asked Yunevich after they left the bioreactor chamber.

She hunched her narrow shoulders. "No."

"There must be a cure here."

"Probably," she said. "But Pavlenko refused to share it. He said he would only reveal it at the proper time. Maybe we can find something in the clinic or his office. I will show you."

She gave him the location of both. He sent Reaper to

investigate the office, as he headed toward the clinic with the others in tow.

"What was Russia's plan when this was released?" Skylar asked. "Just let everyone die?"

"I don't know for certain, but from what I overheard, Pavlenko owned stakes in several pharmaceutical companies. I believe that he planned to share the cure with them when the pandemic had taken hold."

"He would've profited immensely off a move like that, and Russia would've come out looking like the world's savior," Alex said.

"Disgusting," Skylar added.

"We have all done desperate things when we were in desperate situations," Yunevich said.

"Stop the whining," Skylar said through gritted teeth. "We're knocking on death's door because of what you idiots did."

They made it into the clinic, where they scoured the cabinets. He and Skylar scooped every box and bottle of medicine they found into their packs, while Williams found a trash bag and began filling it.

"One of these must work," he said.

But while he noted dozens of different medicines, from antibiotics to painkillers and pills for indigestion relief, he saw nothing that looked out of place in the standard care a facility like this might offer. Which meant either the therapy was a standard drug far more common than he could have hoped— or it wasn't in the clinic at all.

"See anything?" Alex asked the group.

"I have no idea," Yunevich said.

Williams shook her head, appearing defeated. "I know about archaea biology but not therapies for a disease no one knew existed."

"This is insane," Skylar said, pointing her weapon at

Yunevich. "Someone lied. Either she is, or Pavlenko was and there's no cure."

"I am not lying!" Yunevich shouted.

"You want me to believe Pavlenko just knew some secret recipe and kept it locked away in his office," Skylar said. "What? He was just going to tell the pharmaceutical companies what it was in time to help stop the archaea pandemic?" Her chest expanded rapidly like she was out of breath just from talking. Alex couldn't imagine the pain she must be feeling, but she was on a roll. "Manufacturing a new pharmaceutical would take months to produce at a level that would make a difference against a pandemic. I might have dropped out of my biomed program, but I know enough to say that for certain."

Williams looked at Alex with a dreamy expression. The painkillers Skylar had given her seemed to have blanketed her mind in a haze. "I know that a cure exists. Pavlenko told me he was infected by the archaea when he was a child. And he recovered. He took something back then. He was an evil man, but he never lied to me. I think he was telling the truth—and so is Yunevich."

Alex clasped his pack closed again and swung it over his back. "Then maybe it's something already approved for clinical use for a different disease. It might already be in production."

"If you're right," Yunevich said, "then I'm not sure if Pavlenko would have kept it in the clinic. He would not have wanted us to have easy access to it. It might be—"

"Vector, this is Command," Kasim called over the line. "We just intercepted comms from our Russian observers. You've got four Sukhoi Su-57 jet fighters headed in your direction."

"We need time to clear this facility," Alex said. "We haven't identified a cure yet."

"Those Su-57 pilots are on a flight route right over your

position. Looks to me like they heard you guys knocked down their doors, and they're coming in to blow out the evidence. You need to get out of there immediately."

They were so close to finding the one thing that would completely unravel the Russians' plans. And now Kasim wanted them to abandon Future Guard. "We just need to sweep the labs, then we—"

"You don't have time. Those birds are going to be there in thirty mikes. That leaves us a twenty-minute window to clear the area. We cannot let them catch any you or any of our birds there. Do you understand?"

Alex had no choice but to say yes.

SKYLAR LIMPED alongside Williams out from Future Guard and into the arid night. Alex hurried along just behind them, holding onto one of Yunevich's arms so she didn't bolt.

"Romeo Alpha, Vector Two," she called as they exited the facility. "Ready for exfil."

"Copy, Vector Two," a comms officer from Ramstein replied. "Airlift call sign Shadow Hawk incoming, ETA fifteen mikes."

Skylar hobbled toward the bottom of a dune where two of the Reaper Team officers were guarding a group of nearly a dozen people. The people wore ragged clothing, lab coats, and scrubs. She thought she recognized the four scientists who had bolted into the desert at the beginning of the op.

Her ribs still ached. New needles of pain began to thread their way through her insides. She wanted to blame it on her nerves, but she knew the truth. The archaea were already beginning to worm their way through her guts.

"Grayson's on his way," a Reaper officer said.

Skylar managed a nod, jaw clenched. Each breath seemed

more difficult than the last. She wanted to pop one of the pills she'd given Williams, but until they were in the sky and out of this goddamn desolate desert, she needed full situational awareness. Dull instincts and slow reflexes were not worth numbing her pain if the enemy had any last surprises.

A spear of light pierced the dark desert from one of the doors of the Future Guard building. Grayson emerged with the other five members of his team. Two of the men limped, holding onto their comrades for support.

"We gave the science team remote access to everything we could," Grayson said when he reached them. "They haven't found anything yet. None of the people we captured or freed had a clue. Any luck with you all?"

Skylar shook her head. "Story's the same here."

"Is this crap contagious?" one of the officers said, lowering his weapon. "Heard from the scientists we're all contaminated."

"Our team at home tells us it's unlikely to be transmitted between people," Alex said. "Once it's inside you, it settles in your gut. But the junk on our clothes is still contagious. We'll need a full decon and quarantine when we get back just to be safe."

"Great," Grayson said. "How the hell are we going to find this damn cure trapped in some plastic bubbles on Ramstein?"

"Maybe it's one of the medicines we collected," Williams said hopefully.

"Maybe," Skylar said.

But she doubted they had gotten that lucky. Pavlenko was smarter than that. It was probably stashed away deep in that facility someplace they wouldn't have even considered. And now it looked like the Russians were going to blow the whole damn place up before they could find it.

Skylar hadn't even considered what happened next. The pain in her gut reminded her of the ticking clock. Vector

Team's first operation had been a hell of a ride, but it seemed like it would be a short one. At least she'd gone out still fighting, not pushing papers at a desk. That was something.

"Vector and Reaper Teams, this is Shadow Hawk One," a cool voice called over the comms. "Landing in one. Over."

The muffled thump of the Stealth Hawks sounded first before two sleek black choppers descended out of the murky night. Waves of coarse sand scraped over Skylar from the birds' rotor wash. She shielded her eyes, peering between her fingers. The side doors to the choppers flung open. Crew chiefs wearing hazmat suits waved them onboard. Reaper split up between the two helicopters, escorting their new prisoners and the people they had liberated from Future Guard.

"Welcome back," the crew chief said, closing the side door. Skylar, Alex, and Williams settled into seats near him. "Short ride to our connecting flight where you all are going to be hosed down and cleaned up for the journey home."

The birds took off into the night. Williams's eyes closed as she succumbed to the painkillers. Skylar watched the Future Guard facility fade away. The clenching in her stomach grew tighter with every beat of the chopper blades.

Only a few minutes into their flight, Kasim called over their channel. "Russian flight of Su-57s inbound."

Seconds later, a blinding white light flared over the horizon. The whiteness gave way to a huge orange and red fireball, blooming into the night. The sound hit them next in a relentless shockwave, rattling the chopper.

"Good lord," Skylar said.

"Guess it's a good thing we ended up using the chemical agents on the archaea," Williams said, eyes half-opened again. She sounded groggy. "Otherwise those bombs might've sent the deadly bugs airborne."

"Yeah, good thing," Skylar said.

But nothing about this felt good.

38

ALEX SHUFFLED through the chemical sprays and showers set up in a hangar at Ramstein. His guts felt like someone had stuck their hand through his abdomen and were squeezing as tightly as they could. Skylar was barely hobbling along behind him. Yunevich, Williams, Reaper, and all the people they had liberated from Future Guard followed. Doctors and other medical staff, covered head to toe in protective gear, separated the group into various ten-by-ten-foot spaces divided by plastic curtains.

In one of those partitioned spaces, a doctor and nurse checked over Alex's injuries. Another team examined Skylar, and two nurses tried to coax Williams onto a rolling patient exam bed to prepare her for surgery.

"It'll be okay," he said to her over the clamor of the other voices.

Williams smiled dreamily, on the verge of passing out from the anesthesia the docs had given her.

"Watch it," Skylar barked from her cubicle.

One of the doctors had lifted her shirt to reveal ribs

covered by massive red and purple bruises. Another dabbed sterilizing alcohol over the cuts along her face.

"We're going to need X-rays on those ribs," a doctor said.

"We don't have time," Skylar said.

"You might have fractured—"

"They aren't getting any worse right now, but this disease is eating my guts alive."

"We—" the doctor began.

"Look, get us one of the computers the agency left us," Alex said. Another wave of pain twisted through his stomach, and he nearly doubled over. "Hurry."

"Fine. You heard him," the doctor said, pointing at one of his staff.

A handful of nurses guided them past the plastic curtains and into two hospital beds situated just a couple feet apart. They stuck IV needles into the backs of their hands.

"We're trying broad-spectrum antibiotics," one of the doctors said.

That hadn't worked in China, but Alex didn't bother to argue.

The medical staff finally retreated from their bedsides to the monitors in the corner of the partitioned room. They appeared to be debating Alex and Skylar's treatment. From their frantic gestures and urgent tone, Alex could tell these people were out of their league.

On the other side of the partitioned hangar, Team Reaper was being tended to just like Skylar and Alex.

"I guess this is the end," Skylar said. "Always thought I'd go down fighting the enemy, not my own damn body."

Sweat ran down her forehead in thick rivulets, and her skin had grown ghostly pale.

"Don't say that," Alex said. "We'll figure something out."

A few minutes later, a nurse in full biohazard gear hurried

toward them, lugging a thick Toughbook laptop. She handed it over to Alex before leaving them alone again.

While the base personnel had confiscated all the meds he had brought back for their own investigations, he had inventoried them during the flight. Alex had already sent all the images and names of the various pharmaceuticals back to Vector HQ.

"Back to work, partner?" Skylar said. Her chest rose and fell in shallow breaths, her lips trembling.

"You can use that button by your hand if you need to increase the painkillers," Alex said.

Skylar shook her head. "Not going to let anything screw with my head until we figure this out."

Alex patched Kasim in over the comms so they could consult with him and get an update.

"Weber and Park are already procuring every pharmaceutical compound you identified at Future Guard," Kasim said. "They're going to start cell culture experiments to test each drug against the archaea samples we have in-house."

"Good," Alex said. A chill swept through him. He felt the uneasiness of an oncoming fever, but he pushed past the burgeoning physical pain and discomfort. "Also, Pavlenko had stakes in three pharmaceutical companies. If the answer isn't in the meds we brought back from Future Guard, look to see if there are common drugs these companies make."

The drug that cured AGS was likely already in production. That would be the only feasible way to roll it out in a limited timeframe. To achieve the stockpiles and manufacturing capacity necessary to treat the millions or more that would be affected by AGS, it made sense to Alex that all three companies would need to be making it.

Or maybe that was just blind hope talking.

"Morris is on it as we speak," Kasim said.

Alex braced himself as another wave of pain roiled through his gut. "What's happening in China?"

"There are fifty thousand confirmed cases of AGS, and Weber estimates that over the next week, that number will climb into the millions."

Millions of lives, and there was very little left he could do from this hospital bed in Germany beside writhe in pain from the disease burgeoning in his gut.

A few minutes passed before Morris sent him a complete inventory. Alex opened the Toughbook again and scanned the list. Drugs that they had found in the clinic at Future Guard were highlighted in green, and any that all three companies shared were highlighted in yellow.

"We've got about twenty matches, ranging from antimicrobial agents to protein synthesis inhibitors to a couple of antivirals," Kasim said.

"Are you going to test all these drugs in the lab too?" Skylar asked.

"Weber and Park are working on it. For now, they're using surviving archaea from the bone samples you sent back from Ninh Binh, along with the sample from Breners. The tests will be more accurate when we get better samples. But even so, it would take weeks to prove any of these drugs work in the lab." There was a beat of silence. "But with the rate the infections are spreading, I'm afraid we don't have that long."

"Yeah, we'll be dead by then," Skylar said. "What's the plan? Randomly try every drug on this list in infected patients until something works?"

The notion of running expedited emergency drug trials on so many people made Alex sick. Most of these drugs probably wouldn't do a damn thing to help. Plus the side effects of using them against an unknown disease might prove as devastating as AGS itself.

"Do you think we could reach back out to Dai?" Skylar

asked. "Maybe she remembered something else about the cure."

"You're right again," Alex said, an idea forming through the fog of his growing fever. "I think Dai already gave us all the clues we need."

"What do you mean?"

"The story about her brother. He had an allergic reaction to the drug. That might help us narrow it down."

"We don't have the guy's medical records," Skylar said.

"This is a long shot, but she said the only other time she saw him with that kind of allergic reaction was when he'd been given… something. I can't recall."

"Shark liver," Skylar said. "I remembered because it sounded so nasty."

"You think something in one of these medicines would elicit a similar reaction as this man's seafood allergy?" Kasim asked.

"Maybe it's the fever talking," Alex said. "It could be the guy's allergies are entirely unrelated. But it's worth a look."

"If this is the only lead we've got, we need to run with it," Kasim said. "Talk soon. Hang in there, Vector."

Alex did his best to ignore the wrenching in his gut. Every minute that went by, he imagined the population of archaea expanding. Whatever drugs the docs were pumping into him through the IVs weren't working.

Skylar didn't look like she was any better. Her eyes were half-closed, breathing labored. She'd been through hell already. He should have been paying more attention to her injuries. Then again, Skylar should have told him how bad she was hurt. The growing trust between them was a fragile thing, an ember that needed to be tended. Alex vowed that he'd be a better partner on the next mission. If there *was* a next mission.

Park finally hopped on the line. "You guys might be onto

something. We found a drug compound on the list containing squalamine."

"Squalamine?" Skylar asked, eyes barely open now. She adjusted her earpiece. "What's it do?"

"Supposed to kill bacteria, for starters."

"I thought antibiotics don't work on archaea," she said.

"Most don't," Park said. "A few papers in the medical literature suggest a handful of uncommon antibiotics *might*, though. And this isn't just any old normal antibiotic. It was also supposed to have anti-angiogenic properties. A research group investigated it as a potential cancer treatment, and another group tried it out for macular degeneration. Says here that it failed Phase III clinical trials, though."

"Since it passed Phase I and Phase II clinical trials, we know it's relatively safe at least," Alex said.

"You got it," Park said. "Here's where it gets interesting. It's a steroidal antibiotic isolated from dogfish shark tissue. In fact, we found a 2012 paper in the *Clinical Microbiology and Infection* journal that suggests squalamine actually breaks down archaea cell walls."

"Is this it, Doc?" Skylar asked. "Is this the cure?"

"Maybe," Park said. "It wasn't ever used in the clinic for archaea, of course, but I don't see any other compound from those companies with links to shark tissue."

Alex knew the science was still out. And maybe he was just clinging to stubborn optimism. Maybe he just wanted to believe they had actually found Pavlenko's secret cure because the alternative was too much for him to bear.

"We'll know once we start trying this out in patients," Park said.

"I volunteer," Skylar said. "My gut feels like someone's trying to rip my intestines out with their teeth. Don't think I'm allergic to sharks—although, to be honest, I've never tried one."

"We'll work on sourcing it," Park said. "But I can't guarantee anything."

"Great bedside manner, Doc," Skylar grumbled.

Another thought struck Alex. "If this does work, what do we do about people like Dai's brother who might be allergic to it?"

"The Ninh Binh leak happened only a couple years after squalamine was isolated," Park said. "Back then, it was harvested straight from the shark tissue. Current manufacturing methods produce synthetic analogues. That theoretically eliminates the allergy issue."

"Cool, cool," Skylar said. She closed her eyes. Her voice sounded groggy, distant. "So Vietnam wasn't a waste after all, and maybe, just maybe, we actually did some good."

"Yeah," Alex said. He paused, choking back a wave of nausea. "How soon before we know for sure, Park?"

"Weber is telling me right now that she's secured squalamine from a source in Silver Spring. We'll begin lab tests immediately. But since the drug's already in production, we can clear it for emergency use with your doctors. I'm still not sure if it's the right drug yet. You understand?"

Another wave of pain churned through Alex's gut. His muscles contracted then felt like they were being pulled apart, fiber by fiber. His head started to go dizzy with the agony, and he writhed, trying to control himself, knowing he was failing.

"We can't wait any longer," Alex said through gritted teeth. "Skylar and I took a concentrated blast of archaea. We won't last the night."

"We'll get it rolling immediately," Park said. "We just need to find a supplier in your area to get it to Ramstein."

"What do we do in the meantime?" Alex asked.

He felt flush, sweat dripping down his forehead, soaking his patient gown and the sheets around his body.

"Pray that it works," Park said.

Alex ended the call and lay back in the bed. His mind was slowly growing hazier. The pain wracked his body as the world devolved into a murky fugue. He tried to fight the sudden exhaustion, wanting to stay up until he got confirmation that their doctors were ready to try the squalamine on him.

He blinked, struggling to keep his eyes open, turning toward Skylar. Her eyes cracked open just a bit, and she gave him one last smile.

Always a fighter to the end.

He tried to give her a reassuring smile in return. Tried to convince himself that in a matter of hours, they would be on the other side of this disease.

But the pain soon became too much, the infection too aggressive. Medical equipment chirped their frantic alarms. A weakness unlike anything he'd ever experienced washed through him. The last thing he saw was a gaggle of doctors in biohazard suits racing around his bedside.

Then, blackness.

39

GRAND CANARY ISLAND, Spain

AN ORANGE FOGGY cloud cloaked Grand Canary, giving the island a Martian-like appearance. Visibility had just barely cleared enough for safe flights on and off the island. Kasim had ensured that he, Weber, Park, and Reis were on the first plane to land.

A handful of times a year, the Sahara Desert blasted the Canary Islands with a massive *calima* or sandstorm. That sandstorm suffocated the resort-filled islands off the northeastern coast of Africa with hot winds and dusty air that could persist for up to a week.

Turbulence shook the Gulfstream G650, and Kasim tightened his fingers around the armrests. He looked out the window to see the island drawing closer. He could not help but think that they were descending right into the remnants of the very storm they had feared most. The one that had set Skylar and Alex's desperate mission into motion. The one that would take the archaea from the Future Guard facility and spread it across Europe and North America.

And amid all this chaos, his wife was with her sister in Rome. Enjoying a last-minute holiday that he hoped wouldn't be tarnished by a world-ending calamity.

While the hot winds had already begun their journey toward the United States, Kasim was here with his team to find out what the storm had left behind on Grand Canary besides bucketloads of desert dust.

Their plane touched down on the runway with a jolt and taxied to a private terminal. As soon as the cabin attendant opened the door for them, sweltering air rolled in, choking them with orange dust.

Kasim coughed despite wearing a meager surgical mask to keep the sand out of his mouth and nose. He took the first steps down the ramp stairs. Grit settled into his hair and clothes. A black van waited for them on the hot tarmac. He was already looking forward to a shower by the time they loaded into the luxury van. The driver activated the automatic door, sealing out the heat. The air conditioning provided some necessary relief, but Kasim could still detect the metallic taste of the dust.

"This is terrible," Park said. "Almost makes me wonder why people even bother coming to these resorts this time of the year."

"You think this is terrible, you should have been here in the middle of the storm," Reis said. "My family once spent our summer holiday here when a calima hit. For an entire week, we were trapped inside. Every flight was cancelled for days. You couldn't go outside without your skin practically peeling away."

"Sounds terrible," Park said.

"I promise, once this clears in a couple days, you will see just how beautiful the island is," Reis said. "Then you'll see why people come here."

The van traveled north along the island's coast. Through the haze of orange, Kasim saw what appeared to be normally lush plants all covered in thick layers of orange and brown dust. A volcanic mountain rose ominously off to their left, barely anything more than a dark, looming silhouette with the screen of sand swirling on the air.

The twenty-minute ride led them to the University Institute for Biomedical and Healthcare Research at Las Palmas University. They were met at the entrance to the rectangular black building by a pair of Spanish scientists who ushered the group inside. Kasim had used his connections to pull a few strings and reserve some laboratory time for his team under the guise of urgent aerobiological research related to the calima. The overall story was not a lie.

"Here's everything you asked for," one of the university researchers said, opening the door to a lab. "Let us know if you need anything else."

"Thank you," Kasim said.

He shut the door to the laboratory after their two escorts left.

A silver canister sat on one of the lab benches.

Reis walked toward it, already slipping on a pair of blue nitrile gloves. "That is just like the ones we used for my lab."

Weber set her phone on a desk. She tapped on it, and Richard Wagner's "Flying Dutchman Overture" began playing.

"Music?" Reis asked.

"We have a lot of work to do," Weber said.

"That's Wagner, right?" Park said.

Weber nodded.

"Figures," he said. "A German forcing us to listen to German opera music. We don't have anything better?"

"I kind of like it." Reis started to examine the device on the laboratory bench.

"You have good taste," Weber said, putting on her own gloves.

"You're just trying to suck up to her," Park said. "Just wait until she breaks out the Kenny G."

Weber and Park looked over Reis's shoulders as he began to take the device apart to reveal the filters inside. Each of those filters was stained with the same orange dust.

"You told us that Pavlenko wanted you and Williams to engineer the archaea so EnviroProct's sensors couldn't detect it," Kasim said. "Are you sure you can find it?"

"Definitely," Reis said. "EnviroProct's sensors are like using a huge net in the ocean, catching everything and hoping they find a random tuna, for instance. Unlike them, I know exactly what we're looking for. I can isolate the archaea using techniques that are more like using a single line with bait I know that only the tuna will go for."

Kasim had more questions, but he held his tongue. He needed to trust the researcher rather than satiate his own curiosity. That was a skill he'd had to learn while working with the headstrong team he'd assembled at Vector. Each one was brilliant in their own way, but together they could be so much more when they actually trusted one another.

For now, he took a backseat to the scientific mission, and Weber and Park followed Reis's lead. They ran the dust-coated filters through a series of solvent washes that Reis told him would separate any microbes trapped in the microscopic fibers. With some of the samples, he performed another battery of cell lysate and DNA isolation techniques to remove the genetic material from the microbes they found.

After a day's worth of work, they had successfully sequenced the DNA.

Park loaded the data into one of the computers he had brought along. He used a bioinformatics program to compare it to the genetic samples Alex and Skylar had obtained from Kaliningrad.

"Looks like we found the weaponized archaea," Park said, turning to face Kasim. "The genetic sequence is a nearly perfect match, except for a small mutation in the genome."

"That mutation might be from the genetic modification Pavlenko made last-minute to evade the EnviroProct sensors," Reis said.

Kasim didn't want to believe what they were saying. That would mean all the work Vector had done and all the sacrifices they had made were for nothing.

"The archaea still spread," he said. "We didn't stop it."

"Yes and no," Reis said. "All I've confirmed is that we spotted archaea DNA in the dust. DNA is a very stable molecule. Long after organisms die, the DNA within their dead tissues remain for years. Maybe the archaea are actually dead. Maybe we're looking at nothing but their single-celled carcasses."

Weber offered a sorrowful expression. "And if they aren't dead, we'll find out in a matter of days when people on Grand Canary start coming down with AGS."

Reis shook his head. "We don't have to wait that long. We can do another assay to show if the cells are alive or dead."

"He's right," Park said. "A viability assay. Very simple."

It took a couple more hours, but eventually Reis placed a slide on the stage of a fluorescent microscope.

"Look at this," he said.

An image showed on the computer screen next to the scope. All Kasim saw was a black screen filled with red specks.

"I performed a standard Live/Dead assay," Reis said. "Live cells will fluoresce green. Dead ones fluoresce red. I even compared this to a control to ensure the Live/Dead assay was working appropriately. The image you're looking at now is the archaea we isolated from the dust samples."

"They're all dead," Kasim said.

Reis grinned, pumping his fist. "That's right. No living archaea."

Kasim closed his eyes and sat on a stool next to the lab bench. He savored that moment, tasting victory after a long day spent in this cramped laboratory. That sensation flowed through him slowly. A trickle before the dam burst. The only thing holding him back from hooting in joy was the voices he heard in the hallway.

No need to attract any extra attention from their Spanish hosts.

"I can't believe Cruz and Wolfe did it," Park said, an infectious grin plastered over his face. "They actually killed the archaea."

"I just wish Skylar and Alex were here to celebrate with us," Kasim said.

"And Renee too," Reis said.

Weber gave them all a gentle smile, but she wasn't celebrating with them. "I want to be optimistic, but we're looking at just one small set of samples. We'll need to carefully monitor the situation and ensure no unexplained AGS-like symptoms crop up anywhere here in the Canary Islands. We'll know whether we're in the clear or not by the time the microbes from that dust storm finally reach the United States."

"Of course," Kasim said. "We'll continue monitoring the situation here to make sure we didn't miss anything. Keep collecting other samples and running them so I can be absolutely certain when I tell Commander Liang what we found."

Despite Weber's sensible caution, Kasim couldn't help feeling a spark of hope. As the triumphant sounds of classical music flared behind him, he finally felt as though Vector had won a real victory.

THREE MORE DAYS of running samples collected from around the Canary Islands confirmed the same results they had found after their first experiment. As Reis had promised, the air cleared.

Kasim relished in the warm tropical breeze when they took their short breaks between running experiments and when they returned to their beachside hotel at the end of their shift in the lab.

No one on the Canary Islands or neighboring Morocco had come down with AGS. It seemed that the United States, Northern Africa, and Western Europe might not need a miracle cure after all. Team Vector's efforts in Algeria had paid off.

But China was another story.

After another grueling day in the lab, Kasim returned to his hotel room, where he made an encrypted call to Liang.

"Liang here."

"It's done," Kasim said, leaning back in his bed. "No evidence of AGS here. The dust hitting the United States in a couple days should be harmless, aside from the usual respiratory challenges."

"Good." Liang paused. "The Future Guard facility has been absolutely gutted. Nothing's left. Russia is officially claiming there was an accident at Future Guard's terraforming operations causing a catastrophic failure. Same thing happened in China with the second facility there."

"We've seen the last of Pavlenko and his archaea weapons program. But this mercenary group, Archon, I think extends further than what we saw of it on these missions."

"Your report said they showed up in Vietnam."

"They were there in a blink. I have a feeling they're more widespread than we initially thought. They might've only played a small role in Pavlenko's operations, but we'll need to keep our eye on them."

"We will," Liang said. "We'll need teams like Vector on the frontlines for a very long time. You all will remain gainfully employed. If you need something, anything, it's yours."

"Thank you."

"No, thank you, Abraham. Your team stopped what would have been the most devastating bioterrorism attack on the United States in history."

"I only wished we had stopped it sooner," Kasim said. "Then the release of the archaea in China could have been avoided altogether."

"Couldn't agree more. That's why as soon as you return stateside, I need you to report to me. I've got something I may need your help with. This time, I don't want to be too late."

"Yes, ma'am." He paused. "Actually, what's the deadline on this next project?"

"I want to get an investigation up and running in the next week."

"Can you give me an extra five days in Europe?"

"This has to do with the archaea?" she asked.

"No, not exactly."

"Five days?"

"That's right," he said.

"I can give you three."

Kasim ended the call. His time in Grand Canary was coming to an end. But there was one last thing that had to be done before he could go back to the States.

He dialed another number.

"Divya, I want you to extend your trip to Italy," he said.

"What? I leave Rome tomorrow."

Kasim let out a soft laugh. "I don't care what it costs. I've got three days. I know we've got too much wine untouched back home, but what about a weekend in Tuscany? Just you and me."

"I... are you serious?"

"I am."

"I won't believe you until you're here."

"I'll see you tomorrow."

Finally, a promise he could keep.

In the meantime, Kasim considered grabbing some shut-eye. Exhaustion tugged at his eyelids, but his thoughts kept them from closing. He wondered what was in store for Vector next. What Liang would ask of them when they returned.

While advances in biological technologies offered tremendous potential in solving some of humanity's greatest challenges—curing cancer, stopping pandemics, addressing global hunger, and even combatting climate issues—those same technologies could be abused and twisted like Pavlenko had done.

But he held onto the hope that for every monster who might abuse science, there were thousands of others who would use technology for the world's gain—and protect others from those few despicable humans who would fight against civilization's best interests.

A knock on the door dispelled his thoughts, and he jolted up from the bed. He opened his door to see Weber.

"They're finally here," she said.

40

SKYLAR STEPPED out of the Peugeot 508 and took a long breath of the clean air wafting over Grand Canary. It hurt her bruised ribs to inhale so deeply, but she couldn't help it. The seaborne winds carried a salty scent. They teased her with promises of basking on the beach next to the clear aquamarine waters surrounding the island.

After spending the past several days cooped up in Ramstein, she was ready for exactly that.

Alex got out of the sedan, followed by Williams. Her left arm was in a sling, and the bandages over the wound in her shoulder pressed up against the T-shirt she wore.

"I can actually stand without my stomach feeling like it's going to rip apart," Alex said. "I like that."

"Me too," Williams agreed. "And it's a lot nicer here than on that air base."

"Yeah, yeah, I get it. You two feel wonderful," Skylar said. "My ribs still feel like an elephant used them as a drum."

She rubbed her side.

"Kasim promised we would have a few days here to lie

low," Alex said. "Perfect time for some R and R while those ribs heal."

"All I want is to sit my butt down on one of those chairs by the beach and drink a cold beer," she said.

"I'm thinking that can be arranged."

They walked toward the entrance to the hotel. The glass doors slid back before they reached them. Kasim strode out, a wide grin cutting across his face. The excitement Skylar saw in his expression was only eclipsed by Reis, who ran past him.

"Paulo!" Williams hurried to meet him.

Reis met her in a one-armed embrace, careful not to smash her left side. Skylar could not help but smile.

"You're such a sap," Alex whispered to her.

She gave him a playful elbow to the ribs.

"Never thought I'd see you again," Reis said when they finally parted. Tears streaked both their faces. "Are you feeling okay?"

"I am now," she said. "Finally."

They pulled each other into an embrace again.

"Please don't hug me like that," Skylar said to Kasim. "Not that I don't like you. But, you know, the ribs."

Kasim met her and Alex with a hearty handshake instead.

"You two did it," he said. "Everything's working out better than we possibly could have expected."

"What are the latest numbers from the East?" Skylar asked.

Kasim looked around as if to make sure no one was listening in. The only person outside was the doorman, but he motioned for them to move to a secluded area on the beach just past the hotel.

"Deaths in China were limited to a few thousand," Kasim said. "It's a tragedy, no doubt about it, but the squalamine worked on even the worst cases. The companies that were already making squalamine generously donated their entire stock, vowing to continue making the pharmaceuticals until every case in Asia is eliminated."

"Generously donated, huh?" Skylar asked, raising an eyebrow. She doubted there was any philanthropic intent behind the gesture. More like a desperate desire to do anything to avoid the devastating hammer of international justice.

She wished those companies would simply be obliterated. And maybe they would, later. For now, saving all those people suffering AGS had to be the focus.

"A little international pressure will do that," Kasim said. "The US has been working behind the scenes to determine who, outside of Pavlenko, was responsible for the archaea program. Our friends in the State Department convinced a few Russian oligarchs that perhaps donating their stockpiles of squalamine would be more advantageous to their public image rather than charging for it. All it took was showing them some of the government links to Future Guard, and they cooperated easily."

"At least controlling the outbreak limits the economic damage too," Alex said. "Hopefully, the Russians won't get anything out of this like Pavlenko had planned."

"There's certainly a lot less fear and anxiety now that AGS can be cured," Kasim said. "We have other manufacturers pumping out squalamine at record pace too."

He paused, looking between the two operatives.

"Look, there will be time for another full debriefing with you two later," Kasim said. "We'll go over more of the witness statements from the people you and Reaper brought back too. For now, I'll have them send your bags to your rooms. Go clean up. Grab a drink. Relax. You deserve it."

A FEW HOURS after her arrival to their hotel, Renee sat on a couch beside Paulo in Kasim's suite. The man was on a call in another room, his voice muffled by a closed door. That was a good thing because she didn't want someone she'd just met to see her like this. She still could not stop the mixture of tears and joy that undulated through her at the sight of Paulo.

He laid a gentle hand on hers, their fingers intertwined. Only a few days had passed since they had been taken out of Lisbon, but it may as well have been a lifetime.

"Never thought we'd be together again," she said.

"Me neither," Paulo said. "Even when these people took me out of Kaliningrad, I worried they were just another group of terrorists."

"Glad they're on our side," Renee said.

Paulo nodded, and Renee leaned her head on his shoulder. She had a million questions about what their future held. There was a part of her that wanted to get back to work, resume her old life. But another voice in her head told her that it probably wasn't safe. That the kidnappers might target her again.

And with their Lisbon lab destroyed, all their coworkers and many close friends gone, what was left for her there?

Somehow, going back to any academic lab after everything they had gone through just seemed so inconsequential.

She pulled away from Paulo slightly.

"What is it?" he asked, his face drawing up in concern.

"I just… I think I need a new path now," she said. "Lisbon isn't going to be the same."

"Are you saying…." He paused, emotions rolling across his face in waves. "What about us?"

She gave him a soft smile. "I'm hoping whatever we do next, wherever we go, it'll be together."

Paulo let out a soft sigh. "That is my plan."

She let go of his hand and pulled him in close. Their lips

met. She felt a lightness at his touch. The pain in her shoulder almost didn't seem to matter. Everything else in the world faded away. Her whole world became the connection she and Paulo shared.

Until she heard the click of a door.

"Ah, sorry," Kasim said. "I could come back later."

Renee and Paulo broke apart, blushing, but she didn't let go of his hand.

"Do you have news?" she asked

"I got off the phone with our commander." Kasim clasped his hands together, leaning toward them. The man looked like a kind doctor preparing to deliver devastating news to a family waiting outside an OR.

"We're ready," Renee said. "I can't imagine what you have to say is any worse than what we went through."

"Truth is, I don't think we can just let you go back to Lisbon," Kasim said.

"Figured as much," Renee said.

"I understand," Paulo said.

"You both seem far more okay with that than I'd thought. Did I miss something?" Kasim asked.

"I liked my work in the lab," Paulo said. "But you gave me a taste of what it's like to make a real difference in people's lives when the whole world is at stake. How can I go back to a place where my biggest impact is writing a paper that only a dozen other researchers in my field read?"

"And it's about time we move on to the next stage of our lives," Renee added. "We were both applying for faculty positions when *this* happened. Trying to go back to living our normal lives again just doesn't seem, well, normal."

"My only question is, will we get to see our families?" Paulo asked. "They must be worried sick."

"Of course, in due time," Kasim said. "We're figuring out how to deal with that, but we will let them know you're safe as soon as we can be sure we're not endangering you two, or them, by doing so."

"Are you putting us into witness protection?" Renee asked.

"I'm not sure that we need to do anything so drastic yet," Kasim said.

She caught that last word.

Yet.

It meant that even Kasim was unsure what threats might still be lurking in the dark world that she had briefly glimpsed.

"That being said, we will need to keep an eye on you two," Kasim said. "And our commander is impressed with your scientific acumen. You showed remarkable insight into a field we previously neglected. We may have a couple of openings in Fort Detrick for scientists with your specific skill sets. Neither position is a direct report to me, but you will be working with some of the best researchers in the world to uncover biological and chemical threats. What do you say?"

Renee looked at Paulo. From the expression on his face, she knew they didn't even need to discuss it.

"We're in," she said. "When do we start?"

AFTER A LONG SHOWER, Alex eyed the bed in his hotel room. That luxurious refuge with its plush pillows and clean white sheets called to him, promising him comfort that the hospital beds back in Ramstein just could not compete with.

He checked his watch. The only thing more important than the allure of sleep was the promise he had made to Skylar to meet her in the lobby.

By the time he made it down, Skylar was already waiting on a white bench near a couple of potted palm ferns. She gave him a smile, and he offered her a hand, helping her to stand. She winced like an old woman, one hand on her bruised ribs.

"You got ready quick," Alex said.

"Unlike you pencil pushers in the Agency, you got to learn how to clean up fast in the Marines," she said. "When you're bunking with thirty other people, chances are everyone's trying to get into the shower at the same time, or the water's cold enough to freeze your ass off. Sometimes—and very often —both."

"I have a feeling that isn't the only reason you made it here as fast as you did."

Skylar laughed. "You got me. Someone says cold beer on the beach, and I come running. You thirsty?"

By the way she marched toward the nearest bar, Alex could almost forget that she was still recovering from a medical student's study guide of painful injuries.

"I'll just do a coffee," Alex said. "I could use the caffeine."

"Hell, no," Skylar said. "You'll get what I order you, and you'll like it."

Alex considered protesting, but he'd give her this win. Besides, he figured the coffee here wouldn't be anywhere near as good as the drip-coffee Dai had served in that humble home under the karst mountains.

Skylar ordered them two draft beers, and they found a quiet spot at a table near the beach. The sun was dipping below the horizon. A few shreds of orange-and-red light glowed over the waves and the mostly empty sand.

"*Salud*," Skylar said, raising her glass.

Alex met hers in a toast. "Squalamine."

They drank, sharing a few moments of comfortable silence.

"It's nice not to have people poking and prodding us every five minutes," Skylar said.

"A guinea pig's life is not for me," Alex agreed. "And I'm glad they could test the treatment on us first."

"Not like they had a choice. We were on the verge of

death. If they had waited even a couple hours, I don't think either of us would be drinking a beer right now."

"The nightmare's almost over. Pavlenko's gone. The AGS will be erased in a matter of weeks. But I still don't feel right."

"It's that Yunevich woman, isn't it?"

"I made her a promise that we'd protect her family," Alex said. "She might've been guilty, but I doubt her kids had any part in all of this. I'm afraid to ask Kasim if we made good on that promise."

From the look on Skylar's face, he could tell she thought she knew the answer. "Trying to extract a whole family from Moscow... not likely. But look, you did everything you could. Everything you *had* to do."

"I still feel like I swallowed a bad egg."

Yunevich's family weren't the only ones Alex had tried to save and failed. There were all the other indentured researchers who had been massacred in Kaliningrad too.

Skylar looked out toward the rolling waves a few seconds before responding. "I know the feeling. Can't tell you how many calls I had to make before I lost this"—she knocked on her prosthetic leg for emphasis—"that I regret."

"And how did you deal with it?"

"Not sure that I ever really *dealt* with it," Skylar said. "But there's one thing you've got to remember."

"Oh?"

"Keep your eye on the mission. Maybe it's something they didn't teach you when you were a desk jockey. But that's the first thing we learned in Officer Training School. You and I did what we needed to do to save millions of lives. Whatever happened to Yunevich's family is out of our control. But all the families Vector *did* save should count for something."

Alex opened his mouth to speak, but Skylar cut him off with a dismissive wave.

"Look, if I've learned anything, it's that the human mind

loves to remind us of all the screwups and crappy decisions we make," she said. "It doesn't like to dwell on the good things. So you got to look out at the ocean tonight and remember all the people across it that get to sleep soundly because Pavlenko and his archaea were stopped. Think about the difference you made in their lives. And what about Williams and Reis too? Those are the kind of things that are important."

"You're right."

"Always am."

"I wouldn't go that far."

"I'm right on this." Skylar lifted her glass, tipping it slightly to point at him.

Alex smiled.

"And besides," she continued, "if that's not enough to make you feel better, Kasim said Liang's got a new job for us as soon as we get back. We'll have a chance to redeem ourselves."

"That's what I'm afraid of," Alex said. "Plenty more chances for us means there are plenty more threats."

Guilt would always come with this job. But he would survive it.

She took another sip of beer before continuing. "Maybe I'm just putting my foot in my mouth, but I got to think your brother would be proud of what you've done, Alex. You saved a lot of lives."

Alex took a drink while he fought for something to say. But there was only one thought on his mind. "Wasn't just me. You, too, Skylar. No way I could have done that without you."

She knocked back another gulp. "We got a long road ahead of us, don't we?"

The world could be a treacherous place. Alex had no illusions that just because they stopped Pavlenko all the other monsters salivating to take his place had suddenly disappeared.

No, there would be others to fill the void his death had left.

Driven by greed or power or a thousand other reasons.

All that mattered was that Alex knew he would not stop fighting. Not as long as there was a breath in his body.

And if he was going to continue this war in the shadows, then he was glad to have Kasim and Weber and Park on his side.

Most of all, he was glad to have Skylar.

"We can do this," he said finally.

"That's the spirit," Skylar said. "Whatever's next for us, we got this. We always got this."

As they tapped their glasses together, he knew they did.

The End of Biostorm (Vector, Book One)

-Author's Note-

WHILE WRITING my first few books, I also pursued a PhD in Bioengineering at the University of Maryland. I always enjoyed talking science with other graduate students and researchers. There was nothing more interesting than picking the brain of someone whose expertise was in developing bioreactors to generate new living bone tissues or a scientist specializing in parasitic organisms that hijack the host's body like the mind-controlling funguses that afflict some ants.

So when I first got introduced to aerobiology by another graduate student, I was fascinated. I learned that sandstorms originating in the Sahara Desert can spread dust, microorganisms, and even pathogens across the globe. Those storms can spread diseases afflicting everything from coral to humans. The Calima mentioned in the last scenes of the book is a very real phenomenon, and every scientific study alluded to in the book is based on a corresponding published scientific article.

Just as I mentioned in the book, this mass transport of dust carrying all kinds of tiny bugs is not unique to the Sahara. The Gobi and Taklamakan Deserts are also responsible for similar storms affecting eastern Asia. I couldn't help but think what would happen if someone released a more virulent, deadly pathogen into these dust storms. How could we possibly defend against a bioweapon transport mechanism that didn't care about borders or security or any of the other efforts we've enacted to stop madmen and terrorists?

Dust storms and all the microscopic critters they carry can have detrimental effects on the ecosystems where they fall. But they are also vital. For example, the dusts picked up in the deserts of North Africa carry phosphorous produced by microorganisms. Phosphorous is crucial to plant health and growth. Notably, the Amazon rainforest loses tens of thousands of tons of phosphorous each year to flooding and rain. The dust storms traveling from Africa to South America actually replace that missing phosphorous.

As desolate as the deserts may seem, they are actually life-giving resources for forests around the globe. It truly amazes me just how connected all these seemingly disparate ecosystems are, and how fragile the balance is between what appears to be a barren desert and a thriving rainforest halfway across the globe.

The second component of the bioweapon was the pathogen itself. Archaea are single-celled organisms that were previously classified as bacteria. However, more recent research has shown these are unique from bacteria, falling squarely in their own domain. They have metabolic pathways and cellular membranes that are strikingly different than bacteria, despite possessing a similar size and shape. Some of the most interesting extremophile archaea can draw energy and survive in harsh environments including super-heated geysers in Yellowstone and frozen lakes in Antarctica. And of course, archaea thrive even in the digestive tracts of animals and humans.

Currently, not much literature exists on diseases caused by

archaea. But given their presence in the gut microbiome of humans, there are suspected links between archaea and certain afflictions affecting the gut. Of course, since archaea's potential roles in disease aren't well-characterized, there are very few studies on how to stop a pathogenic archaea.

However, the studies Vector's science team mentions do in fact exist. Squalamine, first isolated from shark livers, is thought to disrupt archaea membranes (among its anti-angiogenic and anti-microbial properties). Would it actually work in an engineered archaea bioweapon released in dust storms across the globe?

Hard for me to say, but it's an interesting piece of a scientific puzzle.

What I can say is that the "Great Green Wall"-type efforts around the Sahara Desert and the deserts of China are very real tactics that have been implemented to combat desertification. Each year, millions of acres of usable agricultural land are lost to the spread of arid desert. Agricultural communities are constantly displaced, and food supplies relying on these lands are disappearing.

As a result, intensive terraforming efforts have been used to fight back desertification. These efforts include planting trees and other plants to stabilize the soil along with developing improved methods of water retention and infiltration. Initial efforts and ideas to turn the Sahara Desert, for instance, into something like a tree-filled replicant of the Amazon turned out to be mostly fruitless. But over time, these programs have demonstrated varying degrees of success. People in desert-adjacent communities have learned new ways to regenerate the land by relying on local farmers and novel methods of land management.

Reclaiming this land is important to food production and the livelihood of agricultural communities. But as we know, the dust storms rising from these deserts are equally important to the health of distant forests and other ecosystems.

It's definitely a delicate balance.

Outside the scientific aspects of the story, I drew some inspiration from the Soviet Union's Biopreparat unit. Ken Alibek's book, *Biohazard: The Chilling True Story of the Largest Covert Biological Weapons Program in the World*, evoked plenty of the scenes, characters, and events regarding this fictional modern-day version of the Russian biological weapons program.

However, some of those disasters related to Biopreparat—such as the anthrax and smallpox leaks—are indeed real events.

Similar programs in Vietnam are wholly my own invention, based loosely on the events of these other tragic events.

Finally, one of my favorite parts of these globe-trotting adventures is revisiting places that have left their mark on me in my own travels.

Istanbul is an invigorating and ancient city. The perfect place where cultures collide in a history steeped in rises and falls. You can visit vestiges of the past in places like the beautiful Hagia Sophia and overwhelm your senses in the clash of smells and sights and sounds of the Grand Bazaar, then stroll along the modern chic stores and eateries of İstiklal Caddesi. It's a city that feels as though you can choose your own adventure, whether it's a boat ride down the Bosporus or an evening in a cozy hookah bar chatting with friends new and old, or, perhaps, a visit to a lively Irish pub.

I haven't visited Kaliningrad directly, but I have been through the neighboring Baltic States. I can recommend a road trip through Estonia to Latvia and Lithuania. Tallin is indeed a fairy tale town with a medieval history and a good place to recuperate when you've just escaped a gunfight in a Russian port city. Tallin was in fact the very first European city I ever traveled to. Walk the castle-like walls of the city center and meet people at the many welcoming bars and restaurants off the picturesque town square. Estonia is a fascinating post-Soviet country with a fierce independent streak you cannot help but admire.

The Sahara Desert, of course, is a landscape that feels simultaneously barren and alive. On the surface, you can look out over the sands and never feel so alone; but at the same time, those sands are constantly shifting, the winds howling, the stars glimmering, and the desert almost seems like it has a life of its own. Worth the visit, even if only for a day.

Finally, Ninh Binh is a beautiful province in Vietnam with striking landscapes of jutting karst mountains and lush rice paddies. When I went in 2018, you could stay in a stunning boutique hotel room under those mountains next to green paddies for $30 USD a night, rent a motorized scooter for $5 USD a day, and explore intricate caves, winding rivers, and temples on top of mountains. Certainly one of the most fascinating and gorgeous places I've ever seen. Not to mention, venturing into one of the many family-run restaurants in Ninh Binh is its own highly satisfying culinary adventure.

Ninh Binh seems to just be establishing itself as a hotspot for travelers visiting Vietnam. I'm glad to have spent the time I did there as it transitions from a somewhat sleepy, relaxed locale to a place bustling with tourist activity like Ha Long Bay.

When I was in Ninh Binh, I did not worry about bioweapons or mysterious gunmen. The region is extraordinarily safe and friendly. My only concerns were picking out where I wanted to hike and then grab a beer and bite to eat.

It always amazes me, no matter what topics in science I explore or what far-reaching destination I visit in these stories, just how closely connected everything really is. Our histories and cultures and beliefs, the good and the bad, tend to mix and interact and feed us just like those Saharan dust storms traveling across the Atlantic.

Thank you so much for reading and sharing this story with me.

Anthony J. Melchiorri
   March, 2021

-Dear Reader-

THANK YOU FOR READING *BIOSTORM*, Book One in the *Vector* series. I sincerely hope you enjoyed the series. If you did, would you please leave a review? You can leave one as short or as long as you like.

Reviews are crucial to authors. They help us figure out what people did and didn't like, along with helping tell potential future readers what to expect. I greatly appreciate any and all reviews!

I've had this story brewing for a long time, and I'm so happy it's finally out in the world. Wolfe and Cruz have their work cut out for them in future missions with Vector. If you want to follow along with their next op and hear about what's next, sign up for my mailing list here: http://bit.ly/ajmlist

I won't spam you, and I only email my readers when I've got something new out or some special deal for you. For signing up, you'll also receive a couple of free books.

I love to hear from my readers. If you want to get in touch, there are a number of ways to reach me.

Facebook: www.facebook.com/anthonyjmelchiorri

Email: ajm@anthonyjmelchiorri.com
Website: http://www.anthonyjmelchiorri.com

-Acknowledgments-

THIS BOOK WOULDN'T EXIST without the team of people who have consistently supported my efforts. Their advice, criticism, and conversations helped take the ideas and concepts in this story to the next level. Thank you first and foremost to my fellow cohort of graduate students from my days at the University of Maryland, back when I got my PhD, whose conversations fueled my flights into fiction while we talked about all the most fascinating advances and discoveries in our fields. A big thank you to my editor, Erin Long. She's been with me since some of my first books, helping to develop my characters, pointing out plot holes, and in general polishing the work I send her. Thank you to Virge and Brittany at Red Adept Editing for helping clean up the manuscript. To Frank and Luis, the first people who set eyes on this thriller. To Nicholas Sansbury Smith, who I owe my career to, and so many conversations as we mix real-world science into our fiction. A big thank you to my wife, Katarina, who listens to all my ideas and serves as a sounding board as I prototype the characters and story elements. To my agent, David Fugate, who has been a champion for my books. A big thank you to the Podium Audio team for bringing this work to life in audiobook format. While all these people have played a part in bringing this book to fruition, any stubborn errors left in this story and its telling are purely my own.

Printed in Great Britain
by Amazon